D0811948

A Family Gathering

a story of triumph over tragedy

A literary journey, fourteen years in the making.

Also by Gene Cartwright

I Never Played Catch With My Father
Half Moon, Full Heart

Coming:

The Widowmaker
Quietkill
Alone Again
Harold

in Honor:

Ossie Davis and Ruby Dee

One cannot mention the one without, in the same breath, speaking the name of the other. That fact says all that need be said about the love and life they shared. They were, and are still, one.

One cannot honor the one without honoring the other. And so I am honored to honor them both. They have long been an inspiration to me and countless others. I dedicate this work to them, their inspiring lives, their unquestioned commitment to each other, to their craft, and to the betterment of humankind.

Mr. Davis sought no awards, no public praise, no special honor. His reward came daily, through his unwavering devotion to his calling. Yet, what will leave an even more indelible mark is his great humanity—their great humanity. Both he and his beloved wife were always determined to, by their deeds, not words alone, uplift us all. May it always be so.

Thanks.

Deepest thanks to my editor and devoted friend, Louise Turner.
It is impossible to overstate the extent of your invaluable contributions
to this 'labor of love.' Your tireless work and boundless dedication to
this novel were matched only by my own.

A Family Gathering

third novel by

Gene Cartwright

Falcon Books and Falconcreek Books are imprints of Falcon Creek Publishing Co.

Los Angeles   Houston   Washington, D.C.

First Edition

Library of Congress Cataloging-in-Publication Data
Library of Congress Control Number: 2004117117
Cartwright, Gene
 A Family Gathering: a novel/by Gene Cartwright —1st ed.
 p. cm

ISBN: 0-9649756-2-9
ISBN: 978-0-9649756-2-0 (13 digit)
 1. Title

10 9 8 7 6 5 4 3 2 1

GMW

LA-TX-DC

Published by Falcon Creek Publishing Company - January 2006

Book Design, dust Jacket, artwork by Gene Cartwright. © 2005, 2006 Gene Cartwright All right reserved. Publisher: 13504 Francisquito Ave Suite E. Baldwin Park, Ca 91706 www.falconcreekbooks.com (or www.namewhiz.com)

Printed in the United States of America

Dedication

For the innocent victims of life's tragedies;
for those who struggle with crippling adversity,
and those who have overcome it—lifting
themselves from the basement of their lives.

—

For Bruce Henry,
my best friend when we were mere 'infants'
at George Washington Carver High School, in Baytown, Texas.
And for all those—present or now absent—whose footprints once marked
those slate-grey hallways so long ago. That hallowed institution, once a beacon
of hope in a segregated system, is now gone, destroyed by those with no sense
of history; reduced to dust by those who gave not the slightest damn
for generations to whom it meant so much. Even the tiniest
flakes, from decades-old brick and mortar, have long since
been scattered like cremated remains; made to vanish
by the relentless force of dry summer winds.
And yet, that institution stands,
even now...in all of us.

—

For Willianne Lewis, my longtime friend and confidant,
whose belief in me never falters. You are irreplaceable.
Thanks for reading AFG,
and offering invaluable help and advice.

—

For all those whose paths my life has crossed,
whether for good or ill, and whether charged to their account or mine.
Live long, live well.

—

Finally, and always,
for my parents, Elmer and Marie Cartwright.

A Poem

I Weep No More
©2005 Gene Cartwright

I weep no more.
 Well of tears—bone dry,
 bed of thorns now lies empty,
 absent my presence, waiting, hoping, expecting,
 foretelling my return to its piercing embrace.
 But I have moved on.
I weep no more.
 Wall of fear—once stone,
 blown asunder, now gone forever,
 reduced to dust, crumbled, shambled,
 unable to thwart my will, nor prevent my escape.
 'Cause I have moved on.
I once longed for the serenity of death, the solitude of nonexistence,
 the eternal peace of unbeing—as in never having been. But no more.
 I once sought the tomb of a mindless darkness, unacquainted with
 the informing nature of memory, or the gift of light. But no more.
 I have found my voice, heard my song, seen my spirit leap
 like a geyser toward heaven.
 And I have moved on.
I weep no more.
 Well of tears—bone dry,
 bed of thorns now lies empty,
 craving my presence, waiting, hoping, expecting,
 predicting my relapse to its cruel embrace.
 But I have moved on.
I weep no more.
 Wall of fear—once stone,
 blown asunder, now gone forever,
 reduced to dust, crumbled, shambled,
 unable to shunt my will, nor stay my escape.
 'Cause I have moved on.
I weep no more,
 'Cept for joy, aloud I cry,
 now yearning to be, to live, not die.
 Now cleansed of shame, I weep no more.
 My soul is free. I weep no more.
 My soul is free. I weep no more!

Book One
In Her First Life

"Where was God on May 15, 1974?"

—*Aunt Rose*

chapter one

"I'm runnin' a bid'ness here..."

It usually killed old folk first.

Especially poor ones—"The Disposables:" poor, feeble, often lonely, living alone. Infants were likely next—"Poorborns:" newborns, mostly poor, mostly black. Proof, to many, that even the gods favor the rich.

Then, stray dogs. Mangy mongrels with heads down, ears drooping, tongues hanging, tails dragging. But not cats. Never cats. Could be cats are way too cool and arguably smarter. They always managed to avoid the killer: heat.

Heat rained down, then back up, like invisible hellfire. Hundred 'n four, not a hint of rain. Kind of Arkansas heat that parched throats, dimmed vision, sapped strength, slowed speech. It was brain-baking heat, akin to inhaling furnace blast, minus singed brows and lashes.

It was only May, for God's sake, not August. Yet, the 'Sticks' were already blistering. But then, the *Sticks* always seemed to get more of everything nobody sane ever prayed for. More sweltering heat; more flash floods; more twisters...hurricanes; more mosquitoes; more DDT; more poverty; more garbage dumps; more rut-ravaged, unpaved roads; more broken sewers, more malevolent neglect. One could surely blame God for the heat, the bad weather, even the mosquitoes, but not the rest.

Precious few souls in the Sticks, a.k.a. Oakwood Manor, owned window-unit air-conditioning, let alone central air. For most, central air meant opening the front and back doors and allowing the wind to race through the *center* of their rented 'shotgun' houses. Those fortunate enough to have 'store-bought' air frequently found themselves visited by neighbors who just happened by, and were in no hurry to leave.

Coolest place around was Mr. Bryson Peabo's pool hall and juke joint. His was a well-patronized, 'round the clock hot spot near Miss Ruby's Café and backroom whorehouse. Both establishments dominated the western end of poorly paved Oak Street, the only thoroughfare in the Sticks' red light district, not counting backalleys and trails.

Ol' man Peabo—a grumpy, tattooed, bald, six foot-four ex-Marine with one leg and one fairly good eye—did not allow for 'hangers around' and 'lookers-on.' If you were not spending cold cash, he would toss your ass out into the hot sun, whether you were friend or foe, Jew or Gentile.

"Nothin' personal. I'm runnin' a *bid'ness* here, not the YMCA," he would say, with no hint of a smile, and just before the heavy wooden door slammed closed.

Miss Ruby's was even more popular. Ruby Jean Dandridge was an aging, though still vivacious, vixen who had the natural ability to wow and woo a crowd. True, her café offered unsurpassed, mouth-watering, soul-food fare, but 'after-hours' drew her most devoted patronage.

The fiery, eldest daughter of a Mississippi sharecropper, the Rubenesque Miss Ruby possessed an entrepreneurial spirit and genius to rival that of the wiliest Wall Street wizard. Her place was a cash cow. She knew how to pack 'em in. Her southern cuisine drew widespread praise, and garnered nearly as much addiction as did other 'unwritten menu items' she offered. Of course, few ever admitted to being more than café customers.

And Miss Ruby was no miser. To the contrary, she was a philanthropist. College scholarships, church offerings, and charity events were beneficiaries of Miss Ruby's generosity. And she sought no recognition.

Then, there was the 'Blue Room.' The exterior of Mr. Lonnie Cooper's *Blue Room* was painted blue...had a blue bulb over the door...came on as soon as the sun went down. Despite the Sticks' modest population, Mr. Lonnie's 'honky-tonk joint' had its share of devoted patrons as well.

"LC," as some called him, was a longtime widower. He was suave, well-read, articulate, and a world-class gambler, by his description. He reportedly earned his fortune in all manner of gambling—mostly illegal—from Maine to Seattle. In reality, few believed he had ever traveled much farther than New Orleans. His place was located near the eastern end of Oak Street, opposite direction to Mr. Peabo's and Miss Ruby's. All existed in an air of friendly competition, except on one occasion.

In the summer of '73, Mr. Lonnie added a large, twelve-table poolroom to his operation. Until then, his was mostly a beer joint, nightclub, gambling-in-the-room-in-the-back sort of place. Mr. Peabo's had its specialties, Miss Ruby's had hers. But the Blue Room? Now, that was the place to go for live entertainment—particularly blues acts, and lots of hard liquor, especially on Saturday nights.

There was a division of vice offerings, so to speak, until Mr. Lonnie crossed the line. However, the matter was soon rectified. Mr. Peabo paid an after, after-hours visit, and had a 'Come To Jesus' meeting with the brother—Mr. Cooper. No one else was present. The next day, the tables were loaded onto a semi and carted off to...well, no one ever knew for sure. Things soon returned to normal, and that was that.

To be fair, it must be said, the Sticks boasted more than 'dens of iniquity.' It was, as were many poor, southern neighborhoods, a self-sufficient community. Few things were needed that could not be had. There were two preachers, two plumbers, an electrician, two carpenters, a roofer, painters, masons, two dry-cleaners. There were corner grocers, record shops, mechanics, beauty shops, barbers, seamstresses, baby-sitters, yardmen, cooks, gamblers, undertakers—jacks-of-all-trades. And then there was 'Rainey's'—Mr. Samuel I. Rainey. 'Course the "I" did not stand for anything. He added it so his initials would form the word, SIR. Rainey had the best damn barbecue anywhere in Arkansas, or Texas. Folk would drive for miles, even stand in line for his 'cue.'

Rainey's is where the phrase, 'Finger Lickin' Good' allegedly originated. Hordes of white folk found their way to his door, even some 'Kluxers,' reportedly. Of course, they would grab their barbecue and scurry back out of town. But at least their dollars remained in the Sticks.

Truth is, white folk patronized other businesses as well. Miss Ruby's 'pleasure room' had its clientele—mostly male, mostly white, mostly at night. Proof, to many, that even color can sometimes be overlooked. These 'gentlemen' found their way to the back door, entering only under Miss Ruby's discriminating eye. Even Sheriff Lucas Darden, wearing street clothes, was often reported seen leaving in the wee hours of the morning.

Licensed businesses aside, the Sticks had its share of petty thieves, rip-off artists, hucksters, and...well, smartasses. No other way to put it. But they were severely dealt with by the residents themselves. The place was a village. A poor village, but a village nonetheless.

The Sticks even had a lawyer, well...sort of. That is what he claimed. 'Course no one ever saw Ol' 'Fessor, Lemuel J. Marshall III's license or degree, nor heard of a case he ever tried. But he could talk up a storm. He was full of advice, but never accompanied anyone to court. 'Fessor would write out a little speech to be delivered by the accused, then advise: "You'd be better off pleadin' guilty and throwin' yourself on the mercy of the court." He told this to every client, no matter the charges. If further convincing was needed, he relied on his tried and true: "Now, if you insist on a trial, it'll cost you nearly everything you got if I go to court. Least this way, when you get out you'll have some money left."

But 'Fessor left town rather hurriedly one night. His whereabouts were never discovered. Rumor was, a jealous husband got after him. Seems 'Fessor had bartered his fee for 'favors' with the man's wife. And she still went to jail. The fact the woman was a great cook only fueled speculation regarding the true reason for her husband's rabid anger.

chapter two

In Her First Life - *May 15, 1974 Rural Reedville, Arkansas.*

─────────────────────────────

Fear seized her like a claw.

'Bout a mile from The Sticks, three miles from Reedville, proper, Jonathan Jefferson Reed's old '62 Ford pickup just set there—a rusting hulk held together with baling wire and a prayer. The sun-bleached, blue heap hugged the edge of a large circular clearing, nearly surrounded by a sentry of towering Arkansas pine.

Nothing moved. Nothing. Damn truck looked downright abandoned. Always did, moving or not. The old wreck was an unlikely means of transportation for the son of one of the most powerful families in Arkansas. Not surprising, since Jonathan's parents discouraged him from flaunting his wealth in the face of those who had so little.

Just then, his scrawny, naked, pale-white backside—with nearly protruding vertebrae—appeared in the lowered driver's window. Inside the seedy truck cab, carpeted with fast food wrappers and the decomposed remains of unidentifiable crawling critters, the thick, hot air reeked of musty sneakers, sweaty private parts, and unshaved armpits.

Jonathan kicked open the creaky door and backed himself out onto the parched ground. His wet skin sizzled in the unforgiving heat. He drew the back of his right hand across his dripping brow, swiped it on his right pant leg.

Sixteen year-old Jonathan, whose middle name was given to honor the only President of the Confederacy, was nearly six feet two, barely a hundred thirty pounds, brains and all. Like a soiled mop turned upside down, his stringy, rusty blond hair fell past a pimply face to just above sloping shoulders.

Jonathan closed the door, yanked up his faded Levi's and tucked 'himself' back inside. He zipped his fly; slipped his white, Harley Davidson T-shirt over his hairless, sunken chest; then buckled his overlapping belt. He paused, glanced back at the beautiful, sweat-soaked black girl. She sat slouched in the passenger seat, breathing heavily, staring into her lap with vacant eyes. Her bra was back in place now, but much of her taut, flawless, creamy-brown skin was still exposed.

At 12 years old, Deborah Yvonne Davis had the sweet, innocent face of a young girl, but the fetching body of a woman, years older. It was her blessing and her curse.

Jonathan stared long and hard, savoring the sight of her. His bowed erection was still at full bore. A look of self-satisfaction covered his pock-marked face. With a cocky swagger, he reached through the open window, touched Deborah's shoulder with unsure fingertips. She flinched, leaned away. Her smile was gone. Deep frowns etched her glistening brow.

Deborah was in complete disarray. With her chin pressed against her chest, she slowly arched her supple back, raised her bare bottom, snaked up her white panties and forced down her brown, flower print skirt. Never did look up. The heat-brewed stench rose in nearly visible waves. She appeared ready to puke.

Jonathan straightened his lanky frame and swiped his dripping brow once more. He gazed with expectation toward the distant tree line for nearly a minute. Curiously, as he peered into the distance, he raised his right arm high above his head for several seconds, then sauntered to the passenger side. With his left hand briefly resting atop the roasting cab roof, he again stared toward the tree line.

Deborah appeared dazed, remorseful; her breathing was uneven. With unsteady hands, she tried to straighten her soiled, once-white blouse. She peered into the cracked, side-view mirror and attempted to groom her curly, shoulder-length black hair.

Just then, sour sputum bubbled up, filling her mouth. Deborah leaned forward, braced herself against the dash, and repeatedly spat onto the cluttered floorboard.

Swatting gnats and flies, Jonathan thrust his left hand through the lowered passenger window. He attempted to caress Deborah's contorted face. She recoiled, aimed a questioning glare at him. He loosed a weak smile and folded his bony arms across his chest.

Jonathan had heard things—all manner of things said about black girls. Things, the truth of which, he was set on discovering for himself. They were all hot and wild; full of fire; beyond satisfying, he had heard. He had spent many nights in his room, his mind boiling with steamy imaginings while he pleasured himself to the point of self-abuse.

"The young stuff is best," he was told and believed. Such talk had come from a few boastful rednecks, and several young black boys touting their sexual prowess and eager for a taste of "Vanilla."

Some had even offered to barter: "Chocolate for Vanilla," they said. Jonathan refused such quid pro quo, boasting he needed no middlemen; he could get any *snatch* he wanted. He was a Reed.

Jonathan yanked the passenger door open, leaned back against its unpaneled inside, with its exposed glass, and rusting gears. He slouched, with arms folded, chin extended—looking all proud of himself. He took a deep breath, filled his lungs with superheated, pine-scented air.

"Why are you opening the...the door?" Deborah's feeble voice barely registered.

"So you can go. I got 'a get home, take a bath...change clothes. It's hotter'n hell out here. C'mon, girl! It's gettin' late."

Deborah grimaced then looked away. She took another labored breath, gathered herself, and slowly stepped from the odorous wreck. With her strength nearly sapped, she stumbled. Jonathan held fast, offered her no assistance. He just stood there flicking sweat from his pimpled brow.

Undaunted, Deborah righted herself and aligned her twisted skirt, while aiming an acid-laced stare. Jonathan looked away, avoiding her caustic gaze. He responded with a smirk, combed fingers through his hair then wiped both hands on his soiled jeans.

"You ain't seen me today," he barked, pointing. "You hear? You be sure and tell your friends they ain't seen me either. And don't say one word about what we did here. It would just get *you* in a heap 'a trouble. Who knows, we might even want 'a do this again sometime."

Before Deborah could speak, Jonathan bolted to the driver's side and leaped behind the wheel. He fired the ignition and raced the engine, forcing Deborah to scurry to get clear. She watched in silence as he peeled away, spitting soil and grass from beneath the tires.

With her fists clenched, Deborah stood alone now in the sweltering heat. Her blouse stubbornly clung to her sweat-soaked skin. She felt cemented to the spot, unable to move.

Then fear seized her like a claw. Her eyes began misting. The heat flared mercilessly; trees seemed to swirl. Deborah collapsed to her knees, lifted her head, began sobbing, then praying. With salty sweat pouring—some seeping into the corners of her mouth—she stuttered through the Lord's Prayer. Her voice crackled. Gram d'lena, her late, paternal grandmother—had taught it to her when she was barely two. They would often read scriptures and pray together.

Just now, Deborah could almost see Gram's face. She sensed her grandmother's presence, and felt ashamed. Unclean and painfully ashamed. What ever had possessed her? How could she have defiled Gram d'lena's memory this way? This was not real. It could not be. She felt separated from her inner self, disconnected from the person she always believed herself to be.

Time. Deborah lost all awareness of time, yet knew she had to hurry home. But home was the last place she wanted to be now. How would she ever explain her appearance? How would she account for being more than two hours late arriving from school, and without her friends? What would she say? How would she be able to keep her secret?

Then, panic struck her. Kay, B.B., and Tommy were Deborah's schoolmates. The three girlfriends always walked home from school together. Tommy had joined them this day, of all days.

Surely, all had long ago arrived at the Davis home and found 'Sister Davis'—as most called Mabel Davis—waiting, as was her custom. What must her mother be thinking? What must Kay, B.B., and Tommy be thinking? What explanation had they offered, in light of her mother's certain grilling?

By now, everyone, especially Deborah's brother, Matthew, was deranged with worry. Matthew had likely arrived home from school, found his sister was not home, and insisted he would find her. Always eager to assume his 'big brother' role, he was likely trudging down dusty Crispus Attucks Road this very minute—his .22 Winchester rifle, or Louisville Slugger, gripped in his powerful hands, or slung over his broad shoulders. Not finding her, he would not hesitate to search the woods as well.

Deborah's younger sister, Rachel, was a precocious fifth-grader with a 154 I.Q. She was likely finishing her homework, unimpressed by anything save her own lofty thoughts. For reasons unknown to Deborah, or anyone else, there was little love lost between the two.

Rachel exuded an air of superiority that seemed to exist almost at birth. She was always quick to exhibit, if not flaunt, her brilliance. Even her parents were not exempt from her acid temperament, especially her mother. Rachel treaded much more cautiously with Reverend, and for good reason.

Rachel had adamantly refused to walk home with Deborah and her friends. "They are all so childish and intellectually immature. And they're *boy crazy*," Rachel often complained to her mother—and in that precise language. Mabel Davis did not press the issue. Mrs. Abigail Linton,

Rachel's homeroom teacher, lived less than three miles away. She always drove her 'Ace Student' home evenings.

Then there was Deborah's father, the Reverend Henry B. Davis. God forbid he had arrived home from Pine Bluff to find his daughter was not home, and her whereabouts unknown to anyone. And his mood would certainly not be helped by the loss of his car's air-conditioning the day before. That fact was compounded by Reverend's insistence on wearing long-sleeve white shirts and dark suits, no matter the weather.

Such sobering thoughts quickly inspired a bit of fiction. Deborah began plotting her defense with each unsure step: *Upon realizing that accepting Jonathan's offer of a ride was a bad idea, she got out of his truck and resumed walking home. She then decided on a shortcut through the piney woods, but got lost.*

The story sounded plausible enough, until Deborah remembered Crispus Attucks Road passed less than an eighth mile from the Davis home. No need for a shortcut. No one would believe such a tale.

Rachel would likely be first to point out the flaws of such a story. Not only would Deborah be punished for straggling home hours late, but for lying—an unpardonable offense in the Davis household, as grievous as Satan worship.

So what now? Deborah wished with all her heart it were already tomorrow, next week, next month, any day but the present. Maybe, just maybe, everyone would be out searching for her. She would then be able to slip into the house unnoticed; bathe, change clothes, then face the music later. That thought quickly became her prayer. She pleaded with God to make it so.

Despite the crippling heat of earlier, the evening breeze felt cool against Deborah's tear-stained cheeks. The feeling was short-lived. Piercing pain, then a burning sensation, consumed her lower abdomen and vaginal area. She doubled over, gasping.

Hungry, trembling, her vision blurred, Deborah straightened her frame and waited for her eyes to focus. Shortly, she began forcing herself forward. She willed her way along the fresh tire trail, trudged past the tree-line, and onto the degraded asphalt roadway. Heat waves still spiraled from portions of the bubbling black surface. She paused at the winding road's edge and anxiously searched in both directions.

Then, a startling sound—crackling twigs, rustling leaves. A cold chill darted down Deborah's back. She wheeled toward the tree line. Silence. Dead silence, except for her pounding heart. She took a couple of unsure steps forward, paused, then gazed back down the road.

Deborah prayed no one, especially Tommy, would happen along, and see her this way. His shortest route home was back down Crispus Attucks. She hoped he had already passed, or taken an alternate route.

Almost as quickly as it had come, the creepy sensation eased. An eerie calm washed over her. She was unnerved by its unexpected effect, but doubted it would last. Shortly, with tears winding down her face, Deborah began her dreaded journey home. Vivid thoughts of Gram consumed her; they brought both comfort and condemnation.

All those years, all those treasured moments spent with Gram d'lena, now seemed so distant. Were they ever real? Why did those times with her have to end? Why had God—a supposedly merciful God—taken her grandmother away?

Deborah wished with all her heart Gram were still alive. Her mind, though spinning wildly, remained awash in memories of her beloved grandmother. Her tenderness, her comforting gaze, her unconditional love, her gentle spirit always provided refuge—the refuge Deborah desperately needed right now.

But who was Deborah Yvonne Davis? And who was this Gram d'lena, who meant so much to her? How had this young girl—second daughter of the Reverend Henry B. Davis, and Sister Mabel Davis—come to be at this place, on this day?

chapter three

She stared in stunned surprise, then...

Her eyes were first to answer.

A telling glow. A fluttering of long, thick lashes. A deepening of well-earned lines. A face that beamed like August sun.

The question, softly spoken, fetched a lingering smile. The youthful inquisitor—her own eyes gleaming—waited with head tilted, a thick, curly, black braid grasped between tiny thumb and forefinger. A soft breath exhaled. Silence.

Gram d'lena looked away for a time. She stroked her furrowed brow then paused to allow the sudden swell of emotion to retreat. With her left forearm pressed down against the timeworn tabletop, she leaned forward, gently caressed her granddaughter's upturned face. And while exuding the sort of warming love that can only come from grandmothers, Gram gazed into expectant young eyes and loosed a warm smile.

"Kinda caught me off guard, babygirl. Wasn't expectin' you to ask me such a question right out. Needed a minute to collect myself...let my heart slow down a bit. But, all that aside, the answer is yes. Yes, I still love your granddaddy...love him with all my heart."

Gram's voice grew wispy. Her eyes glistened with a hint of mist. Through the tiny kitchen's open French window, dawn's early light caressed her dimpled face, revealing every twitch and twinkle. The delicate, soft-white, handmade, English lace curtains—drawn but untied—danced in cool, gentle, country breeze.

"And I'll love him the longest day I live. Reckon love is 'bout the most important, most wonderful thing you can give or receive. Can't be bought or sold, only freely given. It's the one gift that leaves giver and receiver...richer. I must sound like a Hallmark card or somethin,' huh?"

"You make all that up, Gram d'lena?" asked Deborah, more in awe than doubt. Never doubt.

"Wish I could take the credit, babygirl. But your granddaddy used to say that all the time. And I believe it with all my heart...made his words my own. I always say, for somebody who barely finished the ninth grade, that man sure had a way with words. Words flowed from his mouth like honey. Like warm, sweet honey. And I still love him...much as I ever did. There's a peace that comes over me, whenever I speak of him. I feel it down to my marrow."

Gram's unsteady voice trailed like a wreath of smoke in the wind. A lone tear spilled. She hesitated wiping it away, determined to not draw attention to it.

"Are you crying, Gram d'lena? You crying? Please, don't cry. I didn't mean to make you cry."

"Must be my hayfever, baby. Gets real bad, come summertime."

Deborah's own eyes began to tear. She reached for 'Marie,' her hand-painted doll with the big brown eyes, brown face and long, shiny black hair. Gram had ordered it 'special' from New York for her grandbaby's fourth birthday. Marie was Deborah's constant companion, a faithful friend who never betrayed a confidence, never awakened her during the night, and never wet her diaper.

"You miss him, Gram? You miss Pa-Pa?"

"God, yes. More than I can tell you, baby. See, when you truly love somebody, and been with them long as me and your granddaddy were together, ain't a day go by you don't miss 'em. You prob'ly too young to understand this, but sometimes when I'm walkin' 'round this ol' house, he spring to mind so quick I have to stop and catch my breath.

"I can almost see his face...can almost touch him. He look so fine, just like that picture of him hangin' over the divan. He's all smilin' and everything, like he own the world. He was one proud man. Hand me that towel, baby."

"Does it scare you, Gram?"

"What, baby? Seein' your Pa-Pa?"

"Yes, ma'am. I don't like no ghosteses."

"Ghosteses?" Gram chuckled. "No, baby. Sometimes it happens when I'm not expectin' it. Kinda' catches me off guard, but it don't scare me none. I just get sad for a few minutes. Then, I think of somethin' funny he used to do, or say, and I'm alright. I ever tell you the story 'bout the apron?"

"I'm not sure," said Deborah, despite having heard the apron story at least a dozen times. She knew it word for word. But Gram loved telling it and she was not about to deny her that simple joy.

Gram's eyes danced, as she folded her arms across her ample chest, and reared back in her specially-cushioned, straw-bottom chair.

"When we lived in our ol' house back in Kirbyville, Texas, your granddaddy loved to tease me. Used to sneak up behind me, loosen my apron strings and go stand in the kitchen doorway. I had a big kitchen, then. You could get six or seven grown folks in it at once. House was fairly good size, too. I sure loved that ol' house. It was so roomy and airy...lots 'a shade trees. Had a front porch. Made a lot 'a mem'ries there.

"We lived on a couple 'a acres, next to ol' man Koontz's place, 'bout three miles from town. C. Rodd Koontz was his full name. Never knew what the *C* stood for. He was one mean ol' cuss. Mean and rich. Had a peg leg. Cursed a lot. Dipped snuff, too. Nasty habit. All that spittin,' juice drippin.' Unh!" Gram scrunched her face at the mention of it.

"But he and your granddaddy always got along. That's 'cause Reverend George didn't take no guff from nobody, black or white. He was kind, but...Anyway, all of a sudden, while I'm busy cookin', my apron would fall to the floor right in front of me. Your granddaddy would double over laughin', like that was the funniest thing he ever saw. I can just see him now. Didn't matter how many times he played his little joke, he laughed just as hard every time. Glasses would shake; dishes would rattle."

"For real?" Deborah returned Marie to the chair next to her.

"Sure as I'm sittin' here. Lord, I do so miss hearin' him laugh."

Deborah stroked Gram's hand lightly. Hers were loving hands, with fingers gnarled by time, ravaged by arthritis.

Gram grew quiet. Both gazed out across the rich green earth straddling Arkansas's Ouachita and Central regions. Her small A-frame house seemed lost in the vastness—a speck on the horizon.

Nearest town, Reedville, was just over four miles away. Nearest neighbor, other than family, was three miles away, just past winding Drawhorn Creek. Gram said that was just fine with her, said she rather liked having a neighbor living so close.

"You scared of dying, Gram?"

Gram sat straight back, thrust her right hand to her chest. Never knew what was coming out of Deborah Yvonne's busy little mouth.

"Dyin'? Not anymore, baby. Stopped being scared long time ago. Reckon it was after Mama and Papa passed away."

Deborah scooted her straw-bottom chair closer to the old, oak leaf-table. The aged, pine floor creaked its familiar symphony. Gram was sure she saw another question form on her granddaughter's determined brow.

"Gram, is 'passed away' same as dying?"

"Well, yes. Reckon that's 'bout as plain as you can put it."

"Then why don't you just say died, instead?"

"Hmm. Baby, you know...I never thought about it, until you asked. Guess it just...just seems less sad when you say passed away. Like your loved ones just faded away, slow like."

"Like in a dream or something?"

"I suppose. Took me a long time to get over losin' my mama and papa, I tell *you.* Didn't think I ever would. Was hard to imagine never havin' them around again. World's a whole lot different without your mother and father. You feel so alone, even if you got sisters and brothers—even ones you still on speakin' terms with. Nothin' can take their place. They say the worst thing is for a parent to bury a child, but I couldn't imagine anything harder than losin' my mama and papa.

"Funny thing is, I soon started to look at life a lot different...started to realize how little of it there is; that there's a lot of livin' to do everyday. God must 'a meant for it to be that way."

"Is there really a heaven and a hell?"

"Now, where did *that* question come from?"

"From Daddy."

"Your daddy?"

"Yes, ma'am. Daddy is always preaching about heaven and hell. He says heaven is way past the sky, but he never says where hell is. I think it must be far away—way past Arkansas, even Miss'sippi, 'cause it takes your whole life to get there."

Gram smiled, shook her head. "You don't say. Baby, most folk who look like me and you...think Mississippi really is...Anyway, don't you believe your daddy?"

"I just want to know what you think."

"Babygirl, you sure ask a lot 'a questions, to be so little."

"Daddy said that's how you learn, Gram. You ask questions, then listen to the answers. That's what Daddy said."

"I guess your daddy ought 'a know. He was the same way when he was comin' up. Would ask one question right after the other. I would sometimes give him food, even candy...fill up his mouth just to give my voice and my ears a rest. He took after his daddy. Should 'a known he was gon' be a preacher, too. That child could talk up a storm.

"He was different from my other children in that way. Used to pretend he was havin' church in the back yard. Had his sisters and brother, even neighborhood children, singin' and shoutin,' fallin' out like they was filled with the Holy Ghost. His daddy made him stop, when he started takin' up offerin's."

"So, is there?"

"Is there what, baby?"

"A heaven and a hell, Gram."

"Now, your brother, Matthew, is outside workin' so hard...washed dishes last night. And you s'pose to be helpin' me shell these peas. I'm lookin' in your bowl and I only see two, four, five, six...less than a dozen peas, babygirl. Now, why you s'pose that is? *My* bowl is half full already."

"Gram d'lena, your hands are much bigger than mine, that's why."

"I see."

"I'm only five and three 'mumfs.' I have little bitty hands. That's what 'Maffew' says. He says I got little bitty hands. You think I got little bitty hands, Gram?"

"Maybe. But they most certainly are growin' right along with the rest of you. Your mind sure ain't little, though. Tell you what, I'll take your bowl and give you mine, alright? See? Now that makes it look like you workin' a lot harder than me."

"I *am* working harder, Gram. I'm just not working as *fast* as you."

"Is that right? Now, why didn't I figure that out?"

"Cause you tired?"

"Must surely be the reason, baby."

"Can I come and live with you, Gram? Please? I can help you do stuff. And I don't eat a lot, 'cept on Sundays. That's when Mama cooks up everything I like. But not as good as you do."

"Baby, you're somethin.' I don't mind your eatin.' And there sure is plenty of stuff to do 'roun' here. But your mama and daddy likely wouldn't take kindly to you leavin' home at such a tender age. Thanks, anyway. I'm sure glad you and Matthew came to spend the night...help ol' Gram out today. With you helpin' me shell peas and Matthew outside rakin' up leaves, I can prob'ly get aroun' to makin' those sweet potato pies I promised y'all last time. You like that?"

"Yes, ma'am. I can shell the rest of these here peas all by myself. You can start making those pies right now."

"Babygirl, you're a doozy."

"Gram, what's a..."

"Shhh. Enough questions for right now. You got some peas to shell," said Gram. Deborah laughed.

Suddenly, Gram d'lena shot straight up, gasped, covered her mouth. Deep frowns carved her brow. She clutched her bosom and sank back into her chair. Her eyes riveted on her grandbaby. What she saw chilled her blood, stole her breath.

Less than three feet away, her beloved Deborah Yvonne appeared cloaked in a dark shadow that obscured her features. Pure evil is what it was. Gram cursed the demonic presence, even as she trembled the length of her body. With jaws clenched, her heart quaking, she summoned the name of God to her lips. In the name of all things Holy, she petitioned the Almighty to build a hedge around her babygirl.

In an instant, two distinct names, two distinct images leaped to her mind: Jude Barsteau, and Florinda Batiste. She quickly dispatched the former from her thoughts, but the latter persisted. Could it be true? Was ol' lady Batiste fulfilling her curse from the grave?

When Deborah was first born, well-wishers often visited the Davis home, bringing gifts. One Wednesday morning, ninety year-old spinster, Florinda Batiste, was among them, cloaked in her customary white, from head to toe. It was well-known that the longtime resident was a Voodoo practitioner of longstanding.

The moment Florinda practically 'appeared' near Deborah's bassinet, everyone shrank away. A hush fell. Gram d'lena observed Batiste staring at the baby, frowning and chanting. Mabel Davis watched, passively. Just as the old woman extended a gloved right hand toward Deborah, Gram glanced at Mabel, then rushed forward. She grabbed Batiste's left arm and nearly dragged her from the house. And without raising her voice, Gram d'lena sternly commanded she never return, nor be caught anywhere near a single member of her family. "Not ever," Gram repeated.

An angry Florinda Batiste started away, then turned, pointed, and yelled: "That baby is got a dark cloud over her, Miss Magdalena. I seen it. You gon' see it, too...all 'a y'all. She's dead! Y'all can pray to that God 'a yours all y'all want, but she's dead! You hear me? She's dead!" Then, despite her years, Batiste, who lived a mile away, left walking, briskly.

The next morning, shock and horror gripped the Sticks. Batiste's charred remains were found in her smoldering shack near Devil's Woods. Some blamed The Klan. Others swore it was a single bolt of lightning. Official cause of the mysterious blaze was never established. Florinda Batiste was reportedly found sitting upright...in an oak rocker. A badly ripped Bible, open to Psalm One, rested in what remained of her hands.

Psalm One:

"1. Blessed is the man that walketh not in the counsel of the ungodly, nor standeth in the way of sinners, nor sitteth in the seat of the scornful. 2. But his delight is in the law of the Lord, and in His law doth he meditate, day and night. 3. And he shall be like a tree planted by the rivers of water, that bringeth forth his fruit in his season; his leaf also shall not wither; and whatsoever he doeth shall prosper. 4. The ungodly are not so, but are like the chaff which the wind driveth away. 5. Therefore the ungodly shall not stand in the judgment, nor sinners in the congregation of the righteous. 6. For the Lord knoweth the way of the righteous, but the way of the ungodly shall perish. —(Authorized King James Version)

But what could not be explained, was the fact neither the chair nor the Bible was so much as singed. Grim photos of the horrific scene, reportedly taken by Coroner, Henry P. Chesney, were never released. Never. Sheriff Darden claimed they were likely misfiled, and that he "wuddn't" about to waste taxpayers' money, nor his precious time, looking for them. Some said he was just plain too scared to even look at the photos, let alone touch them. If true, it may have been a wise decision on his part.

Less than twelve hours after Batiste's remains were carted off to the morgue, Chesney himself fell dead. Heart attack, they said. Only fifty-one years old, the longtime Reedville resident, and Reed family cousin, suffered the attack while examining Florinda Batiste's cadaver.

The bizarre events sparked fear and speculation, regarding evil spirits and demonic curses. Few in the Sticks, or Reedville, were inclined to even speak Batiste's name. To this day, even weeds will not grow on the spot where her hovel once stood. And for about a year following her death, dozens reported seeing what they were certain was Florinda Batiste, dressed in white, and scurrying along the backroads of the Sticks. The last such sighting was on Easter Sunday, 1963.

Now, five years after Deborah's birth, Gram stood staring at this dark shadow. She had heard her beloved mother speak of such evil in hushed tones, but had never witnessed it until now. With fists formed, Gram kept repeating her prayer, commanding the evil spirit to flee.

The baleful omen persisted only seconds. But that was enough to cast a lasting pall. Gram stared at her grandbaby, before turning away until the fear subsided. Why was such an ungodly spirit being visited upon an innocent child?

Gram prayed that whatever evil this dark sign portended would pass quickly and forever. She gathered herself and, with faltering steps, moved to plant a kiss on her grandbaby's brow. She laid warm, loving hands on Deborah's head, then moved to the open window. She was certain that if she remained near the table, the fear branded on her face would not escape Deborah's probing eyes.

A chill coursed Gram's shivering frame, even as she prayed. Deborah gave her a curious glance. Gram took a deep breath, forced a weak smile then turned away. Deborah resumed shelling her peas, as Gram kept whispering her prayerful mantra, summoning the Holy Angels:

"God, I pray your Holy Spirit come now. Deliver us from this evil; drive it from this place. Father, build a hedge around this child for the length of her days. In the merciful name of God the Father, The Son, and The Holy Spirit, I pray. Amen." Gram took a quick breath and repeated her prayer.

Gram d'lena told only one person—a close friend—what she experienced that day. The woman, unrelated to her, vowed to keep her secret forever. Gram had no doubt she would keep her word.

chapter four

Deborah never dreamed she would need a second chance to live her one life.

From the moment
Deborah Yvonne Davis first laid eyes on Gram d'lena, in 1962, a lasting
bond was formed. Their love was instant and eternal. Kindred spirits,
they were—joined at the heart. The instant Deborah began walking,
Gram could barely set foot across the threshold before her grandbaby
would make a bee line for her, toddling as fast as her plump little legs
could carry her.

A stoic Mabel Davis would often watch from the kitchen doorway,
as her daughter bounced on her toes—anxious arms uplifted, head tossed
back—and waited to be swept up into Gram's big loving arms. Gram
d'lena never disappointed. It was enough to make a mother jealous. Some
were certain it did.

Gram had love aplenty, and did not horde it one bit. She adored all
her grandchildren. Yet, for eight years, she and Deborah shared a special bond few will ever know. Best of all, Gram lived barely one quarter of

a country mile away, just north of Drawhorn Creek, two ticks from where John Henry Langston and Crispus Attucks Roads crossed.

Magdalena was Gram's given name—Magdalena Morris. She was right proud of her first name's biblical roots. And was equally proud she had no middle name to disavow. Said a middle name was like a third thumb: unnecessary. And did not tolerate being called Maggie. It was Magdalena or nothing.

"Jesus didn't have no middle name," she loved to point out. "Didn't keep him from doin' his work."

A deeply religious woman, Gram d'lena was solid enough in her faith to have a laugh at the expense of the Son of God without fear of eternal damnation.

—

Gram d'lena was Deborah's paternal grandmother. And until her passing, on June 16, 1970, when Deborah was barely eight, she was the Davis children's only surviving grandparent. She embraced the role with both arms and her whole heart. Was not much else she wanted to be.

"I am most sure I was born to be a grandmother. My grandchildren make me feel more like a mother than when I was motherin' my own children," she told anyone willing to listen.

Gram even looked like a grandmother. She was a buxom, rosy-cheeked, well-bottomed woman with big loving arms that seemed capable of embracing the whole world, with room to spare. She had big, deep, black- brown, smiling eyes with a light gray corona; long lashes, and creamy-brown skin that scarcely had a blemish. Even had a mouthful of "original teeth," as she proudly called them.

Gram wore her mostly white hair pulled straight back into a bun that seemed permanently affixed. On the rare occasion she let it down, it fell past her shoulders. However, for some never explained reason, she wore those 'Old Maid'-looking black shoes. Worse, she wore them with thick, brown cotton stockings that never stayed up. Always seemed to twist and pucker around her ankles. Deborah found it difficult resisting the urge to reach down and yank them up.

But Gram d'lena insisted she was not old. "I refuse to be old. Just plain ain't got time to be old. Bein' and actin' old takes a lot of time and energy, just when you can least afford to squander either. Much easier to act and think young."

Gram was always saying things like that. Deborah clung to every word; she remembered each one, even the precise inflection in her grandmother's voice.

"Life ain't but a minute, no matter how long ya' live," Gram loved to say. "Live yo'self a thousand years ev'ryday," was another of her favorites. Gram had a bushel of such pearls. Most anyone who spent more than a minute in her presence was bound to get an earful, especially if she had a good feeling about you. She would look you up and down, not say a word, just size you up. If she liked you, she would talk your ears off.

Deborah Yvonne loved to hear Gram talk, as much as Gram d'lena loved talking. Nevermind she did not always use proper English, and even loosed a little cuss word every now and then. She had earned the right to speak any way she chose.

One of the last gems of wisdom Gram bequeathed her granddaughter was: "Don't ever stop dreamin,' babygirl. Ev'rything starts with a dream. This ol' world would be a sad place without dreams and dreamers." Deborah took Gram's words to heart.

—

Gram died at age 72, following a severe bout of influenza that left her heart and respiratory system weakened. All who knew and loved her were devastated. None more than Deborah—her babygirl.

Despite her father's pleading, and his assurance Gram was in heaven, Deborah withdrew. She stopped eating, hardly stirred from her bed. The Reverend was concerned about her attending Gram's funeral, but knew he would not be able to keep her from doing so.

Deborah found it inconceivable she would never again feel Gram's loving arms around her, never see her smile, or hear her soothing voice. There would be no more trips with Matthew to Gram's old house. No more sitting at her kitchen table, listening to her stories, feeling the old floors shake whenever she laughed.

The day of Gram's funeral at Shiloh, Deborah planted herself next to the casket during the entire service. No amount of coaxing by her father, or by Matthew, could entice her away. It was as if she were standing guard, protecting Gram d'lena as Gram had always guarded and protected *her*. Deborah would forever remember every detail: Gram's white dress; her long, gray hair in a bun; the faint smile on her face; her hands, with fingers laced, placed across her chest.

At the end of the burial ceremony, it dawned on Deborah that Gram's casket would be placed into the earth and covered. Gram d'lena would be...in the ground, covered up forever? Deborah wondered about the rain. What would happen when it rained? It just didn't seem right that Gram's casket would be soaked from rain.

Sure, these were the simple thoughts of a child, but they deeply troubled Deborah. She darted from the cemetery, even as her mother and Maylene tried in vain to intercept her. She kept running, well past the church grounds, out toward the open fields. Matthew ran full out to catch her. But it was not until he stood facing her, with both arms around her for a time, that she stopped struggling against him.

Deborah refused to return to the burial site. She and Matthew later found their way to the front of the church. Both sat in silence on the church steps until long after the interment had concluded.

—

The night following Gram's funeral was the longest and darkest in Deborah's young life. She was inconsolable, found it impossible to close her eyes, much less sleep. She lay sobbing, with Marie pressed to her face. She kept whispering Gram's name, over and over.

But somewhere near midnight, while suspended between light and darkness, Deborah felt the mattress sink on her side of the bed she shared with her eldest sister, Maylene. It frightened her something awful. Deborah's eyes shot open; her heart nearly leaped to her throat. She struggled to speak—to make the simplest sound, but her voice failed.

There she was—Gram d'lena. She appeared less than three feet away, shrouded in soft white light. It was Gram in every detail, smiling broadly, love shining in her eyes like diamonds.

Deborah's fear quickly eased into an embracing calm. She sat straight up, and stretched out a trembling right hand to touch her grandmother. Gram smiled, lifted both hands palms up and was gone.

A wide-eyed Deborah felt bathed in the warm afterglow. A caressing peace enveloped her, radiating throughout her body. It was all a bit much for an eight-year-old, even a precocious one. Had she imagined it all? Were such things even possible? Was Gram d'lena an angel now?

Deborah desperately wanted to wake Maylene, Rachel, and Gloria and tell them everything, but thought better of it. Her sisters would never believe such a fantastic story. Telling her parents was something Deborah never once considered. She was certain neither would have believed her. She never told a soul, not even her brother, Matthew—her soulmate and protector.

It was soon thereafter, the conversations began: Deborah's guarded communications with her deceased grandmother. At first, they were secret. She took great care to keep them private, pretending she was talking to her doll, Marie.

Mabel Davis' discovery of the true nature of her daughter's conversations brought a harsh, insensitive rebuke, and a warning they immediately stop. The result was a pained little girl with a crushed spirit. Deborah was certain no one could ever provide her the love Gram had shown, and still showed her.

Two years after Gram left to join her beloved husband, George, her old house collapsed, went to sod—fell apart. Takes living, breathing souls to keep a house alive. Deborah reckoned since Gram d'lena was gone, the old place saw no reason to keep on standing.

The Davis children were woefully heartbroken. First, Gram was taken away, then her house. Was not just any ol' house, either. This was Gram d'lena's house—a treasured, sacred place where love ruled. A place where life lessons were taught, and memories born.

A year earlier, nearly everything of material value was carted out of the old place, abandoning it to the ravages of dry *Devil Winds* that echoed like distant wailing.

The now barren earth, where once the simple structure stood, became hallowed ground, especially for Deborah and Matthew. Despite their mother's warnings they stay away from the site, the two frequently stole away and spent hours playing in the ruins. Gram seemed never closer than when they were there.

The Reverend promised his beloved young daughter that she would see her Gram again. "Come Judgment Day," he declared, with a booming baritone that reverberated with the authority of God Almighty. Never told her what day that would most likely be. Still, Deborah believed him. He was her father; his word was beyond doubt.

In the years that followed, memories of Gram streamed through Deborah's mind like liquid silk—ever present, undiminished by the relentless march of time. Gram was, and remained, the solid Oak in her life. Deborah still spoke to her, and heard her calming voice. Her beloved grandmother was always only a whisper away, forever the angel in her dreams.

chapter five

In Her First Life -The Last Day

The day after Dr. King was assassinated, the Klan...

On May 15, 1974,
Deborah Yvonne Davis lived the last day of her first life. When the sun rose that morning, she was a happy, precocious, bright-eyed, twelve year-old school girl in love with life. She was an innocent, gregarious, virgin woman-child on the cusp of teenage-hood. Gram would have been proud.

Like her peers, Deborah often found herself wrestling with strange, new emotions and occasional self-doubts, but was reluctant to confide in her mother. Maylene knew the feeling well. Her own similar experiences served to draw her even closer to her younger sister. She offered a willing ear and a compassionate, empathetic heart.

Unlike Gram, Mabel Davis was not the warm, fuzzy, conversational type given to emotional handholding. Neither she nor Reverend could imagine twelve year-olds facing weighty matters of any kind. Whatever they required could most likely be supplied by a firm right hand, and a healthy serving of 'King James Version,' from Genesis to Revelation.

For years, the only entertainment in the Davis home was provided by the Sears Silvertone stereo, with am-fm and eight-track player. Programs and music were strictly proscribed. No blues, no rock n' roll. Some Motown was okay. But on Sundays, gospel music ruled.

Reverend finally purchased a television set, just in time to watch the 1968 Democratic National Convention in Chicago. Rules for watching were more restrictive than listening to the radio had ever been. Still, the Davis kids had little to complain about, compared to the plight of some of their friends regarding food, shelter, clothing...such things.

Deborah—DeeDee to friends—resolved to paint smiley-faces on her few difficulties. She was surrounded by a God-fearing family, close friends, and nearly untouched by the gloom of adult realities. There would be time enough for coping with problems she often overheard her parents discussing. Besides, she was sure it would take forever to grow as old as they.

—

Growing up in the Sticks was a challenging, yet unremarkable, experience. This oft-referred to 'Colored Quarters' was nestled in the rustic backwash of the backwater called Reedville, Arkansas, fifty-eight miles southwest of Little Rock. For most of its citizens, Reedville was not much to speak of. Few did.

Those lucky enough to escape, jumped the fence and never looked back. Without the unquestioned clout of the powerful, scandalously rich Reed family, map makers would surely have saved their ink.

It was 1974, only six years removed from one of the most violent years in recent American history—the late, 1968. The stinging legacy of the Jim Crow era; the scars of violent, denigrating racism, and its dehumanizing impact on the human spirit was evident in Reedville, as it was elsewhere in the South.

An uneasy peace had long existed between Blacks and Whites. A line of demarcation, drawn by a virulent race hatred as intrinsic as bone marrow, insured eternal racial divergence in Reedville and elsewhere. One would have thought Whites had been the ones enslaved.

At 12 years, Deborah still remembered her sixth year, 1968, with surprising emotional clarity. It was the year innocence died for so many, young and old alike. A not so distant place called Memphis, and the Lorraine Motel, became part of a sorrowful litany spoken with anger and sadness by nearly everyone she knew.

Grown men wept openly. Despair and resignation embroidered nearly every conversation. Few Blacks accepted that a single, scrawny, uneducated white man was the lone doer of the deadly deed. Deborah remembered Gram being lost for words. It was the first time she had seen her cry so mournfully.

The one exception was when she spoke of the racist, 1963 bombing of the Sixteenth Street Baptist Church in Birmingham. That unspeakably savage act took the lives of four young black girls, while they sat in Sunday School. Deborah was barely a year old then. She would later recall that Gram's eyes teared; her voice always thinned, whenever she spoke of the horror. Then came April 4th, 1968.

"But I ain't gon' hate nobody. I can't," she said. "Hate is like eatin' lye. It kills you from the inside. But it won't destroy your enemies one little bit."

The day after Dr. King was assassinated, the Klan held a hastily organized rally out near Shays Creek, three miles south of Reedville. Word was, several Reedville residents and merchants attended, celebrating the cowardly act with fireworks, fiery speeches, and a cross burning that turned deadly. A freak gasoline flash fire erupted, spreading to nearby vehicles. A station wagon exploded, killing a four-year-old boy dressed in a tiny Klan uniform and sleeping in the car's rear seat.

In a display of typically twisted reasoning, the Klan blamed Dr. King. They suggested if he, Dr. King, had not "needed killing," the rally would not have happened; the fire would not have occurred, and the baby would not have died.

The next day's Arkansas Democrat-Gazette told the story in vivid fashion. Scorched remnants of the little uniform were shown on the front-page. It dramatized the insanity of hatred in a way few things could.

Most Blacks, and many Whites, upset by the Klan's activities, avoided Reedville's business district for more than two weeks. It was not an organized boycott, but had the same economic effect. Soon, every store window in town displayed signs—many handwritten—declaring all were welcome, whether they truly were or not.

Across the country, the atmosphere was explosive. Racial tensions reached a boiling point. Several big cities, particularly Detroit, suffered riots, burnings and violence resulting in numerous deaths, and severe economic loss.

The night of Dr. King's assassination, Deborah's preacher-father took to his pulpit, at Shiloh Missionary Baptist Church. He did so, to vent his anger, frustration, hope, and determination to "overcome." He had sent out word that Shiloh's doors would be open. He wanted all his members, and others who chose to come, to meet him there.

They came. In less than an hour, the church was filled to overflowing. Miss Ruby and Mr. Peabo were there. Mr. Lonnie did not attend. But word came that he closed his doors that night. Reverend had that kind of respect from saints and sinners alike. Shiloh had seldom seen such a crowd. Dozens stood in the aisles, while others remained outdoors. Deborah never left Gram's side.

The Reverend Amon Devereaux, longtime Pastor of the smaller, St. John Missionary Baptist Church, opened his church's doors, also. Both he and Reverend were hopeful of diffusing the rampant anger, and preventing possible violent reaction.

However, at Shiloh, not all arrived with bibles tucked under their arms. A few, much more militant congregants, had less godly plans of action. Their anger, rage, and their intent to be anything but passive, had the potential for deadly confrontation. Two dozen or more men, including several Deacons, brought along more earthly artillery in the form of shotguns, rifles, and pistols.

"If the Klan or any other white folk show their faces anywhere 'round here tonight, we gon' arrange a meeting for 'em with the Almighty," someone shouted. Others voiced agreement.

The Reverend, despite his own anger and deep sadness, boldly stood in his pulpit and tried to calm his congregation. He understood the raw emotion, the rage, but denounced vows of violence. He did so, using the lessons of Dr. King himself. "We cannot defeat them, by becoming them."

Reverend began praying. Others joined him. Soon, prayers were being heard beyond the walls of Shiloh. All were moved by Reverend's appeal to those who believed in God's message of "love and forgiveness."

"They intended this for evil," he said. "But God will see that good derives." Even those who had vowed retribution, now clutched bibles, although their guns were never far away.

Not long after relative calm returned, it began to rain—serious rain. A pounding rain fell in torrents, accompanied by peels of thunder and chards of lightning. It fell with such speed and ferocity, none inside were able to leave. Some saw it as Divine intervention.

The unforecasted storm lasted throughout the evening and into the morning. Water and nonperishable food—always stored in the basement—were provided those desiring either.

Then, the lights went out. Just past midnight, power was lost. The outage lasted three hours. Some saw a "white folk conspiracy." Candles were quickly lit, creating an ambiance that begged for introspection and calm. A couple of well-armed deacons kept a lookout, just in case.

Just before sunrise, the storm moved on. The crowd of hundreds eventually dwindled to less than a dozen, including the entire Davis family. Most were determined to get to their jobs, despite high water levels. Few had the luxury of taking a day off from work.

—

The Reverend Henry Bertram Davis' voice was powerful and unshackled. His was the voice of Black people whose own voices were often muted by practical considerations of jobs, and fear of retribution at the hands of their modern-day overseers. In Reedville, that overseer was the all-powerful Reed family. Had to be a plumb fool not to know that. They ruled with the iron-hand style of earlier robber-barons, tolerating no challenge to their authority, from stranger nor kin.

The Reed family, headed by firebrand patriarch, Richard Reed, owned damn near everything, including a stable of flunkies—white and black—who kept them informed. Seemed what the Reeds did not own, had not been invented by man nor created by God.

Not much, except weather, happened in Reed County or Arkansas without their blessings. Much of the Reeds' control over people in the County was derived from the virtual naming of, and or controlling of, the Sheriff's department and all judgeships.

The Sticks—the 'Colored Quarters, so-called'—was patrolled by one Rufus T. (Thaddeus) Bluehorn. Bluehorn, 6'-4," 280 pounds, was a ruthless, greasy, cigar-champing, gap-toothed, self-hating black man brought in from neighboring Pilser County. Folks in the Sticks called him 'Blue Hog,' though not to his face. While he was given full rein in the Sticks, he was not permitted to stop Whites for any reason, even fleeing felons.

Bluehorn lived in a *lean-to* shack on Reed property. His sole responsibility was to "keep niggers in line." You did not want to be stopped and confronted by ol' Rufus T. His reputation for brutality and viciousness toward fellow Blacks was legend.

One would have fared better in a confrontation with a white deputy any day. Black folk unfortunate enough to encounter *Blue Hog,* and survive, would later describe themselves as having been "Bluehorned." That was enough. No further explanation was needed.

So, it was understandable that, in 1972, no one in all of Reedville, especially the Sticks, mourned Bluehorn's horrible death at the hands of killer or killers unknown. On the first Sunday morning in April of that year, his decapitated, castrated hulk was found simmering inside the trunk of his burned out, eight year-old patrol car.

The death scene was about a quarter mile into Devil's Woods, just off the northern end of J.H. Langston Road. There was not even pretense of a criminal investigation. And no funeral. Rumors surfaced that ol' Rufus' remains were dumped in an unmarked ditch, rather than buried in a grave, unmarked or otherwise. And, to no one's surprise, not a soul applied to fill the vacant position.

The Reed dynasty dated back to 1874, thirty-eight years after Arkansas became the 25th state in 1836. Silas Zebediah Reed, Richard's paternal grandfather, and Silas' three brothers, moved their families from central Kentucky to the Natural State. Legend had it, they had been forced out at gunpoint. Reasons were never offered.

Silas, the eldest and the more ruthless of the brothers, soon amassed a huge fortune. Most of the booty came from illegal spirits, logging, cotton, transportation, a string of ritzy gambling parlors, and scores of well-appointed whorehouses—particularly in New Orleans.

Silas soon purchased the holdings of his more docile brothers. His business interests spread like tentacles throughout the South, Southwest, and Midwest. He acquired mammoth parcels of real property, in suspicious deals that fattened bank accounts of lawyers, judges, and government officials.

However, the end came for ol' Silas in a most inglorious manner. He departed this life on September 11, 1923, less than twenty-four hours after being kicked in the head by a one-eared mule he owned. Silas refused medical treatment, ignoring the pleadings of both wife and physician. He thus proved as stubborn as 'Sambo,' the surly, four-legged beast that dispatched him to his reward.

Succeeding generations of Reeds ballooned the family fortune that, by most accounts in 1974, totaled nearly 800 million dollars. Some estimates were several times higher. Richard chose to concentrate on real estate development, insurance, oil and gas, blue chip investments, and political bribery. It had all worked extremely well in the past.

The Reed family epitomized one of two, vastly different worlds. For Deborah and eldest sister, Maylene; younger sister, Rachel; youngest sister, Gloria; and only surviving brother, Matthew, their narrowly proscribed world revolved around church and school—in that order. Wealth and power were merely words in their dictionary.

The Davises lived honestly and modestly. The thought they could be considered poor never occurred to them. What was lacking in material wealth was more than compensated for with love, faith in God, and dedication to helping those less fortunate. And God knows there were plenty of less fortunate to be helped. The needy came in all colors and ethnicities. Extreme hunger has a way of blurring race distinctions, even if only temporarily.

The Davis children were like most kids, yet *unlike* most kids. Being any preacher's kid meant bearing a special burden to walk the straight and narrow. However, being one of the Reverend and Mabel Davis' offsprings meant the burden—having to live between the lines—was tenfold. If the fear of God was not enough to inspire circumspection, the fear of the Reverend's ability to swing his right hand was more than sufficient to compel obedience.

All this proved especially difficult for young Matthew. He was the second child, and only surviving son—a naturally contrary, independent sort who possessed a mind of his own. He was also afflicted with a quick temper destined to get him into trouble someday.

At fourteen, Matthew was obsessed with bodybuilding. It began in first grade, after he was beaten up by a fourth-grader. Now, he was muscular and nearly six feet tall.

Matthew was a quick study. He had the potential to be a great student, were it not for his impatient nature and unwillingness to follow dictates. From the outset, he displayed a knack for testing the limits of his father's love and calm temperament.

"That boy keeps me on bended knee," Reverend often lamented.

A great deal more praying lay ahead. Thank God for Gram. When she was alive, she was always saving poor Matthew from the Reverend's anger. Following her death, only God stood between them.

chapter six

====================================

Any threat to one was a threat to all.

S eparate is almost never equal.

In 1974, seventeen years after the historic events at Little Rock's Central High School, Reedville County's, George Washington Carver Schools remained all black. The campus was three decrepit schools in one: an elementary, junior-high, and senior high school.

All three aging structures were set on a single campus, surrounded by tens of thousands of lush, wooded acres owned by Reed County. The overcrowded facilities were never properly equipped, nor maintained. Water pipes rusted and leaked. Plumbing often backed up, creating pools of human waste and unbearable stench inside and outside the buildings. Hard to do algebra with a hand cupped over your nose.

Following repeated complaints, feeble attempts at repair proved inadequate. So, poor black families pooled meager resources, to address the more urgent problems: those impacting the health of their children.

Plumbers, carpenters, electricians, masons, and others contributed their time, talents, and materiel to improve conditions.

The all-white County School Board never bothered with excuses. The exception was a solitary, courageous, School Board member: Sarah Faubus, a retired teacher from Little Rock. Miss Faubus was forced to resign shortly after privately meeting with black parents.

State Education officials turned a deaf ear as well. All this pointed up the consequences of not having real political and economic power. This issue, and the matter of taking individual responsibility, were subjects the Reverend often preached about, with varying success.

Unfortunately, whenever Reverend lectured more than preached, the offering was curiously smaller; the amens were fewer. Many congregants seemed to prefer a message of fire and brimstone, accompanied by animated oratory—a good whoop.

School textbooks were mostly dog-eared hand-me-downs from better-supplied white schools. Students often found racist drawings and vulgar scribblings inside many of them.

The fact Carver students excelled, despite the adversity, was a testament to their determination, the support of their parents, and the devotion of dedicated teachers.

Few Carver students were much concerned about the larger, distant world beyond them. Rightly or wrongly, they felt the broader 'white world' was not their world—at least not one that offered hope.

The fact that only six days earlier, on May 9th, the House Judiciary Committee opened hearings to consider recommending impeachment of Richard Nixon for his Watergate sins, mattered little to them.

What captured the attention of the entire school, and the whole of Reedville's Blacks, was the fact Hank Aaron broke Babe Ruth's homerun record. 'Hammerin' Hank' hit his 715th homerun on April 8th. The historic achievement came despite vile threats against Aaron and his family. Even twelve year-olds understood, that despite Aaron's successes, many Whites still regarded him as a 'nigger.' Successful alright, but still a *nigger.*

Carver school buses were dilapidated and few. The newer and best were always reserved for white students. They were students whose parents never complained about busing until black students were bused to better-equipped white schools. Overnight, busing became a monster heralding the downfall of western civilization.

Students either walked to school, took the bus, or were driven by parents fortunate to have the time, and a car. Most black parents, blessed to have decent jobs—or jobs at all—were off to work at the crack of dawn. Having decent work usually meant traveling more than one hundred miles round trip to Little Rock each day. Same was true for many poor white families. And there were lots of them. Of course, most would object to being lumped into the same category as their black counterparts.

—

Deborah loved the long, lazy walks to and from school with closest friends, Karetha Jackson and Beverly Brown, respectively nicknamed Kay and B.B. Each was twelve. There was always plenty to talk about, especially the subject of boys.

Karetha was the taller, and equally as vocal and opinionated as Beverly. She wore her hair in a small Afro, and sneaked on lipstick right after school. She would remove the ruby-red gloss just before she reached the Davis home, where they would deposit Deborah. Today, the lipstick had turned liquid and leaked inside her book-bag.

Beverly said exactly whatever came to her mind. Shorter and slightly heavier than her two friends, she exhibited no lack of self-confidence or wit. There was hardly a boy in the entire sixth grade for whom she did not have a one or two word description.

Unpaved Crispus Attucks Road snaked through miles of captivating, wooded, sun-drenched countryside. It finally wound past the Davis house, just under two and three quarter miles from school.

Karetha and Beverly lived only a quarter mile farther. The girls walked as slowly as possible. All were certain that once Deborah got home, Reverend would likely not let her out again, except for church.

Neither Kay nor B.B. had a father at home. In 1969, Beverly's father, Jerome—a onetime college football star with great promise cut short by a career-ending injury—simply walked away.

Karetha's father, Anthony, was on death row in California's San Quentin prison. In 1970, he was convicted of robbing a San Rafael convenience store and killing a woman clerk five months pregnant.

Anthony Jackson's public defender lawyer failed to call a single witness, despite the fact a half-dozen potential witnesses—all black—supported his client's claim to being one hundred fifty miles away when the crime was committed.

Both Reverend—or Preacher, as he was often called—and Sister Mabel Davis regarded both girls as their own. Reverend had the most to do with that. He always insisted on meeting his children's friends. And he was never reluctant to give them the same godly instruction he provided his own family.

Mabel Davis mothered the two girls, filling them with meat and potatoes, while Reverend nourished them with the *Word*. It was at Reverend's insistence, that the girls took to accompanying Deborah to Sunday School and church service most Sundays. He even bought them shoes and what he called 'dress-up outfits.'

—

The stroll home from school was always filled with laughter, and animated conversation covering the full range of subjects twelve-year old girls talk about.

Karetha, exhibiting a bit of envy regarding her friend's physical development, once teased Deborah. She asked her if she rubbed olive oil on her breasts, or powdered them with yeast, to make them grow. Deborah insisted she simply bathed regularly, and with soap. She suggested if Karetha did the same, her breasts might grow as well.

That is the way it often was, whenever these best friends were together. Good-natured teasing would go on and on. Neither ever took offense. The girls were like sisters—friendly competitors, but each rabidly protective of the other. Any threat to one, was a threat to all.

Rapid physiological changes provided a constant source for comparisons. Of the three, Deborah drew most of the attention from older boys, and men, for that matter. However, their reluctance in approaching her was due to Reverend's well-earned reputation for protecting his daughters.

Reverend Davis, the eldest of two sons and the second of four children, was well aware his Deborah was physically developed beyond her years. He was fiercely protective of all four of his girls, but especially Deborah Yvonne—his second girl. He rightly felt she most favored his late mother, Magdalena.

By all measure, Deborah was a child in a woman's body. Her looks earned the catty glares and snide comments of girls and women alike. Her flawless, creamy-brown skin, well-defined curves, and swaying walk, made her the envy of women decades past their prime. What was worse, she was the object of lust for men decades beyond her twelve years.

It was Deborah's good fortune that the depth of her youthful innocence made her practically oblivious to the discontent left in her wake. Her focus was on family, friends, church, and school.

Although she bore some resemblance to her 'semi-sweet chocolate-skinned' mother, Deborah was several shades lighter-skinned than her father, and her paternal grandfather, George. She was clearly more 'milky-caramel colored,' like Gram d'lena.

Deborah was also the lighter-skinned of her sisters, especially Rachel, whose deep, 'mocha-brown' skin most resembled her mother's, and brother, Matthew. While skin color seemed of such focus for others, Deborah often found herself wishing she were several shades darker.

Besides her obvious physical endowments, Deborah was blessed with the ability to clearly articulate her thoughts and ideas in writing. She loved music, and was gifted with a melodious voice.

Deborah's stirring soprano performances, in the choir of her father's church, often left the 'old sisters' weeping and fanning themselves. Their 'Sunday hats' were frequently left skewed, as they leaped to their feet, flailing and shouting while in the throes of the 'Holy Spirit.'

Nearly every Sunday, regardless of what songs were sung by the choir, there was at least one request for Deborah to sing *Amazing Grace*. Deborah always graciously obliged, singing the old favorite in a slow, stirring style reminiscent of Aretha Franklin.

Most often, at the conclusion of church service, while her father greeted departing congregants, Deborah found herself surrounded by worshippers praising her God-given talent.

"God sure used you this morning, baby. You just keep on using His gift for the glory of His kingdom," they would say.

Deborah, though uncomfortable with the endless praise, would smile, repeatedly nod, and thank them, while anxious to get away as quickly as possible.

But the warm feeling such praise showered on her was almost always dampened somewhat by the sight of Rachel, unsmiling, unimpressed, and positioned to make certain Deborah saw her.

Rachel was only a year and three months younger than Deborah. The two were closest in age than any of the other siblings. It was clear she was envious of the affection shown her older sister.

chapter seven

The Long Walk Home

———————————————

"The big eye ain't the only thing he got," Karetha whispered.

M ay 15, 1974
was about as hot a day in May as anyone could recall. Heat waves spiraled from sizzling pavement. Asphalt roads softened to goo. Yardmen, not smart enough to have gotten an early morning start, hunkered under shade trees.

Officials at Reedville County's all-black G.W. Carver School kept students inside all day, avoiding the danger of heat stroke or worse. When the school day finally ended, and the long walk home down Crispus Attucks began, it seemed even hotter.

Mabel Davis had asked the Reverend to shuttle the kids home. However, he was busy attending a Bible conference in Pine Bluff. Said his trip could not be postponed.

During their walk home this day, Deborah and her girlfriends were accompanied by fourteen-year-old Tommy Lee Williams, Jr., a lanky, bright but retiring eighth grader with a crush on Deborah impossible to conceal. Tommy had taken all school year to build up the courage to ask if he could walk her home. He would soon learn that a healthy measure of stamina was also required. Tommy lived over a mile from school, in the opposite direction.

Given her advanced physical development, Deborah had long ago learned—with her mother's coaching—to dampen her natural exuberance. Hemlines were kept low, necklines high.

Yet, little could chill the warmth of her fetching smile, or dim the sparkle in her eyes. And she had the most mesmerizing eyes. They were a deep, doleful black-brown with a distinctive light, gray-blue corona. Only Gram's were similar. Tommy was all but hypnotized by them.

He was different than most boys at Carver. Tommy was shy and easily embarrassed. At school, Deborah would often tease him by staring into his eyes, from less than a foot away, to merely see how long he could hold her gaze. It only took seconds before he glanced away.

Karetha and Beverly followed the pair. Luckily, the tall, bordering pines cast precious shade onto the western edge of the roadway. Tommy carried Deborah's books in her denim book bag he had slung over one shoulder. His own bag was stowed underneath the practice field bleachers. He would collect it on his return trip. It was clear he was struggling under the weight of both the bag and the pressure to carry on a coherent conversation.

Deborah was also less than talkative. Karetha nudged Beverly then cupped a hand to her mouth to stifle her giggles.

"Must be real nice, having some boy carry your books home for you, like you Cleopatra or somebody," she teased. "Especially somebody as cute as Mr. Tommy Lee Williams. I hear he's smart, too. Smart, and cute. And I like his little Afro...not too big, not too little."

"Tommy, you got any brothers? Any cousins?" asked Beverly. "I don't care if they're older than twelve. Thirteen...even fourteen, like you. But they got 'a look as good, and be as smart as you, too. 'Cause we don't want dummies. Later for dummies. I am not doing some boy's homework, no matter how good he looks. Okay?"

Tommy shifted the book bag, but said nothing.

"Excuse me. You don't even do your own," said Karetha.

"Do too."

"Since when? Yesterday?"

"DeeDee, tell this girl I do my homework. I always do my..."

"Please. I am not in this. Just leave me out."

"I do my homework. And I get good grades, too. Let's talk about grades. You don't want to talk about grades."

"Hey, we can talk about grades," said Karetha.

"Well, talk, then."

"What you get on Miss Baker's math test, yesterday?"

"What you get on Mr. Adams' English test?" asked Beverly.

"I asked you first."

"B minus. I got a B-minus."

"B what? No way. You got a C," said Karetha. "I helped Miss Baker pass the papers back, and I saw yours—a big fat C."

"You're not suppose to be looking at other people's test papers."

"It was an accident. I promise."

"Right. Miss Baker made a mistake when she graded number six."

"I don't think so. Miss Baker don't make any mistakes," said Karetha, defending herself.

"Just listen at you. It's *doesn't* make mistakes, not *don't* make mistakes," said Beverly.

"So, you admit it."

"No way! I'm just correcting your grammar."

"You leave my Grandma' out of this."

'That's real funny. You know what I'm talking about. Miss Baker made a mistake this time. I showed her and she changed it to a B minus. I'll show you when we get home. I don't have to lie to you."

"You probably changed it yourself," said Karetha.

"Did not!"

The girls argued a bit more. Neither conceded anything. Deborah appeared embarrassed, but tried to conceal it from Tommy.

"Anyway. Tommy, I was asking 'bout your male relatives," said Beverly. "You got any cousins your age?"

Tommy remained mute. He turned, glanced at the girls, then Deborah, lowered his head passively, and shifted her book bag again.

Deborah chastised her friends. "Will y'all please stop embarrassing me." She struggled to stifle her own persistent giggles. "I didn't hear all this yapping yesterday. Y'all just jealous. That's what it is."

"Jealous?"

"Yes, jealous."

"Whoa! I ain't jealous of nobody. And I do mean ain't, Miss Grammar Queen. I could take *Tommy* if I wanted to," boasted Karetha. "Anyway, you just wait 'til Reverend find out."

Karetha and Beverly snickered. Tommy was in full blush. "Find out what?" asked Deborah.

"You know. Don't play dumb, girl," warned Karetha.

Deborah half-turned, feigned a weak swat at the girls. Both fell back, briefly. "Can't y'all please talk about something else?"

The laughter finally subsided. Short-lived silence followed, which Karetha quickly shattered.

"Guess you know Deborah's daddy is a preacher man."

"I know," said Tommy, kicking stones, sending dust flying. "I'm sure everybody in Reedville knows that. Been to his church a couple 'a times. Even took the Lord's Supper one Sunday. I even started to join church, but I..."

That was the longest run of sentences either girl had ever heard Tommy string together. He sounded positively assertive.

"You started to join but what?"

"Nothing."

"I know. You got scared."

"Did not."

"Yes, you did. You got scared—too scared to walk down to that altar, look Reverend Davis in his face and shake his hand, knowing you've got the big eye for his little daughter," said Beverly.

"The big eye ain't the only thing he got," said Karetha.

"Shut up, girl. You're so nasty," Beverly shot back.

"Why are y'all asking Tommy about my daddy?"

Karetha gazed skyward, pretending not to hear Deborah's question. Tommy said nothing more after that.

The kids continued trudging along, hugging the edge of the partially shaded road, frequently flinging sweat from their dripping brows. Tommy kept shifting Deborah's book bag from shoulder to shoulder. He leaned to one side when he walked. The thing seemed to get heavier with every dusty step.

—

Not one of the gang of four reacted to noise erupting from a weathered, blue pickup truck approaching from behind them. A billowing cloud of dust trailed the rickety thing. Without glancing back, all moved well off the roadbed and kept walking.

"He know you like his little girl?" Beverly prodded.

"Girl, y'all crazy. Me and Tommy just friends."

"That ain't what you told us," said Karetha, giggling.

Without breaking stride, Deborah wheeled around to face the girls. "I'm not talking to y'all anymore," she declared, wagging her finger repeatedly.

"Okay. I take it back. She didn't say it, Tommy. I just made it up," Karetha recanted, with an exaggerated wink.

Meanwhile, the pickup reached the group and slowed alongside. The four turned to see a young white boy all recognized as 16 year-old Jonathan Reed.

Jonathan always seemed friendly enough...appeared unaffected by his family's fortune and position. The kids often wondered why he frequented the Sticks; why he drove a battered truck, and why he wore tattered jeans when he could have anything he wanted. What was it down there, across the tracks that attracted him? A smiling Jonathan leaned toward the open passenger window.

"Hey there! Y'all tired a walkin'?" The girls gave Jonathan a quick glance. Only Deborah waved, though tentatively. All kept moving.

"Hi, Tommy Lee, Miss Deborah...Karetha, Beverly."

"Jonathan," Tommy warily acknowledged. The girls said nothing.

"Pretty hot out there, huh? Must be at least a hundred. Reckon I could give y'all a ride toward home."

Jonathan pulled to the shoulder a few yards ahead. Deborah and the others reached the cab and stopped.

"Nice of you to offer," said Deborah.

"My pleasure. Mine to offer, yours to refuse. Ain't everyday I offer rides in my classic Ford pickup. I'm real particular 'bout that sort of thing. Last person I gave a ride to became homecoming queen this year."

"No thanks," said Tommy. "It's not too far now. Thanks anyway."

"Tommy Lee, you speaking for yourself or for these young ladies, too?" Jonathan flashed a winsome smile. "A person could suffer a stroke out in this heat. Wouldn't want that on your conscience, now would ya?"

Tommy looked at the girls. When neither spoke up, he took a step back. Jonathan was clearly emboldened.

"How 'bout you, Miss Deborah. My father is sending me right past your place. Could drop you off real easy."

Deborah shrugged, looked at Beverly and Karetha to gauge their reaction. Tommy turned away, stared down the road. Deborah eased toward the truck, leaned against the door, turned to her friends, then back to Jonathan.

"Well, I am tired 'a walking. And it *is* hot. Y'all coming with me?"

No one budged. Jonathan reached across the worn, Naugahyde-covered bench seat. He unlocked the door, shoved it open with a thrust of his right hand. To make room, Jonathan tossed several textbooks into the space behind the seat and waited.

"Girl, no you ain't," said a frowning Karetha.

Deborah climbed inside while her stunned friends looked on. They appeared to think she was only teasing Jonathan. She was not.

"C'mon, Tommy," Deborah pleaded.

Tommy seemed torn, but did not move, did not answer.

"Hey, what's the big deal? I'm just getting a ride home. It's way too hot to be walking, anyway. And I'm sure he's a good driver, if that's what y'all worried about."

"The best," said Jonathan. "The best."

Karetha stood with one leg extended, a hand on a hip, her lips pursed. She shook her head in disbelief. For a second, she considered grabbing Deborah by her arm and dragging her from the truck. Karetha found nothing appealing about Jonathan, or his truck, despite the heat.

The kids knew Jonathan often hung out with several older black boys with gutter reputations. What's more, Karetha could not stomach the horde of pimples and zits populating his pear-shaped face. All that, coupled with his reputation for noxious body odor, fueled her uncompromising dislike.

Jonathan eased away. Deborah half-turned to wave through the cab window. No one waved back. Within seconds, the old truck was obscured, by choking dust. Took forever for the gritty cloud to settle. Tommy and the girls turned their backs to avoid inhaling the stuff.

"I don't believe her!" screamed Karetha. "Getting in the truck with pimple-face Jonathan, and leaving you standing here holding her books. And you're still carrying 'em. What's wrong with you?"

Tommy appeared heartbroken and embarrassed. He turned around, glared at the old truck until it reached a bend in the road and disappeared. His bottom lip quivered.

Beverly observed that despite Karetha's comments, Tommy continued carrying Deborah's book bag. She just looked at him, clearly enraged by his *lack* of outrage.

"Tommy! You still holding her books?" asked Beverly. "You crazy? She just climbed in the truck with some...some guy—you know what I'm sayin'—and left you here sweatin' with the rest of us. If I were you, I'd drop 'em right there. I swear. DeeDee's my best friend, but I would leave her stuff right there! I'd leave 'em right smack in the middle of the road," she fumed.

Tommy said nothing, but appeared to be considering Beverly's suggestion. He had to admit it certainly would serve Deborah right. No one could have blamed him. But it was not his nature. It was clear he was prepared to continue.

"I give up," Beverly mumbled.

With a loud grunt, Tommy shifted the bag to his rested shoulder and started down the road. Still fuming, Kay and B.B. ran to catch up. Each voiced anger, surprise, even disgust at the actions of their girlfriend.

chapter eight

Eyes Of A Child

━━━━━━━━━━━━━━━━

Clara Ward and her Singers performed...

T he Davis home
was a modest, three bedroom, wood-framed structure with peeling white
paint. The house was perched on gray masonry blocks, bordered by towering pines, transplanted oaks, and set on a slight rise roughly fifty yards
off dusty ol' Crispus Attucks road.

Over the years, the place had almost doubled in size to nearly twelve
hundred square feet, as the family had grown. It now boasted three bedrooms, and a formal dining room for entertaining the many ministers
and travelling guests who frequented the Davis home.

The expansion had not come without considerable consternation
and controversy for the Reverend. His attempts to get the Reeds to make
larger quarters available were first ignored. When he persisted, he was
told any such remodeling would cost thousands of dollars. After some
heated exchanges, the Reeds agreed to permit the Reverend to under-
take the remodeling at his own expense, and upon their approval of the

plans. After a month or so, a deal was struck, and the remodeling was undertaken. Over the next five years, the same scenario would be repeated at least twice more.

Then came the ultimate insult. After the final remodeling was completed, the Reeds had the gall to raise the rent by more than half. The exorbitant increase was "made necessary by the increased size of the house," they explained. Reverend made it clear he would not pay a cent more than the small, expected, periodic increase. The battle was joined.

Outraged Shiloh members, and other Sticks residents, threatened to withhold rent, and worse: stop shopping at Reed-owned businesses. After several tense weeks, which saw even more than the usual harassment of black citizens by County deputies, the Reeds backed down. The matter was eventually laid to rest. However, few in the Sticks felt the Reeds would not someday seek to avenge their loss of face.

—

Nearest neighbor to the Davises was just under a quarter mile away, elbow close, by country measure. Built in the Spring of 1954, the Davis home was barely four-years old when a tall, dashing, young Reverend Henry B. Davis, and his doting bride, Mabel Strong-Davis, moved in and began their family.

A rough-hewn log fence ran down the east side, 'round back, and straight out west as far as the eye could see. A large, capsule-shaped, white LPG tank rested on a six inch thick, concrete pad several yards from the fence. Sure did not look like a preacher's house. Most surely, not like some of those big-time city preachers' houses.

A long front porch, with a white pine swing on the east-end, stretched the full width of the North-facing home. Could not have a home without a front porch, especially in the summertime, and consider it a real country home.

Several dutiful Shiloh deacons had pledged to paint the house at least once every five years or so. Seemed a shame to not have Reverend's house dressed out in a fresh coat.

But they never got around to the doing of it. Just as painting time came, Preacher insisted they paint some needy congregant's house instead. Said the duty of the shepherd was to tend his flock. Said too much living was going on at Route 5A, Crispus Attucks Road; no time to worry about paint. Said the roof was fine, plumbing worked. Those were the important things.

———

Reverend Davis, now 46, was six feet two, clean shaven, full-faced, balding, broad-shouldered, barrel-chested—a physically imposing man. He had a purposeful glint in his eyes, and was armed with a ready grin and a firm handshake.

Henry Bertram Davis was the unquestioned head of his family. As Pastor of Shiloh Missionary Baptist Church, he was the spiritual, and de facto political leader of Reedville's black community. His imposing physical and moral stature made his voice one to be reckoned with, by both Blacks and Whites.

The Reverend and his wife, Mabel, had lived in the same home for more than sixteen years. All six of their children had been born in the humble dwelling. Their second son, Samuel, was stillborn on August 4, 1964. He lay in a small grave, next to Gram d'Iena's, in the old cemetery next to Shiloh Baptist Church.

The Davises loved this simple home surrounded by the luscious green of the Reed family's sprawling SB-40 property. It was a safe, nurturing place to raise a family. None of the distractions of big city life. No choking vehicle traffic; no drugs, no fear of predators lurking near schoolyards. Their souls were rooted here. A lot of living had gone on within those walls.

———

SB-40 was the sterile designation the Reeds gave this section of rural Arkansas. The land spread for thousands of acres in every direction. Word was, only the federal government and the State owned more Arkansas land. Most of Reed County was indeed Reed land leased to the County.

The Davis front yard, nearly barren except for the flourishing parcel over the septic tank, was dotted with random patches of San Augustine grass. The wear resulted from the yard doubling as both children's playground, and a parking lot. A garage was a luxury few could afford. Few gave the idea any thought. Lean-to carports were common.

The Davis home had long been a gathering place for neighbors, friends, and itinerant preachers, especially on Sundays. And whenever Shiloh held its annual Gospel Tent Revival meetings. Seemed strange to some, that a tent would be raised right next to the church.

However, revivals had a long, storied tradition, especially in the South. Folks remembered and celebrated those days when a big canvas tent was the only church they had.

Legend had it, that shortly after the Reverend's first year as Pastor, in 1959, the famous Clara Ward and her Singers performed at Shiloh, following several appearances in Alabama and Mississippi. Mabel Davis had met Miss Ward in early '58, at an Eastern Star convention in Chicago. She wrote her, invited her, and she came. Shiloh had not seen such goings on before or since.

Visiting preachers often stayed over after Sunday service, enjoying legendary Davis hospitality. Most often, that meant a feast consisting of Mabel Davis' golden fried chicken, peppered mustard greens, fried okra, hot water cornbread, mashed potatoes, candied yams, buttered sweet corn, deep crust sweet potato pie, and peach cobbler covered with a thick, buttered crust. The latter was topped off with a light sprinkling of freshly ground cinnamon, and brown sugar.

Like most black folk in rural Reedville, the Davises had a long-term rental agreement with the Reed family, in effect for years. They attempted numerous times, unsuccessfully, to purchase their home site and a few surrounding acres. The Reeds always refused to sell. No reasons were ever given.

Reverend Davis was not shy about voicing his disappointment about that and other matters. Despite his outspokenness, Reverend was never threatened with eviction or reprisals of any kind. Would not have bothered him in any way. He rightly reasoned, if God could take care of sparrows, He would certainly take care of him, and his family.

Even when he blasted American involvement in Vietnam—pointing out blacks were dying, seeking freedoms for others they did not fully enjoy—most white folk said little. He went on to remind everyone of the shameful treatment of many Black G.I.s in the aftermath of WWII.

On U.S. military bases and camps, captured Nazi officers and officials were often afforded more consideration, treated better than Black G.I.s, who were still segregated from white U.S. soldiers. Many folk in the Sticks had no knowledge of that despicable history.

There were a few whites in Reedville who did not want to be reminded. Some suggested that if the "Good Reverend" and other "Niggras" didn't like America, they could leave. They were likely frustrated they could not threaten him with loss of his job. Reverend could not be fired, except by the members of Shiloh. And that was not about to happen.

Ironically, the only real property the Reverend owned was jointly owned with hundreds of others: Shiloh Missionary Baptist Church and its nearly five acres, including the nearby cemetery. If it ever came to it, Reverend was prepared to move his family onto the property, rather than compromise his beliefs or mute his persuasive voice.

Mabel Davis was, at age 44, a sturdy, handsome, resolute figure. She saw herself as a tower of strength for her husband, a respected personality in her own right. Mabel considered herself a caring woman who approached life, as First Lady of Shiloh Missionary Baptist Church, with ample Christian fervor. She counted herself a God-fearing, faithful woman who embodied the Christian precepts her husband taught.

There was nothing frivolous about Mabel Davis. Through dark-brown eyes set in a full dark face, she could cast a gaze that both handcuffed and arrested in one glance. However, Mabel Davis was not one to display warmth and loving emotion with great ease. That took some effort. While her 'less than affectionate' manner was not intended to convey a lack of love and devotion for her family, that shortcoming was no small matter.

The Davis children, especially Matthew, might have argued the Christian fervor they witnessed from both parents was more than ample. Poor Matthew was constantly receiving sermons, and having his role as a preacher's son defined for him by his father in unyielding terms.

—

On the afternoon of May 15, 1974, Mabel Davis stood on the top step of the shaded front porch, as was her daily custom. She was resplendent in her new Spiegel, flower print dress, and red plaid apron. She gazed expectantly toward Crispus Attucks Road.

Every school day around 4:45, Deborah and her friends would reach the turnoff leading to the house and soon part company, with a promise to see each other the next day.

Most often, before they departed, the children were treated to oatmeal-raisin or pecan cookies, sweet potato or pecan pie, or other delicacies. A smiling Mabel Davis would beckon to them. The kids would dash to the porch, drop their books, and wait while she fetched them heaping helpings and ice-cold milk. Mabel Davis had no reason to suspect this day would be different.

Beverly, Karetha and Tommy were struck speechless when they reached the turnoff and found a stern-faced Mabel Davis standing atop the steps. The three had expected Deborah to meet them, reclaim her book bag and tease them for having to walk home. Mabel Davis did not recognize Tommy, but figured he must be Kay's or B.B.'s special school friend.

A puzzled Mabel Davis bounded down the steps and headed straight for them. Karetha would later recall, her eyes were like saucers, her brow carved with frowns. She appeared ten feet tall.

The stunned trio glanced at each other nervously, then at the rapidly advancing Mabel Davis. Karetha, ever the braveheart, grabbed Deborah's book bag from Tommy and walked ahead to meet her.

chapter nine

The Moment

=====================================

She clutched the sides of her head with both hands.

It was nearly an hour later,
five 'til eight in the evening, when Deborah, soaked, soiled and scared, stumbled the final steps home. She reached the edge of the front yard and stopped cold. The lay and length of evening shadows, the glow in the western skies, the incandescent light evident against drawn window shades—all told her it was much later than she had imagined.

Reverend Davis' shiny, 4dr., white over black, 1967 Chevrolet Impala—all dressed out with fender skirts, whip antenna and chrome tail pipe extensions on dual exhausts—was parked diagonally across the yard in its familiar ruts. The car, his pride and joy, was his one conspicuous concession to materialism.

The short distance from the roadway to the front porch steps seemed twice as far as Deborah remembered. Her feet felt encased in concrete; her temples throbbed. Yet, she forced herself forward. When she reached the top step, she froze again. For an instant, she was tempted to turn on her heels and run as fast as her legs could carry her. But to where? It took a full two minutes before she opened the screen door and forced her trembling body inside.

The creaky door closed behind her. Outside, a sinking sun spawned a streaming kaleidoscope of brilliant color, magically absorbed by puffy, cotton-like clouds that now hugged the horizon. A hot, humid day had at last surrendered to a warm, muggy, but cooler evening. Except for the buzz of airborne critters, all was deathly quiet—too quiet.

—

Five minutes later, earsplitting screams erupted from inside the Davis house, betraying the serenity of the bucolic setting. Deborah's shrill cries spiked in sync with the stinging lashes from Reverend Davis' leather belt, as he laid on stroke after stroke. Every punishing blow was accompanied by angry preachments. Reverend seldom passed up an opportunity to deliver a sermon.

"I didn't do anything, Daddy!" Deborah screamed between lashes. The whipping continued without pause. She bellowed from the pain. However, her cries seemed to only anger her father.

"Don't you talk back to me," he growled. "And keep your hands on that bed. Don't move 'em one inch, you hear me?" The veins in Reverend's forehead and neck stood out in bold relief. "Don't wanna hit your arms if I can help it. As God is my witness, it hurts me to have to do this."

Deborah could not imagine who this was—this man inflicting such pain upon her. He could not be her father. Her father loved her too much, no matter what sins she had committed. She had never seen him so angry, so enraged. Even his booming voice frightened her. "Where did all his anger come from?" she wondered. If he could punish her this way, without full knowledge of what had happened, how much more would she suffer had he known everything?

Mabel Davis showed little emotion. She kept pacing up and down the narrow hallway, outside the closed door to the bedroom Deborah shared with her sisters. Through Matthew's open bedroom door, he could be seen scowling, teeth grinding, eyes narrowing, fists clenching. Maylene and Gloria sat on the bed, on either side of their brother, staring past the open doorway, flinching with every lash. Rachel, nearly as tall as Deborah, but petite and soft-spoken, stood in front of the dresser calmly brushing her hair, and humming a song, likely one only she knew.

Eight–year old Gloria, the youngest, appeared completely confused, even traumatized. She sat quietly but uneasily, peering into the hallway, afraid to speak, even to Maylene. Gloria was further confused, by the concern shown by Maylene and Matthew, contrasted with Rachel's total detachment. While the latter's behavior was not a surprise, the degree of her indifference was pronounced.

Sixteen-year old Maylene, nearly 5'-8," thin, wispy, and with the instincts and caring heart of a mother, could stomach the beating no longer. Tears laced her dimpled cheeks. She brushed them away with uncharacteristic anger and shot to her feet.

"Mama, why is Daddy whippin' Deborah? What did she do to deserve all that?"

Mabel Davis continued pacing...never answered Maylene. She swiped her perspiring brow with a corner of her apron, then stopped in front of the bedroom door. The Reverend was not yet done. His deep, thundering voice reverberated through the door and walls.

"Every Sunday, I get up in that pulpit and preach my heart out, chastising parents about not rearing obedient, God-fearing children. And you do this? It's after eight o'clock! Eight! You know better than to show up whenever you please, lookin' like something the cat spit up. I am duty bound to chastise you," Reverend continued, "Long as every one of y'all live under this roof, you'll do what me and your mother say. You hear me? I don't care if Saint Peter offer you a ride in his personal chariot. And I don't believe you got lost, either. I just flat don't believe it."

An enraged Matthew could contain his anger no longer. He stormed from his room, bolted into the hallway and continued full stride toward his mother. She wheeled around to face him.

"Where you goin,' son?" she angrily demanded—her right hand raised and extended.

"I'm gonna stop him from hurtin' her," Matthew growled through clenched teeth. "She don't deserve that!"

"I know you ain't about to challenge your father. Best you go back to your room and stay there."

An angry Matthew turned slowly, retreated a few steps. Tears charged down his cheeks, angering him even more. Mercifully, the blows ended, but Deborah's mournful wailing continued.

"I said, you hear me?" Reverend repeated.

"Yessir, Daddy. I hear you," Deborah groaned, fearful of further provoking her angry father. She was certain her body could not sustain another blow. The stinging, all-consuming pain in her abdomen and crotch persisted. She wanted desperately to urinate, but held it in. Her stomach cramped; her eyes blurred; she yearned for unconsciousness—anything that would absent her from the moment.

—

The heavy bedroom door eased open. Reverend Davis, wearing a sweat-soaked, long-sleeve white shirt; black, pleated slacks with heavy cuffs, and black suspenders, exited in a sweaty huff. He stalked past his wife, without a glance, and disappeared into the living room. Seconds later, the front door was heard being opened and closed.

Deborah remained on her knees, slumped on the bedroom floor, her forearms resting on the edge of the larger of two beds. She was face down, sobbing heavily.

Maylene leaped to her feet and rushed toward the room. Her mother raised a hand, halting her in her tracks.

"Where you think you going?" she menaced.

"I wanna see 'bout Deborah."

"Don't you worry 'bout Deborah. I'll tend to your sister soon enough. You and Gloria get in the kitchen and get your daddy's supper on the table. Matthew, go to your room. Now!"

"What about Rachel?" asked Maylene.

Mabel Davis did not take the question well. Frowning, she stepped to within an inch of her eldest daughter.

"Did you hear what I said? If I'd 'a meant to include Rachel I would 'a done so," Mabel hissed in a loud, exaggerated whisper.

Rachel, now firmly planted on Matthew's bed, permitted a faint smile to creep across her face. A sullen Maylene motioned for Gloria. The two eased past the 'room,' en route to the kitchen. Each strained to sneak a look at Deborah. Matthew returned to his room, angrily rousted Rachel from her comfortable posture, then plopped down. He sat Sphinx-like on his bed—fists clenched, eyes unblinking.

—

Mabel Davis entered the girls' bedroom and closed the door, leaving it barely ajar. She paused, stared, curiously absent an innate feeling of compassion for her daughter. She then proceeded slowly to the bed. For a short time, she stood motionless, gazing down at Deborah—her expression unchanged, listening to her daughter's pain-filled sobbing,

While Reverend had likely intended his blows for Deborah's posterior, many had clearly missed their mark. Her lower legs were badly swollen with large, raw, raised welts speckled with seeping blood.

Mabel Davis examined them, retrieved a jar of petroleum jelly, cotton balls and a roll of gauze from the dresser. Despite her daughter's wincing and flinching, she applied a heavy covering of Vaseline to Deborah's calves, thighs, lower back, and forearms.

She next tore thin strips of gauze, and tied them around folded gauze pads placed over the layer of Vaseline. For a moment, Mabel Davis appeared moved to embrace her daughter, but did not.

"I know you hurtin,' but I want you to stand up and sit on the edge of the bed," said Mabel Davis, in a firm voice. "Try not to sit on those...on those spots."

Deborah raised her head, loosed a loud groan, and grimaced as she stood and eased her trembling body onto the edge of the bed. Mabel Davis remained standing. For a short time, she seemed conflicted by her daughter's obvious anguish. Yet, she offered no emotional sanctuary from the Reverend's uncompromising brand of physical discipline.

"I'll put some more Vaseline on later," she said, curtly. "You'll stay home from school tomorrow."

Deborah fixed her gaze on her lap, afraid to look up, afraid her mother would read her eyes, as she was keen to do. Right now, she simply wanted to be alone.

The worst was over, she thought. By morning, the welts should be gone, and only *she* would be left to deal with her secret. Deborah was sure Maylene was anxious to come see about her. They would talk later. Maylene loved playing big sister. But Mabel Davis was not yet done. She walked in half circles, back and forth, then stopped directly in front of Deborah.

"Now, I want you to listen real good, child. And you tell me the God's truth. Don't you lie to me," Mabel warned.

"Yes ma'am," Deborah stammered.

Mabel Davis moved even closer. She grasped Deborah's chin, gently forcing her tear-stained face upward. Their eyes met. Mabel spoke deliberately, drawing out every syllable of every word.

"Now, what happened in that truck, exactly?" The question came hurtling out of nowhere.

"Like what, Mama?" Deborah looked away.

"Don't play with me, child. You know full well what I mean. I'm gon' ask you one more time. And I want the truth. What happened in that truck? What, other than you just ridin'? Took a long time to get home."

Deborah knew if she had any chance of being believed, she had to instantly answer. No hesitating. Another sharp pain shot through her crotch. She grimaced, started to clutch at herself but resisted.

"Nothing. Nothing happened, Mama."

Deborah's voice cracked. Tears snaked down her cheeks. She resisted wiping them away.

"You sure? You sure that boy didn't try to do anything to you? You sure?" Mabel Davis leaned down, aimed a laser stare. She took several short, deep breaths, as if sniffing for some telltale scent. She was clearly unconvinced. "Did he touch you, try to...to kiss you or somethin', huh?"

Again, Mabel Davis drew out each word. "Did he try to touch you, try to get you to do anything...anything you know is wrong? Did he? Answer me! Did he?"

"No ma'am."

"As God is your witness, are you dead sure? Look up at me, when I'm talkin' to you. Hold your head up!"

Deborah forced herself to look into her mother's eyes, but could not hold her gaze. She clutched the sides of her head with both hands.

"I'm sure, Mama," she whimpered. "Nothing happened!"

Mabel Davis drew a leaden breath and turned away. Deborah watched her mother walk to the door and close it securely. Her pulse pounded in her ears. She felt numb.

Her mother retreated across the room, threw open the chest's third drawer, lifted a folded white top sheet and returned to the bed. Mabel Davis lingered for a long moment, not uttering a word, just staring at Deborah for what seemed an eternity.

Deborah prayed for some distraction. A tornado, a hurricane—some act of God. Anything to take this focus off her. She sopped her eyes with open palms, sniffled loudly. Her mother hovered over her, menacingly.

"Now, I'm gon' ask you one more time. Are you sure?" Mabel Davis' voice plunged a full octave. Her tone, though stern, conveyed a hint of hope—hope that her suspicions would prove wrong. Or *were* they simply suspicions? Just as likely, was the possibility she was only probing. Deborah prayed it was the latter.

"I'm sure," Deborah whispered, never looking up.

"Well, I'm gon' find out. The last time we talked, you said you hadn't started your monthly time, right?"

"Yes, Mama. I...I haven't," Deborah managed.

"Well, I take no pleasure in this. But I want you to stand up...stand up and take off all your clothes."

"Ma'am?" Deborah's jaw dropped. She felt petrified, frozen to the spot, unable to move an eyelash. Mabel Davis' nose widened; her eyes flared, her voice soared.

"I said take your clothes off, I mean every last stitch. And I mean right now. Then I want you to lay on this bed, flat on your back with your knees drawn up."

Deborah was stunned by her mother's stern command. Her lips quivered. She laced her fingers anxiously, but remained seated. Had she heard correctly? Whatever could her mother have intended?

"I mean right now!" Mabel Davis repeated, as she moved toward her daughter with determined strides.

A feeble Deborah rose and began slowly undressing. Chill bumps dotted her arms. Her every move was labored and exhausting. Her body shook, despite a valiant effort to conceal it.

A tingling sensation coursed Deborah's entire body. She desperately struggled to understand what was happening to her. Why was this day, this moment so unlike any she had experienced? How had she arrived at this place? When would it end? If she just...just prayed hard enough, could not so powerful a God have started the day all over?

While her mother unfolded the top sheet, spread it out atop the quilt, and waited, Deborah slowly removed her skirt, then her blouse, her bra. She glanced up frequently at her mother, then eased her panties down to her ankles. What she saw in the crotch stunned her. Her eyes bulged, her heart sank. She folded the panties quickly and concealed them underneath her skirt.

"Leave your panties out where I can see them," Mabel Davis commanded her frightened daughter in a rumbling voice, reinforced with a stern expression and folded arms.

Deborah felt her chest tighten. A sharp pain shot through her right temple. She felt her knees buckle. Gathering herself, she obeyed her mother, then gingerly climbed onto the bed. Deborah had never felt more naked than she did at that moment. It had been years since her mother had seen her naked. And never by such a harsh command.

Every tortured move sent ripples of pain throughout Deborah's shivering frame. She grimaced, as she eased onto her back, slowly drew her legs up and waited. Why? She was desperate to understand why her mother was doing this. After her father had left the room earlier, Deborah had expected her mother to come to her, but had wished for a soft voice, a kind, gentle, compassionate hand—a loving embrace.

Mabel Davis walked to where Deborah's clothes lay piled on the floor next to the foot of the bed, and paused. She reached down, grasped the panties with her thumb and forefinger, and lifted them as she straightened herself. The panties unfolded, exposing a large, crimson blotch. Shock scored Mabel's perspiring brow. She leaned her head back, turned to one side, loudly exhaled, then took a deep, audible breath. For a moment, it seemed the air stopped moving.

With left arm extended, Mabel Davis slowly turned, stared at the panties, then at Deborah, with unblinking, convicting eyes, but said nothing. The deafening silence seemed eternal. Deborah nearly stopped breathing. Her heart throbbed. Blood? Where had all that blood come from? She could not imagine an answer, except that for some reason, it had come from her. But how? Why?

Finally, without breaking her gaze at her young daughter, Mabel dropped the bloodstained panties to the floor. She stood staring at Deborah, not speaking, her expression unchanged. There was no hint of what was to come. Then as if on cue, she started toward the head of the bed as a frightened, confused child recoiled and shrank against the pillows.

—

The hours crept by like days, despite the time being well past midnight. The only light came from a low-hanging moon, partially obscured by clouds and the crown of the pine forest. The silvery glow streamed through the open window, casting eerie shadows across the room.

Deborah lay on her back, wide awake and staring through bleary red eyes at the rain-spotted ceiling. She was trembling, alternately feeling cold, then warm. And she was afraid—deathly afraid. Any minute, she expected the door to swing open and there would stand her father. He would be beside himself with resurgent anger, having spoken to her mother and been told of her discovery, and her suspicions.

Deborah lay on her tear-soaked pillow. Marie rested on her chest, clutched tightly in both hands. Maylene had brought it to her without her having to ask. Rachel lay on the far side of the same bed, her back to Deborah. Neither had so much as exchanged glances. Maylene had earlier suggested trading places with the smaller Rachel, to provide more bed space for Deborah.

Earlier, Matthew had approached Deborah, as she started into the bedroom she shared with her sisters. It was painful for her to see the deep concern on his face, but she waved him away. He looked hurt, deeply wounded. But more than anyone, Deborah was determined *he* not see her in this condition. She prayed he would understand.

Moments later, a tearful Maylene tried to coax Deborah into talking. Gloria seemed in shock, hanging back, casting oblique glances. They saw the bandages, the still exposed welts on her arms.

Deborah refused to talk, refused to even look at her sisters. Still Maylene persisted, reluctant to leave her sister's side. "You'll be alright. Can I get you anything? Some water? My pillow? You can have my pillow, if you want." Deborah shook her head.

For the longest while, Maylene remained standing next to Deborah's bed, desperately wanting to do something—anything to relieve the pain her sister was suffering. She thought to stroke her face, her hair, but did not, for fear of causing more pain. There was nothing she could do.

Deborah was deeply moved, warmed by Maylene's comforting presence. But she was relieved when her eldest sister finally turned out the light and all went to bed. She welcomed the darkness. It concealed her; it made her feel invisible, it offered her the cocoon-like refuge she craved. And so Deborah prayed. She prayed the morning, if it must come at all, would come slowly.

The pulsing pain in Deborah's lower body had not gone away, although she had earlier insisted to her mother that she felt none. And there was still wincing pain from the fluid-filled welts covering her thighs, forearms, and buttocks. But the deepest pain she felt was inside—inside where even she could not reach.

A sliver of dim light suddenly appeared beneath the closed bedroom door. Deborah's heart spiked. A lump filled her still-parched throat. Then voices—restrained voices, at first. Reverend and Sister Davis were talking. The Reverend was now the louder and angrier. "He must surely know. He must," Deborah told herself. She was now certain her mother had relayed everything to him. She braced for what she knew would follow.

Deborah could not make out what her father was saying, but his tone was chilling. She thought of hiding, but there was no hiding place. She thought of climbing from bed and trying to reach the door to listen. However, she had finally found a position that minimized the pain, and dared not move. Instead, Deborah raised her head and strained to hear.

The Reverend was clearly enraged anew, even beyond his rage of hours earlier. He kept pacing back and forth between his bedroom and the end of the hallway. And he was cursing. Deborah had never heard her father curse. "Cursing is the foul utterance of a sinful soul," he always said.

There was something about a gun. Deborah knew her father kept a .410 shotgun in his bedroom closet. But he would never resort to violence. Reverend had always preached nonviolence; had always spoken of the "power of peace." Surely, she had not heard correctly. Mabel Davis seemed on the verge of tears. She pleaded with her husband to not leave, but without success. The anger in his voice only grew.

Moments later, Deborah heard the front door open and slam closed with a resounding thud. She forced herself up, glanced at her sisters who appeared sound asleep. But Maylene was not asleep. She had found sleep impossible. She remained wide-awake, peering across the room, keeping a concerned eye on her sister.

Seconds passed. The car started; the engine raced; the transmission slammed into reverse; tires spun, and the car shot onto the road. All sorts of tortured thought raced through Deborah's mind. She heard the throaty roar of the Impala's engine fade into the moonlit night. She could only wonder where her father was going, and what would happen when he got there.

However, those thoughts were forced to give way to a stinging, pulsing pain—both on, and beneath the seeping welts. Deborah could not touch them. She did not dare move. She desperately tried to will it all away. She closed her eyes, clenched her teeth, formed fists, and tried as hard as she could to exact her will.

Her efforts seemed to help, but only for a moment. Then the ebb and flow of pain seemed only to intensify. Yet, the physical misery was only one part of her suffering. Just as piercing, or perhaps more, was the fact it was her father who had inflicted this hurt upon her.

The shame and remorse she felt for simply having disobeyed him, for having disappointed him, would have been punishment enough, she thought. She had always taken care to never anger or disappoint him in any way.

Now, in the deepest part of her, Deborah knew that her world—all things familiar to her—had been forever changed. She knew this as surely as she knew her name. And that frightened her in a way that defied understanding.

As her night finally settled into an uneasy, surreal quiet, Deborah could not help but think about how innocently the day had begun, and how horribly it had ended. She prayed, she pleaded with God to make everything go away.

"By morning," she whispered. "if not right away," she petitioned, as if granting The Almighty sufficient time to answer her prayer. Yet, in the center of her soul, she reasoned that God must surely have more important things to do, than hear the mournful prayer of some 12 year old girl from Reedville, Arkansas.

chapter ten

Death Of Innocence
==

If a rose is the sum of its petals, how much less a rose does the loss of a single petal make?

Miller's Café and Five & Dime,
in what passed for a downtown in Reedville, doubled as both Greyhound
and Trailways Bus stations. On Sunday mornings, it was usually a quiet
place, seeing as how most God-fearing folk were either inside or near
somebody's segregated church. White folk were in the white churches;
Black folk were at Shiloh and St. John. The rest were likely nursing hang-
overs, or suffering from acute exhaustion that normally attended a Saturday night of serious sinning.

Miss Ruby, Mr. Peabo and Mr. Lonnie were the ones who profited
from such lasciviousness—adult fun. Preparation for Saturday nights
always started earlier in the week, but on Friday evenings for sure. Suits
and dresses were picked up from Mr. Winston's cleaners. Elsewhere,
hairdos were "dyed, fried and laid to the side." Come Saturday evening,
Oak Street would certainly be no place for kids, especially Davis kids.

Mr. Lincoln Miles' barbershop 'jumped' on Fridays, well into the night. 'Course everybody called him 'Six-fo,' because of his height. Kids called him *Mr.* Six-fo. Every hair had to be in place. Shoes were shined to a glass-like glaze. Soles were finished off in a black lacquer dressing.

Often, patrons and barbers alike traded words, during heated conversations. Topics ranged from politics to the newest 'hot body' in town, and who would likely be first to sample her DNA.

On Saturday nights, style was the name of the game. Both men and women dressed to the nines. Fashion was on parade. And one was careful to not step on anyone's shoes. In times past, many a night—and often a life—had ended too soon because of that single miscue, and despite an apology.

Just past sundown, the joints began jumping, building to a crescendo hours later, around 2 a.m. or so. Mr. Lonnie's Blue Room always cranked up late, and stayed open longer than the competition. The music often traveled far from Oak Street, bleeding into the edge of Reedville itself.

On a few occasions, prior to his demise, Deputy Bluehorn was sent in to try and quieten things down. But even Bluehorn should have known better than to interfere with 'bid'ness.' Some suspect his lapse, in that regard, may have contributed to his premature "Trip to 'Glory."

Crowds were largest when live music was on the bill. Frequently, the live music came from area or regional bands, and hot single acts trying to break into the biz. Many were excellent musicians.

As for the patrons, you were either a player or the played. Everybody was gaming, and enjoying themselves in true Sodom and Gomorrah tradition. The work week was forgotten, misery left on the street side of the blue door.

One entered to the blaring jukebox sounds of the likes of: Muddy Waters, B.B. King, Albert "Defrost" King, Clarence "Gate-Mouth" Brown, Little Willie John, Bobby Blue Bland, Little Richard, Big Mama Thornton, KoKo Taylor and more. One Saturday night, regional favorite, Clifton Chenier, was passing through; he stopped in for a live set. The Sticks went crazy.

Even Miss Lucinda Moss, an elderly sister noted for her ability to 'shout' longer than anyone at Shiloh Church, was rumored to have been in the crowd that night...in disguise. The fact she missed services the following Sunday—ending her ten year perfect attendance record—gave credence to the rumor.

Sister Moss's absence in the middle aisle, third pew, dead center was obvious. That was because her 'three-story hat'—the one with the peacock feathers—was not blocking view of the pulpit for those who sat behind her. She also missed Wednesday Night's Prayer Meeting.

On Sunday mornings, many Miller Café patrons were waiting for the bus. Miller's served what was claimed to be the best pancakes in Arkansas. They offered more than two dozen varieties, featuring about every fruit, nut and flavor there was. But few Blacks dined at Miller's, although two of the three cooks were black. The reason was simple.

In 1969, a black teenager, Tyrone Speed was a frightened, young Army-recruit, on his way to Vietnam, via Okinawa. He nearly spawned a riot, when he swore he saw a white cook spit in his 'over easy' eggs before sending his food out. The cook vehemently denied it, but Tyrone's accusation was all it took. True or not, word spread like typhoid and stuck like Velcro.

By 1974, all 'Coloreds Only' and 'Whites Only' signs were gone from Reedville. But not all vestiges of the attitudes that had produced them had disappeared. You could still hear and see it in the way some store clerks and ticket agents interacted with black patrons. They were often cryptic, scowling, never looking them in the eyes; exchanging money via the countertop, instead of hand to hand.

—

On this bright, cloudless Sunday morning, a handful of passengers waited for the only bus leaving Reedville until Wednesday. There were now just two scheduled stops each week. A few years earlier, the depot would have been teeming with passengers. Not any more. Reedville's population had gone south. So had profits on the route.

Shortly after 10:35 a.m., a clean but aging Greyhound bus, number AK-1893G, lumbered down the otherwise quiet street and eased up to the elevated wooden platform. The destination marquee read: St. Louis-Chicago. The hiss of air brakes, the smell of exhaust and the rumbling diesel engine hung heavy in the morning air.

Nearly all the Davis family, with the exception of Reverend, waited nearby, looking on with pained expressions. Next to Mabel Davis was her younger sister, Rose Simms, 36, a petite woman with a towering presence. She had arrived from Chicago a week earlier.

Aunt Rose exuded an air of strength and firmness that had made her week at the Davis home a turbulent one. She was not at all happy with the decisions that had brought her to Reedville. Rose made no effort to conceal her displeasure.

A silent, unaffected Rachel remained several steps behind her mother, absorbed in a paperback copy of *Native Son* she clutched with both hands. She seemed determined to let nothing engage her attention, except what she deemed worthy.

Deborah stood in front of her mother and Aunt Rose, staring straight ahead through puffy eyes, and toying with the lace ruffles on her powder blue dress.

Aunt Rose had a decidedly regal air about her. She stood erect, shoulders squared, all dressed out in her finest navy blue, Marshall Field's Sunday suit with narrow, gray trim. She wore a modest brimmed, seal-gray hat with a navy band, tilted just so, and navy clutch with heels to match. There was little doubt Rose Evelyn Simms owned whatever ground she stood upon.

Maylene and Gloria quietly brushed away tears, even as their chests heaved with every breath. Both inched closer to Deborah, as the big bus rolled up to the curb. Matthew stood far behind them with arms folded. A deep scowl and furrowed brow revealed his boiling anger. Earlier, he had been pacing up and down the wooden platform with both hands dug into his pockets, kicking anything not nailed down.

For Deborah, the preceding two months had been hell. Nothing bore the slightest resemblance to her familiar. She emotionally and physically withdrew— her song and laughter locked within her. By the end of the school year, her once, honor-student performance had plummeted. Despite being pregnant, she lost her appetite. She only spoke when she had to—including to her kindred spirit, Matthew. He, too, underwent an emotional transformation.

Following the Reverend's severe lashing of Deborah, Matthew refused to initiate the slightest contact or conversation with his father. He simply withdrew, avoiding his mother as well.

Over the two succeeding months, Deborah stopped attending church, with little comment from Reverend. That would have been unthinkable in times past. Reverend Davis now seemed a different man, a different father. He appeared resigned to the awful reality.

It was not easy, but Deborah made sure she and Tommy did not cross paths. And as much as she loved her girlfriends, she did everything to avoid them. However, complete avoidance was impossible, especially with Kay and B.B. Whenever Deborah was with them, she was never the same DeeDee they had known. Fact is, she hardly recognized *herself*. Reverend's 'little girl' had fallen into an emotional abyss.

And what must Matthew think of her now? How had his view of her changed? How would any of them, but especially Matthew, look at her now? Despite none of them knowing the truth of her condition, she was certain she appeared unclean—defiled.

—

The Saturday night before the trip in to Miller's Café, Deborah had not slept a single minute. She and her sisters, with the exception of Rachel, spent most of the night and early morning talking, weeping, and wondering if she would indeed be leaving them.

Mabel Davis had simply told the children Deborah was ill, and would be going to see doctors in Chicago for a short while. Beyond that, they knew little, although Maylene was more than a little suspicious. Maylene had a nose for the truth. Deborah knew the truth, but was sworn to silence. Deborah's best friends: Kay and B.B. were deliberately not told the date of her departure. That was Mabel Davis' doing as well. She seemed determined that as few folks as possible, if any at all, would learn the truth.

Elon Samuels, a young black doctor, newly relocated from Houston's Fifth Ward to Little Rock, examined Deborah and determined she was pregnant. He fought back tears, as he delivered the somber news to a visibly shaken Reverend and Mabel Davis.

Reverend and Mabel's fervent prayers had not been answered. What was more, young Deborah had contracted gonorrhea. Penicillin was prescribed to treat the venereal disease. Dr. Samuels made it clear the baby could also be affected. Only time would tell.

Not much was said during the endless ride home. Reverend drove with a viselike, two-handed grip on the wheel. His jaws were clenched; he kept shaking his head sadly. Resignation enveloped him. It showed in his shrunken posture, the listless tilt of his head, his silence. He was clearly heartbroken, grief-stricken.

The rumble of tires against the roadbed offered the only consistent sounds. Mabel Davis said nothing, never once lifted her eyes from her lap. Deborah saw her parents' deep hurt. She sensed their despair, but *knew* her own shame. She dreaded the idea of facing her siblings. What would their parents tell them? What if she were asked directly?

The thoughts persisted. And nothing could make them, or her fear go away. There was no place to hide. Deborah would soon see condemnation everywhere—in every face, every expression, every word spoken, and not spoken. Fear permeated every waking hour, invaded every dream. She saw each approaching moment as some Trojan horse, concealing the unfamiliar, heralding the unwanted.

Deborah wished it possible to relive May 15th. She would have made different decisions for sure. And the searing pain she now felt would never have claimed her. Most painful was that from that day on, her father never hugged her again, not once.

And Reverend never again told his daughter he loved her. At 12 years, Deborah now wished herself dead. The thought was an anathema to everything she had been taught. Still, she prayed to be with Gram then prayed God would forgive her the prayer.

In her flowering innocence, Deborah had stumbled into another world—a world frightening beyond her comprehension. She was only twelve, and unable to grasp the full weight of the moment, even now. It had all happened so easily, so innocently. A ride home.

Around 2 a.m., on the morning following the news from Dr. Samuels, while everyone slept, Deborah rose quietly from her bed. In a foggy consciousness, she made her way stealthily to the kitchen. She moved slowly, not wanting the old floor to creak, careful to not stumble, straining to see her way.

Without turning on the light, Deborah reached the kitchen doorway, opened a cabinet storage compartment beneath the sink, felt around blindly, and removed a bottle. She next stole away to the lone bathroom, entered, and closed the door gingerly.

By now, Deborah's eyes had begun adjusting to the darkness. She lifted a large bath towel from the rack, rolled it, laid it on the floor stuffed along the width of the door then switched on the light.

A trembling Deborah stepped lightly, as she removed her mother's douche bag from its secret place in the rear of the uppermost closet shelf. Her mother had used it to irrigate her the night—that night after the frightening examination. Now, she climbed into the bathtub, clutching the device and the bottle of bleach.

"God, please let this work," she prayed. With childlike innocence, Deborah prayed for destruction of what was inside her threatening to destroy the only life she had known. Her awareness of what bleach did to clothing was all she knew. But that gave her hope it would work.

She removed the cap, carefully filled the bag, and eased into the tub. She suspended the bag from the shower head, then sat with her legs drawn and spread. Deborah kept telling herself she had to try this—she had to. But what if there was pain—unbearable pain? What if she screamed out and awakened everyone?

Meanwhile, the fumes grew more and more nauseating. Deborah found it difficult to breathe freely, but was determined to continue. Her heart raced as she held the tube in one hand, inserted it, and prepared to release the clamp. "Do it," she kept telling herself. "Do it, now!" she tearfully repeated. "You have to do this! You have to!"

Tears now completely obscured her vision. For several, long minutes, Deborah exhorted herself to go on. She could not. And it was more than her fear of pain, or fear of angering God, that stopped her. It was more than fear of awakening her parents, had she screamed out. Her real fear was that somehow Gram d'lena would know. Gram would know, and would not be pleased.

That fear was enough to dissuade Deborah. That single thought all but paralyzed her. The last thing she wanted was for Gram to be even more unhappy with her than she likely was already. Deborah collapsed in tears. Her body quaked with the full force of her crying, even as she struggled to mute her mournful voice.

—

While they waited, Rose did little to conceal her displeasure at Reverend Davis' failure to see his young daughter off. It was enough that he had decided to send her away. But not seeing her off to a place she had never been, and for whatever reasons, was unforgivable. It was the least he could have done, Rose thought. The fact Reverend was planted in his pulpit did not square with her one bit.

A seething Aunt Rose leaned closer to her sister, aimed a riveting stare. "Sorry, Henry couldn't leave his pulpit for even an hour. God must really be shorthanded these days. You'd think with all those little 'Assistant Pastors' he's got running around, he'd be here."

Mabel was caught off-guard, stung by Rose's comment. "Rose, he wanted to come, but..."

"Right. So, what stopped him? Huh? I don't understand. How could anything in the world stop him?"

Mabel swallowed hard, forced a weak smile. "Listen, Rose. Thanks for everything. Don't let her give you the least bit a' trouble."

"Don't worry about this little angel for even one minute. We'll get along just fine. I'll call when we get home. But you still haven't answered my question," said Rose, leaning closer and whispering.

"What question?"

"Mabel, don't play dumb with me. You know full well which question. I been asking it since I got here. The question is *why?* What is it you're not telling me? Why is Henry so dead set on this? Or is it you? Don't misunderstand, I'd do anything to be of help, but I just..."

"Rose. Rose, listen. I can't say any more than I have already. We just figured it would be best if...if..."

"If what?" Rose insisted. Mabel hesitated, swiped perspiration from her forehead. Rose sighed disgustedly. "Oh, never mind. We'll talk some other time."

"Rose, listen...

"I said, never mind."

Rose turned away from her sister and hugged her niece. Just then, the P.A. blared a new announcement. Both flinched.

"All aboard! This is your eleven o'clock' call for the cities of Memphis, St. Louis, Champagne, Chicago. All aboard!"

Deborah's heart raced. Until this moment, she still harbored hope that her father would appear at the last second and announce a change of heart. She had desperately listened, straining to hear the distinctive rumble of the old Impala. Even now, she dared to look in both directions for even a glimpse of the car.

But there *was* no car, no Reverend. Deborah stood motionless. She closed her eyes and could practically see her father, dressed in his black robe—Bible in hand—enter the pulpit and take his center seat. "Is he thinking about me, right now? Why isn't he here? Why?" she wondered.

Mabel Davis kissed Deborah's right cheek, then rubbed away the ruby-red lip print stenciled on her daughter's face. Maylene and Gloria hurried to their sister's side. The three stood locked in a tearful embrace.

Rachel never moved, although she finally closed her book and tucked it under her arm. Even when her mother commanded she say good-bye to her sister, she steadfastly refused, without uttering a word. She simply responded with a cold stare, never acknowledging her mother in any way. As usual, Mabel Davis gave in, and turned away.

A grim-faced Matthew watched from a short distance, determined to constrain his emotions. After all, he was the only Davis male present. He was 'the man,' he kept telling himself.

Aunt Rose grasped Deborah's hand. Deborah resisted, slightly, glancing up at her aunt with a plaintive gaze. Rose forced a smile.

"Guess that's us, baby. Mabel, we'll call you all soon as we can. It'll probably be late, though. We have to get from the station and out the Dan Ryan. Slow as my Jack drives, it could take a week."

Mabel Davis slipped a crumpled handkerchief from her shoulder bag and placed a timid hand on her daughter's shoulder.

"Now Deborah, make sure you mind Aunt Rose. Do whatever she tells you. We'll be callin' from time to time to see how you gettin' along."

Mabel's words tumbled out in fractured cadence. Deborah nodded a weak *yes* and dabbed her eyes. Aunt Rose waved good-bye and the two started for the bus.

They had only taken a couple of steps, when Matthew rushed forward. He threw both arms around Deborah, practically lifted her off the ground. He next reached into his right front pocket and removed a cross and chain. Everyone watched with moist eyes, as he slipped it around Deborah's neck. Fighting back tears, he kissed her cheek, placed his lips to her ear, and whispered.

Deborah responded with a rush of emotion, then quickly brushed aside a sudden wave of tears. Aunt Rose renewed her grasp on Deborah's hand and the two moved past the others.

When they reached the platform steps, Deborah yanked her hand from Aunt Rose's and bolted back to where her mother stood. "I don't wanna go, Mama!" she screamed. Tears poured. "Please, don't send me away. I won't be bad anymore, I promise. Please, call Daddy. Ask him if I can stay. I'll do whatever you want me to do. Please, Mama! Please!"

Maylene and Gloria were in hysterics. Both pleaded for their mother's intervention. Strangers took note; some shed tears, without knowing why. Rose tried to console Deborah, but she pulled away. Mabel Davis stood fast, her hands clutched in fists, gripping her handkerchief, twisting it tightly. She shook her head, no.

"I can't, baby." Mabel Davis eased closer, but never embraced her daughter one last time. "You have to go to Chicago with your Aunt Rose for just a little while. It's just for a little while."

The public address system crackled then sounded the final call, over Deborah's pained cries. An angry Matthew forced himself away, turned and leaped from the platform. His determined gait carried him hurriedly down the street. He never looked back.

A tearful Rose guided Deborah toward the bus. At the last moment, they boarded then paused at the door before moving to the middle seats.

Deborah took halting steps down the aisle, certain every damning eye was trained on her. It was the first trip she had ever taken without her parents. Aunt Rose ushered her frightened young niece into a window seat. Deborah peered through a cascade of tears at the remnants of her family remaining on the platform. She desperately searched for Matthew. He was nowhere to be seen.

The bus door creaked closed. The driver adjusted his mirror, crunched into gear, then eased away. Mabel Davis lifted her handkerchief to her eyes. A sobbing Maylene and Gloria waved, clinging to each other. Matthew, who had walked away a half dozen blocks, turned his back as the bus passed.

Rose embraced Deborah and fought back tears. She felt angry, and guilty for having any part to play in what was taking place. Her anger was for a brother-in-law unwilling to face the result of his decision.

Deborah's wet face glistened. The last thing she saw was her mother lifting a crumpled white handkerchief to dab her eyes. She would later recall the moment and wonder if her mother's tears were real.

The growl of the grinding engine, the groan of gimpy gears filled the passenger compartment. The aging Greyhound lumbered past familiar sites. Deborah gazed out at the bus' distorted image in storefront glass and wondered when, and if, she would see any of this again. But even more, she wondered how this day could be.

The vehicle soon rambled onto a narrow two-lane highway, and into pastoral, sun-drenched countryside. For Deborah, the unthinkable was now reality. If she were dreaming all this, the dream—the nightmare was persisting far too long. But there would be no awakening. She was leaving her only world, her only reality. Her life had forever changed, and in ways she was far too young to comprehend.

And what of Jonathan's life? Deborah often thought of him. Those thoughts made her boil with anger. What price was he paying? How had his life changed? She doubted he had given a single thought to his role in the private hell she was experiencing.

An even more dramatic upheaval was taking place within Deborah. A new life was developing inside her still-maturing, young body. It was beyond her ability to process it all. She would never know the normal physiological development a young girl undergoes.

And there would be no more whispered, late night conversations with Maylene—gentle, caring, understanding Maylene. Maylene knew things. She read more than just school textbooks; she read library books, magazines, newspapers. And she listened to the news. Maylene was smart without trying to appear smart.

More importantly, Maylene had innate wisdom; she always seemed more mature than others her age. And she was more than a sister; she was a confidant. There were deeply personal things Deborah could discuss with her. Maylene listened with her heart, and never made one feel the lesser for not knowing what she knew.

But all that was now gone. Deborah's first life was over. Despite promises of her eventual return to Reedville, something in her heart told her otherwise. Everything had changed. She was experiencing physical turmoil and emotional upheaval not experienced by women twice her age.

There was no escaping her new reality. Deborah had no clue what to expect from moment to moment. Every unfamiliar physical sensation frightened her. She felt horribly ugly, inside and out, and was already avoiding mirrors. They mocked her, she thought. The person she saw reflected in them glared back at her with shame and condemnation pouring from her eyes.

———

The irritating bus noise and the buzz of passenger conversations soon faded from Deborah's consciousness. Deborah now saw unfamiliar, even strange, distorted sights streaking past her window. She was not sure which were real, which were imagined. And that frightened her even more.

Despite Aunt Rose's warmth and caring touch, Deborah felt alone. She felt painfully alone; encircled by strangers aiming curious, condemning glances at her. They had to have known what was wrong with her. She was certain of it. But they had no right to look at her this way, she kept telling herself.

Momentarily, the thought of Gram rushed to Deborah's mind. Her chest swelled with emotion. She grimaced, closed her eyes and whispered Gram d'lena's name over and over. A peace seemed to embrace her. Mercifully, within minutes, she was fast asleep.

Rose reclined her niece's seat, removed a pillow from the overhead, and gently placed it beneath her head. She lovingly gazed at the angelic face next to her, and whispered a prayer.

Book Two

In Her Second Life

Not even the deepest footprints last forever.

—gene cartwright

Looking forward, looking back.

'Till Morning Comes —Chicago: February 13, 1975

It was shortly after eight in the evening.

Aunt Rose closed Deborah's bedroom door quietly, and slipped down the hallway to her bedroom. Uncle Jack lay sprawled across the bed, snoring and still wearing his street clothes.

A toasty warmth permeated every room of their Yale Street home, making it easy to forget the 26-degree temperature and falling snow. Both had resigned themselves to a sleepless night—a night of waiting, a night of nervous anticipation, a night of praying. They were praying for Deborah Yvonne, a child no longer a child, and the child she would soon bear.

The snowy, February day in Chicago had ended without serious event. Deborah, only hours from the dawn of her due date, had eaten little, despite Aunt Rose's gentle insistence she eat more. A somber Deborah had talked even less. However, she had admitted to Aunt Rose that she was afraid and sad, mostly sad. Rose knew why.

All day, Aunt Rose had been reluctant to leave her young niece's side. Except for Jack's late-evening snow removal from the driveway, neither he nor Rose had ventured from home. That was a great comfort to Deborah. She had little doubt that no matter her own uncertainties, Aunt Rose and Uncle Jack would take care of her. There were countless reasons for her abiding faith in them.

Deborah heard her door close. At first, the sound startled her. She looked about her room. The bedroom, lovingly decorated by Aunt Rose, had been her special haven for nearly eight months. She shared it with dozens of handmade, stuffed animals. It was aglow with amber light spilling from the nite-lite near the window. Deborah had positioned herself in a large, reclining chair, having decided it would be the most comfortable place for her, especially on this night.

The howling wind barely registered with Deborah, as she eased the chair to an upright position, and listened to her heartbeat pulsing in her ears. For the longest time, she sat staring at the light across the room, being entertained with childlike thoughts, regarding the shadows at play.

Shortly, she placed both hands over her now fully extended midsection, closed her eyes, and felt her baby move, now more than ever. A torrent of warring emotions erupted. She grimaced. Deborah was at once, angered, comforted, distressed, and made even more anxious by the movement inside her.

Then, a quietness, a stillness, yet a rhythm—the rhythm of two hearts. And thoughts—thoughts too intense for adults, years older. Once more, they rooted themselves in the deepest parts of her mind and soul. Deborah fought to not focus on events that had brought her to this night. She did not want to be consumed by all that emotion again, not now.

A deep sigh. Another. And another. Deborah placed both hands, palms down onto the chair's armrests, and slowly eased forward. More, then more, until she was able to stand. She remained standing for a moment, then slowly and carefully moved to stand only feet from the full-length mirror, next to the large, triple dresser. She had stood there many times before, but this time was different.

With her eyes closed, she slowly loosened the front buttons of her ankle-length gown. She eased it from her shoulders—first one, then the other. Holding onto the bodice with both hands, she allowed the garment to slip well below the lower curvature of her stomach.

Deborah then opened her eyes, turned left slightly, and stood observing this...image in the mirror. Tears trickled, slowly at first, then more. This twelve-year old woman-child gazed into her mirror and found the person gazing back at her, and the young girl still nestled deep in her heart, were not really known to each other, even now. In many ways, they were yet strangers, and would remain so for years to come.

chapter eleven

Someday never comes.

The impressive Chicago skyline glistened
in the bright, mid-afternoon sun. Lake Shore Drive and Lake Michigan
environs teemed with auto and pedestrian traffic. More importantly, in
the 7th inning, at Wrigley Field, the Cubs were drubbing the Astros 16
to 3. Heaven was smiling and God must have been batting cleanup.

The city was alive, if not exactly well. To no one's surprise, fractious
politics continued unabated. In the wake of the sudden death, six months
earlier, of Harold Washington, the city's first black mayor, few expected
anything approaching civility. After all, this was Chicago. There was a
longstanding reputation to maintain.

Less than twenty miles away, none of this mattered. In a mid-rise
office park with manicured grounds, the avant-garde structures seemed
more a modern art exhibit than an office park. Paul Castle, 38, 6'-3,"
slipped from his white Mercedes. He oozed leading man charm, wore
faded jeans, a white silk T-shirt, and olive-colored Armani jacket.

Moments earlier, the slightly greying Mr. Castle pulled into his re-served space in front of *The Castle Group*, his entertainment and literary agency. Briefly, he sat perusing a thick, manilla file folder, and listening to jazz great, Les McCann's "Much Les" album, on cassette.

Inside the well-appointed, twin level offices—complete with lobby atrium and perpetual fountain—anticipation gripped the two dozen staff, and a Ms. Deborah Durrell—the agency's franchise client. She was beyond attractive. She was downright beautiful, modelsque, regal, yet completely unassuming.

Deborah was radiant, in a two-piece, pale-yellow, short-sleeve sum-mer suit with matching pumps. Her rich, black-brown, barely shoulder-length hair shimmered. It appeared as if she had just stepped from the pages of Vogue. Her diamond studs sparkled in the ambient light. Debo-rah clearly stood apart from the others, and was calmest of all.

The excitement of seeing her second novel, *Silent Song,* reach num-ber five on the New York Times Best-Seller's List, days earlier, had barely subsided. Now, here Deborah was in Paul's office with senior agent and firm partner, Steve Bono, and literary agent, Julie Amada. She was wait-ing for what both had described as "heart-stopping news."

Deborah was excited, but had a way of masking her emotions. The just completed manuscript of her third, and widely anticipated novel, *A Quest For Angels,* had created enormous interest in the publishing world. Steve and Julie—both literary agents—were unable to sit for even a mo-ment. They kept pacing and drinking coffee.

There were other things on Deborah's mind. Steve, who was han-dling film/TV rights for her second novel, was confident of receiving a mega-offer from a major Hollywood producer-director he would not name. He had a superstition about divulging even general details until he had firm offers in hand.

Deborah's concern was for maintaining the integrity of her work, no matter the offer. She had already reaped significant financial rewards. Despite her success, she craved anonymity, the freedom to write without demands being inflicted upon her. That seemed less and less likely, as she became more successful and sought after.

"How do you feel?" Steve asked, stopping next to Deborah.

"Fine. I feel fine." Deborah smiled.

"I loved *Quest.*" It has excellent film possibilities. So does the other two. But this one is really special. It really got to me."

"That means he cried," said Julie."

"I got a little misty. I admit it."

"I still want to change parts of the first chapter," said Deborah, "Especially the first three paragraphs. I still..."

"Everything's fine," said Julie. "You say that about all your manuscripts. You're a perfectionist. But if you keep changing things, you eventually reach a point of diminishing returns. Many of our authors are like you. We almost have to pry manuscripts out of their hands.

"Then, there are others who think they've got another *War And Peace,* after only a single draft. I will say, however, I enjoy working with writers better than I do actors and musicians. Nothing personal, that's just my preference. In my other life, I was a hair-flailing rocker. So, I can talk about musicians."

The nervous chatter stopped. Silence returned. No one spoke for minutes. Steve left for a moment, then returned with his fifth cup of coffee in less than an hour. Seconds later, he left again, to take a call in his office. Julie now sat slumped on the nearby leather sofa reading a copy of Billboard Magazine.

Deborah Durrell had long ago said good-bye to Deborah Yvonne Davis, her former incarnation. The name change was her idea. So was her revised life history she had recited for several years, more recently to a Publisher's Weekly reporter. Paul knew her real name.

Deborah's story had been honed over years of rehearsal, in conversations with those eager to know more about the young woman behind such a powerful, literary voice. Deborah simply omitted any honest mention of her life before Chicago.

For those who insisted on knowing more, she was born in Beaumont, Texas to an unwed mother who died when she was six. Following six more years in a foster home, she was brought to Chicago to live with her aunt and uncle. The end.

It was a somber tale Deborah found difficult, but necessary to tell. Each time she did so, she visualized Gram standing in front of her, frowning, wagging her finger in admonition. Every answer seemed to spawn another question.

Presently, the only question was whether Deborah was prepared to isolate herself again, until she was satisfied with the final draft of the *A Quest For Angels* manuscript. It should only take days, but there were times such efforts would take weeks, if not months. Admittedly, she was a perfectionist when it came to her life's work.

Deborah had been extremely moody of late. Ever since that awful day in 1974, the month of May had always brought on a bout of depression. The month of May always flooded her mind with memories of things best forgotten.

Writing had always been in her soul—writing and music. Gospel music, not pop music. It was her love of gospel and singing in the choir at Shiloh Missionary that spawned and shaped her love of music.

It was Gram's teaching her to read at the age of four that whetted her appetite for the written word. It was life, the painful living of it, that had given heart, body and soul to her writing.

Deborah often referred to writing as her "passport to sanity." There was little doubt of it, even when she was a student at Northwestern University, majoring in English and music. Writing was her life source. Few things could ever occupy the same place in her life, her soul. It was what gave voice to the music in her heart.

—

Paul entered his office with Steve at his side. Deborah and Julie looked up to see a mile-wide smile plastered on his clean-shaven face. He raised his right arm above his head and waved a folder.

"These are offers," he calmly noted. "Three of the biggest publisher's in New York City want Quest. These prove just how badly they want it."

Deborah clasped her hands together. A broad smile lit up her face. Paul stepped forward and handed her the folder.

"This will make you a multimillionaire, if not a mega-millionaire, real soon. I know that's not what drives you. But given the buzz about this book, your being on the Times list already, and our belief in opting for major promotion, over humongous advances, you won't have to worry."

"We want millions of readers and book buyers. The megabucks will come in no time at all," said Steve. Julie nodded.

"I'm not worried about the money." Deborah's mood was light, but reflective. "My midsize publisher has given me freedom. I don't want to lose that, but it's time to move on. I'm grateful they gave me a chance when no one else offered anything but rejection slips."

"Leave the details to us," said Paul. "We'll review the offers and, in short order, decide what comes next. We are, by definition, in an auction as we speak. It could be over in hours, or take much longer."

Deborah closed her eyes briefly, looked at Paul, mouthed a thank you and sat back. "There are days I am amazed that people care about what I write...that they read what I write." Deborah's eyes began to mist.

"Listen," Paul cut in, "there are people out there who recognize great talent. You happen to be looking at three of them. Just wait. You ain't seen nothin' yet."

"Promise?"

"Absolutely. Everybody in this business, who knows anything, agrees with me. Publisher's Weekly is doing their piece on you and your current novel. It should come out in a couple of months. There'll be major reviews of the new book, prepub and post-pub. I know you aren't excited about a long national tour, but your readers are going to want to see you, hear you—even more than now. You can't hide your face any longer. There'll be more expectations with the new book. More media. Lots more.

"Right now, most of your readers have no idea what you look like. They likely see you as they see themselves. And that's great. They love your work. I don't think that will change. In fact, I feel it will only increase."

Deborah stood. She and Paul embraced. Both pointedly stared into each other's eyes for a moment.

"Thanks," said Deborah. "Steve, Julie."

Paul smiled and placed an index finger to her lips. "You're welcome. But it's your God-given talent that's responsible."

Steve winced. "All this saccharin-laced, mutual admiration is making me nauseous. You guys cut it out!" He said, even as he and Julie applauded.

That second, Paul's secretary, Janet Luu, abruptly entered the room.

"Sorry, I couldn't get the intercom to work," she apologized. "Phone, Miss Durrell. It's your Aunt Rose."

Deborah was struck by Janet's somber expression and serious tone. She thanked her, and started for the door.

"You can take it in here. Line one," said Janet, pointing to the phone on Paul's desk. Deborah moved quickly, punched up the line and lifted the receiver. The others left the room to give her privacy.

chapter twelve

_____

"You're scaring the hell out of me..."

Outside Paul's office,
Deborah could be seen, but not heard speaking on the phone. Paul was keeping a wary eye on her, while trying to provide Steve and Julie more details about the offers. Paul saw Deborah's expression plummet. Deep frowns now lined her brow. She raised one hand to her forehead and shook her head dejectedly. It was clear the phone call was not good news. Paul started back into his office.

A somber Deborah slowly hung up the phone. She stood there—her hand resting on the receiver. Paul was now next to her, waiting for her to say something.

"What's wrong? Aunt Rose alright?"

Deborah's bottom lip quivered a bit. Her eyes appeared glazed. Without a word, she swept her purse from the lamp table and quickly moved through the doorway, into the winding corridor. All were stunned...left wondering.

Steve and Julie eyed each other. Both wondered what had so completely transformed everything. Steve asked Paul. Paul hunched his shoulders and shook his head.

"I don't know," he answered, closing his door and starting after Deborah. Paul hurried down the long, S-shaped corridor leading to the winding staircase and the lobby. The corridor walls were adorned with scores of framed records, awards, photographs, and other memorabilia from his twelve years in the business.

Paul found Deborah standing nearby in an adjoining hallway. Her arms were folded; her back pressed against the wall. She was staring at the floor. Paul hesitated, wanting to be as sensitive as possible. Still, he was desperate to know what had upset her.

He approached slowly, placed a caring hand on her shoulder. With the other, he gently lifted her chin. She resisted him slightly.

"Deborah. Sweetheart, you're scaring the hell out of me. What is it? What's wrong? What did Aunt Rose say?"

Deborah remained silent for a long moment. When she did speak, her voice was barely audible.

"I'm not sure I can...can talk about it, Paul. I'm just not..."

"There's nothing we can't talk about, remember?"

"This is different."

"Come with me."

Paul took Deborah's hand, escorted her back to his office, and closed the door. She plopped onto the sofa. He rushed to his desk, dialed Janet, and instructed her to hold his calls. He then rejoined Deborah and eased down beside her. A moment of silence passed.

"You ready to tell me about it?"

"Paul, I need some time, alright?"

"No," Paul was emphatic.

"Excuse me?" Deborah leaned back and stared with eyes widened.

"Deborah, look at me. Look at me, with those amazing eyes." Paul grasped both her hands. "Hey, I just don't want you to go silent on me again. What is it, already?"

Deborah tossed her head back, while reclaiming her hands and clasping them tightly. Paul searched her eyes. She looked away. There was no hint of tears, just a portrait of pain.

Throughout most of the four years he had known her, and was helping to develop her career, Paul had never seen her this way. He was not sure what to make of it all.

"Deborah, you have to talk to me. Please!"

"Talk is pointless."

"Tell me something. At least enough to know what we're not talking about. Right?"

"It'll only lead to more talk about...about things better left unmentioned."

"Let's not do this dance. It's me, okay?"

More silence followed. Paul was prepared to wait as long as necessary. Time mattered little just now.

"It's my...my father," Deborah whispered. "He's ill. Could die. Could die any day. That's it." She spoke dispassionately.

Paul was not sure he heard her correctly. He inched closer, seized both her hands again, had Deborah repeat her answer.

"What's wrong? What happened?"

Deborah lifted her head and turned to face Paul. Seemed an eternity before she spoke.

"He entered the hospital for a heart operation—a bypass. A quadruple bypass. The surgery went fine. But within minutes of being placed in intensive care, he had a stroke—a massive stroke. Aunt Rose says he had suffered from high blood pressure and heart disease a long time. Never did much about it. I never knew any of this."

"Dee, I'm so sorry."

"Aunt Rose says that the same thing took his father, and *his* father before him. She says it runs in his family. She got the call from my sister, Maylene, about an hour ago."

"I am so, so sorry," Paul repeated. "What can I do? Just tell me."

"I'm fine."

"You can't be fine. Not really. Listen, I'll..."

"I said I'm fine. I've more important things to think about."

"Like what? He's your father."

"He stopped being my father a long time ago. He..." Deborah stopped. Her breathing grew labored. Perspiration beaded her brow. She sprang to her feet. "I have to get out of here," she stammered, and started from the room.

"Deborah!"

Paul followed. His genuine concern came naturally. The eldest of six, he had always witnessed a great example of male strength and caring. His cherub-faced, 'Papa Bear' of a father, Mario, had been a successful building contractor. But he was a father, first. "When you care, you care with your whole heart," he always said. Mario's own father had changed the family name, Castellano, to Castle and moved them from New Jersey. "To protect the innocent," he said.

Paul's concern for Deborah was not simply evidence of a lesson well learned, it was much more. And it came from his heart. Their first meeting, three years earlier, almost did not happen. Deborah had queried his agency twice and not received a reply. Instead of following up with more queries or phone calls, she arrived at the office, unannounced.

What captured everyone, was that Deborah arrived with copies of her manuscript, a bio, a detailed marketing proposal, and a bed pillow. Exuding an air of supreme confidence, she declared she would camp out in the office until someone read her manuscript and gave her an immediate response.

It worked. Paul, who was only two hours away from a crucial trip to New York, rescheduled his trip, met with Deborah and read most of her first novel, 'My Path To Forever,' in one sitting. He signed her on the spot.

However, it was her second novel, 'Silent Song,' written while still a Chicago Prep school English teacher, that truly launched her career. Now, here she was—a full-time author, financially secure, and on the threshold of a success she could only have dreamed of years earlier.

chapter thirteen

In Her Second Life

_____

"No one should have to grow accustomed to that."

T he sun was well into its descent, when Paul
and Deborah began their unhurried stroll along Lake Shore Drive. The evening air was cool and only moderately windy. Earlier, during the short drive from Paul's office, Deborah had said little. She stared straight ahead—her eyes riveted on a place far beyond the spotless windshield.

Despite the tragic news, Paul read nothing into Deborah's reaction that suggested she was considering a trip to Arkansas. He was not surprised. Although generally aware of her estrangement from her family, he knew few specifics. She hardly spoke of her life before Chicago.

In the car, Deborah's silence had driven Paul batty. He flicked the radio on and off, adjusted the rear view mirror, drummed his fingers on the steering wheel. Deborah sighed; he stopped.

A natural talker, Paul now felt compelled to say something. When they stopped near a bench to gaze out across the lake, he chose his words carefully.

"I'm here for you," he whispered. "Whatever you need, just tell me. I can book a flight for you whenever you want."

Except for a pained sigh, the offer was met with more silence. For the moment, Deborah even rejected the labor of speech. The simplest verbal response demanded more than she was prepared to surrender. Paul waited.

"I can't claim to understand what you're feeling. Don't really know what you're thinking. But if I were you, I'd probably be undecided, too, assuming you are undecided. This has all happened so quickly. Times like this, families are suppose to come together, suppose to lean on each other. I come from a large, close-knit family. So, it's difficult for me to understand your parents sending you away for any reason."

Deborah grasped Paul's hand firmly; she gazed into his eyes.

"There's a lot I haven't told you about me. And in spite of our friendship, I'm not going to burden you with things even I don't fully understand. I'm not."

"Burden me? You can't burden me. I love you. I keep telling you that, but I don't seem to be getting through. I love you. I-Love-You! Want me to sing it? I will, you know."

"Don't say that, please. Don't say that."

"Don't say it, or don't sing?" Paul asked, lightheartedly.

Deborah released Paul's hand and turned away. He stepped around to face her squarely.

"It's true. Why shouldn't I say it?"

"Because."

"Not a good answer. Because what?"

"Because I cannot honestly say the same thing to you, not the same way." Deborah answered as delicately as she could.

"You meant to say you're not sure."

"Paul, I said what I meant to say. Right now, what I'm not sure of...is myself. Look, you're a wonderful, caring, desirable man. Any woman with half a brain would..."

"DeeDee! Hold on. Thanks, sweetheart. Please don't take this the wrong way, but I don't want compliments. Hearing things like that from the woman I love is like being kissed by my sister. More like a kiss-off."

"Paul, I'm being honest. That was not a kiss-off. I know how to do kiss-offs and that wasn't one. I won't string you along. I can't. I value those three words: *I Love You.* I won't simply say them because the allure of the moment demands them, or begs for an accompanying note to some lovers' duet."

"Look. I certainly don't want you to say anything that isn't true. I know you wouldn't. My persistence is not some attempt to wear you down. If you tell me you don't feel romantic love for me, I can understand that. It won't make my day, but I will understand it. Is it the difference in our ages?"

"Age has nothing to do with it."

"I just wondered. I'm twelve years older than you."

"You're not listening, Paul."

Paul stared at Deborah a long moment before the two walked on. Both remained silent for the longest while. Deborah shattered the silence with a confession that shocked him.

"There have been times, during the last fourteen years, when I have actually wished my father dead." Deborah looked directly at Paul. "That's a terrible thing to say, but it's true. In my heart, I know it's wrong. But for all these years, Uncle Jack has been my father. Aunt Rose, my mother. They took care of me; they fed me; they sent me to school, college. They nursed me when I was sick; hugged me, when I was hurt, or scared, or both. They are my parents," Deborah proclaimed with soaring emotion.

"But there were twelve years spent with your real parents."

"Real parents?" Deborah mocked. "What are real parents? I haven't spoken to my father for more than ten minutes in all those years...to my mother in three years. The times I've spoken to any of my sisters and brother can be counted on one hand. I haven't spoken to one sister at all in the last fourteen years.

"My letters were never answered. And I wrote many. The truth is, I was virtually excommunicated from my family—forced to create another life for myself. And I have. Simply put, I died at the age of twelve, Paul. Do you know what its like to have your life end at twelve, and yet be expected to go on living as if nothing ever happened?

"I know it's an unfair question. Of course you don't. You couldn't possibly know. No one could, unless they had walked the same miles I've walked. I blotted them out—my family, I mean. I simply had to, for my own survival, I stopped caring about any of them, all except one."

"Samantha?"

Deborah simply nodded. Paul could feel the depth of her pain He heard it in her voice, saw it in her face, but felt helpless.

"Listen. I'm not trying to convince you of anything, I promise."

"I understand."

"I'm really not. This is your life. And this is a decision you'll have to make alone. Whatever you decide, I'm with you. I've always felt there was some emotional baggage weighing you down, holding you back in some way."

"Emotional baggage," Deborah chuckled. "I can't deny it, any more than I can deny existing. The two have been synonymous. But after all this time, I've grown accustomed to it."

"That's not acceptable. I'm sorry. Like you said, there's a lot I don't know, but no one should have to grow accustomed to that."

"After wishing my father dead, the possibility he could die soon doesn't give me the feeling I expected." Deborah glanced away. Paul listened, struggling to mute his stunned reaction.

"Fact is, I don't really know what I expected to feel. I know this isn't making sense but..."

Paul searched for words of comfort. Deborah, sensing his frustration, raised an index finger to her lips and smiled.

"Just having you listen to me is enough, right now," she said. Paul needed to hear her say that.

"Father suffered the stroke two weeks ago."

"Two weeks?"

"Two whole weeks," Deborah repeated. "But that doesn't surprise me. Except for Aunt Rose, I'm sure I wouldn't know, even now. The truth is, I wished they hadn't called at all. My life was just fine."

Paul caressed Deborah's shoulders. She tensed.

"Is he still hospitalized?"

"No. He probably should be, but he's not. From what I understand, doctors say they've done all they can do. Besides, his health coverage has been exhausted."

"In just two weeks?"

"Apparently. He's home now, waiting to die, I guess. End of story."

Paul wished for something to say, some sage advice—anything to ease the distress he was sure Deborah felt, despite the feelings she expressed regarding her father.

"Why have they never really talked to you in all these years? Never explained things? Never tried to reach some understanding? You're their daughter. I don't understand."

"Out of sight, out of mind. I don't really exist anymore. And so, the past doesn't exist."

By now, Deborah had grown weary of the conversation and the dark memories it was dredging up. She folded her arms, shook her head repeatedly as if trying to exorcise those recollections.

"I'm sorry. There are things I just…I cannot explain right now."

"You don't have to explain to me or anyone."

"I don't want to think about yesterday. I don't want to think about tomorrow. I don't want to think. I really don't. I just want to be left to exist in my present life. There's no room for anything else."

Paul embraced her. "It's alright," he whispered. "It's alright."

Precisely at sunset, the brisk lake wind swelled. Paul draped his right arm around Deborah's shoulder. And as always, she felt more than a bit uneasy, accepting the slightest display of affection from him. The last thing she wanted was to give him false hope, or to appear patronizing.

Deborah had long ago struck an uneasy balance between her friend-ship with Paul, and her determination things not go further. Allowing more would likely result in every barrier she had erected falling like domi-noes. She could not permit that to happen.

—

The two watched the final spray of brilliant sunlight dance on por-tions of the darkening water. The effect was pyrotechnic. Somehow, the thought of pain and suffering seemed incongruous with the natural beauty surrounding them.

If nothing else, the past several hours had dramatized the fleeting nature of happiness. It highlighted just how difficult joy is to grasp and hold. Much easier to catch a butterfly in a windstorm. One moment, all were enjoying good news, then...

chapter fourteen

In Her Second Life

So, it's Blacks and Whites with attitudes. Each for different reasons.

Fashionable Zeno's restaurant was crowded but quiet, as usual. Paul and Deborah sat nestled in a corner, with an unobstructed view of the lake. A single candle, set in the middle of the cloth-covered table, illuminated their faces.

A soft spray of recessed light washed from overhead. Even softer jazz wafted from more than two dozen, widely spaced speakers concealed in the practically invisible ceiling.

Paul interrupted Deborah's distant gaze. He smiled. She smiled back. He sipped his glass of Zinfandel. She nursed a glass of fizzing ginger ale. Deborah was not hungry, but Paul insisted she eat something. She relented. The problem was deciding what to order. Twice, the waiter had offered more time. Now he was back.

"May I take your order now, sir?"

Paul glanced at Deborah. She shook her head, 'no.'

"A few moments more," Paul answered.

"More wine? Ginger Ale, sir?"

Paul indicated *no* and grasped Deborah's left hand affectionately. She hesitated before lifting and twirling her glass, while loosing a faint and fleeting smile.

"You spoke to your Aunt Rose again?"

"Yes. I called her just before we came here. She and Uncle Jack are fine. She's a little worried about me. I've told you about Aunt Rose." Paul nodded. "Told her I was with you. She said I was in good hands."

"Could you repeat that?" Paul flashed a wide grin and folded his arms across his chest.

"She said I was in good hands."

"The woman's a saint—wise beyond her years." Paul inched closer.

Deborah was aware he was trying to lighten the mood. Truth was, she wanted to be alone but knew Paul was concerned about her state of mind. No way would he leave her, until he was sure she was okay. Paul moved closer, stared pointedly, tried to make her smile.

"You'd better enjoy this anonymity," he said, wagging his finger. "Coming to a restaurant or walking along the lake, or anywhere else, will soon be more difficult, if not impossible for you."

"You seem so sure about that."

"I am."

"Is this another one of those famous Paul Castle predictions?"

"Absolutely. Write it down. Carve it in stone. That's my prediction, which I make without reservation. I predict. Ah, I predict that..."

"What's the matter? Can't get it out?"

"See what you do to me?"

"I'm making you stutter?"

"Amongst other things."

"So what do you predict?"

"I predict your fans will be legion."

"Don't start the Shakespeare thing."

" You'll have to wear disguises when you go out in public."

"I don't know if I'm looking forward to that proving accurate."

Both shared laughter that lasted all too briefly. Paul was aware Deborah's mind had quickly returned to more somber thoughts. She clearly did not want to think about tomorrow, but he knew such thoughts were unavoidable.

"Listen. If you do decide to go to Arkansas, don't worry about the new draft. I don't think we need one. The publishers we've heard from aren't asking for one. You should save that energy for interacting with your editor, whomever that will be."

"What about the new offers? Then later, we'll have to review contracts," said Deborah. "I want to study the details for myself. I need to keep busy; keep my mind occupied."

Paul knew Deborah would not simply rely on the professionals around her. He would have been surprised if she had not wanted to see the contracts for herself.

"You choose which offer, we'll look over the contract; lawyers will look. We may amend them, sign off, then look out Pulitzer," said Paul, with his patented laugh. "Depending on how long all this takes, we can have the publishing contract sent to us in Arkansas."

Paul's words had hardly faded, when Deborah's expression changed. She looked away, looked down, began swirling her drink again. Her reaction did not escape Paul.

"What's wrong, now?"

Heavy silence followed. Paul took a long sip of wine and waited. He was not sure he really wanted an answer.

"What's wrong?" he repeated.

"Paul, I have no intentions of going anywhere. But if I decide to go, I'll have to go alone. I simply have to."

Paul lowered his glass and sat straight back.

"Why?"

"Why?"

"Yes, why?"

Deborah tossed her head to one side and leaned toward Paul.

"Well, I hope you're not thinking..."

"I'm not thinking anything, I just want to know why."

"It's not because I don't think Arkansas is ready to see us together, okay? I couldn't care less about that. It's 1988. I'm sure it's no longer unusual, even down there. Truth is, even Chicago isn't as ready as you think. America isn't either. You've seen the look I get from some brothers, when I'm with you. And I've seen the looks some white folk give both of us. They don't know whether our relationship is business or personal. So, it's Blacks and Whites, each for different reasons. But to hell with them. That doesn't bother me."

"Alright. Fine," said Paul. "I'm convinced. So, why shouldn't I come with you?"

"Paul..."

"No, Look, I don't mean to be pushy or insensitive at a time like this," Paul whispered. "I just want to know why. That's not too much to ask, is it? If you say so, I'll drop it. I promise. I won't say another word."

Deborah folded her arms and stared at him. A moment later, the waiter approached again, then thought better of it and walked away.

"It's not too much," Deborah conceded. "First of all, I'm not at all sure I'm going. Secondly, you've got a business to take care of, and contracts to get for the lawyers and me."

"I can get that done from anywhere on the planet."

"And finally, I don't know what's waiting for me in Arkansas. I'm more than twice the age I was when I left Reedville. An awful lot has happened. And don't forget, no one has invited me back there. I don't expect open arms waiting to embrace me. So, for me to introduce you to that...that uncertainty is both unwise and inconsiderate. I hope you can understand."

"I'd like to say I don't, but I do. I'll tell you what."

"What?"

"I'll take care of things here and come later. How's that?"

"Paul."

"No, Listen," Paul insisted.

"I'm listening."

Paul grinned and rubbed his hands together, certain he had come up with an unassailable argument.

"If you needed me for any reason, I'd be right there. I'd be close by. Where are you going to stay, anyway? I doubt Reedville has a Hilton, or even a Holiday Inn, for that matter," he chuckled.

Deborah could not help smiling. Paul might have come with something better, she thought. An offer of emotional support and having a familiar face to rely upon would have been much better arguments. She may have been hard put to counter such an argument.

"That's not a problem."

"No problem?"

"No. I'd stay in Little Rock, which is where I would stay whether you were there or not. I'd rent a car and drive to Reedville, that is if I were to go at all."

"If you go?" Paul was skeptical.

"If I go."

"Sounds like you've already decided. Which is fine. I think you owe it to yourself to confront this now...come to grips with your past, once and for all."

Deborah did not protest.

"Right?"

"You may be right."

"May be right?"

" It's true that if I don't go, my life will likely never completely be my own. It'll always belong to the past."

"I agree."

" I don't want that, Paul. I don't want to die wishing I had tried one last time to understand all this. I want to end this chapter."

"I understand."

"And there is one other thing I should probably tell you. It explains why I was sent away all those years ago."

"I'm listening."

"Not here, not now. Later."

"You say later, and hope I forget to ask, but I won't."

"No. I'll tell you. I promise. Someday."

"Someday? You mean, someday when I'm old and gray, hearing gone, my walk has become a shuffle, my pants pulled up to my nipples, belt overlapping, my teeth in a jar of fizzing cleanser, my..."

"Stop it, stop it!"

"My glasses thick as coke bottles."

"I said stop it. I get it." Deborah tried to choke back her laughter. She failed, but for only a moment.

What she loved about Paul was his ability to both empathize and lighten the darkest mood, at the same time. Only now, she was in no mood to have her mood altered. Strange, but that's how she felt.

Deborah was emotionally spent. She buried her face in both hands for a few seconds. Paul placed an arm around her shoulder, removed a white handkerchief and handed it to her. She dabbed her cheeks, composed herself, and left for the ladies room. Paul signaled the waiter for the check. When he returned, Paul accepted it, handed him his credit card, and placed a crisp, folded, twenty dollar bill in his palm.

chapter fifteen

Rose, Sweet Rose

"I live here, woman!"

For Deborah, the spacious, cream-colored brick, ranch-style house at Yale and 97th streets was a mansion. It had no front porch, but Deborah did not mind. There was no septic tank, either. What it had was a beautifully manicured lawn, a real garage for two whole automobiles, and space—plenty of space.

Uncle Jack and a few friends built the three bedroom home in 1964, while he worked full-time at Johnson Publishing Company. He was especially proud of the sprawling basement, with its full-size kitchen, full bath, game area and regulation pool table.

The basement also served as Jack's 'Santa's Helper Headquarters' during the wonderful Christmases Deborah enjoyed with Rose and Jack. He would hide nearly a mountain of gifts there, along with his Santa suit. Christmas, snow, Chicago, a towering tree—all decked out. Deborah's first Christmas came during a difficult, emotional period for her. Uncle Jack pulled out all the stops to make sure it was one she would remember.

Then, there were the Christmas events taking place in the city: the trip to the Loop for Santa's arrival; the amazing Marshall Field's Christmas Windows, where the store creates magical, thematic windows depicting Christmas. There were amazing decorations throughout Chicago; the State Street Parade; displays at Bloomingdales, Neiman's and other stores. There were the City's, and the State's tree displays. Mayor Richard Daley had these and other reasons to boast of his city, until his passing in 1976.

Jack and Rose treated Deborah to as many events and venues as possible. For her, and for them as well, it was like a trip to wonderland, a trip to the North Pole. For Deborah, It was almost too much for her to grasp. And this happened not just during her first year, but every year.

At home, Deborah's favorite room was Uncle Jack's kitchen, especially at Christmas. It was a culinary paradise. The aroma of great food wafted throughout. There was the smell of roasting, baking—pies, cakes, cookies—everything. Scented candles were lit throughout the house. The scent of Christmas was everywhere.

The kitchen was a hallowed sanctuary throughout the year as well. Late at night, when the weight on Deborah's shoulders, and the need to empty her heart were unbearable, there was nothing like a 'meeting of the hearts' with Aunt Rose. The two, clad in pajamas, would sip coffee and often talk until dawn.

Deborah credited Aunt Rose and Uncle Jack for a success she happily shared with them. Shortly after Deborah received her first six figure advance, a stunned Jack and Rose came home to find their retired mortgage papers on the kitchen table. And there was more. A new pickup for Uncle Jack—complete with a toolbox, loaded with new tools;—a new Cadillac DeVille for Aunt Rose, all parked in the driveway. Each vehicle had a giant ribbon and bow attached. All that, and a two-week Caribbean cruise. The two were rendered speechless. Even Jack teared up.

—

It was almost midnight, when Deborah arrived home. Rich, black coffee was already brewing. The aroma greeted her the instant she opened the door leading in from the garage. Rose had set out a pair of

Royal Winton cups and saucers. A flickering, scented candle was set in the middle of the table. As usual, the porch light had been left on, as had the table lamp with the tattered shade, visible in the living room's bay window. Rose purchased the shade when she and Uncle Jack were first married. She was not about to throw it away.

To Jack's dismay, Rose saved almost everything she touched. She still had a book of matches saved from her first visit to a formerly segregated Chicago hotel. The basement was a repository for a lifetime of collecting memorabilia. Jack had another, less edifying name for the stuff cluttering his prized basement and garage.

Rose, now fifty-one, showed no signs of slowing. She was as vibrant and feisty as ever. Her eyes still surrendered the content of a heart never able to conceal true feelings well. She tightened the belt on the silk robe covering her silk pjs and eased into the chair opposite Deborah.

"How's your coffee, baby?" She asked. "I can freshen it for you."

"No thanks." Deborah shook her head.

Rose took a slow sip, both hands wrapped around her cup. "DeeDee, baby, I'm happy you decided to go see 'bout your father. After all, he'll always be your father, no matter what. Always."

Silence followed. Deborah finally tilted her head to one side and grasped strands of her hair between thumb and forefinger.

"Uncle Jack has been, and is my father. You've been and are my mother. Now, I know what you're going to say, but it's true. It's not only what you've said *to* me; it's what you've done *for* me"

Rose stirred her coffee and smiled. "We've had this conversation many, times," she said. "I have never wanted you to have bad feelings 'bout your mama and daddy, or your sisters and brother. But I understand how you feel. When I look at you, I see my daughter—my own child. I feel as if I gave birth to you myself." Rose placed a hand atop Deborah's and gazed lovingly as she spoke.

"Aunt Rose..." Deborah's eyes glistened. It almost always came to this. After all these years, the tears were never far away. Rose raised an index finger to her own lips and continued.

"I blame myself for a lot of what's happened over these years, especially your mother and father not coming for you...not taking you back to Reedville."

"Why? What could you have done? It was their decision, not yours. You did all you could. You were, and are here for me. You and Uncle Jack."

"I know. But it was my decision not to say anything to them about it. I certainly could have forced the issue—forced them to at least talk about it. I said nothing all this time. I never once challenged them on it. I feel bad about that."

"I don't want you to feel bad. You have no reason to feel bad. You were not responsible for decisions they made."

"You know, Jack and me couldn't have children. I used to say it was a blessing in disguise. We didn't have to worry 'bout a house full of little crumb snatchers. 'Course that was just our way of dealing with the pain...making jokes, laughing and everything. Then, your mama called me that night. Never will forget it. She had just got word from the doctor." Deborah flashed a look of surprise.

"I never knew she called you that same night."

"She talked 'bout everything she could think of, except what she really called me about. Finally, she said it...told me you were in that way and all. The minute she told me, I knew Henry was going to do *something*. I didn't know exactly what, but I knew he'd do *something*.

"But all this never would 'a happened if your Gram d'lena had been alive. She would 'a chased your daddy up and down Crispus Attucks with a stick...talking about sending her babygirl away." Rose took a long sip.

"They asked you to come get me, bring me here to Chicago," said Deborah. Rose heard the emotion building in her niece's voice, saw it in her eyes. "Then, after Samantha was born, they came for her, not me. There is no forgiving that. Not ever.

"I keep thinking how my own father chose to stay in his pulpit instead of having the courage to come to the depot that Sunday. He always preached about forgiving—about forgiving until seven times seventy. But he couldn't forgive his own daughter even once."

Deborah's voice faded. A tear crept down the right side of her face. The pain was as real as ever. Aunt Rose reached across the table and gently squeezed her hand.

"You have to forgive them, DeeDee, baby. You have to. Even as God forgives us our sins. I know it's hard. Forgiving folks is not easy."

"God forgives us, when we confess."

"But you don't know they haven't confessed."

"They haven't confessed to me."

"I guess your daddy just never learned how to deal with what happened. He was always, and still is, a good and righteous man, at heart. But he lacks the softer touch. And the fact that boy was white didn't make things any better. You know that. We've talked about all this before. That was 1974, and not much had changed, in spite of all that marching and dying. No telling what would have happened if you had stayed there. I shudder to even think about it."

"We'll never know," said Deborah.

"True. Sending you here was the only thing they could think of. And I was happier to get you than they were to send you. You were a fragile, frightened and confused little girl.

"Then, after Samantha was born, they never sent for you. And they never spoke to me and Jack about it. To tell you the truth, I didn't want them to. I know that was selfish. Jack still reminds me, to this day. You were a special blessing to us. You still are."

Deborah dabbed her eyes with a tissue. Rose waited a moment. "As for your mama and daddy, I guess the passing years made it harder, not easier. The years kept passing, and you became rooted here. Same was true for Samantha, down there. You became *our* little girl, and Samantha became theirs. If I live to be a hundred years old., I'll never..."

"But they never asked me how I felt about any of this," said Deborah. "For a long time, throughout high school, and even through my first year at Northwestern, I convinced myself May 15th never happened. It was all a dream. Like...like I had always been here in Chicago, especially, if I blocked out that day. And I did block it out, although it was never an easy thing to do. I was not only separated from...from what was my family, I also lost my two best friends in the whole world: Kay and B.B.

"It broke my heart when Maylene called you...said they stopped coming around...stopped coming to Shiloh after I...after I left. They even left Reedville before graduating. Kay moved away first. B.B. moved a month later. And no one knew where either moved. Maylene said they had asked for the address, here. Sister Davis supposedly gave it to them. I have trouble believing she did."

"I remember telling you about it at the time," said Rose. "But you were in your...silence then. I was surprised you later recalled that. Your leaving changed their lives forever, just like everybody else's. Friendships are so important at that age. You never forget your friends—true friends. I remember my childhood friends, to this day. I wonder 'bout them...where they are, what happened to them, how their lives turned out. It kinda' makes me sad, so I make myself think about something else. And as far as your mama and daddy is concerned, I gave them up to the Almighty a long time ago. It's all beyond my understanding."

"I remember you holding me, telling me 'they' loved me," Deborah recalled. "You told me that, over and over. But I kept thinking...if they really loved me, why did they...how could they just send me away? How? I could never figure that out. I still can't. I've wondered if it were more a desire to save Reverend the embarrassment. *I* was an embarrassment that could only be hidden by my not being there. And they never called me, really...or took my calls. How is that possible?"

"I know, baby. I know. And your mother never explained any of this to me either. It's one of those things that sometimes occur in families. Terrible things happen, and no one talks about it."

"I know. I will never understand that. And I'd be willing to bet they continued to carry me as their dependent, while you and Uncle Jack were the ones taking care of me all these years." Rose did not respond; she looked away briefly. "They also had to grant you and Uncle Jack the authority to make medical decisions for me, but never made sure *you* two were surviving okay."

"Well, the good Lord took care of that, baby. I stopped trying to figure this all out long ago. I still love my sister. Always will. Fourteen years and we've only laid eyes on each other once in all this time. It's like she separated herself from me, too. I don't understand how such things happen in families. Things happen that defy explanation. Far too much left unsaid. Secrets kept just for the sake of keeping secrets. Nobody knows why. It just leaves you shaking your head, trying to figure out the how and why."

A lengthy silence followed. Deborah kept turning her cup with both hands, and staring blankly at its contents. "How much do you think they really love each other?" she all but whispered.

"Who, baby?"

"The Reverend and his wife."

Rose was caught off guard. She lowered the cup she had just raised, gazed into Deborah's eyes. "Your parents? A lot, I'm...I'm sure. Always have. Why you ask?"

"I know I was just a child back then, but I was just thinking, trying to remember ever seeing them holding hands, kissing, or just being playful, you know? And I can't remember a single time. Not once. I'm sure they did, but..."

"Of course they did," Rose agreed. Her tone revealed her discomfort with the subject.

Rose sipped more coffee. Deborah noticed her gripping the cup especially tight. She had not intended to stilt the conversation with talk of the lack of any display of affection by her parents.

"Thank God for you and Uncle Jack." Deborah redirected the conversation. "God knows I love you two so much. I've said it before, but thanks for being here for me all this time. You're my angels. You're my real mother and father. You were both there for me during the most dreadful time of my life—a time when all I knew was fear, whether asleep or awake. You nurtured my hopes, my dreams, shared my tears, embraced me when I needed it most. There's no way to tell you how much you both mean to me."

Tears careened down Deborah's face. Rose was crying, too. "Baby, there are things I'm tempted to say, but I won't."

"What things?"

"I want you to find out some things for yourself. And I feel sure God will reveal them to you. If you change your mind about not wanting anyone to know you're coming, I'll call Mabel and tell her."

"No. I don't want them to know."

"That's fine. And you know if you wanted me to go with you..."

"I know. I just...it's just something I have to do alone."

"You're right. But I want you to pray real hard you won't go with hate in your heart. Remember what your Gram use to say about hate. She said it's like eating lye. And remember, there's a little girl down there who was taken from here many years ago. We don't know what she's been told, but she's innocent...caught in the middle. That's what you have to remember."

"I will."

"I know you will. I know."

For one thing, it's often hard to reconcile the fact I actually have a daughter. It's like I only imagined it all. Sometimes, I feel there's nothing inside me to connect with that fact, not emotionally. Same thing is true with...with the rest of them. Intellectually, yes. Emotionally, no."

"Baby, I wish I could wave my hand and change that—make things different. If I could, God knows I would have done it long ago. And you wouldn't have suffered like you did."

Deborah was warmed and comforted by every word Rose spoke. However, she felt guilty—guilty for still clinging to a secret she had held for seven long years. This trip to Reedville would not be her first since being sent away in 1974; it would be her second. Deborah struggled to push that fact from her mind, but it persisted with a vengeance.

chapter sixteen

The Journey - 1981

====================

Fear and apprehension swelled inside her,

I t all seemed so long ago.

Seven years. Deborah was now nineteen, a freshman at Northwestern University. Each day of those seven years had found her struggling with the memories, the anguish, the pain of her young life following May 15, 1974.

While it appeared, to others, she had moved beyond the roughest part, Deborah often found those memories too vivid to withstand. It was during one such episode, she made a fateful decision she dared not share with Aunt Rose.

It was the Friday leading into the long Labor Day weekend of 1981. Deborah was to have spent three days in Gary, Indiana at the home of her roommate, Janice Penhall and her family. That is what she told Aunt Rose and Uncle Jack. Instead, she boarded a Trailways bus for Reedville, Arkansas. Her decision had not come easily. For some time, the desire to finally reclaim her daughter, and redeem her own troubled life, had consumed Deborah. That was much of what she thought about.

Just what she would do, and how she would do it, had not been thoroughly thought out. But that did not matter; those were simply details. The most important things were that she return and demand all she felt belonged to her.

Deborah was filled with a boldness that countered the doubts assaulting her. Even so, she regretted the deception necessary to act on her conviction. The last thing she wanted was to not be completely honest with her aunt and uncle, but felt she had no choice.

And so she made the trip. Deborah purposely chose a night departure, arriving at the nearly empty Reedville depot just before 10 p.m. Most of the twenty or so fellow passengers were continuing through.

Fear and apprehension swelled inside her, as Deborah exited the bus. She gingerly stepped onto Reedville soil, for the first time since that long ago Sunday. She fought against persistent recollections. Miller's Cafe remained, but was presently closed for the night. The Five and Dime was gone, claimed by competition from the new Walgreens across the street.

The old images invaded Deborah's mind. She resisted, clenched her jaws, closed her fists, her eyes. She forced back the memories. The darkness permitted her to escape seeing the place in the full glare of day. Still, it was not easy to stand there.

Carrying her dark-blue denim tote bag over her right shoulder, Deborah struggled to push forward, past the moment. But a feeling of isolation descended upon her like a wet canvas. "No one knows who and where I am," she told herself. It dawned on her, she was no longer in the protective embrace of Aunt Rose and Uncle Jack. And here in Reedville, there was no one to welcome her, no one to embrace her. It was then, she was consumed with the thought she had made a terrible mistake.

Deborah stood on the wooden platform, peering into the distance, the darkness—dark, except for the dim light from a few, widely spaced power-pole lamps. Moments passed. She sighed deeply, then entered the depot. It appeared to have changed little over the years.

Deborah found only the stationmaster inside. He was parked on a stool inside his small ticket booth. She claimed her suitcase and made her way to the wooden bench farthest from the ticket cage, and sat down. Her heart pounded; her temples throbbed, her mind swirled. What now? What now? She sat stone-still, contemplating the answer.

Seconds became minutes. Deborah was lost in contemplation. She failed to notice the young, pimple-faced ticket agent in baggy khakis, wrinkled, short-sleeve white shirt, black vest, and a pencil stuck behind his right ear. He was standing less than three feet away from her. His sudden appearance startled Deborah.

"Waitin' for somebody?"

The young man could not have been more than twenty. He seemed friendly enough, almost bubbly.

"What?" Deborah gasped.

"Sorry. Didn't mean to scare you. Just noticed you been sittin' here a while. You waitin' for a ride?"

"Ahh, no. I'm just..."

The young man stared into Deborah's eyes. He seemed fixated, mesmerized. She glanced away for a short while.

"You need to make a call? Got change for the phone if you need some. It's over there, next to the Coke machine," he said, pointing toward the far wall adorned with a huge, framed route map.

Deborah flashed a weak smile and shook her head slightly. "No, no, not just now. Maybe later." She knew calling was no option.

The young man seemed puzzled. He started back toward his ticket counter, glanced over his shoulder, then returned to Deborah.

"Well, I'm gon' be shuttin' her down in 'bout an hour. Only other bus due in is one headin' back where you just came from. It leaves at eleven. So, if you change your mind about the phone, let me know."

Deborah said thanks and sank back against the high-back bench. She felt exhausted, tired of thinking, tired of wondering what to do. What if she did call the house? It was *the house*, not home. What if she did call? Even if someone actually answered, what would she say? And what if they refused to believe it was she? Or worst of all, what if they flat out refused to come get her, or denied ever knowing such a person?

The truth was, Deborah did not want to arrive asking for favors, appearing to need anything from anyone. And she did not want anyone to come get her. No. She wanted to simply arrive at the front door, unannounced, boldly asserting herself and demanding her daughter. It would not matter if she were not greeted with open arms. She would see right through the slightest display of joy and excitement directed toward her. She was not there to beg to be returned to the family fold.

An hour drifted past. Deborah was consumed with wonder about Samantha. What would she look like at nearly seven years? All this time, and no one had so much as sent a picture to her, or Aunt Rose. What would she say to her daughter? *"Hi, Samantha! I'm your mother. I've come to get you...take you back to Chicago with me. You're my daughter."*

Deborah was overcome. Tears rained down her face, spilled onto her lap. She tried to wipe them away, but without success. She turned away, not wanting the young ticket agent, or anyone who may arrive at anytime, to see her so over wrought.

It was then, Deborah realized she could go no farther. She had failed. This place, this old bus station would be as close as she would come to Samantha, at least for now. The thought that she was so near her daughter, and what had once been home, left her more pained than ever.

At that moment, Deborah was certain she felt worse now than if she had not come at all. The moment passed. A sense of accomplishment swelled within her. She had acted. She had not failed. She had acted. Even as she made her way to the ticket booth to have her return ticket stamped, Deborah knew she would come back someday. She was only nineteen, but felt many years older now.

Returning to her seat, finding her way through teary eyes, a conflicted Deborah made a vow. Someday she would have the power, the means, the courage to stop at nothing to reclaim her daughter and her life. Someday, she would possess the resources necessary to determine the course of both their futures, asking nothing of anyone. Someday.

chapter seventeen

Determination

Well, she would face that moment when it came.

The sparkling Greyhound bus sat idling
at curbside. The dozen passengers, who had arrived a short time earlier,
boarded quickly. Deborah drew a long, deep breath. She clutched the
handle of her suitcase. The night air had turned a bit cool now. Earlier,
she had donned a light sweater and secured the lowest button. Chicago
would have been even cooler this time of night, the wind many times
stronger, she thought.

Deborah imagined Aunt Rose sitting at the kitchen table nursing a
cup of Seaport Coffee. It was a brand she loved, but found hard to come
by. Uncle Jack was likely sound asleep, snoring his way through another
stand of majestic oak trees.

Finally, all were aboard. The door creaked closed, the engine revved,
gears shifted, and the bus eased away, en route to the Windy City and
beyond. Deborah closed her eyes briefly. She questioned the wisdom of
her decision, and prayed she had wisely decided.

It was then, the young clerk exited the depot, closed and locked the heavy wooden door. He turned to see Deborah planted firmly on the wooden bench a couple feet to one side of the entrance.

"Sure hate to leave ya' sittin' here like this. It being dark and all. 'Course mosquitoes ain't too bad now. They were something terrible up until a month ago. It ain't too likely you'll see a soul 'fore mornin' comes."

The young man was genuinely concerned for Deborah. He belatedly introduced himself as Casey, and handed her a Coke he had taken from the machine. It was an act of kindness she had not expected.

"Thank you. That's kind of you. I'm...I'm Deborah.

"Miss Deborah, you sure I can't call someone to come get ya'? You got folks here, right? I'm most sure they'd come for you real quick, unless...." He hesitated. "Ohhh, they don't know you're comin,' do they? Is that it? I don't mean to pry or nothin.' No business of mine. Maybe you just want 'a surprise 'em."

Deborah shrugged her shoulders, loosed a faint smile. He called her "Miss," she thought. She had no desire to sit on the bench all night. The idea was more than a little scary, but she felt she had little choice. Deborah had not come this far to turn around, despite sound reasoning to the contrary. She could not bring herself to board that bus, without at least trying to reach her destination.

The only activity she observed was a gathering of night bugs fluttering beneath the bulb of the pole-mounted street light. Casey had informed her earlier that Reedville's one-car cab fleet stopped running in town after ten. He offered to lock her inside the building for the night; said he would show her how to get out without a key.

Deborah politely refused. The idea of being locked in a building in Reedville, or anywhere where others had the only key, was not an appealing notion.

Deborah likewise refused Casey's final offer. He suggested driving her to wherever she needed to go...in his pickup. She refused almost before he completed the sentence.

"One more thing," Casey informed her, before leaving. "Most nights, Deputy Orlo Poole makes a turn through town to check on things and all, more or less. It all depends on whether Darlene—his sometimes' girl-friend and his baby's mama—is workin' graveyards out at the new saw-mill. His would-be mama-in-law, Darlene's mama, she usually keeps the kid when Darlene works nights.

"They don't get along, Orlo and Miss Jewel. She's Darlene's mama. If she is workin'—Darlene that is—then Orlo's gon' be patrolling elsewhere, like out near Miss Ruby's place." Casey loosed a short-lived chuckle and gazed skyward. "Got a half moon tonight. Lots 'a clouds, though. Listen, I usually get here about seven. Cab's runnin' 'bout seven-thirty. I'll try to get in 'bout six-thirty tomorrow."

With that local society update and lunar report, Casey bounded down the short rise, crossed the street and entered his Chevy pickup, parked in a diagonal space in front of Walgreens. He backed out, flipped on his headlights, tooted his horn, waved, and disappeared into the night.

The instant the taillights of Casey's truck vanished, Deborah real-ized just how utterly alone she was. And it was not just the fact she was sitting on some bench in front of an empty bus depot in an empty south-ern, backwater town. She felt alone from the crown of her head to the soles of her shoes. The idea of being snuggled aboard that Greyhound Bus was never more appealing than it was that moment.

Every sound was now amplified. Every beat of her heart reverber-ated in her ears like a jackhammer. And she prayed. Deborah sat stone still, clasped her hands in her lap and prayed. She summoned every com-forting thought she could. She imagined the most secure, serene sur-roundings she had ever known: the loving home at 97th and Yale streets.

And what would happen when morning came? Deborah asked her-self that question over and over. She would make her way to the house, somehow. She would go; she would definitely go. She could see herself, suitcase in hand, marching up those steps, up to the front door, and knocking as hard as she could. She would stand erect, head back, shoulders squared. Her eyes would directly focus on whomever answered the door; it would not matter who that was.

She would then...well, she would face that moment when it came. But no matter what, no matter who was there, or what was said to her, her one purpose was to see Samantha. She was seeking nothing for herself. She was not there seeking to forgive or to be forgiven; to be loved or to love, except for Samantha. She was there to finally reclaim her daughter. The desire to see her baby, to hold her, to fulfill her need to be a mother was overwhelming. Nothing would stop her. And no one, including the Reverend, would stand in her way, or matter ever again.

Deborah had her return ticket, and money for Samantha's ticket, with little to spare. All she could think of was getting back to Chicago with her daughter. The inevitable explaining to Aunt Rose and Uncle Jack would come later. Deborah was certain they would forgive her and understand. There was no doubt she would somehow manage both college and motherhood. She would get a decent job, go to school, and be a mother to Samantha.

The thought of seeing Samantha left her excited and winded. Deborah found herself gasping. Just thinking about Samantha had taken her mind off her present dire circumstance. Fear soon subsided, sort of. And concern for her physical safety faded considerably. She would be alright.

—

An hour later, hunger struck with a vengeance. Only half the coke was gone. And food? Deborah remembered she had brought food. She opened her denim bag, lifted a small brown sack containing three sandwiches: one tuna, and two peanut-butter and jelly—her favorite. They may as well have been Caviar and exquisite French pastry. She downed half the tuna and an entire PB&J, chased by the rest of the coke, before ending her filling feast.

Deborah simply wanted to sit and not think for a while. She was desperate to have her mind just go blank. No thoughts, no contemplation, no imagining. Nothing. But that sort of peace would have to come much later, if at all. Not on this night. Not in this place.

Morning could not come soon enough. And yet with each tick of her wristwatch, which was beginning to sound like a giant bass drum, Deborah's trepidation increased a hundredfold. Her mind previewed nearly every possible scenario, regarding what would happen when she reached the house. She prayed Maylene, Matthew, or Gloria would be there. They would likely receive her with greater warmth.

Just then, the distant moaning of a freight train pierced the cool night air. The unmistakable refrain was barely audible at first, but swelled as the powerful locomotives drew closer. The sound grew to a roaring, rhythmic crescendo, then gradually faded as the steel leviathan moved on into the darkness.

Deborah knew that if she were right, it was likely the Missouri Pacific winding its way along multiple tracks dividing The Sticks and Reedville proper. And she thought of Gram, and her magical stories of trains she never had a chance to ride, except via her boundless imagination.

—

Three in the morning. Only once had the silence been disturbed, if one did not consider cricket racket, and other night critter chatter. Just past 4 a.m., fear struck. Her heart stopped mid-beat. A light-colored pickup with two, boisterous, white men inside slowly drove past the depot. They were weaving, country music blaring, voices booming. They sounded drunk, and were arguing. Deborah froze rock-still. She pressed her back against the wall, practically held her breath, and silently prayed they would not notice her. They drove on.

Moments later, Deborah began breathing again. She drew herself into as small a presence as possible. And she could not help thinking that at this moment, while she sat on a wooden bench, her father, mother, and siblings were a few short miles away, likely sound asleep, unaware she was so near.

—

Her eyes shot open; she sat straight up. Deborah had fallen asleep. But when? For how long? Her pulse spiked. The realization she had dozed...frightened her. She stole a quick glance at her watch. It was nearly

5:15 a.m. It was more than a brief doze. More like an hour. The darkness in the eastern skies was beginning to lift. Morning would soon come. Deborah felt emboldened. She had done it—survived the night. A sudden surge of newly found strength coursed her body.

Deborah stood, yawned, and stretched—both arms spread and extended above her head. The early morning air filled her lungs. She strolled a few steps down the platform and stared down the empty street. Just as she started to return, she caught sight of her reflection in the window. It frightened her. Then came an uninhibited laugh and a much-deserved, though fleeting, feeling of emotional, if not physical, relief.

—

Casey returned at 6:30 on the dot. Deborah was glad to see him and the fresh donuts and hot coffee he brought. He opened the Depot, helped lug her bag back inside, and flipped on the lights. While he went about his start-up routine, he inquired about her night.

"Uneventful," Deborah answered.

"Good! That's what we wanted, right?" Casey's voice was the most cheerful Deborah had heard, since leaving Chicago the day before. Or was it two days, now? She could not remember right off. Time seemed all jumbled up—out of whack. Deborah hungrily munched on the donuts, and practically gulped the coffee.

"Careful, " Casey warned. "That coffee's hot enough to melt steel."

Deborah smiled, removed her sweater, and returned it to her suitcase. "What's your last name, Casey?"

"Walton. Casey Walton. Yours?"

Deborah hesitated. "Deborah. I'm...Deborah."

"Pleased to meet ya,' Deborah. "Listen, I'll call that cab just 'fore eight. You relax, eat as many of them donuts as you like. I got 'a do some paperwork. My relief comes in at three. This is my last day 'fore I go back to finish up my senior year at UA—University of Arkansas."

"Congratulations," Deborah offered. Casey thanked her and disappeared into the ticket booth. She continued her much welcomed breakfast and resumed waiting.

The cab—an aging, bondo-gray colored Ford Galaxie with cracked windshield, and missing hubcaps—pulled up in front of the depot at precisely 8:30. Having said her thanks and good-byes to Casey yet again, Deborah sat on the now familiar bench with her suitcase nearby.

The scruffy cabbie—a skinny, frizzled-haired, dentally-challenged man with dingy Skoal cap, faded jeans, Nascar T-shirt, and dirty Roper boots—alighted and approached the platform. He got as far as the rear end of his chariot before coming to a halt.

"You the one needin' a cab," he inquired before loosing a brown stream of liquid from the 'chew' wadded in his right jaw.

Deborah looked at the man and had second thoughts. "Ahh...yes. That's...that's me."

"Alrighty. I'm your man."

With that introduction, the man returned to the driver's door and waited. Deborah remained where she stood, riveting her gaze on the cabbie. Seconds passed. Neither moved. More seconds. Realizing he was not going to win the standoff, the man slammed his door shut, returned to the platform and retrieved Deborah's luggage. He tossed it unceremoniously into the cab trunk.

Deborah proceeded to the cab, opened her own rear door and climbed inside. She had hardly closed the door, when the driver pulled away, readjusted his rear view mirror, and glanced back at her. A deep scowl scored his brow.

"Where to?"

"Crispus Attucks at Route 5A," Deborah answered. She saw the man glance once more into the rear view mirror.

"The Sticks?"

"Crispus Attucks at Route 5A," Deborah repeated.

"The Sticks. No can do, least not down that way. Not 5A."

"Why not?"

"That ol' road's closed right now. They got her shut down on account of a lot 'a logging they doin' up there. Got 'a take ya' another way."

Deborah nodded, and settled back as best she could. The driver seemed none too concerned steering around potholes in the road. It was clear to Deborah, his shocks were seeing their last miles. But the air worked. That was no small blessing. Even at an early hour, the sun had already begun to beat down mercilessly.

Fifteen minutes into the drive, Deborah had no idea where she was. Few houses could be seen from the roadway, owing to the abundance of overgrowth. The road—a posted sign for which she had not seen—was partially paved. Deborah asked the driver where they were.

"This is old Route 5. They've rerouted this thing a thousand times over the years. But I'll get you there," the driver assured her.

Minutes later, Deborah leaned forward in her seat. She was certain she remembered a distant house, set well off the road, as the place where B.B. used to live. She began wondering about her friends. Where were Karetha and B.B. now? Where was Tommy, for that matter? Deborah fought off such thoughts. They only made her sad, she warned herself.

The area began to look more familiar, or so it seemed. Deborah was certain she was only a few hundred yards from her destination. She had kept a wary eye on the cab's meter and felt it seemed to be advancing more rapidly than it should. She ordered the cabbie to stop. He did so, pulling onto the right edge of the roadbed.

"You sure this is it?" he asked, peering into the rear view mirror, as he removed his cap and scratched his balding head.

"I think it's just ahead a bit. I'll walk from here. How much?"

"Seven and a quarter," he answered.

Deborah reached into her bag, located her purse, and counted out seven dollars, fifty cents into the driver's hand. He kept the hand open a few seconds. Deborah recounted the fare, more slowly this time.

"Seven and a quarter. Right?"

"Right. Thanks for the tip."

Deborah nodded. The cabbie threw open his door, retrieved her suitcase, and waited as she exited the cab and joined him.

"Sure you don't want me to wait?"

"No thanks," Deborah answered.

Before she could reconsider her answer, the cabbie was back in the cab, doing a U-turn, and steaming back toward Reedville.

Deborah swiped beads of sweat from her brow, lifted her suitcase, and began walking. Less than a hundred yards down the road, she came to a stop. On her left, and several yards off the road, was the house. Deborah's feet practically turned to lead. Her heart nearly beat through her chest.

"My God. Oh, my God. I'm here," she thought. "This is it." Deborah bit into her lip then clenched her teeth.

The yard grass was a bit high. The trees appeared out of place. They seemed shorter. But then things tend to look different after so many years, especially if one has been *away*.

The piney woods stretched out forever, behind the white house with the black trim. There were no cars, no toys strewn about. Perhaps everyone was already gone, Deborah concluded. She could see the porch swing clearly enough. Good. She would wait there until someone returned. They would be so shocked, stunned to arrive and find her there, waiting. Besides, the wait would provide her more time to think through what she would say and do.

A few yards more. Deborah stopped mid-step. Her heart raced; her eyes bulged, she dropped her suitcase to the ground. She turned in a complete circle, her sight coming to rest on the house. By now, she could clearly see that it was abandoned. It was empty. The house was empty?

Deborah saw the broken windows. The porch swing listed to one side. The screen door barely hung in place on one hinge. A blanket of leaves covered much of the porch. They were gone. No one lived here any more. Everyone was gone!

Deborah stood in the streaming sun and wept. They had all moved away, and she had no idea when or where. And Aunt Rose certainly had no idea. But how could they have just..."Samantha!" she yelled out. "My baby's gone, too!"

Leaving her suitcase where it had fallen, Deborah raced toward the house, stroking away tears that blurred her vision. After a brief sprint, she stopped a few yards from the porch, looked around at the land, the house, the spot where the septic tank should have been. Nothing. She loosed a loud burst of laughter, clapped her hands together then raked them over her face.

"This is the wrong place, the wrong house!" She yelled out. "I'm at the wrong place!"

Deborah continued up to the old house, leaped up onto the creaky porch, and peered in through the broken windows. This was not the Davis home. It was not. Deborah yielded a deep sigh. Somehow, the surroundings had completely fooled her. The similarity in the lay of the land, the placement of the house—it all had looked so familiar.

A dejected Deborah grabbed her suitcase and hurried back toward the roadway. She stood at the road's edge and gazed in both directions. There was no sign of traffic. Nothing. Far beyond where the cab had stopped, the road appeared to stretch into blurred infinity. She had no idea where she was.

There were no shade trees nearby, no relief from the sun, except back at the old abandoned house. Deborah returned to the porch steps to rest and gather her thoughts. She sat there for nearly two hours, staring toward the road, feeling the temperature creep steadily upward. Not a single vehicle passed by.

But Deborah soon realized the old house was no place to rest. If and when someone came along, they would most certainly not see her from the roadway.

And so, with a parched throat, and immeasurable disappointment, Deborah repositioned her bag, placed a firm grip on her suitcase and returned to the road's edge. Again, she looked in both directions. Not a thing. She began the long trek back down Old Route 5 toward Reedville proper. Deborah was hopeful she would remember exactly how to get there, and prayed she would not pass out from the heat before doing so.

The small white compact pulled a few yards past Deborah, eased to the side of the road and stopped. She was startled, stopped dead in her tracks. Deborah had not heard the slightest sound from the approaching vehicle.

The driver was clearly prepared to offer her a lift. So, Deborah struggled to quicken her step, but her strength abandoned her. She then saw the car's backup lights come on, the vehicle reverse several feet toward her, and stop. Deborah reached the passenger side, just as an elderly black woman opened the driver's door and stepped to the ground.

"Just put your suitcase in the back seat, baby and get inside. Aren't you hot out here? Doesn't look like you're just passing through, like me."

"Yes ma'am, I am, I am now. I have to come back another time."

Deborah managed to lift her suitcase into the rear, close the door firmly, and climb into the front passenger seat. The smartly dressed woman wore a yellow blouse and beige slacks. She cranked up the air and repositioned the right side air vents.

"Thank you," Deborah managed.

The kindhearted, rosy-cheeked, white-haired, Good Samaritan introduced herself as Hazel Fontenot.

"Deborah. I'm Deborah."

Hazel explained she was a retired teacher visiting from Lake Charles, and just passing through. She had gotten lost trying to get back to Reedville. She questioned Deborah's being stuck on such a "God-forsaken stretch of road," as she put it.

"How you get stuck way out here? I had to turn around down near old Crispus Attucks, a few miles down," she added. "The road is blocked off...equipment everywhere. And they didn't even bother to clearly establish a detour. We both know why."

Deborah explained she had mistaken the address of a friend, and was returning to Reedville. Although she had little heart for conversation—especially cheerful conversation—Deborah felt obliged to engage her rescuer.

"This place sure has changed since the last time I was here. Lots of families had to be moved...contaminated ground water," Hazel continued. "I hear they've been dumping chemicals around poor folk out here for years. No telling what that's going to do to them...ten, fifteen, twenty years down the road."

Deborah listened and agreed. "You say Cripsus Attucks was a few miles back, in the other direction?"

"That's right. Where is it you're trying to get to?"

"Ahh...the home of some folk I used to know."

"Do they have a car? Did they know you were coming?"

"Yes and...and no, ma'am. I'm not sure anymore."

Well, I suppose I could take you back down that way...see if you could locate the place. Where are you from?"

"Chicago. I'm..."

"Hmm. That's a long way to come...get this far and not reach your destination, baby."

"I know."

"Tell you what. I need to get to Reedville, first. If you want, I'll drive you back out later on. We'll see what we find. I take it you don't want to call ahead. Must be a surprise. Right?"

"Right. Yes ma'am. But...but it's okay. I'll just go on back to Reedville. I'll figure everything out from there."

"If you say so. If you change your mind..."

"Thanks."

Little more was said until they were back in Reedville at the bus depot. Hazel parked, got out, and waited. Deborah removed her things, thanked her and placed her suitcase on the platform.

"Sure you don't want to take me up on my offer?"

"No, thanks. But please let me pay you something—something for gas, anyway."

"Not a chance, baby. I was coming this way all along. You just take care, and be blessed." Hazel's face reflected her concern.

"Yes ma'am. I am already. Your coming along was a blessing."

Hazel smiled, then offered to buy breakfast at Miller's. Deborah politely refused. On any other occasion, she was certain a conversation with one, Hazel Fontenot, would have been a most enlightening and rewarding experience. But right now, she was certain she would not be fit company. She felt tired, empty, angry, disappointed and confused.

The dusty drive back into Reedville had given Deborah time to form and cement a decision. She would return home to Chicago. The fact she had a bit more than three hours to wait for another bus did not concern her, after all that had happened since arriving. Deborah told herself there had to be a reason—a reason for the way things had turned out. Despite her desires, all her long held plans, perhaps there was a much greater plan—one bigger, one grander than her own.

Deborah entered the depot, moved past a score of patrons, and retreated to a seat far from the entrance. She dropped her suitcase onto the floor and slumped down onto the unyielding wooden bench.

A geyser of emotion began swelling inside her. She fought it back, declaring: "I'm not going to cry anymore. I'm not. Not out loud, anyway. Someday. Someday," she kept whispering. "Someday."

Within minutes, Casey was standing in front of her, with a frosty bottle of Hires Root Beer extended in his right hand. "Courtesy of Greyhound and Trailways," he said, with a wide grin.

Deborah smiled and accepted the drink. Casey smiled, then turned and walked away, frequently glancing back at Deborah over his right shoulder. It was the last time she would see him.

Halfway through the Root Beer, Deborah closed her eyes and dozed. The bottle nearly slipped from her hands, waking her in time for her to catch her bus. By then, Casey was gone. She told herself she would never forget him. To this day, she had not forgotten Casey Walton and the kindness he showed her. And he had likely not forgotten her.

chapter eighteen

Lone Traveler

"I live here, woman..."

"**A**ll I can do is send my love
and my prayers along with you. And I do." Rose dabbed her eyes and
toyed nervously with her cup. Her words literally snapped Deborah back
to the present. She touched her aunt's hands and smiled.

"I know. Believe me, I know. Your love and prayers have been good
enough for me all these years. I'm sure they'll see me through this, too."

Rose grew noticeably uneasy with the level of emotion and senti-
mentality their conversation had reached. She eased onto the edge of
her chair.

"Listen, I'm going to bed now. All this crying and going on ain't good
for my image. If Jack sees me all choked up and teary-eyed, he'll know
I'm not the tough ol' broad I've been making myself out to be all these
years. That's all I need at my tender age."

"I've got a feeling he knows already."

"You know something I don't?"

"We both know Uncle Jack has his ears glued to every wall in this house," said Deborah. "Nothing gets past him."

Both snickered, then cupped hands to their mouths. Rose stood, and turned to look over her shoulder. Jack, a robust, 6'- 2," partially bald man with a dimpled smile, filled the doorway. He was decked out in his Chicago Bears pajamas and frayed, teddy-bear house shoes.

"Jack!" Rose blurted, "What are you doing there?"

"I live here, woman," he shot back.

"You know what I mean."

"What are you two cackling about in here? A man can't sleep with all this hen chatter going on."

"Hen chatter? You could say good evening to Deborah, first."

"It ain't evening no more. Good thing I'm off tomorrow."

"Jack, tomorrow is Friday, not Saturday," said Rose.

"Crap! Now why you have to go and tell me that?"

Deborah and Rose looked at each other then down at Jack's tattered house shoes. He had them on the wrong feet. Rose was barely able to contain herself. She sat pointing and laughing. Deborah doubled over. Jack turned around and left without another word.

After Rose and Jack turned in, Deborah made her way down the stairway leading from the kitchen to the spacious, well-furnished basement. She moved quickly to a walk-in closet located on the far side of the larger of the four rooms. A flip of the light switch, and Deborah instantly saw what she wanted: the suitcase. She removed the large, brown leather suitcase, but not in preparation for her trip.

For nearly all the fourteen years since Samantha was taken from her, Deborah had written to her daughter several times a week, and often daily. And the tone and substance matured as Samantha grew older.

She lovingly wrote letters, notes, made cards—birthday cards, Christmas cards, 'any day' cards. She expressed her thoughts in brief paragraphs, in pages, a single sentence, in a single word. Many of the writings bore tear stains; others evidenced an unsteady hand.

Devastated by the fact that letters she wrote her parents and siblings were never answered, her calls not returned, Deborah had no hope letters or cards sent to Samantha would be received by her. She continued to write them, but none were ever mailed. They were Deborah's way of pouring out her heart, her love, her longing, while hoping to someday share it all with her daughter.

On this night, she felt an overpowering need to read the letters again. There were hundreds of them, all packed away inside this large brown suitcase with the heavy leather strapping.

And there were gifts: stuffed animals, a doll—things a young girl receives as she grows older. Later, and more recently, there were small books of poetry, a Bible, photos of Samantha taken by Uncle Jack, beginning with her baby pictures. Especially the ones he had taken during the days and weeks following Samantha's birth.

There was even a photo taken of the two of them—Deborah and Samantha—on the day Samantha was whisked away, back to Reedville. All the film negatives containing this and other snapshots would be set aside and forgotten for years.

Deborah had long hoped, prayed, dreamed, and prepared for the day Samantha would see all these things for herself. Tears welled in her eyes, as she lugged the old case to the center of the room. She eased down onto the floor and began slowly loosening the straps. Soon, she was staring at layer upon layer of unsealed letters and cards. Deborah held some up to the light, then clutched them to her chest...and wept.

chapter nineteen

Journey Into Yesterday

====================================

Deborah's thoughts soon returned to fear-filled imaginings....

Deborah was in no mood
for conversation. She had looked forward to a restful flight to Little Rock, comfortably nestled in her window seat, contemplating what lay ahead. It was not to be. She had drawn the short straw in the form of an obnoxious, portly, good ol' boy on his way home from a Chicago business trip.

The boisterous man with the beer-belly and receding hairline, who introduced himself as Cabe Bender, had been yapping since take off at O'Hare. When he was not talking, he was blowing his nose every thirty seconds. Sounded like a damn foghorn. Something about breathing re-circulated air, he kept saying over and over again. Even when Deborah closed her eyes, he kept jabbering.

"I know quite a few, ahh, Af...Afro-American people. I get it right?"

Deborah shrugged her shoulders. "Oh, my God," she thought, "Not another one. Not another self-styled, pseudo-liberal, white person bent on impressing me with his imagined credentials as a *Progressive*. What's so damn liberal and progressive about simply regarding human beings as human beings?"

"I even worked with this colored, ahh...Afro-American guy once," the man droned on. "We got to be real good friends. In fact, he invited me and my wife Eunice over to his place one Sund'y after church. Not the same church, though," he grinned. "This ol' gal of his could cook like you wouldn't believe.

"I'm talkin' fried chicken, collard greens..." He paused. An annoyed Deborah reached for her stereo headset, as the man droned on. "...snap beans, corn bread, 'tater' salad, the works. An' this ol' boy could sang and dance just like Sammy Davis. Kinda looked like him too, 'cept for the glass eye. You know 'bout Sammy's glass eye, right? I'm not dead sure myself, but that's what I hear tell. Anyway, one time..."

Deborah turned up the headset volume and reclined her seat. She glanced at the man and shook her head. His lips were still moving, but she could barely hear him. She closed her eyes and prayed he would get the message. He did not.

The man seated to Bender's left, also white, seemed equally annoyed and exasperated by what he was hearing. He looked at Deborah and shook his head sympathetically.

—

With some effort, Deborah's thoughts soon returned to fear-filled imaginings of what awaited her. There was no ignoring the anxiety she felt; it grew by the mile. She struggled to comprehend the fact she was actually returning to Reedville. Yet, she in no way considered it as returning *home*. To do so would have required an attitude of forgiveness. Deborah was not prepared to grant forgiveness to anyone.

Nevertheless, the anticipation mounted. So did the anger she had battled so long and thought she had learned to manage, if not overcome. The Sticks held countless memories for Deborah. Some were wonderful; some were awful. How had the place changed? How would she feel in that first, fleeting, emotion-filled instant she arrived?

The old images—never permanently buried in the recesses of her mind—were now clawing their way back to the fore. How would they measure up against a fresh view of this place she had not seen since 1974, notwithstanding her aborted trip in 1981?

Memories streamed into every corner of Deborah's consciousness. Through misty recollections, she could still see the image of her family standing on the platform in front of Miller's store.

Deborah remembered Matthew stalking away angrily, refusing to watch the bus drive away. And she especially remembered Rachel's unfazed, detached demeanor—her refusal to say a single word, not even good-bye. She just stood there, reading a book, hardly glancing in her direction. There was so much about Rachel that defied understanding.

If she closed her eyes, Deborah could almost hear the old bus rumbling down Main Street, and screeching to a lurching stop in front of Miller's Café. That morning, her young heart pounded like a bass drum. She could feel the throbbing and pulsing in her ears, right down to the soles of her feet.

Samantha! Deborah felt a tremor race through her body at the thought of her daughter. How do you say hello to a daughter you have not seen since she was three months old? How do you establish an instant relationship with a fourteen year-old daughter with whom you've never shared a real conversation? You do not, at least not right away. Perhaps never. But *never* was not a consideration.

Deborah wondered how she would feel seeing her mother—a mother whom she still blamed for not challenging her father's decision to banish her. Deborah then quickly dismissed the notion that Mabel Davis deserved to be thought of as a mother, for even one condemning second. And what of her siblings she had not seen for nearly a decade and a half? What had kept them apart, even in adulthood? What had kept them from attempting to reconnect to her?

Finally, how would she feel seeing her father again—the same father who had not bothered to see her off on that awful Sunday—a father now facing death? Deborah's mind was assaulted by the onslaught of thoughts and memories. That moment, she was seized with doubts about returning to Reedville. She could simply end it all right now. She could end this wondering; this reliving of things best forgotten; this self-torture, this pointless journey into yesterday. She could be done with it. But there was...Samantha. There *was* Samantha.

—

Deborah gripped her leather briefcase firmly in one hand, tucked a small purse under her arm, and followed the valet maneuvering her luggage. They quickly moved past the sliding glass terminal doors, and out into brilliant Arkansas sunlight.

Deborah removed the short-sleeved jacket of her beige suit, settling for the comfort of her sleeveless blouse. The blinding glare also immediately forced her into her sunglasses. The wilting ninety-three degree heat, and ninety-one per cent humidity, greeted her with a whoosh! And she instantly remembered the raging heat of May 15, 1974. Just that quickly, her mind whisked her back to that day—a day that, in many respects, had yet to end.

The valet headed straight for a white Lincoln Town Car waiting at the curb with trunk lid raised. The chauffeur, a young white man in a black suit, held the curbside, rear passenger door open. Deborah climbed inside. She marveled at the fact the man was not only conscious, but showed no sign of perspiring.

A smile crept across Deborah's face. She looked about the car and thought of Paul. Once he made up his mind, little could deter him. She tossed her briefcase onto the seat, removed her sunglasses, leaned back and clamped her eyes shut.

Again, Deborah questioned her decision to return to Reedville. No one in Arkansas knew she was coming. She could easily catch the next flight back to Chicago. No one would know. Aunt Rose and Uncle Jack would surely understand her change of heart.

But even as the thought imposed itself upon her consciousness, Deborah knew she had to go on. No turning back, not now. No more running away from the past, no matter how painful. She prayed for strength, certain that nothing could be worse than the events that had brought her to this moment.

Within two minutes, Little Rock National Airport was behind them. The young driver turned right from Bankhead Drive onto I-440 West, en route to Interstate 30 East, the 630W to the Broadway exit, and The Capital—a four-star, downtown hotel on Markham at Louisiana.

The modest Little Rock skyline soon approached. It appeared to Deborah to have changed considerably. Truth was, as a child, she had not seen downtown Little Rock enough to draw a reliable comparison. She could only remember making a half dozen trips there by age twelve.

Deborah's first visit to the big city came when she was five years old. The entire family accompanied Reverend to a sister church, Mount Moriah, where he spoke at a one-day Bible conference.

Memory of the experience remained. Deborah remembered being awestruck by the size of the buildings; by the number of people, and by the width of the streets. When you're an impressionable child, nearly everything seems larger than life, she thought. She smiled.

Deborah slipped her glasses back into place. The smile soon faded, as a whirlwind of thought and second thoughts bombarded her. Manic. That's the word that came to her mind. Manic. She felt downright manic, riding a wave of excitement just thinking about the good times. Then, almost in the same instant, she crashed under the weight of remembering events that changed her life forever.

—

The chauffeur entered the freeway, bound for downtown Little Rock. But just as he neared the U.S. 67/167 exit, Deborah instructed him to take the exit, and head directly for Reedville. No stopping at the hotel. She decided to act while her resolve was still intact. Considering the ebb and flow of her emotions, it would not take much for her to immediately board a return flight to Chicago.

Deborah threw herself back in her seat, removed her sunglasses and stared at the scenery zipping past. All she could think about was Samantha. What would she look like? What would they say to each other?

How would she introduce herself after all this time? Should she have come back just now? She reasoned perhaps she should have called first, spoken to Samantha—prepared her.

Then Deborah remembered her early attempts at calling her parents, and years later, Samantha. Her calls were screened by a telephone answering machine, apparently purchased shortly after she arrived in Chicago. The message seemed clear to her and to Aunt Rose, though Rose never commented openly. Except, she did once loose a not so subtle curse, blasting the "damn thing."

Unbeknownst to Deborah, Rose *did* ask her sister about the answering device; why no one had called Deborah in all those years. She was met with double-talk about *not wanting to conflict with whatever parental guidance she and Jack were providing.* And she said the 'Phone Mate' machine was Rachel's idea. Said she convinced the Reverend it would help keep away unwanted calls from folk imposing on his time, especially when he was preparing his sermons.

Rose made it clear she did not buy the explanation. Her frankness was met with silence, and long periods of time when there was no communication at all. Messages she forced herself to leave...were not timely returned, if at all. The machine remained in use. Rose and Jack gently discouraged Deborah's continued calling, even her leaving messages for Samantha. Neither had any doubt the messages were being deleted. They could see the effect this further rejection was having on Deborah. Her emotional relapse was always possible. It had to be avoided at all costs.

No. No. Deborah concluded it was best she not first call to prepare Samantha, and consequently, the others. Just show up, as she had planned and so valiantly tried to do in 1981. Only this time, she had the will and the means.

chapter twenty

The Journey Continues

===

On May 15, 1975, Samantha was taken.

Deborah was again consumed with thought, unaware of the passage of time and distance. When she did focus, they were well beyond Little Rock. The sedan soon reached their exit leading to a divided four-laner. Two miles later, the car zipped past a highway sign: Reedville, 44 miles. Deborah's heart spiked, leaving her flush. She was now less than an hour from 'home.' This was no dream. She was not imagining this. It was both real and surreal.

Deborah's sunglasses came off to stay. She stared out at lush green fields dotted with small farms. Except for an occasional dip or turn in the road, the car seemed to be still. Deborah wanted to reach Reedville quickly. Yet, delay would afford her time to prepare what she would say, how she would say it, whether she could really do this.

Fourteen years should have been more than enough time to prepare. It was not. Even after the 1981 trip, and her vow to return, the possibility this day would arrive had grown remote.

And what of Samantha? Would all this be too traumatic for her? What did she know? How much had she been told? How much was truth? What were the lies? How had she—Deborah—been explained to her? Again, the thought of seeing Samantha, after so much time, placed a throbbing lump in her throat. Her heart raced.

Deborah never dreamed she would be returning to Arkansas at this time in her life. She was enjoying her ever-growing professional success. Writing was now her life. She felt safe within its cocoon.

Those years in Chicago with Aunt Rose and Uncle Jack had given her a second chance at her one life. She had long ago embraced her new incarnation, accepting that her earlier self had died. Deborah's thoughts turned to those early years in Chicago—a place at the exact end of the spectrum from Reedville.

What was worse, best friends Kay and B.B were not there. Neither were Gloria, Maylene, and Matthew—her protector. To her surprise, she even missed Rachel's strange behavior, somewhat.

Despite her love for her aunt and uncle, Deborah initially resented both of them. She reasoned if they had not been so eager to take her in, her mother and the Reverend would have been forced to find another solution. Perhaps they would have kept her at home, and faced their harsh new realities together—as a family.

Not long after arriving in Chicago, Deborah sank into emotional purgatory. But the worst would come the following year, after Sam was taken away. Immediately after that traumatic event, Deborah descended into deep depression. She soon adopted a vow of silence.

The effects were stark and visible. Her eyes, once so bright, became dark and brooding. She resisted Rose's attempt to coax her to respond. Silence was Deborah's way of controlling some aspect of her own life. Her vow was steadfastly maintained, even when she was alone.

Aunt Rose was sad and perplexed. She prayed the silence would be brief. However, when it persisted, she grew so concerned she and Jack discussed taking Deborah to a child psychologist. Jack, while equally concerned, was not taken with the idea. He argued that what was needed was love, the presence of other children, and the passage of time. Aunt Rose never stopped speaking to her niece with a loving voice. She spoke to and for Deborah, both asking and answering questions. Uncle Jack learned to do the same.

It was during this dark episode, Deborah began writing incessantly. She wrote prose, poetry and songs. Her words gave expression to her feelings. They helped her combat self-hatred—hatred of life, her condition, her yet distorted, swollen body: nose, feet, hands—her whole face.

Nearly all of Deborah's waking moments were spent pouring her deepest thoughts into a diary she swore to never share. The words flowed from her soul like a river. They spoke to her in a voice, no longer her own, but one belonging to the person she longed to be.

Clarence Jackson, an affable, gentle giant with a heart to match, was Youth Group director at Rose's Church. Weeks later, he suggested counseling. Again, Uncle Jack resisted. When he and Rose finally agreed, the results—though slow in coming—were dramatic.

Four months after it began, Deborah's self-imposed silence ended one morning, a few hours before sunrise. A startled Jack and Rose were awakened by the sound of a soaring, melodic voice streaming from down the hallway. They dashed to Deborah's room and found her fully dressed, standing in front of her dresser mirror, and singing.

Deborah stopped and turned around when they entered. The two broke into soft applause, then moved to embrace her, while struggling to downplay their joy. Deborah's dreadful silence had ended, but not the turmoil that had brought it on. Relapse was always possible.

—

Aunt Rose's thoughts turned to the upcoming 1975-76 school term. School and birth records from Arkansas were not transferred until November of 1974. Medical Power of Attorney and limited guardian rights were also provided. Rose decided against enrolling Deborah for the 1975-1976 school year. Instead, she provided home study. Deborah needed time to adapt to her new reality. Besides, she was in her fourth month, noticeably showing, and experiencing 'doubled over' morning sickness.

Aunt Rose saw to it that Deborah maintained the best health possible. She made certain every prenatal appointment was kept. She insisted on a proper diet, ensured every meal was prepared with loving care. The diet part was not difficult. Uncle Jack was the undisputed chef in the family. His culinary skills were unquestioned. Rose entered the kitchen—his kitchen—only with his blessing.

—

The day Samantha was born, Rose, Jack and Deborah arrived at Cook County Hospital just in time, almost. Deborah's water broke in Admissions. Even so, Uncle Jack had to get a little crazy, before he received immediate attention for her. He was ultimately threatened with arrest, after he jumped onto a desk and promised to moon nurses, visitors, anyone who happened along.

Vaginal delivery was never likely. Deborah's young age, size of the fetus, and her pelvic development were key factors. Still, owing to her apparent physical maturity, Doctor Hugh Philburn had earlier explored avoiding a cesarean section. He had a twelve-year old daughter himself, and cringed at the thought of her being in such a circumstance.

An air of sadness permeated the operating room. The entire medical team, especially Doctor Philburn, was somber and subdued as they prepared this 12 year-old *child to* give birth to a *child.*

Early on, many questions surfaced regarding Deborah's pregnancy. A thorough investigation by Child Protective authorities, and law-enforcement, were conducted. Deborah's primary care physician was obliged to notify authorities. However, all agencies were soon satisfied regarding the pertinent facts.

The baby was taken by cesarean. Samantha Yvonne Davis, named by Aunt Rose, was born at 3:22 a.m., February 14, 1975 at Cook County Hospital. She was a healthy 7lbs., 3 ounces, and 19 inches long. She came close to being born on the Dan Ryan Expressway. A big rig accident near 79th forced them to sit in traffic more than two hours. Rose was outwardly calm, but Jack was an emotional wreck—a fact he would later forcefully deny.

In a strange confluence of events, Samantha was taken from Deborah on May 15, 1975. Mabel Davis and Sister Hazel Thorpe, a close friend from Shiloh Church, arrived by Greyhound that rainy Thursday morning. Sadly, but predictably, the coincidence regarding the date never registered with Sister Davis.

On the third of April, Baby Samantha, Rose and Jack celebrated Deborah's thirteenth birthday. Rose invited her neighbor's twelve year-old twins, Kaye and Faye Wilson. There was homemade cake, ice cream, a balloon bouquet, a 'Happy Birthday Banner,' an avalanche of gifts. Deborah, while friendly toward the girls, was in no mood for company. Earlier, she had told Rose she felt fat, unattractive, did not want anyone to see her. Shortly after cake and ice cream were served, the girls left.

Two weeks after Deborah's birthday, Mabel Davis made a rare phone call to her sister. She would be arriving in Chicago on May 15th. During the five minute conversation, she made no mention of the fact her daughter was now a teenager.

Rose offered to save her the trip by bringing Samantha and Deborah to Reedville. Mabel rejected the offer, insisted on coming. Rose tried to prepare Deborah as best she could, explaining that, for the time being, only Samantha would be returning to Reedville.

Mabel's arrival was greeted with both trepidation and resentment. Only the barest hospitalities were extended. Rose was only a shell of her usually effervescent self. Jack served only the blandest, most unappealing meals, and hardly had a complete sentence for Mabel.

Deborah avoided being in the same room with her mother. She asked Aunt Rose if she could take her meals in her bedroom. After considerable coaxing, Rose persuaded her niece to join them all in the dining room. Deborah reluctantly did so, but without looking at her mother directly. The instant she finished her meals, she would leave the room with a terse "Excuse me, please."

In a brief conversation, Mabel Davis promised Rose that Deborah would be "sent for" in late summer, in time for the fall semester. Said she wanted to *give Deborah time to recover without being concerned for the baby.*

Besides, Rose and Jack had been "burdened enough...caring for both," as Mabel put it. Rose had a compound word response for her: "Bullshit." Rose then left the room without waiting for a response.

That afternoon, the women and Samantha were gone. Mabel Davis chose to spend less than a full day in Chicago. It was clear she had only one purpose in coming. And it was best she leave as soon as she did. Her presence was not at all welcomed. She left on Amtrak. Returning by the next available bus would have delayed her departure by at least two days.

Deborah was devastated—inconsolable. She spent her days closeted in her room. The aftermath of Mabel's visit was immeasurable. Rose could barely contain her anger. She later wished she had not been so controlled.

Jack was livid. He remained in the basement while Mabel and her friend packed. He was determined to avoid an ugly confrontation, and an outcome he could not predict. Jack did not trust his ability to control himself. He later refused to drive Mabel to Union Station. Said there was "no way in hell" he would have a part in what he called "baby stealing."

Mabel Davis' departing promise to send for her daughter within a few months rang hollow. Deborah did not trust the woman. She remained in her room, damning her mother in a loud, pained voice. She refused to watch the cab pull away carrying her baby. The bottomless anger, the excruciating loss she felt was indescribable.

During her brief stay, Mabel Davis never once took her daughter aside and spoke to her privately. There was no mention made of the months leading up to Samantha's birth. No questions about what her life had been like since arriving. No mention of her best friends, Kay and B.B., or her sisters and brother. Rose's attempts to raise those subjects were shunted aside with meaningless banter. And no word from her father—the Reverend. Nothing.

The instant Samantha was taken, and each day thereafter, Deborah's heart ached for the sound of her baby. She longed for her crying, for changing her diaper, as Rose had taught her. Deborah missed preparing her formula, standing next to her crib and watching her sleep. She remembered standing and staring at Samantha while tracing her fingers over the delivery scar. "Where is God?" she angrily questioned. "Is he asleep? Is he blind to me? Is my voice too weak for him to hear?"

Minutes after Mabel left for Union Station, Rose entered the guest bedroom and found a bright blue gift bag atop the dresser. At first, she thought Mabel had forgotten to pack something. When she approached, she noticed a small, handwritten note attached. It read: "Deborah." That was all. Rose stared at the bag, then finally forced herself to open it.

What she saw, made her blood boil. Inside was a small doll—a black doll. It was apparently meant for Deborah. Rose could barely contain her anger and disgust; refused to even touch the thing. Swallowing a mouthful of expletives, she closed the bag. And without so much as showing it to Jack, she grabbed it, marched straight to the garage and deposited in the bottom of the garbage bin. Rose never breathed a word to anyone.

—

Deborah stared into nothingness. John drove on, occasionally glancing back at her in the rear view mirror. He observed his passenger's position had not changed for miles. Deborah not only *appeared* transfixed; she *was* transfixed. She was lost in relentless recollection, remembering that Samantha's leaving, though traumatic, was only part of a day of deep emotional torment. There was more.

Suicide. Deborah had once attempted suicide. That fact was never far from her consciousness. It was especially true this day. As the car rolled on, she recalled that near final night—the same night Samantha was taken from her.

Something in Deborah's soul convinced her she would never see her daughter again—that there was no reason to go on. Her downward spiral had begun immediately after Samantha's birth. Doctors, whom Rose consulted, labeled it "Post Delivery Blues." Whatever it was, it was constant and profound. Deborah's emotional roller coaster showed no sign of stopping or slowing. And she wanted off.

On that unwelcomed anniversary of May 15th, Deborah felt deceived by her mother, abandoned yet again. Only this time, there was a pervasive air of finality about it all. The pain was made most unbearable by the taking of Samantha. Sister Mabel Davis had not been there for her daughter during her pregnancy, nor the birth of her baby. Yet, there she was—taking Samantha away, without shame, with no apology, and without any sign of remorse.

On that first night without Samantha, a strange and sad quiet hung like a dark cloud. It was funereal—like what follows when one learns of the death of a loved one. For the longest time, not much was said. Aunt Rose's later attempts to console Deborah were met with cold silence.

Late that night, distraught and deeply depressed, Deborah sat alone in Rose's bathroom, clutching Jack's pearl-handle straight-razor in her right hand. She pressed it against her left wrist firmly enough to draw blood. Yet, the pain never registered.

Deborah kept the razor in place, despite the tears streaming down her face. Her mind reeled. "One, quick, hard slice. That's all it would take," she told herself. It would not take long. A few minutes, and it would all be over. No more crying, no more anger, no more rejection—no feeling unwanted by the people responsible for her birth. She would be free.

That instant, the razor fell to the tile floor. It was as if it were yanked from her hand. The clanking sound, the sight of it on the floor startled her. Deborah had not thought to release her grip. It just happened. She stared at the razor, at the light bouncing off the steel blade. She saw the mark on her wrist, the trickle of blood. For an instant, her arm seemed detached from her body. It was not *her* arm; it belonged to someone else.

Deborah clenched her eyes shut, and saw Gram. Her heart raced. It was as if Gram d'lena were standing next to her, holding a baby—Samantha! Gram was cradling Samantha in her arms. Deborah's heart quickened even more. She forced open her tear-filled eyes, retrieved the razor, held it for what seemed a lifetime. It was only seconds.

Exhausted and sobbing, Deborah rinsed her blood from the blade, closed the razor, and held a wad of tissue to her wound. She would later conceal it and the resulting scar, with a bracelet Jack had given her on her thirteenth birthday.

Remembering all this later, Deborah knew three things had prevented her from tumbling over the edge: thoughts of Gram, of the unspeakable grief her death would have caused Aunt Rose and Uncle Jack, and the likelihood Samantha would someday learn of her actions.

Deborah's suicide attempt had followed considerable thought. Before Samantha's birth, she had considered death her only escape. So deep was her pain, so desperate her desire to be rid of her anguish, Deborah wrote her own funeral program, start to finish. Only Aunt Rose and Uncle Jack would be listed as family. What deep despair must exist, for a twelve-year old to pen her own funeral service, and in such precise detail?

And the plans were detailed, right down to the dress she wanted to be buried in. A white, ankle-length, satin dress with embroidered bodice, three-quarter length sleeves, ruffled collar—all trimmed in white lace. It was identical to the one Gram wore when she was laid to rest. And the song? 'Come Ye Disconsolate.' It was one of Gram's favorites.

For Deborah, there would be no peace on the night of May 15, 1975. After coming so close to ending her life, she fell into fitful sleep near midnight. But, within minutes, she shot awake—sat straight up.

Samantha was crying! Deborah heard her cry out. She flipped on the bedside lamp, bounded from bed and rushed to her baby. But there *was* no baby. There *was* no Samantha. Deborah's heart sank. She gazed into Samantha's empty bassinet and was overcome. She cried out mournfully and slumped to the floor, clutching Samantha's blanket and calling out to her. Rose, who had been unable to sleep and was already headed to Deborah's room, rushed to her side. Amidst her own tears and anguish, Rose knelt down beside her niece. She embraced her, and the two remained there until hours past dawn.

In the days, weeks and years that followed, Deborah would stand before the full-length mirror, stare at her scar, the empty crib. It seemed she had suffered all that physical and emotional pain for nothing.

And her body had paid a seemingly permanent price. There were those ugly stretch marks on her young body. They persisted, despite the cocoa butter, and the 'Mother's Friend' lotion Rose had given her. She vowed no one, not even Aunt Rose, would ever see her this way again. Soon thereafter, Deborah's deep depression so consumed her, she fell into a self-imposed silence. Now, thirteen years later, unexpected events had brought all those memories rushing back. Only days earlier, Deborah was on top of the mountain. Then, before she had any time to bask in the glow of her new success—this.

—

Two years after Samantha's departure, Deborah finally permitted Uncle Jack to remove the bassinet. The decision did not come easily. The crib's presence had been a source of comfort and distress. As long as it remained there, she felt Samantha could never be far away. Yet, seeing it everyday was a reminder her baby was gone. All her attempts at calling to inquire about her were screened. In an act of self-defense She gave up.

Admittedly, during her pregnancy, Deborah endured deep and conflicting emotions about the child she carried. For the longest time, she viewed the unborn baby as an invader—an unseen intruder that, though blameless, was in part responsible for the anguish and torment in her life. The conflicting feelings left her reeling.

Each time she gazed at her body and saw the frightening changes, she all but cursed this...this person growing inside her. Deborah now felt ashamed and guilty for harboring such feelings for a single moment.

Such thoughts, such emotions, merely evidenced the depth of Deborah's inner turmoil. A mature woman would have had great difficulty coping with these issues. And her nightmare began when she was only twelve, not twenty, not thirty. A child.

During the weeks leading to Samantha's birth, and especially at the moment of that miraculous event, a bond formed. It formed and persisted, despite Samantha's departure, and the intervening years. The bond formed, despite the circumstances. Sure, there were times when Samantha—like those who had mangled her life—was rendered faceless. At times, they were all made faceless, purposely blurred to the point of nonexistence by Deborah's need to survive her hell. But, unlike the others, Samantha was always there. Always.

chapter twenty-one

Another World

═══════════════════════

Running without legs, breathing without air, looking through cracked glass.

B y 1988, all visible evidence
of Baby Samantha's existence, except for a single photo, and a pink name-tag bracelet, had long ago disappeared from Deborah's world. Yet, an even more vivid reminder remained: the scar. Despite Dr. Philburn's success in minimizing its severity, and the intervening years, Deborah still could hardly bear to view her own nakedness.

While the Lincoln sped on, the memories persisted. Deborah remembered her first days and weeks in Chicago, especially that first night.

1974. Deborah hardly said a word, from the time the old Greyhound bus left Reedville, until it arrived in Chicago. She slept most of the way. But sometimes she would awaken, sit up, look around at Rose, the passengers, and wonder where she was, and why. Her heart would race, her eyes, widen. Then, it would all come back to her—the where and why. She would shut her eyes tightly and will herself back asleep. All the while, Rose hardly slept. She watched over Deborah, and prayed.

Chicago was quite a culture shock. Nothing Deborah had seen in Arkansas could have prepared her. The air smelled different. The sky looked different. The people were different. Everyone seemed to be in his or her own world, unaware of the hordes around them, all moving without running into each other. They reminded her of ants.

During her first night in her new home, Deborah fell into tortuous sleep fraught with nightmares unlike any she had experienced. In them, every terrible event, every unwanted feeling kept repeating, over and over again. As in her waking hours, Deborah felt as if she were running without legs, breathing without air, looking through cracked glass. What was missing, unlike in her conscious moments, was the ever-present love and touch of her aunt and uncle.

Finally, gasping and frantic, her pounding heart ready to leap from her chest, Deborah bolted awake. Her eyes darted about the large dark space. She had no idea where she was, or why she was alone—alone and in such a large bed. Where were Maylene and her other sisters? Why were they not in the room? And she heard cars outside, close by. Why? Where was she?

It took a moment for Deborah to realize she was not in Reedville. The Sticks were miles and miles away. She was in Chicago. In an instant, she recalled the bus trip with Aunt Rose, the circumstances that had brought her here. She began sobbing, then crying aloud. She drew the covers over her head and curled up in the fetal position.

Marie. Deborah remembered her doll, Marie. She was not there with her. She had forgotten her. But how? How could she have not missed her before now? Deborah clutched her pillow tightly, buried her face in it and cried.

The room light came on. It was Aunt Rose. She spoke out to Deborah softly, taking care to not frighten her even more. Deborah's sobbing became mere sniffles, as Rose approached and gently uncovered her face. Without a word—no questions, nothing except a loving smile, Rose embraced her niece for a long moment, then gently stroked her face. Rose held her again, until she felt Deborah's quaking body ease. No words were spoken. No words were needed. Only silence.

A smile—Deborah's smile. A smile that was reward enough for Rose. She turned on the table lamp and flipped off the room light. She returned, fluffed the four large pillows, removed her house slippers, and lay next to Deborah until the latter was fast asleep. For Deborah, there would be many more sleepless nights. There would be more questions without answers. But Aunt Rose and Uncle Jack would always be there.

—

By the Fall of 1975, Deborah was pouring herself into her studies. She read so much, focused so intently on school, Rose grew concerned that she had little balance in her life. That soon changed. Jack and Rose quickly became the most active they had been in years. Close friends said they seemed reborn.

There were picnics in the park, open-air concerts—which often included a few of Deborah's new friends. Deborah visited every museum, major library event, opera, circus, and select music concert Rose and Jack could schedule, or afford. Deborah loved the Chicago Botanic Garden, the Lincoln Park Zoo, the Children's Museum at Navy Pier, Shedd Aquarium, The Sears Tower Skydeck—despite Jack's queasy stomach— Grant Park, The Hancock Observatory. Jack once slyly suggested Harrah's Casino in Joliet. A stern gaze from Rose caused him to withdraw the idea.

Fortunately, Aunt Rose's church offered a variety of programs for teens. Deborah met most of her friends there. Uncle Jack was not a frequent churchgoer, preferring to spend his Sunday mornings at 'Bedside Baptist Church,' as he called it.

Jack admitted to having problems with preachers—Baptist ministers, in particular. He felt they begged for money too much, and were too adept at finding ingenious ways to keep much of it for themselves.

"How much is in that permanent 'Building Fund' *now?* And why does the Pastor need a 'Love Offering' on top of his salary, new car, insurance, and his annual 'Moneyversary' celebration?" Jack often chided. His and Rose's disagreement on the subject often provided lively entertainment.

Jack, an ardent football and baseball fan, made sure Deborah attended dozens of Cubs, White-Sox and Bears games. Never mind it was more for Jack's enjoyment than hers, she eagerly grabbed her baseball cap, her own glove, and tagged along.

One of Deborah's greatest sports thrills came, when Jack caught a homerun ball in the left field bleachers at Wrigley field. Half a dozen fans were draped all over him. They were clutching and clawing for the ball, but Uncle Jack held on. He handed Deborah the homerun ball crushed by the visiting team. However, in keeping with custom, he had her throw it back onto the field. The crowd cheered.

Jack loved baseball and basketball, but was a football fanatic. Over the years, Deborah came to share his love of sports. There was hardly a 'Bear' statistic he did not know, especially those of Walter Payton.

Payton's retirement at the end of the 1987 season broke Jack's heart. In fact, the Bears lost four Pro-Bowlers after the '87 season. Walter Payton and Gary Fencik retired. Wilbur Marshall became a 'free agent,' and speedster, Willie Gault, was traded to the Raiders.

And Jack loved to rail about the Bears' ongoing quarterback problems. He called it "quarterback by committee." Longing for the NFL 1985 Bears Championship team. Jack knew everything there was to know about the Bears. Deborah's introduction to 'Bears Football' would come in the fall.

Aunt Rose was *the* basketball fan in the house. More specifically, she was a Michael Jordan fan. It was Rose who scored tickets to the 1988 NBA All-Star game, hosted by Chicago. Michael Jordan was the main attraction. Not only did he win his second consecutive NBA slam dunk title, he scored a record 40 points, eight rebounds, four steals and three assists to lead the East to a 138-133 victory. Jordan also earned NBA All-Star Game MVP honors. Aunt Rose had the game program framed for Deborah.

—

From the beginning, Aunt Rose and Uncle Jack assumed the role of parents, and in a way few natural parents do. Deborah was their sole focus, the object of all their love and caring. That first Christmas with Deborah, in 1974, was unlike any before. They were a family.

Aunt Rose beamed, on that Saturday in late summer of 1975, when she and an excited Deborah made their first real shopping foray. Deborah's period of silence had not long ended. She was in desperate need of a new wardrobe, and was especially happy to be rid of maternity wear. But she and Rose needed no excuse. Both had long planned for this day.

Deborah beamed with excitement. Rose was thrilled, just witnessing her niece eagerly try on outfit after outfit. They stopped only for a lunch of Cheese Steaks and fries. By day's end, Rose's Cutlass Supreme over-flowed, including the trunk. Jack had wisely emptied it that morning.

And there would be many more firsts. It was Rose who introduced Deborah to her first nylons, her first pumps—navy blue—her first non-cotton underwear, her first real lessons in personal hygiene, the use of feminine products. She provided Deborah's first visit to a beauty salon, her first manicure, and her first silk robe—one matching Rose's own. The two were like mother and daughter. In reality, they *were.*

Still, all was not sweetness and light. Despite Rose's and Jack's best efforts, there were times when Deborah seemed closer than ever to her emotional edge. Often, when she appeared happiest, a renegade thought or memory would thrust her back into a dark place.

Two months before Samantha's birth, there were troubling signs. Rose was horrified when she entered Deborah's room one day, and found her standing in front of the mirror, clipping fistfuls of her hair with a pair of shears. Rose called out to her, but Deborah did not respond. She seemed oblivious to everything.

Rose dashed to her, threw both arms around her, and held on. Seconds later, she gingerly lifted the shears away, then began stroking away tears streaming down Deborah's face. Deborah was mumbling a nearly inaudible mantra. Rose held her close, pressed her ear to her face.

"I can't look at myself anymore," Deborah sobbed. "I can't look at myself. I'm not beautiful. I'm not...beautiful. I'm ugly. I'm fat. And I hurt all over. They said I was beautiful, but I'm not. I'm not. Don't look at me, Aunt Rose. Please, don't look at me. I wish...I wish I was blind, so I couldn't see the way I..."

Rose placed a finger to Deborah's lips to silence her. She was desperate to find the right words, the right reaction. She guided Deborah to her bed, held onto her, refused to leave her side. They sat together for hours. Rose embraced her niece and prayed, silently. She assured Deborah she was beautiful. She spoke of a beauty that also flowed outward, from within her—a beauty that could not be diminished by what was happening to her body.

"This will soon pass, baby," Rose said over and over. "You *are* beautiful, 'cause God made you. I can...I can just imagine what you see, how you feel. I can't exactly know, but I can imagine, because I love you so much. I can come close. But, I can tell you this much: not only are you beautiful, but there is a beauty that will come from within you—a beautiful child that will love and need you...that will have your blood flowing through his or her veins.

"God will prepare you for that day, and you'll see how all the terrible things that have happened to you, all the things you feel so badly about right now will fade. They will just...just fade away. You will soon look into your baby's eyes and see your own face reflected in those eyes—the eyes of your child. A child as precious as any ever born. A child that God will permit to come into this world. A child that will always glow with the beauty that is you...that is in you.

"I want you to close your eyes now, and we'll pray. You don't have to pray out loud. Just talk to God and let him hear your words...know your heart, and He will take care of you. When you look in that mirror, from now on, I want you to only see Him looking back at you through your own eyes. You have to. We are not our own. We belong to Him—to God. He loves you. And so does your Uncle Jack and I. Never forget that."

Rose and her willingness; her eagerness for her own courage to be Deborah's courage; for her strength to be Deborah's strength, had no limits. As time went on, Aunt Rose helped her through many issues, her first bout with acne, for one. Fortunately, it was a mild case. She taught Deborah how to use makeup—the less, the better, Jack suggested in true fatherly form. Nothing escaped his watchful eye.

On Sundays, Rose and Deborah often looked like twins, just different sizes. They frequently wore matching suits and shoes—heels for Rose, pumps for Deborah; manicured nails, similar hair styles. Jack joked that the two even walked alike. From the beginning, members of Rose's church embraced Deborah. That was especially important when Mr. Jackson first introduced her to members of his Youth Group.

Uncle Jack and Deborah were like two sides of the same coin. Both loved sports. They even watched games on television together, often falling asleep on the sofa. It was Jack who opened her first bank account; started her allowance, taught her to cook.

Jack appointed Deborah his "Chef's First Assistant." Neither would forget the first complete meal Deborah prepared: boneless, skinless chicken breasts smothered in mushroom sauce; candied yams, homemade cornbread, peas, and brown rice. There were scarcely any leftovers. What little there was, ended up in Jack's lunchbox the next morning.

Jack took pride in teaching Deborah to shoot pool. She was ecstatic, the first time she beat her uncle. Years later, she still wondered if she actually won, or if he threw the game.

Uncle Jack's greatest joy came during a fourth of July barbecue in his backyard. He browbeat his best friend, Julius, into playing Deborah a game of pool. To Julius's embarrassment and surprise, she won the first two of three games. Then four of five, seven of nine. Deborah finally had to drop her cue and simply walk away, before Julius conceded defeat. Jack never let him forget it.

Then there were the trips. Jack, who had no particular fondness for driving, became a denizen of the open road. Summer vacations took them to not only the neighboring states of Michigan and Indiana, but New York, Pennsylvania, even Virginia, Maryland and more. They visited nearly all the key sights in Washington, D.C., including the White House.

There was even a brief overnighter in Canada, a soaking visit to Niagara Falls, a tour of the Big Apple. Deborah was fascinated by her visit to Detroit, and especially Hitsville, USA—Motown. She had seen pictures of the location, but standing there was awe-inspiring.

It was as if any minute, she could expect to see Smokey Robinson, The Temptations, Diana Ross and The Supremes, Stevie Wonder, Marvin Gaye, Martha and The Vandellas—even Berry Gordy himself walk out the front door. Motown took on an even more special quality after that.

It was Uncle Jack—a surprisingly patient Uncle Jack—who taught Deborah to drive. Aunt Rose was completely surprised. Her Jack did not have a reputation for being the most patient teacher.

In 1980, Jack and Rose bought Deborah a 1979 Volkswagen Super Beetle. Her joy was unspeakable. The gift marked two unforgettable milestones: Deborah's eighteenth birthday, and ownership of her first car. The 'Bug' was also her reward for her years of hard work, and for being named Valedictorian of her senior class.

Deborah's academic success earned her a ream of scholarships, including a full, four-year scholarship from Northwestern University. Other offers were from out-of-state schools. She could not envision herself living far away from her aunt and uncle.

Back on her sixteenth birthday, Deborah felt she crossed a deeply personal and emotional divide. Still, she could not pinpoint the precise moment, the hour, the day she looked at Rose and Jack and saw them as her mother and father. Perhaps it happened years earlier, but it was on that day, that the full realization fell squarely upon her.

And she thought about things in a more mature, more adult way than ever before. She wondered how Aunt Rose and Uncle Jack had been able to afford all they had done. How could they have afforded all the trips, the clothes, the gifts? And her medical bills with Samantha—even the birth, doctor visits over the years, dental bills, her braces? They were not wealthy.

Uncle Jack had a job he loved, working as a pressman at Johnson Publishing. But it did not provide full medical coverage for Deborah. Aunt Rose was mostly a housewife. She earned extra money at home, doing part-time bookkeeping for a number of small businesses, and was great at her work. Uncle Jack could attest to her frugality and firm-fisted grip on the family purse strings.

Rose's and Jack's labor of love also involved sacrifice. And they did so without Deborah's awareness. The fact she had never thought about it before, was a testament to their success in that regard. And had Deborah not earned a college scholarship, there was little doubt Rose and Jack would have mortgaged everything they owned. They would have cashed in every certificate of deposit Rose had managed to squirrel away, to make sure Deborah went to college.

—

All this and more flashed through Deborah's mind, as the Lincoln sped on. Except for the clanging of thoughts in her head, the only sounds came from the rhythmic rumble of the tires on the asphalt roadway.

Unfortunately, that rumbling sound whisked her back to 1974, back to the tortuous drive home from Dr. Samuels' office with her parents. Before she could resist the memory, she was there again. They had all learned she was..."with child." On that day, even the tire noise seemed but a muffled voice of disapproval, and further condemnation of her.

Then, another thought—a damning fact symbolizing so much that could never be explained. From the moment it was determined Deborah was pregnant, her mother never provided her the counsel one might have expected. There was no insight regarding the unimaginable transformation her young body and mind would undergo. For reasons never given, Mabel Davis left her daughter to fend for herself. There were no warnings, no cautions, no comforting words. There was no advice, no sympathy demonstrated regarding the wretched episodes of morning sickness Deborah suffered. Why?

Ironically, those conversations, and demonstrated care and concern would come later—in Chicago, from Aunt Rose. Rose, who never bore children, but who possessed the wisdom and caring of a mother filled with unconditional love. Rose, who held Deborah's hand, wiped away her tears, whispered comforting words, and never left her hospital bedside during Samantha's birth. It was especially then, Rose became more than an aunt. She became a mother—Deborah's mother.

chapter twenty-two

The Place

_____

"That boy don't forget or forgive nothing."

N ot much had changed.
Except for the recent coat of flat white paint and glossy black trim, the Davis house looked much as it had in 1974. San Augustine Grass now attended more of the front yard.

Three 'Davis family' cars were parked in the only area void of grass. One was covered with a dark, dust-laden tarp. Another was an older Buick Skylark. The third was a weathered Ford stationwagon. Neither appeared particularly roadworthy, to put it kindly. A fourth vehicle, bearing new dealer tags, was set some distance away, along the roadway.

The tall, stately pines; the majestic oaks; the surrounding, sprawling expanse of SB-40, were separated from the Davis house by an aging log fence. All remained. Crispus Attucks Road had been paved in asphalt at least twice, but was again in severe disrepair. The artery, frequently traveled by heavy equipment haulers, was now dotted with potholes that made driving a challenge. One could reasonably conclude that a good rain would likely make the road more suitable for swimming or fishing, than driving. The expenditure of Reed County funds, for even temporary repair, was nowhere in evidence.

Yvonne, a radiant ten year old with long braids and bangs, dressed in faded jeans and blue blouse, sat swaying in the porch swing. Her brother, Charles, 8, in jeans and T-shirt, sat on the steps pounding a worn baseball into the web of a tattered glove. Summer colds had kept both out of school for two days already. More absences appeared likely during these last few days of school.

Inside the neat but congested living room, with its aging wood floors and dated furniture, Mabel Davis sat entertaining an elderly white couple. Her hair was mostly gray; her face, ravaged by the effects of premature aging and stress.

Elkin and Mattie Hoage, both in their late seventies, had stopped to visit Reverend, pay their respects and offer whatever help they could. Mrs. Hoage—a thin, straight-postured, spirited 'talker' with snow white hair styled in a bun, and sporting a bright red ribbon—had brought gifts: a bushel of yellow squash and a croaker sack of cucumbers. A slightly stooped Mr. Hoage had little difficulty with the load. Mabel received the couple, and their gifts graciously. She viewed their visit as a testament to her husband's universal goodwill.

"Mighty glad y'all took time to come by and visit Reverend, to pray for him and all. I'm sure he 'preciates it, too," said Mabel Davis, sitting upright in her rocker, her hands resting in her lap.

Mr. Hoage, a wiry, white-haired gentleman decked out in blue overalls, raked a gnarled hand across his wrinkled, leathery face and placed the other on his wife's shoulder. Mattie Hoage smiled and looked at him with the eyes of a blushing bride.

"I was plumb set on comin' by," said Mr. Hoage. "Told the wife yesterday, I said Mattie, I sure would like to see how Reverend Davis is gettin' 'long. We knowed y'all a long time and everything. You and the Reverend's always been nice to everybody—white and colored. Always treated everybody the same."

Mrs. Hoage seemed impatient to get in her amens. "I remember him comin' up to our house and prayin' for Mr. Hoage that time when he was terrible sick. Our own pastor didn't come 'til Mr. Hoage was 'bout well. Hell, didn't need him then." Mrs. Hoage thrust a hand to her mouth. Her husband frowned disapprovingly.

"Mind 'yore mouth, Mother."

"Sorry, Mrs. Davis. But I'm tellin' the God's truth."

"Oh, don't mind that," said Mabel, trying to set her guest at ease.

The telephone rang. Mabel Davis' attention was suddenly divided between the Hoages and hoping Maylene would grab the phone.

"Sure hope and pray Reverend gets well soon. He's a God-fearin' man if ever I saw one," said Mrs. Hoage. A second ring sounded.

"Thanks for the kind words. I'm sure he'll be alright," said Mabel Davis. She spoke with a ring of hopefulness in her voice. "All things work for good for those who love the Lord."

The telephone rang a third time. Maylene reached the hallway and answered in the middle of the fourth ring.

"Maybe next time, Reverend'll be able to see you, and hold a conversation, maybe even have some dinner with you. Least that's my prayer," Mabel Davis added.

A moment later, Maylene reentered the living room. At 30, she was thin, but shapely and attractive, although the depth of her beauty was obscured by her homely appearance. She wore an ankle length plaid dress; had her long, black hair in a French roll. Strands fell away along the sides of her unblemished, unmade face. She waited for a suitable moment to interrupt. Mabel Davis noticed her.

"Excuse me," said Maylene. "Mama, that was Gloria. She and Reginald will be getting in from Atlanta 'bout 7 o'clock now. Their first flight was canceled. She said there was a problem with one of the engines, but..."

Maylene stopped mid-sentence, having noticed her kids playing catch on the front porch, and causing quite a commotion. She bolted for the screen door—a scowl pasted on her face. Mabel Davis turned back to the Hoages.

"Long as she get here safe. That's all I worry 'bout," she said. "I just ask the Lord to take care of her."

"You right 'bout that," said Mrs. Hoage. "Specially up there in them planes. Lord, you couldn't get me on one of them things for nothin'."

At the front door, Maylene was busy quieting her children. Their enthusiastic but noisy play had demanded her attention.

"You kids get off this porch with all that noise. Y'all know better. Go play over there somewhere. Go on! And don't be throwin' that ball toward those cars either. You hear me? Now, go on!"

"Mr. June Boy, Mama," Charles shouted, as he leaped from the porch. He nearly fell. Maylene never really heard what he said.

Mrs. Hoage leaned closer to Mabel Davis. "Now, the daughter comin' in...she your youngest girl from Atlanta?"

"Sure is. She lives there now. Graduated from Spelman a couple 'a years ago on a scholarship. That was a blessin', for sure."

"I know you proud."

"I am. I'm proud 'a all my children."

Maylene, who had rejoined her mother and the Hoages, frowned upon hearing her mother's last statement. She folded her arms, rolled her eyes and turned away.

It was then, Mrs. Rebecca Miles, a petite, bright-eyed, seventy year-old LVN, dressed in a white uniform she wore proudly, appeared in the passage doorway. She was practically beaming with excitement as she motioned for Mabel Davis. The latter excused herself from her guests and approached quickly.

Mabel Davis followed Rebecca a short distance up the hallway. At the opposite end, a somber Rachel stood watching through her half-opened bedroom door. She was robed in a white, ankle-length dress; her hair partially concealed her face. She gazed silently as her mother and Rebecca disappeared into the master bedroom.

The two women entered and moved hurriedly to a grand four-poster bed that dominated the room. A roll-away bed was set in one corner, draped with a white Chenille bedspread.

Reverend Davis—his face drawn, his cheeks sunken—lay flat on his back, covered with a crisp, neatly creased white sheet. His hair, closely cropped from earlier neurosurgery made necessary by the stroke, was mostly white now. His eyes were closed. An I.V. was connected to his right arm. The fingers of his left hand were curled, his mouth twisted slightly to the left.

A large, gold-leaf, family Bible lay open on the nightstand next to the bed. A red ribbon bookmark lay at the beginning of Psalms. A pair of gold-rimmed eyeglasses rested atop Psalms One, magnifying the words: *Blessed is the man who walketh not....*Mabel paused, briefly touched her husband's glasses, as she passed. The two women leaned over the Reverend, gazed at him intently while they spoke in hushed tones.

"He turned his head a minute ago. Wasn't a lot of movement, but you could see it real clear," said Mrs. Miles, in a soft voice. Mabel clasped both hands together tightly and smiled.

"That's a real good sign," she said. "Real good. Don't wanna get myself all worked up, but that's a good sign."

Rebecca nodded agreement. "Sister Davis, it's not my business, but I really think the Reverend ought to be in a hospital. I surely do. Now, I know they said they couldn't do any more for him, but..."

"Sister Miles, at the hospital in Little Rock, they told us there wasn't much more they could do for him anymore. There was 'bout six or more different doctors, includin' specialists who examined him. They gave him all manner of tests."

"Yes, ma'am, I understand. It's just that...well, they're doing a lot of things these days for people with strokes."

"Well, it's in the Lord's hands now." Mabel Davis stared lovingly at her husband and stroked his brow. "I just pray God's will be done. We've always trusted in the Lord. He ain't failed us yet."

"You know I do believe in prayer," said Rebecca, lowering her head resignedly. She, too, counted herself a God-fearing woman of faith, but had an abiding confidence in medical science. While she mostly kept her thoughts to herself, she could not help expressing herself this time.

Having lost all her children—her two elder sons to fatal confrontations with police, and her youngest to Texas' electric chair in 1969—Rebecca Miles knew God intimately. Fellow Shiloh members marveled at the inner peace she seemed to possess.

"Keeping busy, and praying a lot helps me get through most days," she always said. "Wish I'd 'a had me some daughters, like you, Sister Davis. There's just something special 'bout them daughters, don't you think so? I would 'a spoiled 'em for sure. Don't get me wrong, I loved my sons. But, anyway." Rebecca's voice trailed. Mabel Davis said nothing. Not a word.

Reverend lay perfectly still. Just then, his lips twitched; his head moved slightly. Mabel Davis and Rebecca noticed and moved closer.

"Now, you'll see a little movement every now and then. Sometimes it looks like he's getting stronger. I noticed that over the past few days. Like I said, he turned his head a little bit. It's hard to tell what's going on, though."

"We'll just keep prayin' and believin' in the Lord," said Mabel Davis, "Pretty soon, Reverend's gon' have that thing out 'a his arm and start eatin' real food. You'll see."

Rebecca started to respond, but hesitated when they both heard a car pull up and the engine switch off.

"I hope so, Sister Davis," said Rebecca. "I surely do."

Mabel Davis gave her husband a caring gaze, stroked his forehead again, and started back to her guests. When she reached the living room, the Hoages were standing at the front door with Maylene.

"I'm sorry I took so long," said Mabel Davis. "Y'all leavin' now?"

"'Fraid so. Reckon' I got 'a take this ol' man home and feed him somethin'. He gets downright ornery when I don't feed him right on the minute, like clockwork."

Mr. Hoage grinned and gave his wife a hug. "We gon' keep prayin' for Reverend," he said.

"We 'preciate that. And thank y'all for droppin' by.'

Mabel Davis smiled. The Hoages shook her hand warmly and started out onto the porch. Through the screen door, they all saw a dark-skinned black man, 28, well-built, dressed in paint-splattered coveralls, climb out of a battered pickup truck. He was over six feet, had short hair and a thick, black mustache.

"That's Matthew," whispered Maylene, standing near the front door and peering out. "Looks like he's been working today. Bless his heart."

Neither Maylene nor her mother saw 'June Boy' standing next to a porch roof support clutching a bouquet of wild flowers. He was a mentally challenged, thirty-eight year-old man with the heart of an angel.

Many believed his 'condition' was the doing of Florinda Batiste who, before his birth, angrily blamed his mother for "spreadin' lies" about her. In retaliation, an angry Batiste placed what she called a 'blood curse' on his unwed mother, when the latter was barely three months pregnant. Florinda then openly predicted the result.

June Boy was a fixture in the Sticks...was nearly always seen walking, pulling a large 'Red Flyer' wagon loaded with gardening tools. He always wore denim overalls, work boots, long-sleeve white shirt, and a smile. He was known to have healing hands, when it came to sick birds and small animals. And his amazing knowledge of flowers and plants was never understood. Some swore he had a 'gift.' Word was, he would close his eyes and simply hold them, or gently stroke them. Within hours, not days, they would most often recover. Of course, few gave much credence to the rumors.

Maylene was first to acknowledge him. "June Boy! You're back."

"Yes'm, Miss Maylene...Sister Davis. I ahh...I got these flowers for Reverend. Got some...some Cypripedium pubscens, some Sanguinaria canadensis, and...and some..."

"Some what, June Boy?"

"Some...some Glandularia Canadensis," June boy proudly stuttered, pointing out the botanical names of the flowers he held.

"Thanks, June Boy."

"They more pretty than the ones I brung yesterday."

Maylene smiled and shook her head with wonder. "I don't understand a thing you just said, but I do believe you're right. You know more about plants and animals than anybody around here. Thanks, June Boy. Yvonne, come take these inside and come right back."

"Miss Maylene, can I see Reverend? I...I can make him well. Alls I have to do is just...just touch his hand and...and pray. I can..."

"Well, he's resting right now, June Boy. Maybe you can see him next time. You talk to Mama about that. You remember what she said the last time. Oh, thanks for the flowers, and for praying for Reverend. We'll see you in a few days. Be sure and say hello to your mama."

June Boy turned to leave, spotted Matthew, and began shaking like a leaf in a hurricane. He frowned, began lacing his fingers and moaning. Maylene quickly moved to his side.

"C'mon now. Don't you mind Matthew." Maylene patted June Boy on his shoulder. "He just got a little upset with you when he thought you were taking things off his ol' truck that time. It's okay. Just go on. Go on. Go that way, 'cross the yard to the road. I bet he doesn't even see you."

June Boy leaped to the ground and took off across the yard, his tool-filled red wagon in tow. He kept glancing back toward Matthew. Within seconds, he was gone. Yvonne returned to join Charles.

The Hoages exited the front door and quickly spotted Matthew. Their smiles vanished. Mattie and Elkin fixed their eyes on him, as they clung to each other and eased down the steps to the ground. Both turned back to Mabel Davis, waved to her nervously, and continued to their shiny, new black, Buick Roadmaster.

Matthew squared his shoulders, clenched his jaws and walked right past them. After he passed, he cast a look of deep disdain back at them, glaring until Mr. Hoage started his car. Maylene loosed a sigh of relief, shook her head and turned to her mother.

"My God, I'm so glad that boy didn't say anything to those old folk. He would 'a scared 'em to death for sure. Lord, the last thing we need is for a couple of white folk to die in this front yard, with Matthew anywhere in Reed County, or Arkansas, for that matter."

"That boy don't forget or forgive nothin'," said Mabel Davis. "And won't go to church to save his life. Lord, help him."

"He's *your* son."

"He's *your* brother."

"That's not *my* doing."

Charles and Yvonne greeted their uncle excitedly. Charles tossed the baseball to him, just as the Hoages pulled away. Matthew paused to stare at the car until it was well out of sight. He mumbled a few expletives under his breath and turned back to the children.

"Let's play catch, Uncle Matthew," said Charles.

Matthew tossed the ball back to him and headed toward the porch. Charles struggled with the pitch.

"You can't catch, boy. You almost dropped the ball. Guess I'll play catch with your sister in a little while. Bet she won't drop it."

Matthew reached the porch and collapsed onto the top step. Maylene and her mother remained standing behind the screen door.

"Hey 'Lene...Mama. How's Daddy doin'?"

"Your daddy's the same, I reckon. Moved his head a little...tried to open his eyes a while ago. We just got 'a keep prayin'."

Matthew stared at the ground, both hands clasped firmly on one knee. He leaned back against a porch column and sighed heavily.

"That's good to hear. Say 'Lene, why you name that boy Charles?"

"What in the world are you talkin' 'bout?"

"Sounds sissified, if you say it right. Char-rulls. You have to say Chalz so it won't sound fruity. Should 'a named him somethin' else."

"Should 'a named him Matthew, right?"

"Hmm. Nothin' wrong with that, I reckon. Even Mama know I'm right. 'Course she ain't gon' say so while I'm sittin' here. Never want to admit when *I'm* right. But I love her anyway. I love you anyway, Mama. You're my best girl."

"Boy, you still crazy as ever," said Maylene, laughing.

"Tell ya what," said Matthew. "Around Reedville, being crazy ain't required, but it sure helps."

"Meaning what?"

"Meanin' there ain't no jobs, no money. That trickle down crap ain't trickled down. Bush called it voodoo economics, at first, then sucked up to Reagan like a newborn calf so he could run with him. Pretty soon, these crackers roun' here, and the few dumb-ass niggers that voted..."

"Matthew!" Maylene interrupted.

"They gon' have to graze like cows just to keep from starvin,' Matthew went on. "The only ones makin' out these days...is Wall Street. Surprise, surprise!"

"Matthew, watch your mouth. Don't be saying that word," Maylene chided. "I hate it."

"Now just what word would that be, Big Sister?"

"Don't mess with me, Matthew Jeremiah Davis. You know what word. The 'N' word. One of the worst words you can say. Worse than cuss words. I don't like it when white folks say it, and I don't like it when black people say it either."

"Who you callin' black?" joked Matthew.

"You! I'm calling *you* black. What you want me to call you? Afro-American? Negro? Colored? What? Tell me," chided Maylene.

"You can call me whatever you want. Just call me for Mama's chicken and dumplins," said Matthew, laughing. "I can smell 'em from here."

"You're laughing, but I'm serious. Find some other word," said Maylene. "Charles is standing right there, staring down your throat and listening to every word you say. He thinks you can walk on water."

"Smart boy. Listen," said Matthew. "There are black folks, and then there are niggers—black and white. You know what I'm talkin' 'bout. You can use whatever word you want. And I ain't lyin' bout the jobs either. They ain't no better in Reedville or Little Rock or nowhere else. And I bet Bush wins in November. You just watch.

"See, what y'all don't understand is, most white folks will vote for the devil himself, if he act like he's gon' keep a boot on a nigger's neck. Why you think all these damn Southern Democrats are turning Republican? It's 'cause most black folk are Democrats.

"And on top of that, they want to tell us who to vote for, and who our heroes ought 'a be. They say: *Oooh, if all them Niggers are Democrats, I don't want any part 'a that shit. Unh-unh. No sir. Hell no!* So, they wrap themselves in the flag, act like the second amendment was given down by Moses, and proceed to beat everybody else across the head with the cross. They claim to be so holy...God-fearin'. They claim God is on *their* side. Bullshit! Don't get me started."

Maylene looked at Charles. "Charles Edward Rollins, get yourself back over there and play. Nobody called you over here. Go on!"

"Maylene, let them kids learn how it really is. Don't sugarcoat it. And make sure they learn in school...make a good life for themselves. Got 'a know the true history of things. That's the only way to survive the crap out here. And even then they gon' have to fight."

"That's good advice for you too, son. Never too late to learn."

"I know, Mama. I'm tryin' everyday. I am."

"Lord, why did I say anything?" Maylene chuckled. "Let me change the subject. A minute ago, I was scared you were gonna say something to Mr. Hoage."

Matthew spat at the mention of the name. "Maylene, I still say you ought 'a change that boy's name. Right, Mama?"

"You work today, son?"

"See there? I knew she was gon' change the subject. Yeah, Mama. I worked. Got two more houses to paint. One in Reedville, the other down in Stamps. Don't know if I'm gon' drive down that far, though."

"That's a blessin', son."

Matthew remained silent. He sat staring at the ground, drawing circles in the dirt with his right foot.

"Ol' man Hoage and his ol' lady come to do their Christian duty, visitin' po' sick and shut-in colored people?"

"Son, all white folks ain't devils, and all black folks ain't no angels either. I got 'a keep prayin' for you. You still ain't forgive him for what he done that time?"

"I ain't talkin' 'bout all white folks. I'm talkin' 'bout one in particular. Why should I forgive his ol' wrinkled, rhino-lookin' butt? We had a deal. I spent three hundred, twenty-seven dollars, and seventeen cents on paint, brushes and stuff. I hired a helper—Cleophus Johnson—and showed up on time to do the damn job. Sorry, Mama. I mean, the doggone job we agreed on. I get out there and the Reed Brothers Contractors was all over the place.

"I should 'a known better. Anybody who would name their son, Heinous...I mean, think about it—Heinous Hoage. What in the world did they think that word meant? And on top of that, people say Florinda Batiste was the midwife. Accordin' to the stories, the boy was goin' 'round bitin' off the heads 'a live birds and chickens. Then he killed himself when he was only thirteen—on Friday, the thirteenth. Now that's weird. Forgive him? The ol' fart never apologized. I'll forgive him when he dies."

"Wasn't that over a year ago?" asked Maylene.

"Seems like yesterday to me."

"It was a whole year, Matthew."

"So?"

"So, maybe the Reed Brothers gave Mr. Hoage a lower bid or something. You ever think of that?"

"Bull! But even if they had, he should 'a told me somethin' or other. Besides, he paid twice as much as I bid on that job."

"How you know?"

"You don't believe me?"

"I'm just trying to help you get over this. And you're right. He should 'a said something. But how'd you find all this out."

"Big Baby Jesse told me."

Maylene's jaw dropped. "Wait a minute, Matthew. Wait. You're telling us you're basing all this on what Big Baby Jesse told you?"

"Why not? He worked for the Reeds up until three months ago."

"Matthew, he operated a backhoe part-time, until his butt got too big to fit in the seat. Then he worked no-time. How would Big Baby Jesse know what was bid on that job, anyway?"

"He knew someone in the office—this girl he was messin' with. She told him everything, even showed him a copy of the bid."

"What girl? Some white girl? Must be. 'Cause ain't no black girl working for them. And you believe that lie? He ain't never had a girlfriend anybody ever knew of. You know how Big Baby Jesse's always stretching the truth, trying to make himself seem more important than he is."

"But 'Lene, that don't make him a liar about this. You know, you never did like him."

"Name me two people who did, besides his mama and daddy."

"Damn, 'Lene. That's cold."

"Alright. Fine, little brother. But even if he's telling you the truth—which I doubt—I say that's an awful long time to hold something in your heart against somebody."

"That don't matter none. What's a year? And what's time got to do with anything? I'm still pissed at what they did to Nat Turner."

"Nat Turner? Just listen to you."

"You got a problem with that, big sister?"

"Your sister's right, son."

"Right about what, Mama?"

"About forgivin' folk. God wants us to have a forgivin' spirit...be slow to anger and quick to forgive."

"Mama, answer me somethin,' alright? Who's been more forgivin' than black people? You think about all that lynchin', the rapes, the hatred, neglect, disrespect, and everything we put up with in this country, and still puttin' up with. We're almost invisible to those in power...until election time. It's a wonder black people don't shoot white folks on sight."

"What you sayin', son? What kinda world would that be?"

"Besides, they got the most guns," said Maylene.

"I'm not sayin' that should happen, Mama. But what if things were reversed? You think they'd forgive and love us?"

"Son, I'm just sayin' you have to be concerned about your own soul. You have to, baby. You know I'm right."

"I *am* concerned."

"Then you have to *act* like it...have to make sure your heart is right. That's what your daddy preached."

"My heart is right. My heart always been right."

"Don't always seem like it. And what about Samantha?"

"What about Sam, Mama?"

"She's real sensitive. She got feelin's. And she hear you talkin' 'bout white people like they got tails and horns. I know she never says anything, but you ever wonder how she feel, knowin' she half white? When you talk like that, you're talkin' 'bout her, too."

Matthew bristled, clenched his teeth. "Mama, you can call her half white if you want to. But out there, right out there...past that yard, she's just as black as the rest of us. I hope y'all ain't lettin' her think otherwise. You know I love Sam. But black is all she's ever known. And black is all she ever gon' be. We all have to teach her to be proud of that."

"Matthew! Son, she's old enough to know she's got black and white in her. Now, that's the plain truth of it. I'm not talkin' 'bout what other folks think. You have to learn to see people like Christ sees all of us. Let love shine in your eyes and in your heart, son. Think about where your soul will spend eternity. I know you don't want to hear all..."

"Mama, I hear all that. What I'm sayin' is..."

"No, no, no, son. Like I said..."

"Mama, you make it seem like I..."

"Listen, now. I ain't gon' let you outtalk me. I know you don't want to hear all this. But I have to tell you. I'm duty bound to tell you what thus sayeth the Lord."

Matthew held his tongue long enough to make sure his mother finished speaking before having the rest of his say.

"Mama, I hear you. I respect you, but let me tell you 'bout what sayeth Matthew. I hear you talk about where I'm gon' spend eternity. Look, I'm sorry, but I just don't have that 'sweet bye 'n bye' attitude like you good ol' church sisters. I believe in the here and now. I live in the here and now, not in the hereafter. Least not yet."

"You can't blame white folk for everything that's wrong, Brother. We can blame them for a lot, but not everything. Black folk need to step up to the plate everyday," Maylene jumped in. "Especially those who have become successful. We have to do what's good and right for us, too."

"I understand that. I got no problem with that. We all know some sorry ass—Excuse me, Mama. I mean, sorry black folk who don't do a 'dat gum' thing but moan and groan. There's folks like that in every race. I'm not givin' any excuse to people like that."

"But we're talking 'bout *us* right now," said Maylene.

"Right."

"And another thing. You need to start going back to church, Brother," Tell me something, how long it's been since you had your behind in a church pew?"

"Alright, here we go. I wondered how long it would take to get around to that. Listen, I know all about what the Bible says about...about not *forsakin' the assembly with fellow saints* and all that. But let me tell you this. Way too many of y'all so-called saints—you know, the ones who always there everytime the church door swing open—they don't understand that you go to church to worship. You serve God when you leave. It's what you do after church service is over that make a difference.

"The same folk with bibles stuck under their armpits on Sundays never open 'em after they leave church. Ol' man Hoage and his wife are Bible-thumpin' Christians, just like a lot 'a others. The Reeds are big-time Christians, too. Always talkin' 'bout the cross, and the flag. That don't mean a thing. They walk around with their noses in the air, won't look you in the eye. Most the time they don't even *see* your black...black butt.

"They can almost step on you, and never even see you. Now, I ain't sayin' they all a bunch of phonies, but too many of 'em are. I always been able to get help from sinners a lot easier. Never understood why, but it's true. Ask yourself how even Christians would treat Jesus if they walked by him, saw him standin' on the corner wearing a dress, some raggedy sandals, and needin' a shave, a haircut and a bath. They'd probably think he was some gay, homeless hippie."

"Matthew…" Maylene started, but Matthew wasn't done.

"And another thing. We hear all this stuff 'bout Republicans…'bout the religious right, the Moral Majority. I guess that means the rest 'a us belong to the immoral minority. I don't understand. I mean, if I could talk to 'em I'd say: you screw over the po' to help the rich, and you call yo'self righteous? You support folks who screw up the air, the water, like you don't have to breathe the same air, and drink the same water as the rest of us, and you say you righteous?

"You worry more 'bout the unborn than you do folks who are alive and strugglin,' but you righteous?" Matthew was on a roll. "So, tell me somethin'. When Jesus was here on earth, was he a liberal or a conservative? Huh? That's what I wanna know. Who made his golden chariot? Who was his chauffeur? What country club did he belong to? Who was his fashion designer? Who handled his stocks and bonds?"

With that, Matthew stood up and strode across the porch. He kissed his mother on the cheek and hugged Maylene. Both struggled to contain their laughter.

"Well, I think we just heard a sermon. We got ourselves a preacher here. Lord, have mercy, Maylene. What we gon' do with him?"

"Don't ask me." Maylene shook her head with resignation.

"Son, I don't know that much about politics and all, but I repeat. All white folk ain't evil. And even the bad ones can change."

"Change? Mama, zebras don't grow up to be giraffes. They are what they are. You can paint 'em…stretch their necks, but underneath they still zebras. Besides, you can't stretch reality that far."

Mabel laughed aloud. "Lord, I got to give it to you son, that's one I ain't heard before. I'm done with it. You can have it, Maylene."

"Anyway," Matthew pressed on, changing the subject, "Mr. Peabo says he might be thinkin' of sellin' his place. I might try to buy it. He's gettin' on up there…tired of bein' on his feet all day and…"

"Feet?" Maylene interrupted.

"Alright. I mean his *foot*…all day. That's another cold shot. 'Lene, you act all mild-mannered and everything, but you can be brutal."

"I'm just being exact," she replied, doubling over. Mabel looked away to conceal her own laughter.

"Anyway, I know I could run it...make a lot of money, too."

"Oh, really?"

"Really."

"And just what do you plan to use for money to buy the place, Lil' Brother. I know ol' man Peabo ain't gon' sell for peanuts. No way. Whoever buys him out is gon' have to come with it. They don't call him 'Big Dollar Bill' for nothing."

Matthew cracked up, nearly choked. "That just shows how much you know, 'Lene."

"What's so funny?"

"You are. You what's so funny. They call him 'Big Dollar Bill' for another reason, which I cannot mention in front of Sister Davis here. Miss Ruby gave him the name. Said if he was gon' be one of her customers it was gon' cost him extra—Big Dollars. I rest my case."

"You're just making that up," said a snickering Maylene.

"Swear to God. Ask anybody on Oak street."

"I don't go on Oak street. And you shouldn't either, grown or not. You been sneaking 'round there every since you were little...since before Daddy chased you out of Peabo's, when he found out you had a job there sweeping up the place after school."

"Don't remind me. It was honest, hard work. That's how I kept a little change in my pocket. I should 'a been congratulated." Matthew waved Maylene off. "Enough of this," he mumbled. "I didn't stop by to cuss and fuss about some ol' wrinkled butt white folks, and the size of Mr. Peabo's ahh...leg," he said, clearing his throat repeatedly. Let me look in on the old man...go get cleaned up. Anybody call Chicago yet?"

Matthew lumbered toward the front door. There was no answer to his question, just an exchange of furtive glances between Maylene and her mother. Both knew how explosive and opinionated Matthew could be. Each were always prepared to be surprised by his views and comments. He seldom disappointed.

chapter twenty-three

The Long Road

Comes A Stranger

On rural, two-lane Highway FM270, the white Lincoln Town Car zoomed past a rusting highway sign: REED-VILLE, ARKANSAS—2 miles. Deborah held her sunglasses in her hand and stared out, hardly blinking. The car was now only minutes from her destination, and a moment she anticipated with both joy and dread.

Earlier, Deborah thought she recognized certain turns in the road, a distant clump of farmhouses. But she could not be certain. A thirty-mile per hour speed limit sign appeared to streak by. The young chauffeur slowed. Deborah had warned him the local Sheriff likely had little tolerance for speeders, especially those in big fancy cars.

A minute later, Deborah watched another sign loom in front of her: ENTERING REEDVILLE, ARKANSAS Population: 3,977. Her pulse spiked. A lump formed in her throat. She drew a long breath, clasped her hands together tightly, and sealed her eyes shut. The chauffeur glanced at her in the rear view mirror. A curious look covered his face.

"Just drive through town slowly when we get there." Deborah's voice was weak, barely audible. "I want to see if I remember any of this place. I used to live here, once upon a time. I was only twelve when I left. As I recall, the place we're headed should be only a few miles outside of town."

The young chauffeur nodded and proceeded slowly. He soon reached the turn leading into what still passed for Reedville's business district. The car crept down Main street, past small businesses and shops.

At first glance, it appeared to Deborah not much had changed. Many establishments were abandoned and boarded up. There were few pedestrians, some vehicles—mostly pickup truck traffic. On the street, several people nodded and waved, even as they gazed with curiosity at the big white sedan.

"Turn right, here." Deborah quickly realized her mistake. "No! Left! Turn left. I'm sorry. It's been so long."

The chauffeur nodded and smiled. "I understand."

"What's your name?"

"Jonathan."

Deborah groaned and shook her head in disbelief. Of all the possible names. What were the odds of that?

"May I call you John?"

"That's fine, ma'am."

"John, did I tell you I was twelve when I left this place?"

"Yes, ma'am."

"You can drop the ma'am. I'm only twenty-six. I'm a little nervous. Do I seem nervous? I haven't been back here since 1974. That was fourteen years ago. Well, more or less. Fourteen long years." Deborah's voice drifted. John turned left and proceeded.

"I don't mean to pry, ma'am. Sorry. I said it again. But why did you leave? And why haven't you been back before now?"

"You're not prying. It's a long, long story. There's not enough time left in the whole year to tell it to you. Maybe I'll write a book someday."

"Well, welcome home."

"Thanks. That's my first welcome. Hope it won't be the last."

Deborah gazed with searching eyes, as the car moved slowly past the last strip of businesses. Within minutes, they reached a residential area populated with large, attractive homes surrounded by lush, green, well-manicured lawns set well off the road.

—

Matthew and Maylene stood next to their father's bed, staring at his still form. Matthew shook his head, partly in frustration, partly in anger. He was frustrated at not being able to do more to ensure better medical attention for his father. And he was angry for feeling impotent, unworthy of the position he held as an only son.

Matthew felt himself a failure for not having educated himself; for not having found success, for still being stuck in the Sticks. He was angry alright—angry at himself, his father, at damn near everybody, at times. The years had gone by, leaving too many things unresolved.

For the past ten or fifteen minutes, Matthew and Maylene had been discussing Deborah. Such a discussion was rare, before now.

"I'm sure Aunt Rose told her," said Maylene.

"I ask myself how somethin' like this could go on so long. All these years," said Matthew. "Years you can't ever get back. When we were kids, that was one thing. But we should 'a said something long before now. It don't make sense, no matter how you cut it. No matter what we say."

"I haven't talked to her—my own sister—in years," Matthew went on. "Everytime I look at Samantha, I think about her. It don't make sense. Never did. And I can't explain it. Can you? Why does it always take sickness and death?"

"We all took our lead from Daddy," said Maylene. "No two ways about it. I don't remember the last time I heard him say her name. Wish I knew what happened to the letters she sent. I found out they existed when Mama let it slip a couple of years ago. I looked for them, but couldn't find a thing. Sometimes, this all seems like a dream—like a nightmare. Seems like none of it ever happened."

"But it did happen."

"I know. And it's still happenin' right now."

A somber Matthew moved to the other side of the bed. He stood staring at his father for what seemed minutes.

"Y'all still prayin'," still asking God to come down and heal his faithful servant? 'Cause he ain't answered yet. Maybe he don't hear you. Maybe he's too busy answerin' white folks' prayers. Ever think about that? Huh? Think about it!"

"Matthew, stop it! That's blasphemy. Respect Daddy. And please, don't let Mama hear you talk like that. Prayer and her faith is all she's got to lift her, to keep her going," Maylene said in a harsh whisper. She motioned Matthew away from their father's bed.

"Mama's not in here right now," Matthew answered. "It's me and you. And Daddy can't hear me."

"How you know that?"

"I just know. Besides, I'm just talkin' to you."

"What's wrong with praying? Don't you pray?" asked Maylene.

"Nothin' wrong with prayin', unless that's all you depend on. Yeah, I pray. I pray for Daddy...for all my family. I pray for little children who ain't got food to eat. I pray no redneck calls me nigger, so I don't have to shoot they ass.

"See, I realize I ain't exactly the forgivin' kind. And I don't pretend to be. I pray my ol' truck keep runnin' one more day. I pray to God I can find a way to get rich. Yeah, I pray. I pray a lot. I got bruised knees from all that prayin', but I got no answers, alright? So, I have to ask myself why I keep on prayin'? And if askin' that is a sin, well I guess I got one more thing to pray about, huh?"

Maylene placed a compassionate hand on Matthew's shoulder. "I'd love to be rich too," she said. "Who wouldn't? But you know what? Rich people have their troubles too."

"Yeah. But bein' po' ain't one of 'em. Fact is, the only people I ever hear talkin' that crap is po' folks. Think about it. Po' black people do more prayin' than anybody. God could use a answerin' service just to keep track of us *prayin' colored folk.'* And just look!"

"It ain't God's fault. It's what you do when you get up off your knees that makes the difference, Matthew."

"Well, swing low sweet chariot. That's my point. Some people get up, but then sit down on their *be-hinds*. Like they expect God to come knockin' on the front door like the Avon Lady. I'm out here everyday, bustin' my black ass. I hear all this bull about black folks being triflin' and lazy...on welfare and crap. Hell, we work! We wanna work, dammit. Hell, this country was built on our backs, fertilized with our bodies and our blood. But you just listen to the damn right wing politicians."

"Matthew, try not to curse in here."

"What? Hell and damn is in the Bible."

"Not the way you're using it."

"Well, God can strike me down if he want to. Anyway, you got a bunch 'a redneck politicians preachin' to us 'bout family values, after doin' everything they could to destroy our families. Don't get me started. I'm out here everyday. And I wanna work. I leave my damn pride at home everyday when I go out here. You know what it's like to have some redneck tell you he don't even want you haulin' his damn trash? Huh?"

"Matthew, Listen to me." Maylene's voice softened, She touched Matthew's shoulder caringly. "Brother, pick up a book sometimes. Read. It's not against the law anymore. Educate yourself. I tried to tell you to go back to school a long time ago. You remember?"

"Yeah. To be what?"

"Anything you want to be."

"Where am I gon' get the money to go to school? Scholarships? Sell my General Motors stock? Can't get no loan. And I want to go back. That's why I'm workin.' But it ain't gettin' me nowhere. So I keep on workin', lookin' for more work and gettin' nowhere. But I got friends that do a couple a' grand a day, on a bad day."

"You talking 'bout Leroy Mims and his cousin. What's his name? Ahh...got one leg longer than the other one. You know who I'm talking about. Tyrone! Leroy and Tyrone. Some real good friends. You better be careful 'round those two pillars of the community—with their big gold chains, and peanuts for brains. They always have to keep watching their backs...watching for cops, and for thugs like themselves trying to take what they got. That what you want?"

"Obviously not. And I don't really hang out with them."

"Then you have to trust God and yourself, Matthew."

"Right now, God ain't givin' me a reason to trust him."

"Matthew, You can't give up, no matter what folks do to you. You have to make your success your own responsibility. As long as you are alive, you have a chance. You are alive, aren't you?"

"Sometimes."

Maylene sighed resignedly. Several long minutes of silence followed. She reached for both Matthew's hands and held them in a gentle grasp.

"Brother, I'm...I'm gonna shock you."

"What do ya' mean?"

"Now, just listen to me for a minute. Okay?"

"Alright. I'm listenin'."

"What I mean is this. I love you. I love you and I can feel what's eating at you. I listen to things you speak about. I hear the deep anger—the frustration in your words, in your voice. And you know what? I actually agree with a lot of what you say. And...and even the parts I disagree with, I can understand. But Matthew, you have to find a way—a way to release things."

"Release what?"

"The anger. Some of the anger...the frustration. You're so intense. Too intense sometimes. You need to be able to release a lot of that, you know? I pray for that...for you. I look at you and sometimes it's like you're so...so wound up. You're almost frothing at the mouth."

"Like I've gone mad or somethin,' huh?"

"Well, sorta. You scare me. I mean, I be hoping you don't have a heart attack, or burst a blood vessel or something. Don't get me wrong, I love your unshakable belief in what it is you believe. It's not easy for you. Never has been. I know the difficulty you face as a black man in America. And I applaud you and brothers like you who have not surrendered your dignity and your fire. Too many of us black women are too quick to damn, and too slow to praise.

"If there's one thing everybody knows, it's that you can always be depended on to be yourself. There's no put-on with you. But you have to find some inner peace with all that's not right in this world. I know that's not easy. But that doesn't mean you give in or give up. It means that you find a way to fight your battles without letting the battles fight you—and win. *You* win!

"And another thing. A good woman who loves and believes in you can go a long way to making life sweeter than you can ever imagine. I'm not saying a good woman can make a *bad man*...good. But she can sure help make a *good man*...great. And that's what you need in your life. There's so much good in you. You have so much to offer. Don't lose it, ever. Am I making sense?"

Matthew did not respond, at least not verbally. He just stood quietly, looking squarely into Maylene's caring eyes. Finally, he hugged his sister, kissed her cheek and left the room. Maylene watched him leave, then eased closer to her father's bed. She stroked his face gently, while brushing salty tears from her own.

—

Deborah's car glided over a double set of rails, onto a shell road, and past dingy, unpainted, shotgun shanty houses all lined up like dominoes. A half dozen black children, all under age six, played in grass-barren yards that fronted deep drainage ditches that overflowed whenever it rained.

Deborah waved. The children waved back to her excitedly, as the shiny, white car drove by. Deborah stared at the soiled faces until she could no longer see them.

Two and a half miles later, the car turned onto unstriped, asphalt-worn, Crispus Attucks Road. It was still bordered by towering pines that had somehow escaped harvesting. A solemn Deborah looked out, and remembered right away. She felt her emotions swell.

"Stop here for a second, please."

John appeared surprised, but pulled the vehicle well off the old road-way, stopped, then started to open his door.

"Don't bother. I'm fine," said Deborah, halting him mid-step. She opened the right, rear passenger door and stepped lightly to the ground. John wore a puzzled expression. He figured there was something special about this place. But from the looks of the area, he could not imagine what that could be.

Deborah moved slowly to the middle of the road and stopped still. The growing sound of her heartbeat began to fill her ears. She stood glancing in one direction, then the other, then drifted along the edge of the roadbed a short distance. Deborah stopped and looked around wist-fully. She began turning slowly, in a full circle. It was all coming back. Little had changed.

The sound of the pickup truck gaining on her and her friends; the sound of animated conversation and childish laughter; the prickly heat and perspiring brows—it was all there.

A mild gust of warm wind caressed Deborah's face. She held fast and, once again, could almost hear distant but resonant voices. She could almost distinguish each word spoken by her friends on what had seemed just another day. Her heart nearly burst free; her emotions seemed set on consuming her. And the fact she was again in Reedville was never more real.

For years, the voices of her friends, Kay and B.B., had replayed in Deborah's mind over and over and over. And why hadn't Tommy been just a little bolder, more assertive? Why had he not insisted she refuse Jonathan's offer? If he had, would it have mattered then? Why had Bev-erly and Karetha not been more vocal in ridiculing her? Would it have mattered that day?

Despite pondering the unchangeable past, Deborah knew those questions had only one answer: it was her decision. It was her responsi-bility, despite her young age. No one else was to blame. No amount of dwelling on 'what-ifs' would change a thing.

Still, it was an exercise to which Deborah had grown quite accustomed. Even when she resisted it, by reminding herself of the futility, there were times when the temptation to engage in "what-ifs" was irresistible. This was one of those times.

Deborah immediately felt a chill course her body—a coldness that made no sense, given the heat. She shut her eyes tightly and waited. The sensation soon passed. After several minutes of quiet, she returned to the car. John cast a wary glance at her. It was not until Deborah looked up into the rear view mirror and nodded, that he pulled back onto the roadway and drove on.

chapter twenty-four

Road's End

===========================

"My God, we all lost that, didn't we?"

Mabel Davis and Maylene
stood just inside the living room, peering through the screen door. Matthew was clutching a large, covered Pyrex dish filled with chicken and dumplings, and standing on the porch. Rebecca Miles had returned to the Reverend's bedroom.

Charles and Yvonne were banging around in the swing, singing some obscure nursery rhyme as loudly and off-key as they could. Matthew cast a slight scowl toward them. They quickly lowered their volume.

"How's Gloria and Pretty Boy getting from the airport?" Matthew asked, referring to his youngest sister and her boyfriend.

"I'm sure they're renting a car. Suppose to get here just after dark. It's 'bout three now," said Maylene.

"Just wonderin' if I need to go pick 'em up. I don't mind playin' chauffeur for once. 'Course I'd have to borrow one of these cars. No way Miss America gon' ride in my ol' truck. And my Rolls Royce is still bein' built.

Anyway, thanks for such a great supper, Sister Davis. You can still burn, girl. Listen, y'all call me when Miss Gloria and her 'fee-an-cee' get here."

"I'll 'Sister Davis' you," said Mabel Davis. "And he just her boyfriend. Besides, we can't call you 'til you get your phone put back on. And another thing. When you gon' get a wife so you can invite us to supper once in a while? You need to get a good job, get married to a good girl...have me some grandbabies? That's what we need 'roun' here. Some new blood...some babies?"

"Talk to your daughter standin' next to you?"

"Don't look at me," Maylene snapped. "I'm done with babies."

"I'm talkin' to you, boy," said Mabel.

Matthew pretended to not hear his mother. He wheeled around, jumped from the porch and dashed toward his truck.

"Can't hear you, Mama," he shouted back over his shoulder, then broke out in loud laughter.

"I know full well you heard me! That boy's a mess," she said, turning to Maylene.

Matthew cranked his truck and backed out into the street, causing a white Lincoln Town Car to brake. Deborah braced herself, thrusting her hand against the rear of the front passenger seat.

Matthew started away then slowed to gaze through his dirty cab window. "Probably just somebody doing a turnaround," he thought, then tore away.

From their vantage point behind the screen door, Mabel Davis and Maylene stared with growing curiosity. The sedan wheeled in, crept past the mailbox and onto the yard. The women turned to each other.

"Now who in the world could that be?" asked Mabel. "Don't recognize that car at all. You?"

"No, Mama. Got Arkansas plates, though."

John wheeled onto the yard and stopped well behind the parked cars. An anxious Deborah pressed her hands to her chest and gazed through the windshield. Her palms were clammy. Her breath came in gasps. Her temples throbbed.

"This is it," she whispered. "My God, after all this time, this is really it. I'm here." Deborah was struggling to make the moment real. "Okay. Alright. So what now? What do I do now? Oh, my God. I don't think I want to be here.

In a single breath, all the doubts about returning home came flooding back. Deborah felt overwhelmed by them. "This isn't my home," she told herself. "This is where I was born, but it isn't my home. Chicago is home. Home is where Aunt Rose and Uncle Jack live...where my friends are. I shouldn't even be here. And It's not too late," she thought.

"All I have to do is tell John to back out and drive away from here. He would do it without question. And the two people peering from the doorway would be none the wiser. They would simply think someone pulled in to make a turnaround."

While Deborah embroiled herself in second-guessing, John killed the engine. His doing so startled her. But it was still not too late. On her command, and with one twist of the key, they could be gone. Despite what Aunt Rose said, coming back here was not a wise idea, she thought.

Frozen in place, Deborah stared out the tinted windows, absorbing the view in front of her. She fought to compare the scene to what she had long imagined the place would look like, and drew a blank.

There was no emotional jolt, no new awakening, no rekindling of even a flicker of passion about this place. What Deborah did feel was immeasurable anticipation about seeing Samantha. Her heart simply could not stop pounding. She tried taking deep breaths. Nothing helped.

Deborah saw the children, the house, trees everywhere. She noticed the once familiar porch swing, observed the two female figures standing in the screened doorway. All the images assaulted her consciousness more rapidly than she could reconcile them. Fighting to calm herself, she grimaced, formed fists, dug her fingernails into her palms as forcefully as she could withstand.

"Don't lose it, Deborah. Please, don't lose it," she exhorted herself.

Through the screen door, Maylene and her mother watched impatiently. They observed that neither the car, nor those inside it had moved.

"Whoever it is, they sure ain't in no hurry," said Mabel Davis. "Must know we watchin' 'em."

"Maybe they're lost," said Maylene.

"Wouldn't take 'em that long to figure that out, now would it?"

The pair saw the chauffeur open his door, step out and walk around the rear of the car to reach the right rear passenger door.

"Somebody's gettin' out. A white guy. Young lookin,' too," Mabel Davis noted.

"Kinda skinny to be driving such a big car," noted Maylene.

"He's drivin' the car, not pushin' it, Maylene."

Deborah's door eased open. She slipped on her sunglasses, grabbed her jacket, paused a long moment then stepped out slowly. She turned and gazed over the car's roof toward the house, while donning her jacket. Maylene nudged her mother; their eyes widened. John closed Deborah's door and waited.

"Mama, that's a black woman, I think. That young guy's her chauffeur. She must be somebody. Wonder who? And what's she doing way out here in the Sticks? Must be lost for sure."

"Reckon we 'bout to find out. Bet she ain't from Arkansas. I'll tell ya' that much," Mabel Davis offered.

Deborah was shaking. She took a deep breath, filled her lungs with scented summer air, hoping to ease her apprehension. Realizing she could delay the moment no longer, she started toward the house, step by ponderous step. She felt profoundly alone—a stranger amongst strangers. John looked on from his open driver's door.

"Who is she?" Maylene wondered aloud.

"Nobody we know. That's for sure," said her mother, while the two women kept staring.

No one spoke. The children stopped swinging. All were watching and waiting, as the stranger drew closer. Deborah was about twenty feet from the porch steps when she stopped and removed her sunglasses again. She could clearly make out her mother's image behind the screen door, and had little doubt the other woman was her sister, Maylene. She was certain neither had yet recognized her. And perhaps they would not, even if she spoke to them.

The idea occurred to Deborah to simply ask if they knew the whereabouts of some fictitious family. They would be unable to provide the information. She would thank them and leave. Period.

Deborah had no idea how long she stood staring toward the house and the front door. Suddenly, the screen door flew open, nearly came off its hinges. A piercing scream rang out. Maylene was beside herself. She was leaping up and down, squealing like a banshee.

"Deborah!" she yelled. "Deborah! Oh, my God."

Maylene loosed another piercing scream. She clutched at her chest with both hands. Tears streamed from her eyes. Mabel Davis was startled by her eldest daughter's sudden outburst. The children sat riveted, not sure just what to make of what they were seeing and hearing.

"Mama! Mama! It's Deborah!" screamed Maylene. "My God, it's Deborah! It's her, Mama! Oh, my God."

Mabel Davis clinched her hands into fists, gazed with lips barely parted. Maylene shot farther onto the porch, stumbled forward, leaned against a post for support. She shook like a leaf in a tornado, fought to catch her breath, while clinging to the porch column to steady herself.

"Deborah?" Maylene managed. "Deborah? My God, it *is* you. It's you! It's you!" Maylene's shrill voice crackled. Her face contorted with stunned disbelief. Mabel Davis nearly turned to stone.

Deborah's arms fell to her sides. She shifted her feet, to be certain she was still standing. It was as if her mind and body briefly parted company. Tears formed, even as she cursed them. Maylene bounded down the steps. Halfway down, she wheeled around to face her mother.

"Mama! Mama, it's Deborah! It's Deborah! My God, she's come home!" Maylene shouted. "Deborah's home!"

Maylene vaulted the final steps and rushed to embrace her sister. She grasped her shoulders with both arms extended and stared at her with disbelief. It was nearly impossible for her to fully comprehend what was taking place.

"Maylene." Deborah whispered.

Maylene grasped Deborah's hands—drew her closer. Mabel Davis remained rooted to where she stood.

"You're home! My God, you're...you're home!" Maylene kept screaming. "I can't believe what I'm seeing, can't believe I'm saying these words. You're home! You're standing right here in front of me. Lord, I need to catch my breath. Somebody, please tell me I'm not dreaming."

A teary Maylene pressed a hand to her chest. "I didn't even recognize you at first. Mama didn't either. I didn't even know who you were, until you stopped right here and I got a close look. I saw your face, your eyes. God, just look at you. You look so beautiful. I know I'm repeating myself. I can't believe I'm standing here looking at you!"

"It's me. It's me," said Deborah, her voice thinning. Maylene turned toward the screen door, beckoned to her mother.

"Mama? You comin' out?" she asked plaintively, then turned back to Deborah. "My God. I know I'm staring. Can't help it. Girl, you look like a movie star, I swear. Car, chauffeur, designer clothes, everything. I'm sad to say I wouldn't 'a known you if I'd passed you on the street. That's the truth. Lord, my little sister...a grown woman. Just look at you. Just...just look at us. Guess we're not children anymore, huh? We all lost that, didn't we? Our childhood, I mean." Maylene swiped her cheeks.

"You look well, Maylene. You haven't changed much. Taller, but nearly as thin as I remember. These years have been good to you."

Even as she spoke, Deborah felt her words sounded clumsy. She was unsure just what she felt. Everything seemed dreamlike.

"Thank you," said Maylene. "But I know I could use a make-over. My own daughter talks about me bad...says I'm too plain."

Deborah stole a quick glance at her mother who remained standing in the doorway. "These your kids?"

"Here I am, going on like nobody's here but me and you. Yes, those are my kids. That's Charles; he's eight. And that's Yvonne. I gave her your name...gave her your middle name. She's..."

"Ten. I'm ten," said Yvonne.

"I'm so excited; my heart's beating so fast. Can't even remember my child's age. You kids come here. Meet your Aunt Deborah. C'mon, now." The children hurried forward. "Guess you saw how we were looking at your car when y'all drove up. I told Mama I didn't know who in the world that was. Mama said, I know she's not from Arkansas." Maylene laughed.

"Hello," said Yvonne, standing in front of her mother. Charles hung back some distance away. Deborah grasped Yvonne's hand.

"Hello. You're a beautiful girl, Yvonne. I'm your Aunt Deborah."

"How come I've never seen you before?" asked Yvonne. The question surprised both Deborah and Maylene.

"I've been...been living in Chicago," said Deborah. "It's wonderful meeting you. You look just like your mother."

Maylene turned to Charles. "Come here, Charles. Say hello to your Aunt Deborah. She's seen little skinny, dirty-faced boys before. Come on over here!"

A reluctant Charles obeyed, stopping at Maylene's side and draping an arm around her waist. Say hello," Maylene prompted.

"Hello," said Charles.

"What a handsome young man you are, Charles."

"Thank, you, ma'am."

"They're beautiful children, Maylene. Both look just like you."

"Thanks. I have to give both their fathers a *little* credit, though. But wait 'til you see Samantha. She is so gorgeous. And so sweet. You'll see. She's not here right now, but..."

"Maylene!" Mabel Davis called out.

"I knew Sam's name would get her attention for sure," said Maylene, stepping to one side and leaving a clear path between Deborah and her mother.

For a time, the only sound Deborah heard was the wind rustling through leaves of nearby trees. No one moved. Mabel Davis remained cemented to her spot. Maylene fixed her gaze on her sister and shrugged with disbelief. Deborah stared at the woman in front of her and wept inside. This was not the moment for an outward display of emotion.

chapter twenty-five

Road's End?

===========================

A maze of fuzzy childhood memories invaded her thoughts.

Deborah moved uneasily, and without invitation, toward the aged porch steps. The short walk to the porch seemed to take an eternity. She kept staring at the ground, as if searching for faint remains of her footprints left a lifetime ago.

Her pulse quickened. She clenched her fists, stopped three feet from the door, and wondered how she had gotten that far. There was roaring silence. Not even chirping birds, nor occasional vehicles rumbling down old Crispus Attucks were heard. Words crystallized in her mind, but resisted forming on her suddenly dry lips.

Finally. "Hello...Mother." Deborah managed the words, forcing life into her wavering voice. But the word, "mother," did not come easily; it surprised her. She heard it escape her lips, but it sounded foreign to her, empty. It rang hollow. The estrangement she felt was palpable. It had shape, form and weight. It had substance, approaching tangibility. It was painfully unreal. Despite her best efforts at civility, she and her mother were both strangers. They were all strangers. No amount of pretense could make it otherwise.

Mabel Davis cleared her throat, as Maylene stepped onto the porch behind Deborah. The kids remained at the foot of the steps, staring at the stranger introduced as their aunt. They were fascinated by this beautiful woman in the fancy car. Why had they not met her before?

A numb Mabel Davis was slow to respond. She reluctantly slipped from behind the screen door, stood with her back pressed against the jamb. With fingers laced, she planted herself like an oak, absorbing the sight of this...stranger. But this was no stranger. It was her daughter, now a full-grown woman. A mother, in her own right.

Seconds passed like tortuous minutes. Mabel Davis fidgeted with her hands. Her bottom lip quivered. She bit into it to conceal its movement and steady her nerves.

"Wish I'd known you were comin,' she said, in a subdued, monotone voice that gave away little. The words did not flow with ease. "I look an awful mess. My hair, this ol' dress, this...this 'ol house. I must look terrible. Wouldn't guess I was a preacher's wife."

So these would be the first words Mabel Davis would speak to her after all these years, Deborah thought. Some mumbo-jumbo about her dress, her hair, the house? "How...how are you?"

"And I'm wearin' these ol' beat up house shoes. Ain't like I don't have some new ones. It's just that these here just feel so downright comfortable and all."

"That's not important."

"Mama, I'm sure Deborah don't care 'bout that," said Maylene.

Mabel Davis fussed with her hair, then the dress. Still, she declined to step forward or look directly into her daughter's eyes. Deborah moved closer, but stopped when her mother flinched.

"Well, I reckon you better come on in," said an unsmiling Mabel Davis. She remained beyond arms reach, avoiding eye contact. She held the tattered screen door open as Deborah entered. Maylene followed, closing the door behind her.

"Lord, I cannot keep this screen door fixed for nothing. Those kids keep wantin' to come in and out 'a here without usin' the handle. Mr. Sibley was supposed to come fix it, but he's been busy addin' on to Sister Jeter's house. He'll get around to it sooner or later. I could get Matthew to fix it again. He fixed it last time, but he's been busy paintin' houses all over the place," Mabel rambled.

Once inside, she motioned her second-born daughter toward the old sofa. And with far less warmth than she would have afforded a common stranger. She was likely in shock, although her dour expression offered no insight.

Deborah sat on the edge of the sofa. She cast glances about the room, searching for familiarity, but feeling alien to her surroundings. She felt as if she had been transported back to a past shrouded in uncertainty, locked in the unanswerable. A mute Mabel Davis sat in an upholstered chair across the room. For a strained moment, no one spoke.

"Seems so strange to me, being here," said Deborah, breaking the silence. "Everything's so...big when you're a child. The trees seem much shorter now. The house even seems smaller. And I remember this room."

"I notice those things, too. Funny how that is, huh, Mama?" Maylene said, trying to draw her mother into the conversation. Her effort was fruitless.

Mabel Davis smiled weakly, nodded then returned her gaze to her lap. More awkward silence followed. Deborah continued surveying the room. Old family pictures adorned the mantel above a seldom used fireplace. She saw no photographs of herself, not even her sixth grade class pictures once so prized by her father.

Where were they? She wondered. Deborah remembered her school pictures were always there. Had her name been removed from the family Bible as well? Had the photographs been stored away somewhere, banned from view?

An army of tiny figurines and other dime-store keepsakes were arrayed atop the crowded mantel. Deborah felt a sinking feeling in the pit of her stomach. And again, she wished she had not come.

On the wall, immediately behind the now burgundy, brocade sofa, a framed, velveteen Jesus hung next to a cheap, plastic framed, Woolworth's picture of Dr. Martin Luther King, Jr.

On an adjacent wall, above a newer Sears & Roebuck, Silvertone console stereo, with cassette player, was a colorful tapestry depicting the Lord's Supper. Next to that, was a plastic-framed, faded photograph of President John F. Kennedy. Deborah remembered all except the velveteen Jesus, although she was sure it must have been there in '74.

What was gone was the old, pale green sofa and the thick, yellowing, protective plastic that once covered it. The old sofa was once Mabel Davis' prized possession. Deborah remembered that only grown-ups were ever permitted to sit on the thing.

Deborah shattered the renewed silence. "I see the old 'Churchmobile' is gone. Never thought that would ever happen."

"Churchmo...You're talking 'bout Daddy's old '67 Chevrolet?"

"I think it was a '67."

Maylene laughed aloud. Her mother remained silent. "I forgot all about the Churchmobile. Church was 'bout the only place we ever went in it. Mama, when did Daddy get rid 'a that car?"

Mabel Davis was not anxious to be drawn into the conversation. She heaved a long sigh before answering.

"'Bout six years ago, I reckon. Gave it to Matthew. You remember that," she said, curtly.

"That's right," Maylene continued. "Couldn't believe he did that. Daddy loved that thing; had a name for it: *Buster.* You remember. He called it Buster. Daddy named all his old cars. He named the new one, too. 'Course it ain't really new. Daddy's never owned a new car. It's a 1983 Chevy Caprice...blue. Calls this one Ol' Blue. It just sits there now.

"The Buick belongs to Mama." Maylene kept going nonstop. She was clearly nervous, excited, and not sure what to say. She seemed to feel if she stopped talking, no one else would say anything. "Matthew starts it up every now and then," she added.

Deborah seized the opening. "How *is* Matthew?"

"Hmm. He's fine. Well, let's just say he's better than he was that Sunday you left. Lord, he changed that day, for sure...hasn't been the same since. None of us have. But let me tell you. That afternoon, when we got home, he grabbed that . 22, headed straight out back—past where that old pile of railroad ties used to be. Did-not-say-a-solitary word to anybody. Nothing. Mama called out to him, but he acted like she wasn't even in the same county. Right, Mama?" Mabel was clearly not happy with Maylene. "Girl, I was too scared to say anything myself. Matthew always could get a little crazy sometimes.

"'Bout a hundred yards out, he started firing. He wasn't shooting at anything in particular; he was shooting at everything and everybody. He was aiming at the woods, but the woods weren't his target. While he was out there, Daddy came home. He heard the gunshots and looked out back, saw Matthew, and started out to get him. Mama tried to tell him to just let Matthew be. But you know Daddy. He was dead set on getting Matthew to stop.

"When he got pretty close, Daddy called out to him in a stern voice. Matthew wheeled around, rifle still aimed. Girl, my heart jumped into my throat. We could hear Daddy yelling at Matthew to put the rifle down, but Matthew didn't—least not at first. The two of them just stood there. Seemed like forever. Both looked like they were frozen still. Me and Mama were standing on the back porch...looking and praying. Girl, we had no idea what was going through Matthew's mind. He was just not himself that day, or since.

"We were scared. Least I was. Anything could 'a happened. Matthew was already angry with Daddy. I mean, *really* angry. Finally, he threw the rifle down, and then took off toward Samuel's Oak, walking as slow as he could. He did not run, you hear me? He walked. I think he wanted Daddy to know he wasn't scared of him anymore.

"And he didn't come home until way past dark. Daddy just...just came back to the house like nothing had happened. He was walking real slow, looking at the ground. But you could see something in his face, in his eyes. Something changed between him and Matthew that day, for sure. I remember thinking...he lost a daughter and a son.

"Hours later, Matthew came home, went to his room. Didn't say anything to anybody. And Daddy didn't say anything to *him*. Fact is, neither one had much to say to each other after that day. I cried for both of 'em. Still do. Done a lot 'a crying over all these years. I'm plain tired of it. I'm bone dry. "

Maylene seemed to be reliving the incident, as she recounted the story to Deborah. She told it in a way that made it come alive.

"How is he, now? Where does he live?"

"Matthew's changed a lot. He's a lot taller, heavier, meaner—a good-looking black man, though. He don't live too far from here. Ain't gon' ever live too far from Mama's kitchen," Maylene laughed. "That was him leaving in that little truck, just as you drove up."

Mabel Davis sat squirming and fidgeting. She appeared particularly unhappy with Maylene's detailed answer to Deborah's question about Matthew. She had listened without comment, but not without contorted facial reaction.

"Back to the Churchmobile," said Maylene. "See what happens when you ask me a question? Anyway, Matthew only had Daddy's old car two weeks before he totaled the thing, coming from Fort Smith in the rain. Mama had tried to convince him to not go, 'cause the weather was looking bad all morning. But Matthew was determined to do exactly what Matthew wanted to do, no matter what.

"Daddy was so mad. Matthew didn't have a scratch nowhere, except to his ego. Wouldn't come around here for a month. I live in Little Rock now. I used to call Mama, asking if he'd come by. She'd say *Nooo, child. Not in a while.* Matthew finally got over his embarrassment."

"Is he married?"

"You serious? Matthew? Married? Ain't no sister in her right mind gon' put up with Matthew Jeremiah Davis. He's too ornery. Got a mind like a bear trap. He's gon' be so shocked when he finds out you're here. I can't wait to see it. And Gloria's flying in from Atlanta this evening. You probably wouldn't recognize her. She's the same, except for the glamour-girl look and the big hair. She still pretending she's five-nine, instead of five-four."

Maylene rambled on excitedly. Deborah focused on her mother, hoping to detect some connection with her. Mabel Davis again fixed her gaze on her lap. Maylene observed her. She prayed her mother would say something—behave like a mother happy to see her daughter.

Maylene ended the brief silence. "What about your chauffeur? He's been standing out there a long time."

"He's fine. He's being well paid to wait."

A long silence.

"You don't plan to leave no time soon, do you?"

Mabel Davis broke in. "Maylene, I'm sure your sister would like to go see her daddy right now. And see if that young man out there wants a cold drink or somethin'. He ain't gettin' paid to die of thirst." Maylene suppressed a snicker as she left the room.

Deborah turned to her mother. She spoke in as calm a voice as she could muster. "So how have you been all these years?"

Mabel Davis' blank expression hardly changed. She seemed determined to appear unaffected. Kept looking away, unable or unwilling to engage Deborah's pointed gaze.

"I know you came here to see 'bout your daddy. I'll take you in there directly. But I just...a lot has happened over these years. I'm glad you decided to come see your father. You've growed into a beautiful woman. We sure owe Rose and Jack a lot. The Reverend and me...we did what we thought was right, back then. We prayed about it and..."

Deborah chose her words carefully. "Look —and I really don't know how to address you—I'm not here to make anyone feel guilty. I had to come to see...to see Father. And I have crucial decisions to make."

Mabel Davis' eyes flared. She eased to the edge of her seat, clasped her hands. "Well, for one thing, your daddy can't talk, least not for a while. And as far as Samantha is concerned..."

"You mean, my daughter? My daughter, Samantha? Oh, we'll talk about her. But what about you?" Deborah leaned forward, lowering her voice. "*You* can talk to me. I'm here now. Despite all this time, I really did not expect open arms and a loving embrace. But I do expect something. Am I being unreasonable?"

Deborah paused to give her mother ample space to respond. Mabel Davis said nothing. She just sat there—sat there and said nothing.

"What are you thinking?"

Again, no response. Just an offset gaze. Deborah waited. Silence. She could hear the ticking clock inset, on the framed Lord's Supper picture, grow louder and louder.

"Who do you see sitting here before you? Who am I to you?"

Again, no answer. Just a wringing of hands. Mabel Davis shifted uneasily in her seat. She glanced at the empty doorway, as if hoping, praying Maylene would reappear.

Deborah stood. Mabel flinched again, composed herself quickly, but never looked up. Deborah moved to the front door, gazed out briefly, then returned to sit facing Mabel Davis.

"Please, tell me something, *Mother.*" A long pause. "Did you feel nothing...from the beginning, despite what father said. I mean, as a mother watching her daughter—her own flesh and blood—vanish from her life? Did you not feel something deep down in your soul that said...this is wrong? This is just wrong! Or was your duty, as the obedient, compliant wife, stronger than your instincts as a mother? Or were you the driving force? Tell me! What was it?"

Mabel finally managed a response. "You don't understand."

"Understand? Understand what? What is it I'm not understanding? Please enlighten me."

"You just...you just don't understand. And I can't...I can't really explain it. But..."

Deborah muted her sigh of exasperation, recognizing the futility of further questions. She returned to sit on the edge of the sofa, still staring down her mother. Mabel Davis looked away.

"You can't even say my name, can you?" But then why should you, after all this time?"

Deborah paused.

Silence.

"I have a life. I don't weep anymore," Deborah declared. "I don't mourn for my lost years, not like I used to. But I...I just have so many things to ask you. I just want to know, did you spend nights, even a single night thinking about me, wondering what was going through my twelve year-old mind and heart?" Deborah's voice was rife with emotion. She riveted her eyes on her mother.

Mabel Davis found it hard to hold her daughter's gaze. Frowns lined her wrinkled brow. She began fidgeting with her hands again. Her breathing appeared uneven.

Deborah stood again. "Did you miss me? Did you pray for me...ask God to remove the fear, the shame, and the pain...take all that away from me? Especially after you came to Chicago and took my...my baby away? You cannot know...you'll never know how painful that was. I had no power, no rights—despite having given birth to her. Having Samantha, for even that short time, made me feel needed. Someone really needed *me*. My daughter needed me. And you took her away. You...you took her away. I never saw her...her first steps, heard her first words, have her look up at me and call me..."

Deborah stopped to gather herself, to temper her emotions. She took a deep breath. "But you have to know, I've survived. With the love and care of Aunt Rose, Uncle Jack, and God Almighty, I have survived. And I've...I've mostly turned out okay. I graduated high school on time, with honors. I graduated from college. I have a decent job, one might say. And I...I have grown to not only like, but to love myself. It took a while, but I got there."

Deborah had not realized her fists were clenched, or that she had closed half the distance between herself and the stranger in front of her. She had not intended to vent so emotionally. The words simply erupted from deep inside her.

Yet, as pointed as her words seemed to her, they were quite tempered, not nearly as explicit, nor as explosive as they might have been.
Even so, Deborah quietly chided herself for losing her cool so soon after
arriving. The scowl quickly faded from her brow. Her intense expression softened. It was then, both she and Mabel Davis were interrupted
by the sound of coughing coming from Reverend's bedroom. Mabel
bounded to her feet and bolted from the room. Deborah hesitated, stared
at the vacant doorway, then slowly followed.

chapter twenty-six

Reunion

===============================

"Where are you, daddy?"

T he room.

Inside the large, airy bedroom, with its aging wallpaper and polished hardwood floor, Rebecca and Mabel Davis stood next to the Reverend's dark-mahogany, king-size, four-poster bed.

Across the rectangular room, the big bay window framed the edge of the pine forest, and a gaping swath of pastoral SB-40, like a painting. Deborah stopped just inside the doorway, next to Maylene.

"He coughed twice, turned his head to one side like you see him there," Rebecca explained. "I checked him, and suctioned him. He's okay now. It's a little warm in here, but other than that, he's fine."

Mabel Davis' eyes glistened with hope. Except for minor movement, it had been weeks since the Reverend had so much as coughed. This seemed the positive sign everyone was eager to seize.

"He didn't open his eyes, did he?" she asked.

Rebecca shook her head, no. Deborah avoided looking directly at her father who lay still, beneath the snow-white sheet. She remained only feet from the door, unable to force herself closer just yet.

Deborah felt like an intruder, as she stood looking about the room and reminiscing. A framed picture of her great-grandparents hung over the old oak chest. An army of fuzzy childhood memories invaded her thoughts.

Maylene was quick to observe the distress on Deborah's face. She hurried to her, grasped her right hand, squeezed it gently, and the two inched their way to the foot of the bed.

Deborah draped one hand around the nearest bedpost, closed her eyes then at last permitted her gaze to fall flush upon her father. This was the moment she had at once craved and feared, even before learning of her father's illness. All her earlier imaginings had involved facing him eye to eye, confronting him about fateful decisions that had changed her life forever. But never like this. Not with him unable to even see her, much less respond.

Rebecca noticed Deborah for the first time. "How're you, ma'am?"

Deborah was staring at her father, and so belatedly reacted to Rebecca's greeting. The Reverend bore little resemblance to the man she once knew. His remaining hair was almost completely gray. His face was drawn, his left hand curled, his mouth—twisted, slightly.

"I'm fine. And you?" Deborah finally answered.

"Pretty good, for an old woman. You with the County?"

"No. No, I'm..." Deborah's eyes were fixed on her father.

"I'm sorry, Rebecca," said Mabel Davis, "This here's my daughter, Deborah. She lives in Chicago."

"Sister Davis, I didn't know you had a daughter in Chicago. I knew about your baby girl in Atlanta, about Rachel, and of course, Maylene. Pleased to know you Miss Deborah."

Deborah shook Rebecca's hand then eased closer to her father's side, avoiding a direct view. Her pulse quickened; her palms grew moist, a prickly sensation covered her. Rebecca turned to Mabel Davis.

"Sister, Davis, I checked the Reverend's temperature and blood pressure a few minutes ago. I exercised his arms and legs about an hour ago. I try to keep them from stiffening up on him. I also emptied the U-Bag. Now, he's probably going to need turning before I get here tomorrow, unless you want me to come earlier. Of course, I'll still need help with him. Ain't as strong as I used to be. Getting on up in age. I'll be seventy-eight, come November. Everybody says I don't look a day over sixty-five. Lord, I wish."

"You can come in the afternoon. I'll get Matthew to turn him for me in the mornin', if he comes by."

"You sure?" asked Rebecca. Mabel Davis nodded.

"Guess I'll be moving along. Got groceries to pick up. Would send my husband, but Lincoln never gets what I tell him, and most everything I don't," said Rebecca, gathering a plastic tote-bag containing her purse and personal items.

"Thanks for everything, as always," said Mabel.

"Sister Davis, is the Women's Auxiliary meeting tonight? I promised Sister Jeter I'd let her know."

"Not tonight. Next week, sometime. I'll make the announcement this Sunday mornin' for sure."

"Pleasure making your acquaintance, Miss Deborah. See y'all tomorrow. If it rains, Ray Lee will bring me. I don't drive in the rain."

Ray Lee was Rebecca's only grandchild. She and her second husband, Lincoln, a.k.a. Mr. Six-Fo, had raised him. Mabel Davis accompanied her to the front door.

Maylene remained with Deborah at Reverend's bedside. Neither spoke, until Maylene turned to her sister. "I know we'll talk later, but I have to tell you..." That was as far as Maylene got. Her voice abandoned her. Tears filled her eyes, and she turned to leave.

Deborah followed her to the door. "It's okay," she said, softly.

Maylene forced a smile through her tears. "I'm sorry. Sometimes I'm surprised I have any tears left. My heart...my heart is so full right now. I'm so happy you're here. I prayed for this day."

"It's good to see *you*. But none of this is real for me. I have images I still carry in my mind. I feel...feel out of body, standing here in this room."

"I really do understand. Look, I'll leave you in here with Daddy. Take your time. You didn't come this far to hurry."

"No. Please, stay," Deborah insisted.

"You should have some time alone," said Maylene. She embraced Deborah then left the room, gently closing the door behind her.

Truth was, Deborah did not yet want time alone with her father. She was not ready. Just being in the house siphoned nearly all her energy. Every part of the place was a reminder of not only happy times, but of events leading to those final days and that...that Sunday.

After several moments of deep reflection and self-urging, Deborah returned to the Reverend's bedside. For what seemed an eternity, her teary gaze fell upon a father she had not seen since age twelve—and saw a stranger. That riveting image tore at her heart. The Reverend seemed so diminished, so frail, so...so lifeless.

A surge of pity rose within Deborah. It surprised her, angered her. It angered her because it stood measure for measure against the years of what was undeniably hatred of her father.

Deborah inched closer, and saw this...this man through a kind of emotional haze. With thumb and forefinger, she lifted the top sheet, revealing the Reverend's upper body. She saw his right arm, the I.V. entry, his tightly curled fingers on his left hand. Deborah stared at the I.V. stand and the bottle poised above the bed. Finally, she mustered the strength and the will to touch her father's left hand, then recoiled. There was little warmth, just a cold, lifeless sensation. However, Deborah soon found herself stroking his hand gently, repeatedly—transferring her own warmth. He had no reaction, but the coldness lessened. She covered him.

Deborah shuddered at the realization that this man was indeed her father. Yet, in her mind, it was impossible for her to make the leap from 1974 to 1988 and have it make sense. Any minute, she expected her *real* father would boldly stride into the room—shoulders squared, eyes flashing—and evict this stranger from his bed.

A geyser of emotions swelled inside Deborah. She turned and made her way to the old mahogany dresser. She quickly found herself gripped by her contorted image in the double mirror. A deep scowl etched her brow. She saw narrowed, fear-filled eyes; a portrait of pain and uncertainty. It frightened her.

Deborah tore herself away, turned toward her father, who remained motionless, except for the barely noticeable rise and fall of his chest as he breathed. She stood there, subconsciously breathing in sync with him, until she realized her sympathetic reaction, and forced in a deep breath.

As she made deliberate note of her surroundings, Deborah wondered how she had come to be in this room at all...in this place. This was not Chicago. This was certainly not the home on Yale Street. This was not *her* home, she declared to herself.

It was nearly ten minutes before Deborah returned to her father's bedside. She had long wondered what she would say when she saw him again. What words would she use to tell him of the hurt she had suffered so long? What would he say to her? How could he possibly explain it away? Would he even try?

Reverend Henry B. Davis was always an imposing figure, literally and figuratively. How would she find the courage to say what was in her heart without cowering? All that was now moot.

Deborah remembered how, even at twelve, a frown-filled glance from Reverend could intimidate her so, even though she always knew she was his "little girl." He often told her so. Everyone said so.

"That little girl has got her daddy wrapped around her little finger," they all said. Yet, if that were true, how could he have sent her away— shut her out of his life with such resolve and finality?

"I never wanted to see you like this, Father," Deborah whispered. In that instant, she knew she had, for the moment, lost the battle to suppress her feelings. "I know there were times I wished terrible things. But the words, the vengeful thoughts—they all came from deep hurt and pain I felt, and still feel. All those years, there were so many things I wanted to say to you; so many questions I needed to have answered."

Tears blanketed Deborah's cheeks, some pooling beneath her chin. Others fell like raindrops onto the top sheet covering her father.

"Where are you?" Deborah whispered in a harsh tone, clenching her fists. "Where are you, Father? I want to see the father who sent me away. I want to see the father who wouldn't come to the station the day I left. You let me leave, and never said good-bye. You always said I was your "little girl," but you never even said good-bye to me. That's the father I want to see—the one who excommunicated me from this family.

"That's the father I want to talk to. I need to ask him so many questions. But you're not him. You're not that father anymore. So, whom do I turn to for the answers I need? You? Open your eyes! Open your eyes and talk to me. How dare you? How dare you? You have even denied me this! Both you and God have robbed me again!"

Angry, hurt, emotionally spent, Deborah turned away. She soon found herself in the farthest corner of the room—her back to the Reverend's bed. She took a deep breath, exhaled slowly.

"I am not going to cry, not anymore I'm not. I'm not!" Deborah declared. She shut her eyes against her tears and wiped them away.

Silence. Stillness. A turn from the corner. A gentle breeze. Caressing sunlight from the large bay window filled her gaze. Through the open window, Deborah gazed beyond the old wooden fence, across fields blanketed with wildflowers and tall sweet grass.

An unexpected, even unwelcomed calm sought to invade her spirit. She thought to turn away, but did not. But she was angry, she reminded herself. She had a right to her anger. It was hers. And was well-earned.

Deborah stared toward the edge of the deep pine forest and found herself transported back to a time now lost to the ages. Clinging to feelings she felt justified in possessing, she resisted wishing for those days—days filled with blue skies, and marshmallow clouds—days when she was still the apple of her father's eye.

Those were days that once seemed endless. Gram was alive...always there, always giving, caring, loving, asking nothing in return. Those were times filled with youthful innocence, a world of wonder where wishes came true. Everything seemed so peaceful and poetic then. Time nearly passed unnoticed. But that was then.

Deborah turned from the window and stood staring back at her father across the distance. Part of her wondered about the last time he had gazed at the old forest, at the array of flowers, or at the blue sky, for that matter. Then, another part of her opposed such thoughts.

She also wondered when he last walked up the path to the house and imagined her running to greet him, or remembered her leaping into his arms, as she had done so often. Had he longed for her? If so, why the years of complete and utter silence?

Deborah felt herself wanting to leave the room, but unable to do so. Even in his condition, the Reverend's presence gripped her. She returned to the cluttered dresser, again avoiding looking at her image in the mirror. Momentarily, her eyes fell on a framed, 8"x10" picture of her mother and father. It was taken a month after the two met at a church social in Kirbyville, Texas.

Reverend was born and raised in the small East Texas town. Mabel met him after she arrived there from her hometown of Chattanooga, Tennessee, according to Mabel. She never said much more than that, even when asked about that period of her life. In fact she said little about her past, especially her parents.

In the photograph, Mabel and Reverend appeared so vibrant, so young. Even younger than her own twenty-six years, Deborah thought. And they seemed so much in love.

Another photograph—a special one. Deborah remembered it was always there atop the dresser. It was a frayed picture of Grandpa George and Gram d'lena. She searched for it, but it was nowhere to be found. Where was it? Who would have moved it? Why? Deborah held the framed photo of her parents in both hands for the longest time, before returning it to its place.

The old dresser was always like a treasure chest. Deborah stared at it and remembered. She remembered when, as a child, her parents' bedroom was always forbidden territory—the door, always closed. You did not dare enter, except by invitation. And once the reason for said invitation had been served, you were obliged to leave immediately. No trying to survey the room on your way out, although the temptation to do so was often overpowering.

However, on the rare occasion she dared venture inside without an invitation, Deborah recalled being captivated by the sight of the huge dresser and its large, shiny brass pulls. They were so tempting. What mysteries, what hidden treasures would tugging on them reveal?

Deborah started away, but found herself drawn back. Her eyes focused on the brass pulls again—especially on the top center drawer. She moved closer, glanced over her shoulder as if to assure herself she were not being watched. She then grasped the pull and drew it gently to her.

Finally, one childhood fear was overcome, one childhood mystery soon to be answered. What she saw, stole her breath. Inside the drawer, face up, lay a disfigured Marie. Marie—Deborah's doll given her by Gram d'lena. Marie's once brown face was now half-white. Someone had applied white paint to the left side of Marie's face. The shocking effect was dramatic, mystifying, sobering.

"Why? Who?" Deborah wondered aloud.

A possible explanation leaped to her mind. This could not be the handiwork of an adult. It had to be Samantha. If so, this was perhaps her youthful way of expressing some burning quest for identity, perhaps.

Wait! What about Rachel! Deborah thought of Rachel. She was certainly capable of such a thing. But what would she be trying to suggest? But Rachel would want others to know. She most likely would have thought it ingenious, and wanted others to know of it. Still, the doll *was* hidden away in her *mother's* room.

If past actions were indications, Mabel Davis would do almost anything to protect Rachel. She may have discovered the doll and hidden it. Would she have acted to protect Samantha? Who *was* responsible?

There was no way to know the truth of any of this. And Deborah saw no point in making an issue of it now. She had always intended to take Marie with her to Chicago, and was certain she had placed her doll in her suitcase. Deborah was devastated, when she arrived at Aunt Rose's and discovered Marie was not in any of her luggage.

A concerned Aunt Rose offered to buy her a new doll, one almost as beautiful as Marie. Deborah made it clear, she wanted no other doll; only Marie would do. "It was from Gram," she kept saying. "It was from Gram. Gram d'lena gave it to me."

Rose understood and called Mabel that first night. After informing her sister they had arrived safely, Rose spoke about Marie, and Deborah's disappointment she had been left behind.

Mabel voiced no regard for the disappointment Deborah felt, did not even ask to speak to her daughter. Rose made clear just how distressed she was, but that brought no expressions of concern from Sister Mabel Davis. Rose thought her sister's reaction quite strange, and could not understand her unwillingness to answer questions about the doll.

Although Mabel promised to locate Marie—'it,' as she put it—and send *it* later. Deborah's doll never came. However, Rose did not relent. She brought up the matter on at least two other occasions, but with the same result. No Marie.

Finally, after much effort, Rose convinced Deborah to accept another doll. It was not an easy task.

"Just think, baby. Marie will always be there waiting for you...there to greet you when you return. She'll be right there, all smiling, hair all shiny and everything." Rose knew Deborah was not the five year old she was when Gram first gave her Marie, but felt her simple reasoning would be well received.

It was not easy, but Deborah finally accepted the picture Rose so delicately painted. She finally grew to care about her new doll, although she never gave her a name.

However, a couple of months later, in an act of pure love and kindness, Deborah gave the doll to a five year old girl in Rose's church. The young girl, Savannah, had lost her older and only brother, Malik, and all family possessions, in a tragic fire. She was certain Savannah would treasure the doll as much as she still treasured Marie.

Tears now filled Deborah's eyes. She caressed her beloved doll—her only remaining physical link to Gram d'Iena—and fought to contain her emotions.

She failed. It seemed, for too many reasons, tears were never far away. These were tears shed for the abrupt end of her childhood, for rites of passage, lost forever—rites a young girl experiences as she progresses into womanhood. They were also for a baby she had missed seeing become a young girl, blossom into a teenager; for a daughter she never had the chance to know. The tears were for the mother rooted in her own soul—the mother she had yet to fully become.

And now, if her imaginings were correct, these were tears shed for the pain, and the heartbreaking quest for identity Samantha had surely suffered, and perhaps still suffered.

So what right did *she* have to—for even one moment—consider herself a mother? She had not been there all those years. It was a thought that haunted Deborah. Despite all the reasons, all the knowing, the question persisted like a faint whisper that remains audible despite competing noise. Why would Samantha not hate her...refuse to even see her, let alone accept her as her mother?

A thousand more thoughts invaded Deborah's mind. She kept staring, thinking, wondering about Marie's disfigured face. Minutes passed. She finally eased her beloved doll back into the drawer for now, taking great care to return it to its original position.

Still, she continued gazing at the gripping image, permitting it to sear itself into her consciousness. After a moment, she forced herself to close the drawer, then quietly slipped from the room, deliberately avoiding a parting glance in her father's direction.

chapter twenty-seven

Home

=================

She bore a striking resemblance to Lena Horne...

Deborah had barely reentered the living room, when an exuberant Maylene bolted through the front door. Yvonne and Charles were a half step behind her. The sound of a car engine masked most of what Maylene was saying.

"It's Samantha!" she blurted. "Deborah, It's Sam. Sam's here! Oh God, I hope I don't cry. I try to be tough, but I'm really a crier, girl. Miss Jasmine Baker—Sam's voice teacher—is bringing her home. Hope you're not as nervous as I am. Mama told me not to say a word, so I'm gon' hush my mouth. Don't want her mad at me for a whole month—which is exactly what would happen." Maylene drew a needed breath.

Mabel Davis entered from the kitchen. She paused near the old sofa, peered out beyond the screen door. Deborah clutched her chest with one hand, and eased down onto the sofa. Maylene joined her. Mabel Davis did a half-turn toward Deborah.

"There's something I ain't had a chance to tell you yet...'bout Samantha. I just hope...well, I just hope you don't say anything to upset or confuse the baby."

"I don't understand. What do you mean?"

While Mabel fumbled for an answer, Samantha and Mrs. Baker exited the car and were approaching the house. Both cast curious glances at the Lincoln and its chauffeur as they passed.

Samantha, with sparkling hazel eyes and milky complexion, was a tall, beautiful, soft-spoken 14 year-old with shoulder-length, golden brown hair. There was little doubt of her mixed parentage.

The instant Deborah laid eyes on Samantha, even at a distance, there was a quickening of her heart—a flutter. It was the same feeling she experienced the first time she felt Samantha move inside her womb. It was akin to the feeling that consumed her the moment she first held Samantha in her arms, within minutes of her birth. Now, in the twinkling of an eye, and despite her soaring anxiety, she felt they were again one.

For a moment, Deborah hardly saw Mrs. Jasmine Baker—an attractive, 67 year-old retired teacher, and Samantha's voice teacher—accompany Samantha to the door. *Miss* Jasmine, as most addressed her, bore a striking resemblance to Lena Horne, and had the presence and personality to match.

Mabel Davis and Maylene stepped out onto the porch to greet them. Deborah remained inside with Charles and Yvonne. Jasmine Baker was all smiles, so was Mabel Davis. The latter's effusive disposition; the loving way she greeted and embraced Samantha; the way she ran her fingers through her granddaughter's hair, and stroked her face so warmly, was not lost on Deborah. She was struck by the vivid contrast to her mother's earlier, dour persona, and the one she was now displaying. Maylene took note as well.

"Sister Davis, I want you to know this young lady is developing into a real songbird," Miss Jasmine beamed. "You all should be proud. Hope she keeps it up."

"I will," Samantha promised.

Deborah was beyond nervous. She leaned forward, strained to get a better view of her daughter—her baby, while resisting the temptation to join the others outside. What she felt defied description. Her heart pounded; her palms were soaked; her mind spun with joy, anticipation, and outright fear.

"Samantha's real good 'bout practicin' and everything," said an exuberant Mabel Davis, exuding a mother's pride.

"That's what I want to hear," said Mrs. Baker. I can always tell when she's been doing her homework. And how's the Reverend doing today?"

"I think he's doin' a little better. Hard to tell, though. We just keep prayin' and hopin'...trustin' God."

Maylene was a wreck. She seemed about to burst. Finally, she could keep quiet no longer. "Mrs. Baker, I hope you're not in a hurry. My sister's here. I'd like you to come in and see her, if you got time."

"Aunt Gloria's here?" Sam beamed, clapping her hands.

"No, Sam. She's coming later," said Maylene."

"Don't keep Miss Baker standin' here all evening, Maylene," Mabel Davis broke in. "C'mon in. I know you in a hurry. It'll just take a minute."

"Nonsense. I've got plenty of time."

A puzzled Samantha kept staring toward the doorway. Mabel Davis held the door open as all entered. She then walked past them to stand in the middle of the room. Deborah slowly rose to her feet. An excited Samantha stepped forward. Her eyes locked on Deborah.

Those few seconds seemed a lifetime. Every nanosecond, every nuance was individually experienced and preserved in Deborah's consciousness. She felt flush, as she took in the magnificent image and living presence of her beloved daughter. *Her* daughter—the baby in the bassinet. The tiny human so dependent on her those first few months. How could she possibly be the same child?

This child, so radiant before her, was the past brought rushing into the present. At that moment, Deborah's being in Reedville, her being in this house, her *being, became* real. All second thoughts about having come to Reedville vanished in an instant.

Deborah struggled to resist the overwhelming urge to burst into tears. She now stood near her mother's old rocker, and could only see Samantha. Once again, everyone else faded from the room; only the two of them remained.

The sound of Deborah's pounding pulse filled her ears. Her breathing became halting, erratic. She struggled for at least the outer appearance of calm. Mabel Davis was first to speak. She did so with an energy and volume that appeared to surprise even her.

"Miss Baker, this here is my daughter, Deborah Yvonne. She just got in from Chicago...came to see 'bout her daddy."

Maylene moved to the sofa and plopped down onto the edge of the cushion. Samantha stared at Deborah with laser intensity. Excitement leaped from her face. As Yvonne looked on, she appeared nearly as excited as Samantha. Charles quietly made his way back outside.

"You're my sister, Deborah?" Samantha asked, flashing a huge grin and moving toward her. "You're my sister? Oh, my god! Wow! My sister! I finally get to...to meet you. After all this time, I finally get to meet you. No one told me you were coming. Why didn't someone tell me?" Silence.

"Sister?" Deborah's joy was suddenly overwhelmed by flaming anger and rage—a rage she knew she had to control, if only for the moment. A stunned, pained, curious expression gripped her face, even as she embraced Samantha, whose height nearly matched her own five feet, seven and a half inches. Deborah closed her eyes, squeezed her daughter tightly. She was reluctant to let go of Samantha's own crushing embrace.

"Sister? Sister? She called me sister." Deborah felt all eyes upon her. She replayed the word—mouthed it several times. It was all clear. She now knew what Samantha had been told about her all those years. She smiled, but wanted to scream out the truth as loudly as she could. She dabbed away tears, but thought to take Samantha's hand, and without stopping to pack her clothes, whisk her away, never to return.

With Samantha only inches away, Deborah peered into her daughter's eyes and saw herself. "It's...it's so wonderful to see you, Samantha." Deborah fought to filter the anger from her voice. "I have wanted to see you for...for forever. I can't believe you're standing here in front of me, and...and I'm really looking at you after..." Deborah paused.

"It's so great meeting you, too" said Sam, clutching Deborah's hands in both her own. "Now, I've finally met my whole family. I asked to come to Chicago every summer, but Mama either said we couldn't afford the trip, or that you may be coming back here soon. And I've never met Aunt Rose or Uncle Jack, either. But, anyway... you're here now! That's the important thing. " Samantha locked both arms around Deborah's waist.

"I've thought a...a great deal about you, Samantha. You're...you're beautiful." Deborah cleared her throat, swiped away more tears, and stepped back to take in the sight of this beautiful, bright-eyed teenager, her daughter. That thought was nearly impossible to reconcile.

"This is my daughter," she kept thinking. "I gave birth to this beautiful child standing in front of me. My daughter. Mine. So much of me is there in her face...her eyes. I see myself in her. Am I the only one who sees that? I cannot be the only one," she thought. "Of course, everyone else knows the truth. Everyone, except Samantha."

Deborah had never felt so much rage and contempt for anyone, as she felt for Mabel Davis, just now. It took all the strength she could summon, to bridle her emotions. What should have been a moment of pure joy, had been adulterated. Deborah was determined to focus on the joy.

"Sorry it took so long to meet you," she said, smiling. The words did not come easily. Deborah turned to look at Mabel. She looked away. For the moment, the lie lived on.

"Wait a second," said Mrs. Baker. "Wait, I know this child. Despite that Midwest accent, I well remember you. Don't tell me this is little Deborah? Baby, I was your sixth grade teacher. I can not be the only one here who remembers."

Deborah's smile radiated. The two embraced, just as Charles reentered from outside, slamming the screen door shut. But Deborah could not take her eyes off Samantha. She fought to simply breathe naturally.

"No ma'am. I remember you. You were the best teacher we had in the entire school."

"Honey, I wish you had been around here to remind everybody else of that fact. I likely would not have retired when I did," Miss Jasmine laughed. "My, my. You have grown into such a beautiful young woman. Has it really been that long?"

"Fourteen years."

"I'm nearly fourteen," Samantha blurted. "I must've been adopted right after you moved to Chicago. How come you never came to visit?"

It seemed the air stopped moving. No one spoke. Hardly anyone breathed. Maylene thrust her right hand to her mouth and looked away. Mabel Davis lowered her eyes, cleared her throat. Deborah was visibly affected by the question. Perspiration blanketed her brow. Miss Jasmine immediately took notice.

"Adopted," Deborah whispered. Samantha, Charles, and Yvonne were the only ones who did not grasp the moment. "Adopted." Deborah waited for her heart to begin beating again. "Samantha, you light up this room. You *are* beautiful."

"Thank you, ma'am. I mean, Deborah. I have to get used to having another sister. This is so cool."

"And I'll have to get to know you, too," said Deborah, fighting to steady her voice. "There's so much we have to...to talk about." Deborah glanced at her mother. A nervous Mabel Davis looked away.

"I can't wait. Mom mentioned I had a sister in Chicago. I saw your picture in her photo album once. When you were little, you looked a lot like me," said Sam. Deborah flashed a quick smile, not sure how much of this she could take without imploding.

"Listen, I really should be going now," said Jasmine, looking for an opening to make her exit. "Deborah, it is so good to see you after all these years. Will you be here long?"

"A short while, I think. It all depends on how my father does."

"Of course. Well, I insist you come visit me. Maylene knows where I live. Have her tell you," said Jasmine. Maylene nodded.

Suddenly, Samantha loosed a shrill scream; thrust both hands to her chest, startling everyone. She kept screaming, jumping up and down.

"Samantha!" yelled Mabel Davis. Everyone wheeled to face Sam.

"I don't believe this!" Samantha chortled, bouncing on her toes.

"What is it, child?" Mabel Davis demanded.

"I know you! I know you!" Sam bellowed. "You're Deborah Durrell! Oh God! Mom, she's Deborah Durrell! You're Deborah Durrell! You're the writer," she said, pointing and jumping up and down. "I saw you on television at Janet's house! I saw you! We read your book in school. We read 'Silent Song.' I did a book report on it. Oh, my God!"

Mabel Davis and the others were stunned silent. They stared at Samantha as if she had lost her mind.

"Durrell...Book? Samantha, what are you talking about?" asked Maylene, standing.

Mabel Davis tried to calm Sam as well. "Samantha! Samantha!"

Samantha grabbed both Deborah's hands and continued bouncing up and down excitedly. "It's you! Wow! I knew there was something about you. I couldn't figure it out. I kept staring and staring. Oh!" Sam shrieked. "Wow! I can't believe this. This is too unreal. Mom, this is Deborah Durrell, and she's my sister? God! My friends are going to die. I have a famous sister and no one said anything? Why? How...how is that possible? Didn't you know?"

"Samantha! Settle down," said Mabel Davis. "Settle down! What on earth are you talkin' 'bout?"

Jasmine Baker stepped closer to Deborah and gave her a hard look. "I've read Deborah Durrell. I've read both 'My Path To Forever' and 'Silent Song.' Deborah Durrell is on the New York Times Bestseller's list. But are you, I mean..."

"Yes, ma'am," Deborah whispered.

"Durrell is your pen name?"

"Yes ma'am." Deborah was visibly embarrassed.

"This is so wonderful. It is truly unbelievable, and absolutely wonderful. Nothing pleases a teacher more than having a successful student. This is unbelievable. I'm sounding like Samantha. I'm not in the habit of repeating myself. But I can't help it. If I were as young as Samantha,

I'd be jumping up and down, too. I am so happy for you. Your books are so realistic, so warm and emotional. They don't read like fiction. I cannot wait to read *Where The Winding Road Ends.*"

"Thank you."

"I am so proud. And I pray your father gets better."

Deborah had not expected to find herself the center of attention regarding her career. But here she was. All eyes in the room, including her mother's, were fixed on her.

A smiling Jasmine Baker turned to a wide-eyed Samantha and placed a hand on her shoulder.

"Samantha, I certainly hope you survive all this excitement. I suppose I'll still see you day after tomorrow? And Yvonne, I hope you're feeling better soon. You and Charles. Well, good-bye all."

Yvonne smiled. All Samantha could do was nod yes and grin. Mabel Davis accompanied Jasmine Baker out onto the porch. Samantha fanned herself with her open hand, then dropped to the sofa to catch her breath. Deborah joined her.

"You're Deborah Durrell!" Sam repeated, gasping and clutching her chest. Why didn't I know this? And why not use your real name?"

"Writer's often do that. It's not important, right now. I'm just anxious to hear all about you. I want to know everything."

"And I'm anxious to know more about you, too. I still can't believe you're standing in my mother's living room, and I'm...I'm actually talking to you. You're my sister! I'm trying to process this through my brain." The look on Samantha's face was indescribable. Deborah smiled, even as she fought desperately to not cry."

chapter twenty-eight

When It Rains

The mention of it cast her into a dark place.

A solemn Mabel Davis stood on the porch and waved good-bye, as Jasmine Baker eased away in her brand new, midnight-blue, Cadillac motorcar. Miss Jasmine was looking all fine and regal. Always did. Even at sixty-seven years, she still turned heads, made tongues wag—even caused a few hearts to flutter.

Unbeknownst to her there were men, years her junior and senior, who sinned in their hearts at the sight of her. They were left wondering how even more beautiful she must have looked years before. Her flawless, creamy-brown skin was as taut as any forty year old's, perhaps more.

Miss Jasmine surely had her share of catty, female detractors, though none ever offered a reason for finding fault with her. She was not pompous, conceited, or anything of the sort. Most anybody in Reedville County would attest to that. She just...had a special air about her. And she always drove Cadillacs. Said they suited her just right; said her aim was to look as good moving as she did standing still. And she surely did.

Mabel Davis turned to reenter the house, when a red BMW 320i, trailed by a billowing dust cloud, turned off Crispus Attucks and onto the Davis property. It pulled hard onto the yard, and lurched to a sliding stop next to the Lincoln.

Jeb Liddy, a paunchy, tree-stump of a white man in his early forties, popped out in a flash. He wore brown khaki slacks, a white short-sleeve shirt with button-down collar, a blue necktie—loosened, and a slightly frayed, wide-brim straw hat. Mabel Davis did not recognize the car or the man.

Liddy ripped a crumpled white handkerchief from his rear pocket, dusted his car's hood, wiped his brow. He gave the big Town Car a curious glance before starting toward the house, clutching a manila folder in his left hand. Mabel Davis waited, gripping a porch column and shading her eyes with her free hand.

"Yes sir. What can I do for you?"

"How're you ma'am? Real scorcher we got today, ain't it?"

"Reckon we seen hotter. What can I do for you?"

Liddy propped one foot on the middle step and removed his hat, revealing his partially bald dome. He wiped his head and brow, replaced his hat and leaned forward, resting a forearm on his leg.

"Well now, Ma'am, I would really like to speak to the man of the house, if I may."

"Afraid I didn't get your name," said Mabel Davis.

"Oh, sorry ma'am. Here's my card." Liddy removed a business card from his shirt pocket, handed it to her. She accepted it with clear trepidation, examined it closely. "Name's Liddy—Jeb Liddy, Reed Development Comp'ny. We own this property and most of the rest 'round here. Y'all rent from us—the Reed Comp'ny, that is."

Mabel Davis studied the card then started to return it to Liddy. He motioned her to keep it. "Mr. Liddy, we pay our rent on time. Always have. Most often, we pay a few months ahead of time. Rent's not due for two months. If you'd called, I could 'a saved you a trip out here to the Sticks. And that little shiny red car of yours wouldn't be gettin' dirty and banged up on that ol' beat up road there. Road's pro'bly a lot better where you live. Didn't y'all get the payment?"

"My visit's not about rent, ma'am."

"Name's Davis—Mrs. Mabel Davis. My husband is the Reverend Henry B. Davis, Pastor of The Shiloh Missionary Baptist Church. Expect you would 'a known that."

"Yes ma'am. Mrs. Davis, I'm pleased to make your acquaintance. Now, may I speak to your husband—the Reverend?"

"Reverend's not well. You'll have to speak to me."

"Fine."

Liddy removed a sheet of paper from the folder tucked under his arm. "Here's a copy of a letter we sent to you folks, I guess 'bout two months ago, according to the date here."

Mabel Davis took the letter and examined it carefully. While her mother read, Maylene appeared at the screen door.

"As you can see there," Liddy continued, "this property, well as other SB-40 property as far as you can see, is to be developed. Vacation of, that means leaving of said property—this property—is to be effected within sixty days of notice. Failure to do so will result in service of a writ of unlawful detainer and forcible eviction by the duly appointed Sheriff of Reed County. Same letter was sent to your neighbors more than a month and a half ago. We never heard back. So we figured there were no questions."

A frowning Maylene threw open the screen-door and joined her mother on the porch.

"What is it, Mama?"

"Ma'am, it's a letter telling your mama..."

"My mama? Excuse me. I'm talking to my mother—Mrs. Davis, to you. Thank you, very much" said Maylene. Liddy took a slow step back and wiped his brow again.

"I never got any such letter," said Mabel Davis. "And none of my neighbors ever said a word about any such letter. If they'd gotten something like this, they would 'a said plenty."

"I'm very sorry, ma'am. Y'all got less than two weeks to vacate the premises. Otherwise, forced eviction will be the order of the day."

"You sayin' we got 'a move? After more 'n thirty odd years...takin' care of, and addin' on to this place, is that what you're sayin'?"

Liddy stood straight up, took a couple of nervous steps backwards.

"You seem a little jumpy, Mr. Liddy."

"I'm just...actually now, this is not my saying all this, ma'am. I'm just doing my job."

"You done?"

"I also have this other document I have to leave with you, ma'am."

Liddy removed an eviction notice from the folder and handed it to Mabel Davis. Maylene cast a brief glance back at Deborah, who remained inside. Deborah took note and stepped out onto the porch. She was reluctant to do so, but felt oddly compelled. Maylene handed her the first letter, while Mabel Davis examined the eviction notice.

"This says we got to quit or something."

"It means move, ma'am."

"In ten days?" Mabel Davis read aloud. "Who sent you out here with this? How do we know you who you claim to be?" she asked, handing the notice to Maylene. Deborah looked on.

Liddy grew noticeably more nervous. "Everything's on this here card," he said. "And the letter says who I am. Phone number's right there. You're welcome to call my office, if you like."

"Mr...." Maylene began.

"Liddy. Jeb Liddy, ma'am, Reed Development Comp'ny."

"Mr. Liddy, my family has lived on this property more than thirty years. Their rental agreement has been in force for every bit of that time. They've remodeled this house three times, at their own expense."

Liddy appeared unsympathetic, despite his initially cordial manner. "I understand, ma'am. Y'all also have to understand that such an agreement can be terminated at the discretion of the landlord. I am certain the rental agreement, and its amendments have been looked into by our Corporate Counsel. Otherwise I wouldn't be here."

"Who's the head of your company?" asked Deborah. She felt drawn in by Liddy's dismissive manner toward Maylene, if not her mother. After all, they were just women, and black at that.

"Ma'am, you mean, our Corporate Counsel?" asked Liddy, adjusting his glasses, straining to get a closer look at his questioner.

"That's not at all what I asked. Who is your Chief executive officer, and or President?"

"That would be Mr. Jonathan Reed. He's President. His father, Mr. Richard Reed, is Chairman and CEO. But you won't be able to talk to either one of them, of course. Others handle these matters."

Deborah's eyes flared. The unexpected mention of Jonathan's name angered her. Her mother and sister exchanged knowing glances.

"Jonathan Reed?" asked Deborah in a subdued voice.

"That's right, ma'am. I'm really not obliged to do anything except deliver these papers. I've said 'bout all I have to say. I suggest you call the office and speak to a Mr. Bud Shuttlesworth. His number is right there."

"You may go, Mr. Liddy. Be sure and tell your employer that our attorneys will be in touch." Deborah pointedly advised.

"Attorneys?" Liddy's eyes widened.

"Attorneys."

Liddy doffed his hat, swiped his head again, then beat a quick retreat to his car. He kept glancing back over his shoulder, nearly tripped just as he reached for his car's door handle.

A downcast Mabel Davis reentered the house, leaving Maylene and Deborah standing on the porch. They watched her until she disappeared from view. Maylene quickly grasped Deborah's hand and led her down the porch steps.

"I know you want to see a lot more of Sam right away, but come with me. It won't take long. See if you remember any of this."

So reluctant was Deborah to leave Samantha, she first thought to ignore Maylene, but followed. The two reached the grounds, then started toward the old log fence separating the front lawn from the fields. Deborah kept staring at her sister, and wondering who this...this person was.

Meanwhile, Yvonne and Charles carried another cold drink, and more oatmeal-raisin cookies to John. He still had the car running, the air conditioner cranking full blast. By now, he had finally removed his suit jacket, tossed it across the front passenger seat, and was listening to an Otis Redding cassette on the car stereo.

chapter twenty-nine

In The Company Of Strangers

====================

"The lying started from day one,"

Captivating! The view that greeted Deborah
and Maylene came straight from National Geographic. Brilliant green
countryside, majestic trees, branches swaying in the warm wind. Colorful wildflowers carpeted acre after rolling acre. Thought-filled silence
prevailed. Maylene, and Deborah—now minus her jacket—trudged
along the faded path taken a thousand times as kids: the shortcut to
Gram's old house. The walk ushered in a rush of recollections.

During endless summers filled with endless hours, and space not
limited by boundaries, the Davis children would explore and roam at
will. Reverend imposed few rules on their playtime, as long as assigned
chores were done, and done well.

Deborah searched for familiar landmarks. However, except for the
overgrown path along the aged fence line, she found few she could be
certain about. Maylene kept asking if she remembered this or that area,
a particular turn in the path along the old fence.

Following another spell of silence, invaded only by persistent rustling of leaves, the sisters headed up a gentle rise toward a dominating landmark visible for miles. A tree. A massive, towering, oak tree dedicated to their deceased brother, Samuel. Deborah recalled that when she was eight, Matthew carved all their names deep into its trunk. Time had finally obscured the markings.

Maylene was still seething over Jeb Liddy's unexpected and ill-timed visit. The timing could not have been worse. Deborah had other thoughts.

"Mama and Daddy don't have a lawyer, and no money to get one," Maylene lamented. Deborah did not immediately respond.

"We'll...we'll try and find one," she belatedly offered.

"Ain't no white lawyer around here gon' go up against the Reeds. And the only black lawyer I know personally is Tommy."

Another name from the past all but leaped out of the shadows. Deborah's eyes widened. "Tommy?"

"Tommy Williams. He was that cute boy in the eighth grade. You remember him. He was tall, shy...had a little afro, and had this monster crush on you."

"*The* Tommy Williams I knew...is a lawyer in Little Rock?"

"No. New York."

"But that won't help here."

"He's got a home in Little Rock. His mother lives there. When his daddy died, he bought it for her. Paid cash, too. I hear he's a big time lawyer...represents athletes, actors, music stars," said Maylene.

"Sounds like he's a sports or entertainment attorney."

"Maybe. Anyway he's extremely single and real good looking."

"Good for him," said Deborah. "Tommy Williams. Help is certainly needed. And quickly. Someone not intimidated by the Reeds. Someone not afraid to represent us."

"You said *us*," Maylene smiled. "You said *us!*"

"I only meant..."

"Tommy usually spends the first part of every summer in Little Rock," Maylene continued, tilting her head to one side and smiling.

Deborah folded her arms and loosed a loud sigh. "So, I'm her sister? My daughter, Samantha, believes I'm her sister?" Deborah's eyes practically glowed red. "All these years, that's the lie she's been fed, and you went along with this, Maylene? All of you? No one told her the truth? Who are you people?"

Maylene clutched her chest. "Deborah, I can't blame you for feeling..."

"All this time, I...I imagined she felt I had abandoned her...didn't want to have anything to do with her. And...and this?"

Maylene bowed her head, wrung her hands, did nothing to stem the flow of tears streaming down her face. I can't tell you how terrible I feel and have felt...so beat down, for so long by what went on here."

Deborah hardly heard her sister. "I am trying to stay calm, as in control of my feelings as I can...not march into that house, take my daughter, and leave this...this place. It's impossible to explain what I'm feeling. I look at you, at your mother, this place and I feel...I feel alien. I'm a stranger. A few hours cannot erase fourteen years of exile. The twelve years I spent here are now worlds away. There is no bridge leading from there to here."

"No, no. I can see one. I can. We just have to..."

"It's an illusion, Maylene. And I will not embrace illusions. Truth is, nothing good can come of my staying here longer than necessary. I've seen father. He can't answer my questions...tell me why he sent me away. Did he ever talk about that, ever explain that? Did mother? If so, I'd like to know. And I never heard from any of you. Why?" A brief, agonizing silence. Maylene had no answers. "I've seen mother, you—everyone except Matthew and Gloria. I want to see them, but my main purpose is to spend as much time with my daughter as I can. There are decisions to be made before I return home."

"Back to Chicago? You can't mean that. You *are* home. We can..."

"Home? It's clear everyone has been living their own lives without allowing for even my existence. Whatever part Samantha and I play in each others lives will depend on many things. I am determined to have her know who I am. But I'm...I'm afraid. I have to do this the right way."

"Deborah, I understand how you feel. I..."

"I wish that were possible, Maylene. I'm sure you *want* to. But even I don't understand. I don't mean to take out everything on you alone. In many ways, I feel that all this talking is pointless. It's more important that I ask the questions, than get any answers. I doubt I could trust any answers, anyway. Even before Samantha was *taken* from me, I lost all connection to this place, to my...my birth family. I died. I died, Maylene. And I had to rebirth myself."

"But we're still your family," Maylene pleaded.

"Family? For all these years, *my* only family has been Aunt Rose and Uncle Jack. Aunt Rose struggled to help me keep my feelings of abandonment, my deep hurt, my intense anger from turning into hate and resentment. I owe both of them more than I could repay them in two lifetimes. Family? *They're* my family.

"I take no pleasure in the truth of this. But after a time, I didn't want to hear any of your names spoken. And yes, I even changed my last name. Just hearing it spoken was a painful reminder. Can you understand that? I wanted to forget this place." Deborah paused to steady her voice. " I constructed new realities that allowed me to feel wanted and loved. I even forced myself to surrender thoughts of reuniting with my own daughter. I created a new world. This feels so...so strange. I hear myself pouring this out to you, and I ask...why? We were children when we last talked to each other this way—sharing our innermost thoughts and all." Deborah briefly looked away.

"I missed that so much," said Maylene. Her voice faltered. "We always shared things. The sharing made me feel needed, important—like a big sister. That meant a lot to me. And you always seemed to look up to me. All these years, I've felt I failed you...let you down. Deborah, I want you to talk to me about it...whatever is on your heart."

"It's hard to talk about this. But I had to come here. I had to come, for my own well-being...to move on."

Maylene's eyes teared. She grasped her sister's hands, then embraced her tightly. Neither spoke for a time. Maylene took a small step back, wiped her eyes with open palms. Deborah waited, unsure what to expect next. "We ahh...haven't spoken about Rachel at all," Maylene said. Understandably, she felt the need to redirect their conversation.

Deborah's jaws clenched. She turned to face her sister squarely. The fact Rachel's name had not come up had not escaped her. Rachel was perhaps the most estranged of all her family. The two had never been remotely close. Theirs was an arms-length relationship Deborah never understood. She had no idea where Rachel was now, or how she was.

"Rachel." Deborah mused. She had not spoken her name once in all those years. Not once. The mention of it conjured up unwanted thoughts. "Let me ask you something, Maylene. Do you have any idea why she always had such hatred for me?"

Maylene appeared surprised by the question—taken off guard. She let the words resonate. "Hate?"

"Hate."

"God, I do wish I knew why she seemed to resent you so much. I don't know if *hate* is the word I'd use. But I have to rely on how you feel."

"It was hate," Deborah insisted. "Hate. And I never understood why. I honestly do not recall a single warm moment we shared. I do remember one thing: the snide remarks she often made about my...my color."

"Color?"

"My skin color—the fact my skin is lighter than the rest of yours. You never noticed the difference? Rachel certainly did. And I had no choice but to take notice. I heard others mention it often enough. I never thought I was *that* much lighter. But I used to wish I were darker, like I remember Matthew, or mother, even father, for that matter. I'll be honest, I used to wonder why I was different."

"That's just the way you were born. That's true for all of us."

"I know that. I knew it then. But I wanted to be less different. There were many who made a big point of my appearance—my color, my hair texture. Well-meaning folk would say: *You're such a pretty girl, such gorgeous eyes. I just love your skin, baby. And you've got such good hair. What a beautiful little doll you are.*

"I know they thought they were complimenting me. But they were saying all these things about features I had nothing to do with. The truth is, I longed for a few kinks, here and there. I never said much about it. But when I was younger, it bothered me a lot—the talk and all. If I'm truly honest with myself, I have to admit it made me feel like...like..."

"Like what?"

"Like I didn't fit in completely. Not with the rest of you. And the...the venom Rachel heaped on me just made it worse. Then, as if that were not enough, well...1974 happened." A long, palpable silence followed.

"I never really knew all this," said Maylene. "

"How could you not have known?"

"I never questioned the difference in your color...your hair. I did hear stuff, but I...I ignored it. Black folk are like a...a chocolate rainbow, right? I mean, we all know Gram d'lena was about your color. Grandpa George was darker...looked more like daddy," said Maylene. "Daddy is not as dark-skinned as mother. And on, and on, and...you know? I never understood the obsession people have about this. It pains me that you felt any way different...for something you had no control over. It's crazy."

Deborah briefly turned away, then back to Maylene.

"It's amazing."

"Amazing?"

"Amazing that I'm standing here talking about all this to you. I have not talked about this to anyone, except Aunt Rose. I've rewritten my life history just to...to survive, emotionally. But standing here, it's like I'm back there—back in the past. And it's real...too real. All of it.

"When I think about that part of my childhood, I cringe. I'm angry, fearful just wondering what Samantha must be experiencing everyday. I ask myself: What has her life been like? What mean things have been whispered about her, behind her back, to her face. How does she see herself, other than as a young girl who does not know who her real mother is?

"And I wonder how much worse it would be if Rachel were around her. How would she treat her, knowing she's my daughter? If my being different, so-called *high yellow* or *yella*, as they say—and I hate those words—if that was part of what made Rachel treat *me* the way she did, then what about Samantha?"

Maylene drew a deep breath. "She's here."

"Who's here?"

"Rachel."

"Rachel? Here in Little Rock?"

"No, here...in this house. Right now...in Matthew's old bedroom. Been living here for the past year. She tried to talk Sam into giving her *our* old room, but Sam wasn't having it. Rachel stays in that room nearly all the time. Hardly ever comes out. I'm sure she knows you're here, though. Question is, whether you'll even get a chance to see her."

Deborah was stunned. Maylene could see the shock etched on her face, the look of incredulity in her eyes. Before Deborah could ask, Maylene hurried to explain. Rachel's sudden return to the family home was not a result of their father's failing health. It was due to several, traumatic events in Rachel's own harried life—events that sent her spiraling into an emotional meltdown.

Rachel, a Jackson State University graduate with a degree in education, appeared to be headed toward a successful teaching career, and a happy life. She was engaged to be married, was working at an elementary school in Jackson, Mississippi. Six months later, her fiancé, Jamile, abandoned her during the fourth month of her unexpected pregnancy. He offered no explanation.

Two months later, he resurfaced and begged to be forgiven. It soon appeared they would reconcile and continue their wedding plans. But tragically, during an armed robbery attempt, would-be thieves murdered Jamile just outside the entrance to a 7-11 convenience store. He had stopped to buy beer. The killing was wanton and senseless.

Rachel was devastated. She plunged into deep depression. Near the end of her fifth month, she attempted suicide with an aspirin-alcohol overdose. She lost the baby and never recovered, emotionally.

"No! I don't want to hear anymore."

Deborah placed a hand on Maylene's arm. "As awful as all this is, I'm unable to relate to this as having happened to someone I know. And I can't help thinking that I've been living in my own hell. Rachel is someone I don't know. I don't think I ever really knew her. As terrible as this may sound, after hearing all this, I feel as if I were reading about it in a newspaper...watching it on television. I'm sorry, I have to be honest."

A lengthy silence followed. Maylene and Deborah peered into each other's eyes, both were searching for that *something* neither could define. Perhaps a sign of connection—reconnection.

"I still can't argue with any of that. And you're right about one other thing," said Maylene. "None of us can ever understand what you've felt all these years. And there is no way to explain how or why all this has gone on, even into our adulthood.

"Me and Matthew were talking about that earlier, before you came. Some things just make no sense, and cannot be explained no matter how you try to fix it up. This is certainly one of them. And I feel so guilty."

"I am not here to make anyone to feel guilty. Feelings of guilt are a matter of conscience, for those who have one."

"And I do. But I'm just hoping there's enough living left for us—time to change things, right the wrongs. I pray we still have a chance at a future—a real future. That's what I pray for everyday. Always have. Most of our lives are still in front of us, right? Deep in my heart, I believe that. I also realize we have to face the past. And I thank God you're here. Deborah, you can't just leave. You belong here. As hard as that may be to know, we deserve to be whatever family we can still be. Besides, we've...we've never even gone shopping together." Maylene loosed a nervous giggle.

"Imagine that." Deborah forced a weak smile.

"And on top of everything else, we got to deal with the Reeds now."

"I'll...I'll see what I can do. Then I have to move on."

"I understand." Maylene was excited, and surprised.

"Maybe I can provide a retainer...find a lawyer. Right now, I think I'll go hug my daughter for a long time, then release my prisoner out there, go to the hotel and get some rest. I'm at the Capital on Markham."

"It's a shame," said Maylene.

"What is?"

"That it took Daddy getting this sick, before we...before we could come together again. I don't know why it always happens this way. And he's not really getting better. Mama can't even see it."

"Why did she bring him home so quickly? If it was because the insurance coverage exhausted, I'm sure a thousand people, here and around the country, would have...Nevermind. So, everyone's praying, I'm sure."

"Night and day. Prayer chains everywhere. Mama's relying on her faith. I don't know who she would be without him. I can't imagine Daddy not being here, either. Parents suppose to live forever. I'm sure you never expected to see him this way. "

Deborah checked herself quickly. "No. In fact, I wasn't sure I'd ever see him, or any of you again, period. But you're right. When I walked into that room, I didn't see the man lying there...as my father. I couldn't. Not the way I remember him. *That* man is now a stranger to me—an imposter. I mean, I know it's him but...it's impossible to explain."

Maylene looked away briefly. "He should 'a stayed in the hospital. At least there, he had a chance of getting better. Not here. I know the insurance ran out, but..." Maylene stopped abruptly.

Deborah carefully measured her next words. "Listen, I ahh...I'll take care of any medical costs, if that would help you convince...your mother to hospitalize him again. I agree with you. He needs around the clock, expert medical care."

Maylene was taken off guard. "You would do that? I mean, it could cost thousands—tens of thousands."

"I could and...and would. You may mention it to Sister Davis; see what she says. But it has to come from you, not me."

"I will. I will. And God bless you, Deborah. You know, I've been trying to imagine how you must feel being here. I wondered how I would feel—if I would've had the courage to come back, considering everything that's happened. I don't know the answer."

"It was not easy. And it's not easy now. I'm at war with myself, with my feelings. I'm happy seeing my daughter. But I'm angry, I'm confused, I'm trying to not hate anyone. I don't belong here...in this place, in this family. I noticed even my photos have been removed. When did that happen?" Deborah paused. Maylene lowered her gaze. "I don't expect an answer. Before I left Chicago, I kept telling myself to rid my mind of the slightest expectations. Reality seldom equals the expectation. I stood in that front yard and I looked around, curious to see if I would feel some spark of reattachment to the place of my birth."

"Did you?" Maylene's query had a hopeful ring.

Deborah closed her eyes, tilted her head up for a moment. "No. And I shouldn't allow myself to even wonder about those things. The only feeling of attachment I value now...is to my daughter."

Maylene's expression fell. "No one else?"

"No. Why should I? What I want is to know myself, who I am in the deepest part of me. I want a quiet place where no one has expectations of me, and I have none of myself, except to lose myself in my writing. And I want to know my daughter. Nothing is more important."

Maylene briefly glanced away. "I have so many regrets about what amounts to half our lifetime already."

"Maylene..." Deborah had wanted no part of sentimentalities.

"I can't begin to tell you what it means having you here," Maylene went on. "And now this thing with the house. I'm sure Mama's glad you spoke up. Maybe we can talk to the Reeds, get them to change their minds. Maybe get them to sell just the land the house sits on."

"I don't think that's going to happen," said Deborah. "You all need an experienced lawyer to act quickly. Maybe there's some loophole in the agreement. I'll make some calls when I get back to my hotel...come up with some plan we can discuss when you stop by. I'll do what I can, make the decisions I have to make regarding my daughter, then I'm gone."

Maylene seemed conflicted. "I'd love to go back to your hotel with you right now. But Mama would swear I had abandoned her and dumped the kids on her. She usually doesn't mind keeping them. All this has made her nerves real bad. She gets real frustrated...ain't always fun to be around. There's a lot on her mind these days, especially now. Visiting you at your hotel sounds great. You coming back tomorrow, right?"

"Yes. I have to see my daughter. I need time—time to decide just what to say to her. More than anything, I want as much time as it takes. And I do want to see Gloria and Matthew. After what I heard earlier, I'm not sure how or where to begin." Deborah looked away to conceal the anger--driven tears welling in her eyes.

Maylene eased an arm around her sister's shoulder. "She's a doll, ain't she? Sam's always acted more like a big sister than an aunt to Yvonne and Charles. She's always seemed so mature for her age, even when she was just a little girl. And speaking of Matthew, I wouldn't be surprised if he showed up at your hotel, once he knows you're here. I would 'a called him, but he doesn't have a working phone."

"I'm anxious to see him. Tell him I said so."

"I will. You two were always so close. And he's been so protective of Sam. Guys are afraid to even look in her direction. He's the same way with 'Yvonne, too."

"Sounds like Matthew."

"Speaking of Matthew..." Maylene's smile faded; her expression deepened. "You asked me if he was married. And I said, ain't no sister in her right mind..."

"I remember."

"Well, I couldn't really say all I wanted to say about that, what with Mama sitting there and all. The truth is, there was one young girl who would have married him. I have no doubt. And Matthew surely would have asked her, someday."

Deborah's saw tears well in Maylene's eyes. "You say *would have.*"

Maylene hesitated. "You have to bear with me. I always get a little...actually, more than a little teary whenever I talk about it." She looked away briefly, took a deep breath, and forced a smile that soon disappeared.

chapter thirty

A Love, Lost

"I have never heard him speak more eloquently than when he speaks of her."

"Nearly two years after you were... after you left, Matthew met this wonderful girl."

"Where? Here in Reedville?"

"No. In Little Rock. One Sunday, Daddy took him to a revival at Mt. Moriah Baptist Church. Matthew huffed and puffed...didn't really want to go, but had to go anyway. Afterwards, he was glad he did. 'Cause that's where he met Joyce."

"Joyce?"

"Joyce Marie Whiting—the love of his life. The minute he and Daddy got back, we could tell something had happened. And it wasn't because of the Holy Ghost, that's for sure." Maylene threw her head back and loosed a hearty laugh.

Deborah listened, while Maylene told how Matthew's meeting Joyce that Sunday changed his life. Joyce's father, Reverend Jeffrey Whiting, Sr. had recently moved his family, including wife, Helen; his only son,

Jeffrey, Jr., and only daughter, Joyce, to Little Rock where he assumed new duties as pastor of Mt. Moriah."

"Where were they from?"

"Houston. Fourth Ward, in Houston. For Matthew, it was love at first sight, girl. I'm telling you, from that day on, every other word was Joyce Marie, Joyce Marie. And when we all met her a month later, we knew why. Mt. Moriah visited Shiloh one Sunday, and they had dinner here at the house. Poor 'Brother' had no chance whatsoever. He was smitten for sure.

"She was an amazing young girl...was so beautiful, 'bout my color, 'bout my size, not quite my height. Had long black hair she kept pinned in a loose bun, sort of. And had these...these dangling curls that fell away on both sides of her face, and in the back. She was beautiful. I know you hear people say that, but she truly *was*—inside and out.

"And she had such a sweet, gentle spirit. The two of us got to be real good friends. She said I was like the sister she never had. Was soft-spoken, had bright, dancing eyes—a doleful look that...that just warmed your heart. She was somewhat shy, but had an inviting personality...a laugh you couldn't forget. She had brains and beauty...very smart. But she never flaunted it. Reminded me of you in so many ways. And loved her some Motown, especially Smokey. I think that made Matthew just a little jealous, if you ask me. He tried not to show it, though.

"At the time, Matthew was...he was sixteen; so was Joyce. All that serious, tough, no-nonsense side of him had to give way to a side we had not seen before. He was always caring, concerned—always looked out for folk he cared for. You remember that about him. But this was a new Matthew. He plain fell in love with her, and she fell in love with him. It was truly something to see."

Deborah's heart brimmed as she listened. She was hearing and seeing a dimension of her brother she had missed witnessing for herself, but had often wondered about.

"Matthew found every reason he could, to go to Little Rock. He even joined the choir, the science club, the baseball team. I'm sure he enjoyed all that. But it also meant he could get to Little Rock, whenever Carver competed with Central High. Joyce enrolled there that September, after all her papers were transferred from Jack Yates High School in Houston.

"By the time he was seventeen, he had his driver's permit and was bugging Daddy to let him drive on his own. But Daddy said he had to wait 'til he was eighteen. That nearly killed him. He could not wait, girl. You hear me?

"Of course, that didn't stop him from getting to the big city, by hook or crook. And when he did turn eighteen, he would talk Daddy into letting him drive Buster to Little Rock every chance he got. That boy put so many miles on that car. We were all surprised Daddy gave in to him like he did."

"So what happened? Why did they break up?" Deborah was anxious to know everything." Maylene grew silent.

"Now, this is the part that...that breaks my heart."

"Why?"

"Joyce was a...a brilliant student. Matthew was so inspired by her, his grades shot up. He even became a member of the Honor Society. Now, we all knew Matthew had the potential, but he was so tied up rebelling against Daddy and just...just being Matthew, he never gave it a chance to develop. Not until Joyce Marie came along.

"She was offered scholarships to some big schools: Stanford, UCLA, University of Texas, Harvard...in mathematics. For her, math was like breathing. She decided on a full, four-year scholarship to UCLA. Matthew was happy, but sad about her going away. But he adjusted, thanks to Joyce assuring him 'bout their relationship.

"Anyway, she was done with all her courses by January. Her brother, Jeffrey had graduated the year before; he was a year older. He had moved back to Texas to attend the University of Houston. Joyce left to visit relatives there that spring. She was only supposed to be gone for only a week." Maylene's voice grew thin. Her speech slowed, and her eyes teared badly. "We never...we never saw her again, after that."

"Why?"

Maylene took a deep, breath and closed her eyes for a few seconds. "Because...because she was killed."

"She was..."

"Killed, murdered...shot down in cold blood."

Maylene barely finished her sentence before the tears burst through. Deborah's heart sank. For a moment, silence ruled.

"My God! Why? What happened? Who..."

"A guy—some twenty year-old who lived in Joyce's neighborhood in Houston...had gone to Jack Yates. He claimed to be in love with her...had assumed a relationship that was never there. We later learned he had been angry when the family moved...even threatened to follow her here. Guess no one took him seriously. When he found out she was back in Houston, he called, said he wanted to see her...wish her the best.

"He went over to her aunt's house. Joyce Marie was there alone with a younger cousin, who was in one of the back rooms. Her brother, Jeffrey, had just left...hadn't been gone ten minutes. The young girl-cousin said they talked for a while; everything seemed okay. Then, he started telling Joyce Marie he loved her; he wanted her to stay in Houston. She told him she was going away—that she had a scholarship to UCLA. She told him they could be friends, but that was all. He didn't want to hear that. He got mad, started cursing her, shoving her around. He got louder and louder. The cousin peeked into the room, saw what was happening, got scared and called the police.

"But before they got there, the guy told Joyce that he knew she was going away because...because of some other guy. He then told her that if he couldn't have her, no one could. In a split second, he took out a gun, and...and he shot her in the head—point blank. Just like that. He just...just shot her. The Medical Examiner said she died instantly. The police caught him a half hour later, brought him back to the scene. The twelve year-old cousin identified him. Poor child was a wreck, but she identified him. 'Course none of that did anything to bring Joyce back. She was gone. Sometimes, I have a hard time believing all this actually happened...that I didn't dream it all up, you know?"

The story drained both teller and listener. Deborah brushed away tears and embraced her sister. Maylene was clearly reliving the awful tragedy as if it had just happened. After a decade—ten, long years, it was still as painful as ever.

"Poor Matthew," Deborah whispered. "How did he find out?"

"Jeffrey called soon after he called his parents. They were devastated. His mother had to be hospitalized. We all were—folk at Mt. Moriah, at Shiloh, everybody at Central High. It was so awful. Matthew...Matthew just dropped. He just let go—fell back on the sofa. It was like he didn't have a bone in his body. It scared us so bad. I remember taking the phone. Poor Jeffrey had to repeat what he'd told Matthew. I nearly had the same reaction. I lost it. Matthew stormed out, ran all the way to Samuel's Oak.

"Couple of days later, after arrangements were made, Daddy asked him if he wanted to go to Houston...to the funeral. Matthew said no. No way he wanted to see Joyce Marie in some casket. The smiling, radiant face he last saw was the only one he wanted to remember. He never asked about the guy; didn't even want to know his name. Didn't want to see the Houston paper that covered the story; didn't want to know about the guy's trial, or what happened to him. All he knew was that...that the girl he loved—this beautiful 'Earth Angel' who loved him—was gone.

"I don't mean to go on and on with this. It's...it's one of the saddest things I've ever dealt with. Matthew struggled for a long, long time. He almost quit school, but he knew that would not honor Joyce Marie at all. So, he toughed it out. We all did. He's never found a special someone since. In fact, I don't think he ever expects to.

"Every once in a long while, he'll mention her name. But that's rare. A couple of years ago, he talked to me...said he plans to visit her grave someday. She's buried in Hearne, Texas. Her parents were from there. Both of them moved back to Houston right afterwards. We last heard from Jeffrey about five years ago. He called, told Matthew that both his parents had passed away. He was living in Atlanta at the time. I don't know where he is now."

"Are there any pictures of her...of Joyce?"

"Only ones I know about are the ones Matthew put away. No one knows where. And there's the one in the 1978, Central High year book. He put his copy of that away as well. And I never bring it up. It's still too painful for him.

"He once told me, he sometimes smelled the fragrance Joyce used to wear. No one would be around. He just...it was like she was right there. I told him, that's because she *was,* and would *always* be. He seemed alright with that. And he never mentioned it again, although I do believe it still happens from time to time...her presence, I mean. I'm sure there are songs he hears—songs Joyce used to love to hear—that always take him back. Truth is, even I can't listen to certain Motown music, especially Smokey Robinson, without thinking about her. And that's a lot of great music. It used to make me real sad. But now, whenever I hear it, I mostly just see her big smile, then I smile."

"All this...in two years," Deborah reflected.

"Two years. 'Bout a year after they buried Jozeta Brock. Don't know if you would remember her."

"I do. Her brother, Waymon, was in my class. What happened to her?"

"She was...murdered. Her body was found just off Crispus Attucks one Friday, just before dark. Some boys came across her in this...this pine clearing. Somebody left her there, after they'd done their business with her. She always was a little fast, but she didn't deserve that. It was terrible. Never caught whoever did it. I doubt they even tried, really."

Deborah's heart skipped, at the mention of the piney woods clearing. She could not help but wonder if it was the same clearing—the one familiar to her. She had never disclosed full details of that day, and likely never would. Deborah had more questions now, but chose not to ask Maylene.

Both were emotionally spent. Deborah fought to not think more about Jozeta Brock, or who may have killed her. A long quiet followed. For Deborah, what was remarkable was the fact an indelible portrait of Joyce Whiting was now forever etched in her heart. And for all the sadness *she* had personally known, she found herself wishing she had been there to help ease her brother's pain and suffering.

chapter thirty-one

A Love, Found

"She is my daughter."

"We've been talking all this time, and you haven't mentioned a husband. Are you married?" Deborah broke the silence, redirecting a conversation with Maylene that had nearly sapped them.

Maylene laughed and clapped her hands together. "Yeah, twice. But after divorcing David, my first husband, I decided I was not going to take any more abuse. He left town when he found out Matthew was looking for him. Served him papers at his mother's, in Arkadelphia. Three months later, I had my divorce. I swore the next man who hit me was gonna eat a .45 slug or worse. I'm serious. What about you? You married yet...engaged?"

"No. No, not yet. Ahh, what's your husband's name?"

"John Rollins. He's a sweetie. Everybody calls him J.R. He's from Mississippi. My friend, Clarise, introduced us years ago. He's Charles' daddy...a real good man. But I still don't depend on him for everything.

You *can't,* girl. I'm an x-ray Tech at a hospital in Little Rock. I'm on a two-week vacation. Pay's good. J.R. is somewhere in California, right now."

"Why's that?"

"Happens two weeks or more out of every month."

"I'm confused."

"He's a big rig truck driver," Maylene chuckled. "He drives all over the country. Should be pullin' into Blythe, California right about now. He'll be callin' me before long. That's one thing about him. He'll call me, night or day."

"Sounds like you have a great marriage. I'm happy for you."

"But it's tough on both of us...the kids, too. He takes his big Peterbilt on the road and I take my big vibrator to bed. They both got high mileage. It's like the Fourth of July when he gets home." Maylene laughed.

"I'm happy for you." Deborah allowed a brief smile. However, it was only seconds before her mood turned solemn again.

"You gon' tell Sam the truth?" Maylene's question was unexpected.

It took a moment for Deborah to respond. "She has to know. The lying...the deception has to end."

"Let me say this," said Maylene. "If I was her, and I ever found out on my own, I'd probably hate *you* and Mama. No matter how the truth hurts, she's got to know, sooner or later. I wish I had...had the courage to tell her. But she would want 'a know why she never heard from her real mother, after finally meeting her."

"She *is* my daughter," said Deborah. "But all these years she's been told she's adopted. She thinks she's my sister. This is just...I'm trying to reconcile this. In my heart, I know what I want to do. I have to figure out how to do it without causing my baby, Samantha, any more pain. But no matter how painful the truth may be, I cannot leave things the way they are, and just go on with my life. I would have no life, not without my daughter, not now."

Deborah's voice trailed. She walked away several steps, stopped to gaze into the distance. Maylene started toward her, but stopped. A long minute passed. Deborah returned to stand a few feet from Maylene.

"The lying started from day one," said Maylene. "That was how Mama and Daddy explained Samantha to everybody. We kids knew it was wrong, but we had to go along. I remember wondering what happened to all those sermons about telling the truth. It bothered me to see Daddy standing in his pulpit preaching about truth, while knowing what I knew. 'Course everybody probably knew it, too."

"Hearing Samantha...my daughter say what she said, was one of the hardest things I've ever had to hear," said Deborah. "After she was taken from me, I felt *I* had abandoned *her*. I imagined she would someday demand to know why that happened. Except for the rare phone calls from Mama to Aunt Rose, there was no communication at all.

"At first, I wrote letters, but they were never answered. I wrote letters to Samantha I'm sure were destroyed. I'm glad I never mailed others. It's impossible to understand how they could hide the truth so long,"

Maylene listened. She had her own suspicions regarding the letters. The undeniable fact was, her mother was first to see every letter that arrived at the Davis house. She always emptied the mailbox.

"The truth died around here over fourteen years ago," said Maylene. "We've been living lies ever since. Sam's always been a very intelligent child. I sometimes wonder what she really knows."

"I know she has to hear the whole truth," said Deborah. "I just want what's best for her, not what simply satisfies me. And she's old enough to be trusted to allow her feelings and thoughts to be known."

"I agree. She does deserve the truth. In fact, we all need a heavy does of truth around here."

"I'd rather it came from her grandmother," said Deborah. 'She's the one who...who has masqueraded as Samantha's mother, denied me...to my own daughter. It's her responsibility to look her in the eyes, and tell her the truth." Deborah's resurgent anger was transparent.

"You're right, she should be the one to tell her. But I can tell you that's way too much to hope for. No way it's gon' happen. No way. The lie is so deeply rooted. And there's something else: Sam's father. She's got 'a know about him, too. Sam's probably the only one who doesn't know who he is. I'm surprised she's never asked questions about that, as far as I know. This isn't going to be easy. I look at you...think about all that's happened, and I cannot imagine being twelve and having someone take away 'Vonne when she was a baby, then make up some story about who she was. I think I would've...just died. Gon' take a lot of praying, and a lot of truth-telling to change any of this. And I sure hope you change your mind and stay a while."

Deborah and Maylene hugged each other warmly, dwarfed by the giant oak behind them. Its massive limbs resembled outstretched arms. Its long, wide shadow seemed a sanctuary. Neither sister appeared anxious to leave its reach. After a time absorbing the quiet beauty, the two started back toward the house.

"Yvonne and Charles seem like such great kids. And I'm sure they're just as smart as they look and sound, too. My guess is you started them reading at a young age."

"Right. I did. I practically had them with a bottle in one hand and a book in the other. That's the only way. I had both of them reading...way before they were five years old."

"I'm not surprised at all. Oh, I meant to ask what happened to the picture of Grandpa George and Gram...the one Father always kept on the dresser."

Maylene did not respond right away. Her expression fell. Finally, "You mean, the one in their bedroom?"

"Yes. It was always there."

"Oh, you probably just overlooked it. Mama keeps so much stuff piled on that old dresser, it's hard to find the mirrors sometimes."

"And what happened to the picture of me, the one that was always on the mantel...in the living room? Or did I overlook that one as well?"

Maylene drew a labored breath. "Sure hope we can get a good lawyer to help us out."

Deborah waited a few seconds before responding. "We will." Maylene's not so subtle change of subject did not escape her. It only deepened her puzzlement.

"Oh, by the way," Maylene went on, "you know that old porch swing out front?"

"You mean, the one on the porch?"

"Oh, that's right, huh?" Maylene chuckled. "True. What I wanted to tell you is, be careful. Sometimes, without warning, Matthew comes over and paints the thing."

"I don't understand."

"Well, several years ago, while we were in church one Sunday morning, he came by and painted the old swing, chains and all. We came home from church, and Mama—for some unknown reason—headed straight for the swing. She plopped down on it wearing her brand new dress...sat right onto a fresh coat of white paint. What tipped her off was the fact black paint from the chains got all over her hands. She jumped up, screaming: *Lord, have mercy! I'm gon' kill him. As God is my witness, I'm gon' kill that boy!*

"We all knew it was Matthew's handiwork. For one thing, Mama should 'a smelled the paint, except she had a cold and was all congested and stuffed up, you know. Her dress was brown, at first. When she got up, she was flailing around, looking like a zebra. White stripes from the slats were all up and down her back and bottom. She was fussing...was mad as she could be. Even Daddy had to laugh. Girl, I'm tellin' you, Sister Davis almost lost her religion that day."

Maylene doubled over, telling her hilarious story. Deborah could not help but share her sister's infectious laughter. She did so without conscious restraint—no thought of anything but the story. For a brief spell, the only sound heard was that of laughter. And that was good.

chapter thirty-two

Reflections

───────────────────────

Moments later, the two fell into steamy embrace and...

It was dark, well after nine when Deborah, resplendent in a shimmering, white silk bath robe exited the bathroom of her hotel suite. She entered the living room in full stride and drew open the drapes to reveal a star-filled sky.

Earlier, before leaving her mother, Deborah reentered the house and found her still avoiding direct eye contact. Mabel Davis busied herself in the kitchen, washing dishes that were already clean, and rearranging everything not nailed down.

With Maylene looking on, Deborah started down the hallway toward the bedroom where Rachel remained cloistered. Once there, she stood motionless, her right palm pressed against the door. Deborah could almost feel a disturbed presence on the other side. She started to knock then turned away. There would be plenty of time for whatever seeing Rachel would surely bring.

Before leaving, Deborah said good-bye to a still elated Samantha. She was in her room studying, and was reluctant to let her 'aunt' go. She had a million questions. Deborah promised to answer all of them later.

During the several minutes she shared with Samantha, Deborah had the strangest sensation someone was listening outside the bedroom door. However, she resisted the urge to open it quickly, and expose the eavesdropper.

"Tomorrow. You'll be back tomorrow!" Sam insisted.

"Absolutely," Deborah assured her.

Sam made a cross over her heart and waited. Deborah did the same. Both laughed and hugged each other again.

—

Charles and Yvonne were perched on the front porch steps, reading, as Deborah started to leave. Instead of a quick good-bye, she sat down next to them for nearly twenty minutes. They were thrilled. Surprisingly, Charles was the more talkative. He peppered Deborah with question after question—about Chicago in general, the Cubs in particular. His excitement bubbled over when she told him of her love of baseball, and her many visits to see the Cubs play.

"Did you ever catch a foul ball?"

Deborah could only laugh. She happily recounted those memorable experiences she had shared with Uncle Jack—and in vivid, play by play detail. Charles was all ears.

Samantha, who had been quietly standing in the doorway awaiting Deborah's departure, walked out to join them. She sat next to Yvonne, whose gaze never left Deborah. Yvonne was fascinated by her aunt's appearance, but more by the fact she was an author—a real author.

"You actually write books—novels? I mean..."

"Yes, I actually do. So can you, someday."

"I can? That is so...so amazing. You have to promise to tell me how you got started and everything. I don't mean right now, but later."

"I promise. And because you two love to read, I'll also see that you get whatever books you want."

Charles and Yvonne beamed, as if Christmas had arrived early. Deborah saw their excitement, and was certain she was as thrilled as were they. She was also elated to have another chance to see Samantha, and get another good-bye hug.

The privacy and isolation of the hotel room was welcomed. Aunt Rose had been unusually quiet during their phone conversation. Deborah described her 'homecoming,' in selective detail. Some things defied translation. Uncle Jack spoke sparingly, before handing the phone back to Rose. When the two said their good-byes, Deborah was sure she detected weeping in Rose's voice.

Deborah's hotel suite was beautifully appointed. A large black vase, filled with a dozen roses, adorned the glass coffee table. The television set was on...volume set to barely audible. Deborah had just turned from the sliding glass doors when the phone rang. She lifted the receiver, kicked off her shoes and plopped down onto the plush sofa. It was Paul.

She was anxious to hear his strong, steady voice. He was the third dependable link to her familiar. Inside his high-rise Lake Shore condo, he clutched the phone, and sipped a glass of Chardonnay.

The lavishly appointed two story living room, with vaulted ceiling, was dominated by a white, Baby Grand piano. The piano faced a ceiling high mirror, near the approach to the raised, formal dining room. Paul, wearing black, silk pajamas, stood barefoot near the glass door leading onto his 24th floor balcony. From this lofty perch, Chicago at night sparkled like ten thousand diamonds.

"You get the flowers?"

"Yes. They're beautiful. You think of everything."

"I try. Listen, I've got great news. Are you sitting?"

"Paul, what is it?"

"Are you sitting?"

"Yes."

"Good. Got another round of offers today. I'll fax copies."

"Great! So I should get them in the morning?"

"By ten."

"That's good to hear. And I know you're not going to tell me more, so I'll just wait." Deborah was thrilled. Yet, her voice lacked the level of excitement Paul expected.

"How'd everything go today?"

Deborah hesitated. "Emotional, extremely emotional. Draining, surreal—unbelievably surreal."

"And your father?"

"He's still comatose. They say his eyes flash open, sometimes. Paul, it was so hard to look at him. Almost impossible to see in him the father I remember."

"I'm so sorry, sweetheart. Did you see Samantha?"

"Yes. I...I saw her." Deborah's voice wavered. "She is so beautiful. There's a lot I have to tell you. I've decided to..."

"Tell me when I get there. I'm leaving for Little Rock tomorrow."

"Paul, don't come. I'm fine. I can handle it alone."

"You don't sound fine."

"That may be true. It's been an emotional day. But I'm fine."

"I'm just listening to the way you sound. Besides, we agreed. No more arguments, alright? See you tomorrow. I'm hanging up."

"Paul..."

"No, no. I'm hanging up, Dee."

"Paul, I'm thinking of..."

"Good-bye, Dee."

"Paul..."

"I'm hanging up so you won't try to talk me out of it. Good-bye."

Paul made a kissing sound and hung up. He tossed the phone toward the sofa, watched it land on the floor and just stood staring at it. His smile quickly faded into a distant, pensive look.

Seconds passed. Paul turned to see a brunette beauty—wearing only a smile and red spikes—descend the spiral staircase. She reached him, removed the wineglass from his hand, downed the remaining Chardonnay and tossed the glass to the floor.

Paul said nothing. He stood there taking her all in, curiously dispassionate. The gloriously endowed young woman inched closer, slipped her arms around his waist, then began loosening the drawstrings of his pajamas.

Paul seized her hands, slowly brought them to his chest. Surprise filled her eyes, as he held and caressed them.

"Okay. Alright. Is it the perfume? Don't you like what I'm wearing?" she asked, playfully. Paul remained unsmiling.

"It's...fine. I just can't..."

"Shhh. It's okay. It's okay. Must have been *some* phone call."

Paul removed his pajama top and placed it around the young woman. She kept staring at him, puzzled by his demeanor. As he watched her, she retrieved the wineglass from the floor, returned it to the bar, removed another, and poured more wine.

Meantime, Paul made his way out onto the balcony. He stood gazing at a sea of sparkling lights—the dazzling sight of the Windy City at night. The young woman soon joined him, standing just behind him, sharing the view.

—

Deborah sat perched on the sofa, staring blankly at the television set. A female news anchor was speaking, but she barely heard the story. Her mind was still absorbing the fact that after more than thirteen years, she had once again gazed into the eyes of her daughter, and embraced her. Little else mattered, just now.

She kept staring at the television. A graphic inset of Vice President George Bush appeared over the woman's left shoulder.

"The 1988 Presidential Campaign appears to be well under way. Vice President Bush is clearly determined to exploit his advantages, while Democrats try to forge a game plan to retake the White House."

As the anchor droned on, the Vice President was shown at one of his many campaign visits to flag factories. Deborah stared into nothingness. She never saw nor heard what followed the story: A Jonathan Reed, Senate campaign commercial featuring his family.

chapter thirty-three

Out Of The Closet

═══════════════════════════

"If Gram had been living, none of this would 'a happened,"

T he roar of silence was deafening.
Mabel Davis had finished putting away the dishes and was wiping down the countertop in her kitchen. A poker-faced Maylene was mostly milling around. She kept staring at her mother, shaking her head sadly. Finally, she could hold her tongue no longer. But before she could utter a sound, her mother turned to face her.

"Out with it, Maylene!" Mabel Davis stared down her eldest daughter. Maylene had not expected such directness. "You been piddlin' around here, mumblin' and going on for the past three hours. Speak your mind."

Mabel Davis stood there, scowling, and drying her hands on her lace-trimmed, checkerprint apron. Maylene hesitated, then figured it was best they have it out.

"Alright, Mama. Fine, since you put it like that. I notice you haven't said a solitary word 'bout Deborah since she left. All this time, and absolutely nothing. Not a single word since she left here. Why is that?"

"Now just which Deborah would you be talkin' 'bout, daughter? Deborah Davis or...or Deborah Durrett?"

"Well, I'll be. Now, here it comes." I was expecting that one, Mama. It's Durrell, not Durrett. And I don't blame her one bit. I'm talking about Deborah—the daughter you gave birth to. That's which Deborah. Why haven't you said anything?"

"Been too busy cleanin' up and...and listenin' to you mutterin' and goin' on. Somebody's got to do some work 'roun' here."

"Well, I'll just shut up my mouth so you can express yourself." Maylene cocked her head to one side, and planted her hands firmly on her hips. "I'm gon' shut up so I don't miss anything. I want to know how you feel about seeing Deborah after all these years. You haven't even talked to her on the phone in more than four years. And that was for 'bout five seconds. She just happened to answer the phone. And even then, you just asked to speak to Aunt Rose."

Mabel Davis closed an upper cabinet door and moved closer, squarely facing her eldest daughter. "Maylene Renee, if there's somethin' particular on your mind, why don't you just come on out with it. Stop signifyin' and goin' on." Mabel wiped her hands on the apron again, folded her arms and waited.

Maylene leaned back against the counter. "Thought you were gon' give more of an answer than that. Alright, Mama. I'll tell you what else is on my mind. It's time to be honest...time to straighten all this mess out, once and for all. Time to answer all the questions about secrets that have been hidden in this family's closet all these years."

"Look, some things is between your daddy and me." A stern Mabel Davis was clearly not expecting Maylene's direct assault.

"Mama, with all due respect—and I do mean that—I don't understand how you can say that. What happened in '74 changed all our lives forever! We were a *family*. We were old enough to be told the truth. We deserved to hear the truth from you and Daddy. But we weren't told the truth. Deborah wasn't sick. She was pregnant! We had to hear things from other people—gossip, strange looks.

"Then, bingo! Samantha," Maylene went on. "We wanted our *real* sister back. Instead, we got a baby that didn't look anything like any of us. Y'all brought a stranger home, Mama. A beautiful baby but still a stranger. It was like she was suppose to replace our sister—her own mother. And not once did anyone ask what we felt. We didn't matter. Nobody believed she was adopted. Nobody. Even June Boy knew better than that."

"You ought 'a hear yourself. And leave that baby out 'a this."

"What baby? And I'll tell you something else. Do you realize Samantha sounds just like Deborah when she sings? Especially in church. Sometimes, I have to get up and walk out when she's singing, 'cause I can't help thinking about Deborah. She even sings some of the same songs, too. Don't tell me that never crossed your mind."

"Hold on, now. You keep your voice down, before she hear you," Mabel Davis warned.

"Right. Of course. We certainly wouldn't want that to happen, now would we? Know something? That's the trouble, Mama. We've kept our voices down too long, already. You went to Chicago and came back with your granddaughter, not your daughter. Why? How? Why didn't y'all bring Deborah home, too? We wanted to know, then. And I want to know now. I'm also sure Deborah wants to know."

"Why are you just now askin' me 'bout that?"

"This isn't the first time, Mama. Maybe you're listening for the first time. But this is definitely not the first time. And when we were kids, we were too scared to ask. We figured if y'all could send Deborah away forever, you could send us, too. Then y'all made it seem like Deborah didn't want to come home, like she didn't want anything to do with us. Long before we grew up, it was clear there wasn't gon' be any answers. Besides, from the beginning you seemed more concerned about Samantha than your own children."

"I said leave Samantha out of this."

"Leave her out?"

"You heard me."

"How? How can I leave her out, Mama? How is that even possible? She's right in the center of everything—always has been. And I love her, dearly. None of this is her fault. But I do remember how for thirteen years you proudly proclaimed that she was your daughter. *Your* daughter, not your granddaughter, and not Deborah's daughter. Your daughter—adopted from some...some mystery woman, I guess."

"Now you wait a minute. First of all..."

"And we all knew it wasn't true, Mama. Everybody knew it wasn't true. And we all saw how you used to fuss over Sam. You used to talk about how good her hair was...how easy it was to take care of and all. I guess you meant it was good, compared to our nappy, kinky hair. Was that it? You think that didn't affect us...hearing that? You used to talk about how pretty her skin was. Was that because she's half white? Was that what it was, Mama?"

"Now, that's enough. You hear me?" Mabel Davis barked, stepping closer to Maylene and wagging her finger.

"And what about your other grandkids?"

"Now, what's that s'pose to mean?"

"What it means, Mama, is that I don't recall you ever making a fuss over Yvonne or Charles. Not like Sam. I know you love them both, but there's always been a difference. Let's be honest."

Mabel Davis' mouth flew open. "What? I don't believe I'm hearing this. I do as much...have always done just as much for your kids as I do for Sam. Now, if you're comparing me to the kind of grandmother your daddy's mother was...well, times have changed. She never had the responsibilities I had—had and have. All she had to do was sit in that house, cook and sew, tell stories, and pamper you kids to death. I can't believe you said that. That is just..."

"Well just let it all come on out, Mama. I'll say this: thank God for Gram. Whether she had the time or not, she *took* the time. There is a big difference. What I said earlier is true. And there's a lot more. But back to Samantha. That child has got to be told the truth 'bout Deborah...about her real mother. If you don't, I will."

An angry Mabel Davis grabbed Maylene's arm. "Now you listen here. Don't be raisin' your voice and preachin' to me. I am still your mother. Always will be. And you'll do no such thing. These are different times today than it was...even in 1974. When all this happened, we not only had to consider our family, but every black family in this town. I know we could have done some things different, and I told Deborah that. But at the time, we did what we thought was best for everybody."

"But what about the rest of those years, Mama? How was leaving Deborah in Chicago—never seeing her family for fourteen years—best for everybody? It wasn't best for *her*, and it sure wasn't best for *us*. So, who was it best for? I don't understand that, Mama. And I guess it was shame and guilt that kept us—kept me, Matthew, and Gloria...not really sure about Rachel—from doing something about it even after we were grown. Good Lord, I'm thirty years old now. I was sixteen!"

"What did you mean—you're not really sure about Rachel?" Mabel Davis' brow was scored with deep frowns.

Maylene shook her head, briefly looked away. "You know what it means, Mama. All the while Deborah was here, Rachel never came out of her room...never opened the door. I kept thinking about that day Deborah was...was sent away. Rachel actually seemed happy, wasn't the least bit upset, not like the rest of us...standing there, pretending to read that book. We've never talked about that either. And she's never had a kind or warm word to say about her since then. Why is that? She's had an attitude toward Deborah since day one."

"Now, you look here..."

"And why was she born so soon after Deborah? I've always wondered about that. All the rest of us are at least two years apart, except for Deborah and Rachel. Why?"

Mabel's eyes nearly popped from their sockets. "What do you mean, why? You know, you got a lot 'a nerve. That ain't none 'a your business. None! Funny how your...your sister shows up, and all of a sudden you done come outside 'a yourself."

"My sister...my sister is also your daughter. Remember? And what's so terrible about me wanting to know about that?"

"What you got against your sister, Rachel?"

"You're changing the subject, Mama. You do that a lot whenever you don't want to answer something." Mabel didn't respond. Maylene exhaled, loudly. " I don't have anything against Rachel. That kind of question should be put to her, not me. Ask her why she hates Deborah. The girl needs serious help, if you know what I mean."

"Maylene, the trouble with you is you're always seein' things where there's nothin' to see. Your sister, Rachel, has always been quiet...kept to herself. And after the terrible tragedy she's been through, she's still tryin' to deal with gettin' her life right."

Maylene was unrelenting. "Tragedy, Mama? Look, I understand how losing Jamile tore Rachel apart. After all, he was the only man who ever really paid any attention to her, as far as anyone knows. And she was determined to hook him. I wouldn't be surprised to find out she *tried* to get pregnant. Her *attitude* is what scared him away the first time he took off. Then, she practically tracked him down...with hound dogs."

"Well, I guess you been blessed with the *gift to* know these things."

"No, Mama. I just got the gift of plain sight, and the gift of common sense, that's all. Anyway, we all grieved for Jamile. But you want 'a talk about tragedy? Let's talk about what Deborah has been through for fourteen years. I cried when Rachel lost her baby, which she conceived outside of marriage, and without condemnation from anyone at this address. I've tried to help her as much as anybody.

"But it's more than that. A lot more. Rachel needs serious psychological help. Now that's a fact. She's always acted strange toward Deborah. 'Strange' is too mild a word, but it'll do for right now. And to tell the truth, you didn't treat her much better today yourself."

"You sure said a mouthful. I know you not preachin' to me. Look, we never stopped lovin' Deborah. She's my child, same as all 'a y'all. I gave birth to her. But we did what we thought was best for everybody. And I don't wanna hear you say that about Rachel again. You hear me?"

"You mentioned love. I'm not sure I know anything about the kind of love you talking about, Mama. How you think Deborah saw love in the way things happened, going way back? Huh? How? I do know *this*. If Gram had been living, none of this ever would've happened. She would've turned this place upside down. The truth is, nobody would've even mentioned sending Deborah away."

Mabel Davis' eyes narrowed to black slits. She clenched her jaws tightly. "Hold on. You forgettin' whose house this was, and still is. Your grandmother had a lot of influence on your daddy. But I was and am his wife. When your grandfather died, your daddy brought her here to live near us. And I agreed to that," said Mabel. "Your daddy's brother and two sisters didn't want anything to do with takin' care of her. So it fell to your daddy."

"And why was that?"

"They were mad at her. And they'd all stopped speakin' to your daddy by then, every one of 'em. A brother and two sisters, and they all treated him like some disease. He was so hurt by it, but wouldn't let on, not at first. It really got bad after your grandmother passed away. But before that, it started when your Grandpa George got low sick and it was pretty certain he wasn't gonna make it. Your grandmother named your father as the sole executor for your granddaddy's, and her own estate.

"That did it. I mean, that did it. They turned against him...went to court to try and have things changed, tried to trick your grandmother into giving your Uncle Melvin her 'power of attorney.' They tried everything. Even refused to sign papers they were s'pose to sign. It was a mess. Now, he was the ring leader—that Melvin. Those sisters were mean ol' heifers, themselves. But that Melvin, now he was the worst of the lot.

"He was the second son...always jealous of your father...resented everything he succeeded in...smilin' in his face and stabbin' him in the back at the same time. And he never could keep a wife—with his chitlin' eatin,' gold tooth wearin,' beer belly-hangin,' cross wearin'...wears all them crosses, like that's gon' get him into heaven. And never been near a church in his life, 'cept when he was gettin' married. Wears more crosses 'round his neck than you find at a Southern Baptist Ministers' Convention. Shit! Lord, I shouldn't be talkin' like this. Got me cussin.' Only time I ever say a bad word is when I talk about *his* ol' fat...Lord, forgive me. Anyway, he goes through wives like some folks with colds go through Kleenex."

"What about Daddy's sisters?"

"After a while, they all just stopped talkin' to him. Your daddy couldn't do anything right by 'em, far as they were concerned. Funny how a little money and few measly possessions can cause such turmoil. Folks you've known all your life, shared a womb with. They change on you...become what they really were all along."

"So, where are they now?" asked Maylene. "I don't think we ever saw any of them more than three or four times. We hardly ever knew our cousins, except for Kevin—Uncle Melvin's only son. And we were all grown by then."

"That sure wasn't your daddy's fault. Your aunties and uncle gave their children their disease...fed them the same hate and all. They all grew up just as silly as their parents. Your daddy's Baby 'Sista,' Corine, and Melvin are the only ones left now. People like him live forever...'long with cockroaches. Even Kevin couldn't wait to get away from his daddy."

"So, none of them wanted to help take care of their mother?"

"That's what I said. They tossed her overboard like a dead fish. That's why it all fell to your daddy. He loved his mama, but she did not run this house. The decisions we made would 'a been made no matter who was still alive. You hear me? I don't wanna hear another word on that subject again."

"You never did like her, did you?"

"Like who?"

"Gram d'lena. Mama, every time her name came up—even as little kids—every time we talked about her, or asked to go to her house, you had this...this *strange* look on your face. I remember it well, too. You even got upset sometimes, because Daddy spent so much time with her—his own *mother*. Why was that, Mama?"

"That's a bunch 'a nonsense."

"Is it, Mama? Deborah and Matthew spent more time at Gram's house than me or Gloria or Rachel. When they would ask to go, you always got this look. I can't describe it, but it was real. And you used to talk about how much Daddy doted on her, too. I don't think you *ever* went up to her house. Were you jealous of her, jealous of how close she was to Daddy?"

"You know what? I am through talkin' about this."

"But I *do* want to talk about it, Mama."

"Go ahead! You can talk all you want, Maylene. You can talk to that sink if you want to. I'm done talkin' 'bout this."

"Fine, Mama. Well, let's talk about something else. Let's talk about Mr. Jude Barsteau. Who is Jude Barsteau?"

The question caught Mabel Davis completely off guard. Her eyes flared; her fists clenched. She took a deep breath, and moved within a foot of her eldest daughter.

"Where did you hear that name? Where did you hear that name?" Mabel Davis demanded, with a harshness unfamiliar to Maylene. She flinched at her mother's angry tone. "I said where did you hear that name? Answer me!"

"I don't remember, exactly."

"Why'd you bring it up?"

"I'm not sure."

"You must 'a had a reason."

"It just came into my mind, I guess. I think I heard Gram mention his name a long time ago. She wouldn't talk about it either."

"Well put it out of your mind! I do not wanna hear that evil name spoke in this house ever again. You hear me?"

"Who is he?"

"What is it about never don't you understand, Maylene?"

Maylene was puzzled, but more determined than ever to find out who Jude Barsteau was. For now, she let the matter drop.

"Well, let's talk about Deborah some more," she said.

"I thought you'd said all you meant to say. Whatever happened in the past...is in the past."

"The past? I don't mean any disrespect, Mama. But what about now? How you think Deborah felt when she found out her daughter's been told she's adopted? I was looking at her. It was like somebody just shoved a knife in her and twisted it. You weren't looking at her."

"This ain't for you to judge, Maylene. God is my judge."

"Well, I know I'm not God, but we have to make judgments every-day. I love you, Mama. But you're wrong. And I have to say it. I'm only giving back what we were taught once upon a time. You and Daddy taught us well, Mama. Trouble is, I actually listened to all of Daddy's sermons. I took 'em all to heart. You can't look me in the eyes and say all this has been God's will."

Endless silence. A subdued Mabel Davis returned to the sink and began re-rinsing dry dishes.

"Something's got 'a be done, Mama—for all our sake."

"You can say whatever you want, but she's not takin' her."

"What do you mean?"

"Just what I said. I hope she ain't thinkin' she's gon' take that baby when she leaves. She belongs right here."

Maylene's countenance fell. She seemed deflated, for the moment. Her mother's words resonated in her ears.

"Mama, I don't know what to say to all this. This is so...so pitiful."

"Pitiful?"

"Yes, pitiful. First of all, there is no baby in this house. Sam is nearly fourteen. Secondly, she doesn't belong to you. Now that you've men-tioned it, I don't think getting Sam away from Reedville is such a bad idea. And she would probably be eager to leave here. But I also do not believe that's what's on Deborah's mind right now."

Mabel Davis clenched her teeth, said nothing more. She turned away, lowered her head. It was difficult to know whether her sudden silence was due to anger or remorse. Maylene wondered if she had been too candid, but then dismissed the thought. She would have been even more forceful, except for her desire to not disrespect her mother, or her father.

Just then, a haggard Rachel stepped into the kitchen doorway. She was, at 5'-6," a petite framed, arguably attractive woman with doleful, expressive eyes, despite her decidedly dour demeanor. Her twigged hair—mostly black with a touch of gray—fell unevenly around her dark-mocha face. She remained expressionless, her arms folded, her body leaning lazily against the doorjamb.

"Good morning to you, too." Maylene said, facetiously.

Rachel ignored her sister and turned to her mother. "I'm sensing a little tension here. Did I miss something, mother?" Rachel's voice was soft, barely audible. "Well, did I?"

"Yeah, you did. Your sister. Your sister, Deborah was here...finally came home to see 'bout her daddy."

Rachel raised her right hand to her chest, in mock surprise. Her eyes widened. Maylene was convinced she had known.

"Are you serious? Someone should have awakened me. I hate I missed the reunion. And after all these years. Where is she?"

"She'll be back," said Maylene.

"Good. I'm hungry, mother. Matthew leave any food this time?"

"How'd you know Matthew was here?"

"Excuse me?"

"I thought you were asleep." Maylene noted.

Rachel chuckled. "I was."

"Then, how did you..."

"Honey, Matthew comes by practically every evening. You know that. Everybody knows you can practically set the Atomic Clock by him." She started toward the refrigerator.

An exasperated Maylene loosed a loud sigh, then walked to her mother, who stood scowling—arms folded. And despite Mabel Davis' rigid posture, her angry expression, her refusal to look at her daughter, Maylene kissed her on the cheek and left the room. Rachel loosed an exaggerated snicker. Maylene never looked back.

chapter thirty-four

Face Off—Next Morning

"It can be a damn trap. You hear?"

Deborah emerged from her hotel bedroom,
wearing a white blouse and seal-gray business suit. She moved to the
desk, removed a business card from her matching handbag, lifted the
phone and dialed.

"Good morning, Reed Company. May I help you?" answered a perky
female voice. Much too perky, to suit Deborah.

"Jonathan Reed, please."

"One moment, please."

"Be there!" Deborah, commanded as she fiddled with the business
card, turning it over and over in her hand. She did not really plan to
speak with him...just make sure he was there.

"Mr. Reed's office. May I help you?" asked a second female voice.

"Jonathan Reed, please. Deborah Durrell calling." Deborah was certain he would not recognize the name, and not take the call.

"Would you hold, please?" The voice was pleasant enough.

Deborah was anxious, but not nervous. She took a deep breath and sighed, more from anger and exasperation than anything else.

"Miss Durrell, Mr. Reed is in a meeting right now. May I ask what this is regarding? I'd be happy to take a message."

"He *is* in the office, though?"

"I'm sorry, is there a message?"

"No. No, thank you."

Deborah hung up, put the card away and dialed the front desk. Her rental car was ready, equipped with a mobile phone as she had requested. She grabbed her handbag and hurried down to the lobby.

Before leaving the hotel, Deborah spoke to the Concierge, informed him she was expecting a package and or a fax. She instructed him to hold them for her. Outside the hotel, she was greeted by a valet. He escorted her to her Lincoln Continental, opened the driver's door, and held it open until she entered.

Five minutes later, Deborah was exiting the hotel driveway and talking to Maylene on the mobile phone. Mabel Davis had declined her offer of help for her father, but readily accepted her assistance in getting a lawyer. As for medical care, she was still willing to 'Trust in God.' Deborah did not have a reaction to the news. She was not surprised.

"I know none of it makes sense," Maylene was conceding the obvious. "But are you staying? Please, say yes." Deborah did not answer. "We need you here. Samantha needs you, too. 'Course, I don't have to tell you that. Her whole life is in front of her. No matter what's happened before, we can't let our lives continue to be built on lies. I know you feel the same way I do. You're being here makes that possible."

"I'm taking all this, one day at a time. That's all I can, or will promise. All I know is, I'm here today."

For the moment, that was good enough for Maylene. Tommy was scheduled to arrive at any time. Deborah purposely muted her response to the news, not wanting to encourage Maylene's inclination to play matchmaker.

Under Maylene's probing, Deborah disclosed she was en route to the Reed Company's offices. Maylene was both surprised and concerned. She reminded Deborah that The Reed family was the most powerful, and politically connected in the state. Most Republicans, and Democrats seeking statewide office, sought Richard's blessings, or his promise to not oppose them.

Deborah was not at all dissuaded. Her plan was set. Maylene repeated her caution, ending the conversation by insisting her sister be careful. Deborah promised to call later, then continued the short drive from her hotel to the Reed Company offices.

More than a half-hour later, inside the Reed Corporation's high-rise headquarters building at Broadway and Capitol streets, the 24th floor elevator door opened. A radiant Deborah stepped out boldly, yet with considerable trepidation. She started across a wide corridor toward a set of glass double doors. Deborah had spent nearly thirty minutes sitting in her car, thinking about this moment—wondering, praying, crying, and eventually steeling herself for what lay ahead.

Through the inch-thick glass, Deborah saw the name: REED COMPANY, INC. It was emblazoned in brass lettering on the wall above the semicircle-shaped, polished burl, receptionist area. She took a deep breath, eased open the door and entered. A beaming young woman with a small flower in her hair flashed a toothy smile.

"Hi, there. Welcome to the Reed Company. May I help you?"

"Yes. I'd like to..." Deborah started, but was interrupted when the young woman raised an index finger and took a call. The wait was brief.

"Sorry. Who are you here to see, ma'am?"

"Mr. Reed. Jonathan Reed."

"I'm terribly sorry. He's not in. And I don't expect him back today. Did you have an appointment?"

"I spoke to his secretary a half hour ago. He was in a meeting," said Deborah—her tone conveying her suspicion.

The young woman appeared uneasy. "I don't know what to say, ma'am. Leave your number, and I'll pass it to Mr. Reed's secretary."

"I'll wait," said Deborah. She turned and started toward a leather sofa a few feet away.

Simultaneously, two men, engaged in robust conversation, entered the suite. One was Jonathan Reed, 30, 6'-4," wearing dark suit slacks, a long-sleeve white shirt, and red tie. The other man, the shorter of the two, was his father, Richard Reed. The elder Reed, 66, was distinguished-looking, balding, and white-haired. He wore an eggshell-white Italian suit, had an amazing resemblance to actor, Robert Duvall—even sounded like him.

"It's virtually an unlimited credit line," Jonathan was saying. "The cap's way out there. Some S&L's got plenty of money right now and I aim for us to get all we need. Don't worry. After I'm elected, I'll have to create some distance."

That voice. Deborah's heart spiked. She paused near the sofa, then turned to see the receptionist's reddened face, as the two approached.

"I like the flexible cap. But it can be a damn trap," Richard warned. "You hear me good. Deregulation or not, we have to be cautious. We don't have the friends in Washington we used to have. I expect we will again, someday soon. But we have to be extremely cautious."

That instant, Jonathan caught sight of Deborah, and was immediately distracted. Deborah was not sure if it was because he recognized her, or because she was female. Richard kept talking. His son's gait dramatically slowed.

"I want multisource financin' on this thing. We don't want to appear too cozy with a single S&L," Richard droned on.

Deborah instantly recognized Jonathan. The sight of him made her nauseous. From the instant she saw him, a thousand tortured thoughts, spanning fourteen years, ripped through her mind like a Kansas tornado. She had long wondered what she would feel...what she would say, if and when she ever laid eyes on the "bastard" again.

Without warning, raw hatred, and a thirst for revenge seemed set to erupt. It took all the self-control and determined self-interest she could muster, to suppress her feelings. A surprising calm soon descended.

Everything happened within seconds. Almost without realizing it, Deborah started in Jonathan's direction. Her determined approach drew a wary glance from Richard.

"Excuse me, Jonathan! Jonathan Reed!" Deborah called out, forcing an air of cordiality into her voice. Jonathan wheeled around, and came face to face with Deborah for the first time since May 15, 1974. He squinted, peered at her curiously. She stared into his narrowed eyes, examined his face, his expression—all in a flash. The familiarity sickened her.

"Yes, I'm Jonathan Reed. I'm afraid you have me at a disadvantage." Jonathan struggled to hold Deborah's gaze. Richard looked on with mounting curiosity. His reddened brow wrinkled with deep frowns.

"I don't think so," said an unsmiling Deborah.

Jonathan kept staring, as if finding it difficult to recognize the woman standing in front of him. "I'm very sorry."

"I'm Deborah. Deborah Davis."

Eyes bulged. A look of recognition. A stunned expression gripped Jonathan's flushed face. He swallowed hard, turned beet- red. His jaw fell, lips parted, "Wait! Wait a second," he chortled, drawing closer, staring intently at Deborah. He straightened his tie.

"Deborah? Deborah Davis?"

"You know this young woman, Jonathan?"

"Yes, father. Ahh...from many years ago. As I recall, Deborah here is one of the Reverend Henry Davis' daughters. Deborah, this is my...my father, Richard Reed. Daddy, they lived on part of that big SB-40 section in Reedville. If I'm not mistaken, Deborah's been living up north...in Illinois, since...since, well, for a lot of years. That right, Deborah?" Jonathan looked as if he were seeing a ghost.

Deborah nodded, as she took note of Jonathan's deep unease. The fact he knew where she lived surprised her somewhat. Richard flashed a brief, obligatory smile then glanced at his watch.

"Welcome back to Arkansas. Guess you're here to help your family make movin' arrangements. That right?"

"No."

"No. I see. Well, what brings you to Little Rock? If I might ask."

An anxious Jonathan cleared his throat before Deborah could respond to his father. "Father, why don't we continue our conversation a little later. I'll just visit with Deborah for a bit. I'll c'mon down to your office, directly."

"Fine," said Richard, tersely. "Don't forget that meetin' with Chuck Stone at 1 o'clock. And I have a 3 o'clock at the Rose law firm right after that." Richard Reed turned on his heels and walked away abruptly, without a parting word to Deborah. He glanced back at her warily.

Jonathan cleared his parched throat. "Good to see you, after all these years. You cannot blame me for hardly recognizing you at first. My god. You have certainly changed. I must say I am more than a little surprised, to say the least. Didn't think I'd ever...ever see you again."

"I'm sure."

"Ah, If you have a moment, we can visit in my office. I've got a little time before my meeting. Wow. Ahh..what brings you here?"

Deborah ignored the question, as Jonathan escorted her down the busy corridor, drawing curious gazes from everyone they passed. Inside his outer office, Jonathan paused at his secretary's desk.

"Susan, hold my calls will you, dear?"

Susan was an attractive, full-figured, dimpled, auburn-haired woman in her early forties. Except for a slightly over made-up face, she seemed pleasant enough.

"Yes sir," she said, handing Jonathan a fistful of messages. He opened the door to a spacious office featuring a spectacular view of the Arkansas River. Momentarily, he directed Deborah to a leather armchair in front of his oversized oak desk.

The minute she entered the room, Deborah's attention was drawn to a large architect's model resting on a table and mounted underneath a clear Plexiglas canopy. A 'JOHN REED for U.S SENATE' bumper sticker adorned one wall. She also noticed a framed photo of Jonathan and a woman she presumed was his wife, along with a son who appeared about five or so, and a daughter, who looked to be about seven or eight. They seemed the perfect family. Perhaps a little too perfect.

"Can I get you something? Coffee? A soda?"

"No, thank you."

Jonathan dropped the messages onto his desk, released a poorly masked sigh and sat down uneasily.

"It's been an awful long time," he said. "You look absolutely wonderful, if I might say so. Life must be good."

"Thank you. I'm doing just fine. I see life is still extremely good for you. You're running for the U.S. Senate?"

"I'm giving it my best shot."

"No piddling stepping stones like Governor, or the House of Representatives for you, right?"

"I've always aimed for the stars. No use changing now. Any other day, I'd be out campaigning. But I got stuck in the office today. Guess it was supposed to be. Otherwise, I would have missed your visit."

"If you win you'll likely be one of the youngest ever elected to the Senate." There was nothing complimentary in Deborah's tone.

"Never thought about it. Of course, my opponent has raised the age issue. I simply use my version of the Reagan response. The matter hasn't been brought up again." He grinned and winked.

"Good for you."

"I'm sure you didn't come all the way down here to hear me discuss my political campaign experiences. How's your family?"

"Funny you should ask. My family is the reason I'm here."

"Are they well?"

"I'm sorry. But I must be blunt."

Jonathan paused, then sat back in his chair. "Then, please do, by all means." A nervous smile swept across his face, then faded.

Deborah sat forward, pointed a stern gaze at Jonathan. "Yesterday, one of your trusted employees—a Mr. Jeb Liddy—served a 'Notice to Vacate' on my parents. The notice gave them ten days to leave their home. We were stunned. Then it dawned on me...this must be some grievous error—some awful mistake. One I'm sure you'll be happy to immediately correct. I mean, these things do happen from time to time, right?"

Jonathan forced a smile, leaned all the way back in his chair, began twirling a pencil he lifted from his desk. Seconds passed. He moved forward, resting both forearms on the desktop.

"It's been a...a long time," Jonathan began. "Believe me, absolutely nothing would please me more than granting your request. But, sadly, I cannot...not on this."

"I see. Why can't you?"

"That architect's model there," he said, proudly pointing, "represents a project that's gon' pump a lot of money into that area—into the entire State of Arkansas. We need that land...all that land. It's indispensable to our long-term plan. Governor Clinton's office has given us complete support. It's a magnificent development. We wanted to call it Whitewater, but that name's been taken already."

Deborah paused to choose her words carefully, to retain full control of her emotions. Jonathan increasingly appeared ill at ease.

"That may be," she at last responded, "But I have a father who is near death, and a mother whom the years have worn down. They've lived more than thirty years in that house...on that land. Now, you and your company want to throw them off. We can't allow that. We won't."

Deborah heard the fervor and conviction in her own voice. She sounded every bit the devoted, concerned daughter. Still, she knew, in her heart, what was truly driving her. It was not only an innate concern for her mother and father she was briefly permitting herself to feel, it was the powerful, undeniable desire to exact revenge.

Jonathan's smile faded. He pushed back in his chair, stood slowly and proudly strode to the scale model. Deborah remained seated, but turned in her chair. Jonathan's air of superiority stirred a fire inside her. She fought to restrain her instinctive urge to lash out, determined to remain in control. Her inner burning was a controlled burn.

"Listen, I am truly sorry 'bout your daddy—The Reverend."

"Of course."

"I had no idea he was in poor health. But we did send letters to all your people out there. They never answered. Not one."

Deborah stood and moved to the edge of the desk. "What do you mean by *all your people?" Her* question was pointed.

Jonathan tossed his head back and flashed a quick smile.

"The Negro...ah, the black folks on our land out there. Now, please don't get offended. I'm just trying to get it right. Okay? We've lent a helping hand to them for many, many years. Many times they didn't have rent and we carried them."

Deborah walked over to the model display, determined to remain cool, but impassioned. "Let me help you get it right, Jonathan."

"Right? In what way?"

"Just listen. These people, including my parents, are the same people who purchased this property *for* you over the years. These people paid taxes for you and your family. They helped to create the life-style to which all of *your* people have become accustomed."

"Deborah, I beg to differ."

"And now, they...they don't count. Is that it? You just get rid of them? Plow them under like a failed crop, right? That's not moral, ethical, or politically astute. Tossing poor people out onto their backsides, during an election campaign, is not exactly a desirable photo-op, is it? I'm surprised your handlers haven't cautioned you...advised you to at least wait until after the election."

Jonathan started back to his desk. Deborah followed. "That is absolutely not the way it is," he said. "This here development is gon' put a lot of poor people to work. Just in case you haven't noticed, in spite of a so-called economic recovery in this here country, Arkansas remains in something near a doggone depression. Now that's a fact.

"Governor Clinton is doing the best he can, but we have to do our part. The fact we're undertaking a project like this, at a time like this, is a leap of faith, I assure you. I don't like the idea of rooting people out of their homes, but I got no choice. None!" Jonathan insisted. "Anyway, right now, I'm not involved in the family's business operations."

Deborah took her seat, and sat with legs crossed in the most lady-like fashion. She immediately noticed beads of sweat forming on Jonathan's wrinkled brow.

"And exactly what is this...this development?"

"You mean..."

"I mean, what are you planning to build? A medical center? A cancer research center? A flag factory?"

Jonathan cleared his throat. "Well actually, it's a Pro golf resort, a four-star hotel, some residential with modest to luxury homes."

"Let me make sure I've got this right," said Deborah.

Inside Richard Reed's closed office, he sat hunkered at his desk. A scowl covered his face. In an open desk drawer, an audio deck was recording the conversation in Jonathan's office. Deborah's voice could be clearly heard.

"You're planning to build a luxurious golf resort, hotel and, of course, some highly unaffordable housing. I'm sure the dozens of black golfers on the PGA Tour will jump for joy. And all those busboys, caddies and waiters will be tickled pink."

An angry Richard Reed thrust a middle finger high into the air, then pounded his desk furiously.

"I don't know what else I can say or do," said Jonathan. "We would sincerely like to help, but we can't afford to make exceptions. We can't. The most we could do, perhaps, is try to help find a small place somewhere for your folks. There's some land out near Shays Creek. We may see our way setting a few acres aside." Jonathan wiped his brow. Deborah shook her head, sadly.

"I do appreciate your gracious offer," said Deborah, in a mocking tone. "But no thanks. You know, I seem to recall hearing news reports that the EPA and key environmental groups determined major portions of that area are contaminated. I am certain you are completely unaware of all this. Several companies are believed to have made illegal chemical dumps out there for years. You're far too kind."

Jonathan could hardly sit in his chair. He squirmed; his face turned crimson; he clenched his jaws, his fists—squinted, as he waited for Deborah to finish. "I don't have to tolerate this," he thought. "Hell, I am soon to be a United States Senator—the youngest; perhaps even President of these United States, someday. I am on the cover of Times Magazine, for godsake."

Jonathan leaned forward in his chair, determined to seize control of the matter. "What you have heard is a slew of unsubstantiated claims not borne out by the facts. We—meaning my family, 'cause I am no longer personally involved—have done extensive analysis that show no such contamination anywhere in the area."

"You could sell them several SB-40 acres, however. Think of the positive political impact that would make."

Jonathan laughed then cupped his hand to his mouth. Deborah remained stone-faced. His grin evaporated.

"I don't mean to be disrespectful, but I doubt there's enough money between those folks out there...to make a down payment on an outhouse, let alone that land. That's prime real estate."

"Of course. Whatever could I have been thinking?"

"Besides, our selling any part of that property is totally out of the question."

"Perhaps," said Deborah, coolly.

"Sorry I can't help. I truly am. It was great seeing you. Give my best to your family. If you change your mind..."

"Is that your family?" Deborah pointed to the photograph on Jonathan's desk. Jonathan beamed with pride.

"Yes it is. My wife and two kids."

Deborah stared at Jonathan. He clearly found it difficult to hold her gaze. She flashed a faint smile.

"Are they the only children you have?"

"Of course they are." Jonathan's eyes widened. "I'm afraid I don't understand the meaning of your question, Deborah."

Again, inside Richard's office, the elder Reed leaned closer to make sure he didn't miss a word. His eyes narrowed. A deep scowl lined his seasoned face.

"Oh, I think you know very well what I mean, Mr. Jonathan Jefferson Davis Reed. I think you know very well."

Jonathan swallowed hard and adjusted his shirt collar. His nostrils flared. His eyes narrowed. Deborah stood.

"What are you saying?"

"Let me ask you. Do you remember when you last saw me?"

Jonathan stared at Deborah for what seemed forever. He rubbed his chin briefly, shook his head slowly. "Ah...no. I can't say that I do. I really can't. Should I?"

"You will."

"It's been so long, I..."

"It's been fourteen, long, painful years for me, Jonathan. Fourteen years. I'm back, now. Not for long, but long enough. Long enough to set everything straight. And I do mean everything."

Jonathan's eyes flared. He leaped to his feet, as Deborah turned and started for the door. "Hold on a minute! Are you threatening me in some way?" he bellowed. "Well, are you? 'Cause if you are, I advise you to think long and hard about that. I surely do. You hear me? Do you?"

Jonathan lost it. While Deborah calmly continued through the doorway, Jonathan followed, calling after her in a most undignified manner. His secretary, Susan, was aghast. She thrust one hand to her bosom, the other to her mouth.

"I said long and hard!" Jonathan repeated. "Do you hear me?"

Jonathan's words cast a look of shock on the faces of those who *only* heard his last words. It was as if the music stopped. Deborah slowed her pace and continued down the long corridor. A soft smile crept across her face. Seconds seemed like minutes, before she disappeared.

A grim-faced Richard stood observing his son from the corridor beyond Jonathan's office, and just outside his own. It was clear he was angry and exasperated by what he had heard and seen.

Jonathan wheeled around to see his father and a dozen others watching him with open mouths. For a moment, he just stood there, as if wondering what the hell had just transpired. The others were no doubt wondering the same. Jonathan was fuming...angry for allowing himself to be goaded into making such a complete ass of himself.

He wheeled around, stormed back down the empty corridor, past a calm, smiling Susan, and into his office. Swearing under his breath, Jonathan slammed the door. It closed with a resounding thud. A rabid Richard Reed reentered his own office and kicked his door closed.

chapter thirty-five

Aftermath

─────────────

"I sincerely hope you are not lyin' to me..."

Within minutes, Deborah was outbound
and en route to Reedville. She breezed through moderate freeway traffic, savoring her memory of the look on Jonathan's face. But her satisfaction was dampened, knowing he still planned to evict hundreds of families from SB-40 land, especially after what had just occurred.

Deborah eased into the middle lane, then dialed the hotel to see if
her package had arrived. It had. She again asked that it be held in the
safe until she arrived. Just as her call ended, she noticed a State Trooper's
cruiser closing fast behind her—headlights flashing. Deborah's heart
fluttered. She glanced down. The speedometer read 75 mph. Instead of
braking, she eased off the accelerator, expecting the inevitable.

With the trooper's car looming in her rear view mirror. Deborah
moved to the slow lane and prepared to brake. She thought about the
earlier phone call alerting her she was being watched. And she recalled
Maylene had reminded her of the Reed's awesome power. For a moment,

she thought it may have extended to the State Highway Patrol. But the officer zoomed past and exited just ahead of her. Deborah finally exhaled. She then called and ordered a new rental car be delivered by morning.

———

Back at Reed headquarters, a stern Richard Reed sat on the front edge of his desk with arms folded. Jonathan, in his full suit now, entered looking thoroughly chastened, although struggling to appear unaffected. Deep frowns were still embedded in his glistening forehead.

"Now, what in the hell happened out there? I am completely baffled. I shouldn't 'a had to call you in here," Richard grumbled. "After what I, and everybody else just witnessed, I expected you'd come in here on your own...explain all this mess."

"Explain what? There's nothing to explain."

"Bullshit! I repeat, bullshit! Let me remind you that you are a candidate for the United States Senate, not the...the local, goddamn school board. Jeezus! What's more, you are the leading candidate—the odds on favorite. A lot is ridin' on what happens between now and the November election. What if some nosey-ass reporter had been in the building...sniffing around? Maybe even some Republican infiltrator. Look, the Donald Segretties of this world still abound. Dirty tricks did not end with Watergate, despite Chuck Colson's 'Road to Damascus' experience. We cannot screw this campaign up with self-inflicted wounds. Now what the hell happened?"

"It was nothing more than a little argument over the eviction of her parents from part of SB-40."

"SB-40 my Confederate ass!" Richard barked, springing to his feet. "I have never seen you so angry before. Not ever. So, you tell me what in the hell that gal said that got you to make such a damn fool a' yo'self?"

Jonathan had not expected such a spirited reaction from the Ol' Man. He moved to the chair in front of his father's desk, and plopped down.

"These people are always crying 'bout something...always looking for white folks to give 'em something—a damn handout. All I said was, hell no! Fear of being labeled racist cannot change what we plan to do.

Funny thing is, most of them Negroes out there are gon' vote for me in the general election anyway, if they vote at all."

"That right?"

"Right."

"I see."

"Well who else they gon' vote for? A damn Republican?"

"You pretty cocksure, aren't you?"

"It's not that. Just look at the past. We may not be perfect, but what the hell have Republicans ever done to earn their votes?"

Richard thrust both hands into his pockets, and moved to stand behind his chair. He stared at Jonathan without blinking.

"Somethin' just ain't addin' up here. You shouted a very angry warnin' at her. Weren't exactly the best choice of words to be yellin' to a woman either. Never seen you like that before. So, convince me. Set my mind at ease."

Jonathan dragged both hands across his face. "I just let her get to me, is all. It was stupid. I'm sorry."

"I sincerely hope you are not lyin' to me. 'Cause if I find out you are, I will be...let's just say I will be one highly upset 'Cracker.' You hear? Now if you got a problem, I want you to find the balls to take care of it, or find somebody with balls who can. And unless you wanna have tongues waggin',' and blow this damn election, I don't think havin' some Negro woman visitin' you in your office, 'specially one who gets to you, and looks as good as she does, is very smart."

"I had absolutely no idea she was even still alive, much less right here in Little Rock."

"I don't wanna hear it. Had no business invitin' her into your office for a private visit. What could you possibly have had to say to her that could not be said in the lobby...in two seconds?"

"Alright, Daddy. But there's no problem here. I promise."

"We need you in the Senate. And I'm not about to hand your opponent anything he can use to Roto-Rooter our butts with."

"Everything is just...just fine."

"Just hunky-dory, I reckon. You think I'm makin' too much 'a this?"
"Honestly?"
"No, dammit! Lie to me, why don't cha.' Hell yeah, honestly!"
"Well, just a little."
"Well, I been aroun' a lot longer than you." Richard started for the door, then turned back to Jonathan, who was still seated. "As you well know, I got this...this antenna inside 'a me. You've seen it before. It's pretty damn accurate, too—as you well know also. It just goes...up. I don't manipulate it in any way. Never have. In fact, sometimes...sometimes I wish I didn't have the damn thing. But I do. So, I pay attention to it...careful attention. I really shouldn't blame it for my sleepless nights; for the fact that I got more hair missin' than I got left. And the fact that what's left is damn near all white, now. Know who I blame, huh? I blame the people in my life—those who set it off. And right now, that sonofabitch is up...way up. Now, don't try and bullshit an ol' turd like me. You damn sure there's nothin' you wanna tell me? I'll take the rest 'a the afternoon off."

Jonathan forced a weak smile, stood and started toward the door, minus his usual swagger.

"Everything's fine, Daddy."

Richard nodded, but did not appear convinced.

"Unh-huh. Just remember, we all have our hard-earned reputations, and generations of honor to maintain. Anything—and I do mean anything, or anyone—that threatens that reputation must be dealt with in whatever way is necessary. There are business associates, and supporters we do not want to upset. Appearance and perception can be more important than reality. Am I clear on this? Am I?"

"Clear."

"We'll sure as hell see. Now, don't miss that meetin' with Stone. He met with McDougal yesterday. And I want to hear more about this Democratic Leadership Council stuff. You gon' have to take a position on that. By the way, Governor Clinton's birthday is August, nineteen. Make damn sure you send a Hallmark card, and a nice gift. Nothin' cheap, like that ugly-ass necktie, and Cubic Zirconia cuff-links you gave me...for mine."

chapter thirty-six

Recollections

"You never know what's comin' out 'a Matthew's mouth," said Maylene.

Five vehicles were now parked
on the well-worn lawn in front of the Davis house. Energetic conversation, spiked with raucous laughter, spilled from inside. Yvonne and
Charles sat on the porch. She was reading a new book; he was breaking
in a brand new baseball glove: gifts from their Aunt Deborah. Both were
unaffected by the commotion coming from inside.

An hour earlier, Deborah and Matthew enjoyed a front porch reunion that threatened to consume every Kleenex in Reed County. Not
many had seen Matthew shed tears—ever. The instant he stepped out
of his truck and spotted his sister on the steps, he lost all inhibitions. He
was overcome with emotion that could not be contained.

Matthew stood in front of his truck, both hands covering his face,
weeping unashamedly. It was an emotional display none had seen him
exhibit before. It was Deborah, despite her own constrained, but tearful
reaction, who finally walked out to the yard to meet him.

The two stood locked in embrace for what seemed minutes. Deborah gazed into her brother's face, and her tears welled all over again. His was no longer the face of a fourteen year-old boy—her protector and best friend. He was no longer the "Maffew" who always accompanied her to Gram's. *That* Matthew was gone forever. He was now a man: six feet-three, bearded, fiercely opinionated, angry, and intense.

Deborah could only see the glow in his eyes, the smile on his face. He gazed back with eyes filled with both joy and regret. She wished it possible to instantly bridge the chasm created by the years of separation. But it was a void no wishing could fill. Time had formed it; only time could fill it.

The two of them had always been inseparable. Deborah remembered the countless trips to Gram d'lena's, the joy of seeing her standing in the doorway—arms outstretched as the two approached. Yet, despite all, there was no denying things had changed forever. There were moments, since her arrival, when Deborah had the inescapable feeling she was in the throes of a dream. A dream from which she could not awaken. And again, she questioned her decision to return to Reedville.

—

Inside the living room, Gloria and her boyfriend, Reginald, sat side by side on the love seat. Deborah and Maylene sat next to each other on the sofa. Matthew was perched on the arm of the sofa, next to Deborah.

Rachel had borrowed her mother's car and driven to Little Rock, leaving minutes before Deborah arrived. After all those missing years, Deborah's decision to speak face to face with her most estranged sister would have to wait still longer.

Reginald, 24, 6'-1," was wiry, handsome, straightlaced, intellectual, well-dressed, and sported a pair of wire-rimmed glasses. He had a decidedly professorial look about him, and had the skin tone, complexion and hair that qualified him as 'double high-yellow.'

Gloria, at 5'-4," 125 pounds, was the quintessential fashion horse. Everything about her screamed fashion chic. She looked fresh out of a salon, instead of having recently stepped off a flight from Atlanta. Neither her lashes, nails, nor her 'big' hair, appeared to be completely her own—the part that likely came with a receipt, that is. Still, Miss Gloria Lynn Davis made it all look damn good, and she knew it.

"I just want to thank all of you for not ever calling me 'Little Sister,' said Gloria. I know youngest sisters are always referred to as 'Little Sister.' I always cringe when I hear it."

"Naw, you mean Lil' Susta," Matthew corrected her. "That's what you really mean. And it's not too late, you know. That name really does fit you. I bet Reggie thinks so." Gloria shook a fist at her brother.

Matthew drew an instant bead on Reginald, patiently awaiting an opportunity to pounce. But presently, having all his sisters together for the first time in fourteen years, he was uncharacteristically emotional.

"Never thought I'd say this," he said.

"What is it now?" asked Gloria. She then immediately regretted having asked the question. "I can't believe I asked that," she quickly added. Matthew feigned indignation and hurt.

"You never know what's comin' out 'a Matthew's mouth," said Maylene. Y'all just here for a little while, but I have to hear chapter and verse from the 'Book of Matthew' everyday. Don't get me wrong, I love him dearly. But I think all that DDT they used to spray around here finally got to him."

"DDT?" asked Gloria.

"Yeah," said Maylene. You don't remember? They use to spray that stuff all over the place...tryin' to kill mosquitoes."

"Seems like I do."

"I remember," Matthew jumped in. "They claimed they were tryin' to kill mosquitoes, but..."

"Matthew!" Maylene broke in.

"Anyway," Matthew continued. "They use to come around, 'specially in the summer...in the evening time. They had this white, Reed County pickup truck with this DDT tank and hose in the truck bed. These two white guys would drive real slow through the Sticks, spraying this big cloud of white stuff that would cover everything.

"Stuff looked like smoke. You could smell it, too. Had a funny smell to it. Lot 'a kids would be runnin' behind this truck and disappearing in the spray. You couldn't even see 'em 'til the truck pulled away and all of a sudden these little black faces started poppin' out 'a the cloud of spray. If you didn't know any better, it looked like the truck was spittin' out little *colored children*."

"Boy, you crazy," laughed Maylene.

"Insane," added Gloria, shaking her head and holding a hand over her mouth to stifle laughter.

"We were breathin' that stuff all those years. Had no idea what it was we were being sprayed with," said Matthew. "But we survived. White folk must be scratchin' their heads, sayin: Damn! What we got 'a do to get rid of 'em? We made slaves out of 'em; we hung 'em; we broke up their families; we tried to keep 'em from learnin,' we sprayed 'em with DDT. And they still here. Man! We can't get rid of 'em. They just like cockroaches. We just stuck with 'em."

"Matthew, I am not going to pass out laughing at you. So please, let's talk about something else," Maylene suggested.

"Alright," Matthew agreed. "Hey, like I was sayin' before my sanity was questioned, I never thought I'd say this, but I have some intelligent, gorgeous sisters. I still think I would have loved having a brother, but I'm lucky to have them. And they're lucky to have me."

Maylene and Gloria pretended to faint, then broke into roaring laughter. Deborah smiled. Reginald sat quietly observing. Oddly, the two of them had a couple of things in common: both were strangers, and both seemed to share similar intellectual plateaus.

On several occasions, Deborah noticed Reginald was observing her, discreetly. "He must be wondering just how I fit in here," she thought. There was no way to know how much he knew, or did not know about the Davis family.

"What did we do to deserve all this praise?" asked Maylene. "I guess the Rapture is 'round the corner."

"Must be. Remember when we were little," said Gloria. "He used to talk about how nappy our hair was—except for Deborah's—used to laugh when Mama would comb it into a thousand little Buckwheat twigs that went every which way."

"I remember," said Maylene. "Mother would try to put little ribbons on it. The twigs would come loose and she'd put saliva on her fingers and..."

"Saliva?" chided Matthew. "You mean spit! It was plain ol' spit! Don't try to clean it up. We all family here, even Reggie. Right Reggie?"

Everyone laughed. Reginald flashed a wary smile and leaned back.

"Anyway," said Maylene. "She would put a little spit on the tips of her thumb and forefinger then twist the ends to try and make them stay together. It never really worked. And sometimes the little plaits—she called them plaits—they would be so tight your head would hurt. Felt like your scalp was gonna split. Even the skin on your forehead would be tight as a drum. You could hardly blink your eyes, for fear of ripping your eyelids."

"Matthew didn't think we were so gorgeous then," said Gloria.

"That's 'cause y'all weren't," Matthew answered. "Y'all thought you were. Like the time 'Lene got in trouble for puttin' Mama's lipstick all over her face. She then put one of Mama's giant bras on right over her dress. Thing looked like twin hammocks."

"I remember that!" Gloria piped in. "I helped her put it on."

"They put it on so tight, she couldn't get it off," said Matthew. "So when Mama came home, 'Lene had this big overcoat on tryin' to hide the bra. But that was dumb, 'cause it was in August or somethin'—dead 'a summer. Mama knew somethin' was wrong right away. The girl had the coat buttoned up to her neck. And was drippin' with sweat. She was two degrees from explodin'."

"Mama made me keep the thing on 'til Daddy got home," said Maylene. I thought he was gon' kill me, but he didn't. He laughed for a solid hour. I could've had a heat stroke."

"Reginald, you must think this is all a little insane," said Maylene. "You got sisters or brothers?"

"No, no siblings."

Matthew rolled his eyes. Maylene struggled to contain herself.

"I'm sorry," Matthew chuckled. "You don't have any what?" The question seemed to catch Reginald off guard.

"It means he's an only child, Matthew," said Gloria, laughing. Maylene covered her mouth and looked away.

"I knew that."

"Matthew, why don't you tell us about you and that Royal Crown Men's Pomade hair dressing fiasco?" said Gloria. Everyone echoed her suggestion.

"That's the thanks I get," said Matthew. "I give y'all a compliment and you turn on me. I don't remember nothin' about that."

"I do," said Maylene.

"Who asked you?" Matthew replied. Maylene ignored him.

"One time—I guess Matthew must've been 'bout eleven—he saw this picture of Jackie Wilson in this old Jet Magazine. So he sneaked into Daddy's room and got a can of this thick, gooey, sweet-smelling hair stuff Daddy used to use. Stuff must've been twenty years old, even then. He put gobs of this stuff all over his head then put water on it, slicked it down and everything. Mess looked like glue. He thought he was sharp, girl. Then he got Mama's good broom."

"You mean her brand new broom," said Gloria.

"Right. You know how Mama was 'bout her new brooms. And still is. Anyway, Matthew put this glue on his hair..."

"C'mon 'Lene," pleaded Matthew. "Stop exaggerating. It wasn't that bad. It wasn't like glue." Maylene waved him off.

"I'm tellin' this story. If it looked like glue, stuck like glue, it was glue," she insisted. "Anyway, he got Mama's new broom and went stood in front of her big mirror. He pretended the broom was his microphone, and he was Jackie Wilson. He was jumping and hollering and trying to do leg splits like Jackie. Honey, Mama came into the room and..."

"No, it was Daddy," Gloria corrected.

"Right," Maylene agreed. "Daddy walked in on him. Matthew looked into the mirror and saw Daddy standing behind him. It scared him so bad he dropped the broom. It crashed into the mirror. Mirror broke into a gazillion pieces. Glass went everywhere, child."

"When Daddy got through with him, Matthew couldn't sit on his behind for a week. Had to stand up at the dinner table," said Gloria, doubling over laughing.

Everyone was in stitches. At that moment, Mabel Davis entered from the kitchen, drying her hands on the huge plaid apron she wore. While laughter roared on, she stood grim-faced, arms folded.

"Matthew, get your butt off the arm of my sofa," she ordered. Matthew jumped straight up. Maylene and Gloria were still doubled over. By now, everything was funny.

"Food's cookin' now," said Mabel. "Y'all can eat in a little while. I know those sandwiches ain't gonna hold y'all for long, especially those children."

"We're okay, Mama," said Maylene. "We're just sitting here talkin,' teasing Matthew 'bout old times."

"I heard well enough. Wish y'all would tone it down some. Your daddy's still low sick, you know."

A hush fell on the room like a boulder. Mabel Davis headed back to the kitchen. No one spoke until Matthew broke the silence.

"Reginald, you're lucky."

"How so?"

"How so? Well, I was always outnumbered five to one. Six to one, when the ol' man was well. But I love 'em all, includin' Rachel. I'm sad to say, I haven't seen Deborah in a...a hundred years, seem like. But somehow, it's just like she was always here, 'cause I kept her here in my heart."

Silence returned, for a brief time. Despite the laughter and teasing, emotions were being worn on the surface. Matthew hugged and kissed Deborah. Although she resisted the emotional tug of war going on inside her, she clung to him for what seemed an eternity.

She then removed a small cross and chain she wore around her neck and handed it to Matthew. That morning, Deborah had debated whether to wear it or not. Matthew recognized it right away. He held it delicately in his brawny hands. It was the one he had given her that Sunday morning fourteen years ago.

Matthew took a deep breath, leaned forward, placed the chain lovingly around his sister's neck. Once again, he whispered in her ear. Each failed to choke back an onrush of emotion. Tears flowed freely. Silence filled the room. One could hear hearts beat.

Deborah saw both joy and sorrow in her brother's teary eyes. And he saw his reflection in hers—a reflection, not as he presently was, but as he was long ago. It was an image of himself that had eluded him all those years.

"Wow. I didn't mean to start all this," he said.

By now every eye was wet. Matthew hugged Deborah again, and for a long while. Maylene bounced up, headed for the kitchen.

"I'll see if Mama needs some help."

Deborah stood, started for her father's bedroom. Throughout the raucous reminiscing by her siblings, she endured a feeling of abject detachment. It seemed clear all were careful to mention only those things she would also remember.

Deborah found herself focusing on those lost years—the times not shared. What memories had been lost? What 'growing up' experiences had she not shared? Notwithstanding the moment shared with Matthew, she felt like an outsider—a total stranger. And again she questioned the wisdom of having returned to Reedville.

Samantha. Deborah thought about her daughter constantly. She whispered her name, and her heart raced, her eyes teared. Excitement and wonder filled her to overflowing. And once more, she understood why her coming was her only choice. But that feeling was accompanied by a new anger, a new rage. The big lie, all the lies, the cruel deception Samantha had been fed all these years.

Her sister? Deborah could not stop thinking about the fact her own parents—these righteous people—had denied her existence; they had all denied her. And in the process, they had denied Samantha the knowledge she had a living, breathing, caring mother—a mother with a name, a face, a longing to know her.

But why? That one, haunting, persistent question was always stirring in Deborah's mind. Even her reinventing herself did not purge it. Sleep offered only the briefest escape, if she were lucky. Often, it was there in her dreams, her waking hours. Nearly always there.

The question begged for truth. However, the truth would have meant Reverend and Sister Davis confessing to other lies, admitting old wrongs, explaining the unexplained. It would have meant answering questions they had been unwilling or unprepared to answer. That was especially true for Mabel Davis—Sister Mabel Davis. First Lady of the Church, Mabel Davis. *"That* Mabel Davis," Deborah thought, angrily.

Deborah was filled with a compote of emotions. Once more, she strongly considered immediately ending the charade, despite the likely trauma such a decision may have had on Samantha. She silently prayed for inner calm, no matter how brief. She prayed for direction and resolve; prayed, even as she doubted an answer would come.

Almost instantly, her mind was consumed by the image of Gram d'lena. Deborah's prayer could only have been so answered. A peace came upon her in a way that overshadowed all else, for the moment.

—

Meanwhile, Matthew turned to Reginald. "So, ahh...I understand you graduated from Morehouse, right?"

"Correct. I'm presently in Meharry Medical School," said a tentative Reginald. He was stiff as a steel rod. And clearly uncomfortable with Matthew's rough-hewn, earthy personality.

"That's great."

Matthew leaned forward, stared at Reginald pointedly. "Little Susta' graduated from Spelman on scholarship...assistant to the Mayor of Atlanta, now. And you gon' be a doctor. That's wonderful."

"That's my goal."

"Outstandin'! I love to see brothers and sisters get ahead. But it's a lot harder for the brothers, though. Right? Most white men see black men as a threat. We make 'em uneasy. You know I'm right. They want to keep us dumb, on drugs, and killin' each other.

"And some of us are stupid enough to go along. Most times, they can't even look us in the eye. You ever notice that? Even when they shake your hand, they look away. And they shake your hand real funny, too. Like they can't wait to get it back out of yours. Like they gon' turn black, or maybe you gon' steal a finger or two."

"Well..." Reginald started.

"But they not threatened by black women at all," Matthew went on, "That's why they quicker to give sisters jobs, while brothers get froze out. Then, if you ain't a so-called success, the sisters freeze you out...won't even talk to your ass. I'm not sayin' that's true in every case, but more than it should. Right?"

"I suppose that..."

"Hold up, hold up. There's one more thing. And this has to do with successful black folk who do make it to the top, or at least a few miles from the bottom. Why is it that so many...they refuse to reach down and lift up? It's like they feel...Hey, I got out, so you get your ass out...on your own. Now, I'm not sayin' they all like that, but too many...way too many. Right?"

Reginald stole a glance at Gloria, who remained uncharacteristically quiet—one hand shielding her face.

"Don't be looking at her. Speak up for yourself, my brother. Don't you think I'm right...I mean, about all that?"

"Well, I suppose you do have a point. Although I..."

"Although what? It all goes back to white folk teachin' us to think less of ourselves...goes back to slavery. We have to fight that. Mama thinks I hate all white people. I don't. Just those that deserve it. Like the bible says, there's times for all things: war, peace...livin', dyin', love, hate. What?"

Reginald cleared his throat and peeked at Gloria again. "Nothing. You...you do make some good points."

"You damn right, I got good points. Look, like I said, I don't hate white people, not all of 'em. I'm just sayin' if black people had done to white folks what they did, and are still doing to us, they would feel the same way I do. Still, you got some of 'em who act like we held *them* in slavery...like we hung their asses and stuffed their balls in their mouths. They act like we keep them from gettin' jobs or bank loans or whatever. If anybody got a right to be pissed off, it's us."

"I understand what you're saying, but what we..."

"But, what?"

"But..."

"Listen, what kinda chance you think Jesse's got?"

Before Reginald could answer, Gloria left for her father's bedroom. Reginald immediately had the look of a rabbit caught in a steel trap.

"Jesse?"

"Jesse Jackson! You think he got a chance?"

"I think he makes some valid and important arguments. I have no problem with Mr. Jackson. However..."

"However? However, what? If he was white he'd be president in a heartbeat. God's truth. Right?"

"Perhaps, but..."

"But what?"

chapter thirty-seven

A Lasting Image

"His eyes are open!".

Gloria entered her parents' bedroom
and found Deborah standing next to the Reverend's bed. She quietly
moved to her sister's side and placed a hand on her shoulder. It seemed
she just wanted to touch Deborah—make her presence real. For a time,
there was only throbbing silence punctuated by deep breaths.

"None of this is real for me," said Gloria. " Your being here...him lying there. It's so hard for me to look at Daddy like this. I see him so
clearly the way he was—so full of vigor, jumping up and down in that
pulpit, preaching hellfire and damnation; the choir behind him like they
were as much a part of his sermon as he was.

"When he'd finish, I was ready to run down that aisle, throw myself
on the altar and join church all over again, every Sunday. Other times,
he would do more teaching than preaching. Most folks preferred the
preaching. At least it seemed that way." Gloria squeezed Deborah's shoulder affectionately.

Reverend lay still. His lids were mere slits, his mouth slightly twisted. Gloria grabbed a tissue and dabbed drool from the corner of his mouth.

"I can still hear the last thing he said to me that Sunday morning I left," said Deborah. "I hadn't been able to sleep at all the night before. I kept thinking any minute he would come get me, sit me down and say: *Now listen daughter, I hope you learned your lesson. With God's help, we'll get through all this together, with...with you here where you belong.*

And I would have been so happy to hear him say I could stay. I would have said anything, done anything. But he didn't say that. He didn't say anything like that. All he said was to obey Aunt Rose. And whatever happened later would depend on whatever the Lord said. I guess the Lord never told him to forgive his twelve year-old daughter and bring her back home."

Deborah's voice trailed, as she stepped away from the bed. Gloria followed, placed a hand on her sister's shoulder. "I'm having a hard time—a hard time realizing your being here is real. And I can't imagine what it's like for you."

Deborah nodded. "I'm sure I won't really understand just how I feel until I'm back in Chicago. It's impossible to take this all in."

Gloria stepped around to face her. "I just want to look at you. It's...it's so hard to describe how terrible it was watching you leave that Sunday. I was only eight, but I remember. I get chills when I think about that day. And yet I absolutely have no explanation for how we let so much time pass without trying to set things right. I guess, in some strange way, the same father who sent you away is responsible for bringing you back."

Deborah struggled to dampen her emotions. "I suppose that's true," she said. Several silent seconds slipped by.

"I'm sorry for staring," Gloria apologized.

"That's okay."

"How long are you staying?"

"I'm not sure. A few days, a week maybe."

"Have you talked to Rachel?"

Deborah shook her head, no. "I haven't even seen Rachel. I'm not sure I will. And I'm not sure she cares one way or the other. We were never close. I don't think she was at all unhappy I was no longer here. She's dead to me." Deborah paused to permit Gloria's reaction.

Gloria seemed lost for words. Her eyes darted about the room, briefly. She struggled for a response. "I guess...I guess I was too young to remember much about then. But I do remember how much I wanted to...to be like you and Maylene. What I remember most, is that you never treated me like...like I was just a little sister. You made me feel I was as old as you were. When you left, there was such a...such an emptiness."

Before Deborah could say anything, Gloria glanced toward the Reverend and was stunned to see him staring back at her. His eyes were open; his lips were parted and quivering. Gloria's jaw dropped.

"Deborah! Deborah!" Gloria blurted, pointing frantically. "Daddy's eyes! They're open!"

A startled Deborah wheeled around. The two dashed back to the bed. "His eyes are open! Is he trying to talk? "

"I think so," said Gloria. "Mama!" She bolted from the room, yelling out to her mother at the top of her voice.

Deborah's heart raced. Her eyes fixed on her father's face. She reached out, lifted his right hand from beneath the sheet gently, and stroked it softly. Her own hands trembled; tears pooled. She stared into her father's eyes deeply, searching for some sign he could see and recognize her.

"Father, can you hear me? Can you see me? It's me, Deborah. Can you say something to me? Can you...squeeze my hand?"

Gloria returned with her mother, Maylene and the others, including Rebecca and the children. Reginald stood several feet back, while the others crowded around the bed. An excited Mabel Davis clutched her chest with both hands. Deborah took a step back.

"Thank you, Jesus. Thank You! Praise God!" Mabel Davis chanted. "Can he...can he really see and hear us?" she asked tearfully. Rebecca moved to her side.

"Sister Davis, I don't know. It's so hard to tell. His pupils do seem to be reacting to the light, but..." Rebecca moved her right hand back and forth above the Reverend's eyes.

Reginald moved closer, leaned over the bed hoping to observe movement. "Well, he does seem to be following my finger ever so slightly. Not much, but some. He does appear to be tracking. Looks like there is some pupil response," said Reginald. "The rapid blinking could be a result of light sensitivity. No way to judge visual acuity. We may be only a faint blur to him, or he may actually recognize you all. Strokes can seriously damage cognitive ability. I sure would love to have him in a hospital."

"What does this mean?" asked Mabel Davis. "Is he getting any better? Is he gon' be alright? Is he?"

"I sure hope so, Mrs. Davis. But I'm not a doctor, yet. All I can do is pray like all of you. Recovery from a stroke can be tedious, full of ups and downs. Intensive treatment is required."

Deborah and Maylene exchanged glances. Both then focused on their mother, who avoided their gazes. Deborah stared long and hard at her ailing father. Although barely open, his eyes seemed fixed squarely on her. His face twitched; his lips parted again. He appeared to be trying to speak. Everyone crowded closer, praying they were about to witness a miracle. Gloria turned to Deborah. "He's...he's looking at you. I think he's trying to say something."

Deborah leaned farther over the bed, and gently held her father's left hand in both her own. She felt his fingers move slightly, or perhaps she only imagined they moved. She chose to believe they had. "He moved his hand just now," she said. "I felt it move."

Mabel Davis' face beamed. "Help him, Father," she whispered, then moved the final step to stand next to Reverend's bed. "God, help him."

Yet, despite all her expressions of concern and elation, Mabel Davis never placed a hand on her husband. She never once touched him. Seconds later, a small tear trickled from Reverend's right eye.

"He's crying, Mama," Gloria blurted. "He must know we're here. I'm here! We're all here. You're going to get better. Can you hear me, Daddy?"

The Reverend's eyelids fluttered several times, then his eyes closed firmly. More tears trickled down the right side of his face. Deborah dabbed them away with a tissue Rebecca handed her, then wiped away her own.

Reginald felt compelled to temper the elation he saw on everyone's face. "He's okay," he said. "He's probably extremely tired. What you just saw consumed a lot of energy."

Rebecca tucked the sheet underneath the Reverend's chin, Gloria stroked his brow gently. Mabel adjusted the top sheet fold. "I think we ought 'a let him rest now," she said. "Thank God, he's gettin' better. The Lord does answer prayer. He does."

Before leaving the room, Rebecca checked the I.V and adjusted the pillows underneath the Reverend's head and upper back. Then, one by one, the others, including Mabel, slowly filed from the room. Deborah remained with Gloria and Maylene for a short time. The three embraced, only steps from their father's bed. A grim-faced Matthew stood near the dresser, staring blankly at the wooden floor.

chapter thirty-eight

The Visit

===================

"That wasn't what killed him, though."

Deborah's car was parked
in the driveway of a large, white, wood-framed, two-story home. She remembered having passed by it the day before. The majestic, multi-gabled structure, with its wide porch boasting swings at either end, was set well off the road, surrounded by a gently sloping green lawn.

An elaborate greenhouse was nestled at the rear, at the end of a winding walkway, and slightly to the east side of the sprawling main house. Deborah faintly remembered the huge estate being home to a former Reedville Mayor, and Reed family kin, back in the late sixties, and early seventies.

The elegant structure, and several others in the area, were large, stately homes located far away from the railroad tracks and The Sticks. They were homes most Blacks, and poor Whites could only dream of owning. In summers, such homes gleamed, sparkled from weeks of spring cleaning, and fresh painting, done by those who returned to cramped, unpainted shanties at day's end.

Inside the greenhouse, Miss Jasmine and Deborah were immersed in lively conversation, even as Jasmine continued snipping, watering and rearranging her family of plants and flowers. She was justifiably proud of her green thumb.

"I am certainly thrilled to hear about your father," she said. "Let us hope and pray it's the first step on the road to his full recovery. I can imagine how important it is to have him know what a fine young woman you have become."

"Thank you. Yes ma'am. It is."

"Now, if we are to get along, you have to stop this *yes ma'am* business," said Jasmine with a wide grin. "I am plain ol' Jasmine. And if the inhibition growing out of the fear I instilled all those years ago makes such informality impossible, a simple yes or no will do nicely. Agreed?"

"Agreed."

"Are you sure I can't get you some tea or a soda? I make some great tea. Mr. Baker used to drink it all day long. That was not what killed him, though, lest that be construed as a belated confession. For the record, it was congenital heart failure. Same thing took his father."

"I'm sorry."

"Honey, it was ten years ago, come the 24th of November...on his birthday, almost to the hour. I gave myself all the time I needed to grieve, then vowed to get on with my life. I went on. I loved Eddie. He knew I loved him. But, he would have wanted me to go on with my life. And I was not about to disappoint him on that score. That did not include remarrying. Raising one husband was plenty for me," Jasmine concluded with a wave of her gloved hand.

Deborah laughed. She could not help recalling that when she was in sixth grade, Jasmine Baker was more renown for her strict discipline than her sense of humor. She always commanded attention and respect, by the sheer force of her personality and presence. A disapproving glance was usually always enough to encourage compliance with forestated rules. However, on the rare occasion, when that failed, she would double the homework for the entire class. The offending student then had the anger and venom of the entire class to contend with. Even Principals and administrators were deferential to her. And she never once raised her voice above its normal level.

"Now, how about some of my famous tea?" asked Jasmine, smiling. "I think it's safe. I'll try it first, if you like."

Deborah accepted, with a broad smile. Jasmine removed her gloves, and the two moved to a white, wicker table with four matching chairs. Jasmine offered Deborah a seat, and poured two tall glasses of tea with lemon twist After sweetening the drink with raw sugar, Deborah eased her chair forward and took a big swig.

"Delicious."

Jasmine sipped her own. "Well, now. It *is* pretty good, if I say so myself. Once in a blue moon it's awful, then I use it as weed killer. It is a lot less toxic, but it does the job. Guess today is your lucky day," she said. Both laughed. Jasmine gazed at Deborah for a long moment.

"Samantha is your daughter, isn't she?"

Deborah was jolted back in her chair; tea spilled from her glass. She set her glass on the table, used her napkin to clear the small spill. "I saw it on your face...at your mother's, when Samantha greeted you."

"Yes. Yes, she is. Samantha is my daughter, not my sister." Deborah answered, proudly and sadly. Even as the words, *my daughter,* slipped past her lips. She felt her heart race.

"Please excuse my directness. I don't know how to be otherwise. Been that way all my life. I'm the one who proposed to Eddie, my husband. That was definitely not the thing to do back in '46, you know. He called me crazy. I never denied it."

Deborah lifted her drink again, smiled self-consciously.

"As quiet as it's been kept, and mostly out of respect for your parents, there is hardly a black person in Reedville County, who did not suspect that was the case. And the white folks certainly had raised eyebrows when they saw Samantha with your folks. Some of them likely took deathly ill. Especially those Gilmore brothers and their bunch. They were just about the most hate-filled rednecks I have ever seen in my life. They made people like Lester Maddox and George Wallace look like life-time members of the NAACP."

"I can't say I'm at all surprised," said Deborah, "I would've guessed many people reacted in that way."

"It was just that less than a year after you were sent away, your folks were saying they had adopted this...this brand new baby. Now, we all know black people come in all flavors. But, this baby clearly had direct Anglo parentage. That was clear. And there was the question of how such an adoption would have been handled here in Arkansas anyway. Later, when Sam started school, I had a chance to see her birth certificate."

"What did it say?" Deborah was anxious to know.

"It listed you as the baby's mother, and the father as...as unknown."

"Unknown. I suppose I expected that."

"But even before you left, most people heard the truth."

"The truth?"

"From Tommy and your two girlfriends. They explained the Reed boy had convinced you to accept a ride home and...Well, I do not have to tell you what happened after that. Most everybody able to walk upright and eat with a fork surmised what had happened. But, again, out of respect for your parents, no one openly questioned the veracity of their explanation. And the talk never went beyond the Sticks."

"Over the years, I've pushed much of that day aside...forced it into the darkest corners of my mind."

"I can understand," said Jasmine. "I cannot begin to imagine what these past fourteen years have been like for you."

"It's impossible to say, especially in the early years. After a time, it wasn't death I feared, it was life."

"Of course. Of course. My God, you were only twelve then—a mere baby yourself."

"But at this point in my life I feel my entire future happiness depends upon me facing my past."

"That could be unnerving for some people." Jasmine's voice dropped to a loud whisper. "There are those who would likely do anything to see the past remains the past."

"I've considered that. But I know in my heart it's time to set things straight. It's time to stop living lies. Until I saw Samantha...looked into her eyes, I was planning to leave tomorrow. I can't now."

"It must be especially difficult to have to return home and find your father the way he is now."

"I almost didn't come."

"Why did you, besides for Samantha? I know you must still love your father, despite everything."

"Love and hate."

"That's completely understandable, dear."

"My coming was as much for me as for him. I suppose I didn't want to later regret not coming back here, if..."

"If your father—God forbids—passes on?"

"Yes."

"You know, I understand some of what you have gone through, in a personal way. You see, back in Tennessee, my father was one of those fire and brimstone preachers, too. We lived within a stone's throw of Clarksville."

"Clarksville?"

"That's right. You ever been there?"

"No. It's just that Mother is from near Chattanooga."

" Is that right?"

"I've never been there, either. But, I *have* heard of Clarksville"

"Of course. I'm proud to say it's the hometown of Wilma Rudolph. She put us on the map, that's for sure. On Sundays, Papa would dress up in his fine, blue-surge suit—almost always wore a blue suit of some kind, except for funerals. And he would deliver what people called a real stemwinder." Jasmine Baker laughed. But Deborah was sure she saw something other than laughter in her eyes.

"I don't believe I ever knew you were a preacher's daughter."

"Not many people here know much about me," Jasmine proudly noted. "One should always keep certain personal facts just that—personal. Like I said, Papa could bring the house down. Those good ol' sisters, with their wide-brim hats and painted faces, would be shouting and fainting all over the church. And we were not even Baptist. We were Episcopalian. Back when I was a little girl, I thought that was some sort of disease. I couldn't even say the word."

"What about your mother, your sisters...brothers?"

"I never knew my mother—not my birth mother. When I was ten, I learned she was a married English missionary my father met when she came here from London. When the time came, after I was born, she returned to England. I never heard from her. Two months before Eddie and I were married, I learned she had died six years earlier. Someday, I'd like to go to England...visit her grave. Don't know why. It's just something I feel I want to do before I die." Jasmine took a long drink of tea.

Deborah felt badly for her, but was not certain what to say. "Any bothers or sisters?" she asked again.

"No. My father married my adoptive mother when I was three. As far as I am concerned, she was always my mother. But because she was dark-skinned, and I looked...well, almost white, people thought she was my nanny. Even black people constantly asked if she was really my mother. She never got angry, would always answer *yes*, proudly, and without explanation."

"She loved you, unconditionally."

"She did, indeed. And I loved her right back."

"Are your parents still alive?"

"No. Papa died in '69. Mother passed away six months later. But I am not going to get all teary-eyed talking about my ancient history. You have this gorgeous, intelligent, talented daughter who is quite curious. But I have had some concerns for her. I don't know what your mother has told you, but it has not been easy for Samantha."

"What do you mean?"

"Well, you can imagine. Black people look at her and say one thing; white folks say something else. And they don't always whisper. Kids can be especially cruel. But others have done their share of gossiping, too, particularly in those early years. It has gotten better. Sam always tries to rise above it all. She is an amazing young lady. Fortunately, she has several close friends. That helps. And she trusts me enough to share her thoughts from time to time. I listen to her. I always listen to her. And I often learn more than I teach."

"Thanks so much," said Deborah. And I'm so happy you're sharing this with me. I'm ashamed to say I know so little about her."

"I'm sure you plan to have a long, long talk with Samantha. I know she must be a major part of that 'facing the past' you spoke about. More tea, hon'?"

"No thanks," said Deborah. "I know Sam has to know, and soon." Jasmine nodded agreement.

"I know I'm probably talking too much. But you know how it is in a small town, most especially a small southern town. Even in 1974, it would not have been easy to accuse the son of a prominent white family of being the father of a black baby. Of course there's a sordid history of such things, going back to slavery."

Deborah nodded. "What you just said about the past is true. But today's a new day for me."

"You're right. Whether people are ready for it or not, today is a new day," said Jasmine. "At least I'd like to believe that's true. Sometimes I find it difficult to see what is so new," she said, as she reached across the table and squeezed Deborah's hand. "Come with me. I'll show you around the house." The two stood. Jasmine started away. Deborah took a long sip, before placing her tea glass down. "You can bring that with you," said Jasmine, glancing over her shoulder. Deborah retrieved her glass and hurried to catch up. The two started from the greenhouse, and out into brilliant daylight.

"And how did you find your sister, Rachel?"

"Ma'am?"

"I mean, she's still recovering from everything. Shame. She was always the quiet one. In fact, the word strange comes to mind. She did not seem to be as easily affected by things as the other children. I always felt she internalized her feelings well beyond what was healthy. A person needs to release pent up feelings, at least once in a while. You two have a chance to talk?"

"Not yet. I think my showing up unexpectedly was a shock to everyone's normalcy."

"Normalcy? Honey, what normalcy? You are in Reedville, Arkansas. I can assure you there has been little I would characterize as normal around here, especially over the past few weeks and days. Murder has a way of destroying feelings of normalcy."

Deborah's ears perked, as Miss Jasmine refilled her glass.

"Murder?"

"Yes, murder. Do not tell me no one told you."

"No."

"No one?"

"No one."

"Well, I suppose, with the present health of your father, everyone is rightly focused on his condition, and your being here."

"Who was murdered?"

"Willie Montgomery. I don't know if you would remember ol' Willie. He was at least four grades ahead of you, chronologically, that is. Must have been Maylene's classmate. He was always tall for his age...skinny, dark-skinned, had a loping walk, grinned a lot, had a gold tooth. Never seemed to have both shoes on at the same time, if you get my meaning. He was always in one bit of trouble or another. Always hung out with the wrong crowd."

"What happened? Who killed him?"

"No one knows. He was found a week ago, out near the edge of Devil's Woods, just off Langston Road. Was not far from where Deputy Rufus Bluehorn was killed years ago. Those woods are worse than the Bermuda Triangle, as far as turning up dead black folk. Then, there was the Brock girl who was killed not far from your folks' place, just off Crispus Attucks, more than twelve years ago—Jozeta Brock. Her brother, Waymon would have been in your class. At least two more black girls vanished, and were never heard from again: Elmira Stucey, and Crezette Winston—Mr. Winston's daughter. You may remember, he owned the cleaners. They disappeared three months apart, back in late eighty-two."

"I can't imagine what it must have been like around here."

"It was awful. Not one clue, regarding what or who was behind it all. Forgive me, but I digress a bit. Back to Willie. Seems somebody put a shotgun to ol' Willie's head, and just blew out what few brains he did have. I shouldn't talk like that. Anyway, he was found dumped in a drainage ditch, butt naked...had a corn cob shoved in his mouth. Now, that sounds like something you see in movies, if you ask me."

"Who do the police think did it?"

"Police? Darling, you have been gone for a while. The sheriff will not spend a single man-hour trying to track down poor Willie's killer. About the only justice he is ever going to see will be found in the hereafter. Nothing will be done in the here and now. Death at the hand of killer or killers unknown. That's the way it was recorded, I am most sure.

"The strange thing is, Willie hadn't been living around here for fourteen years. As I recall, he disappeared about the time you were sent away. His mama died three years later. He didn't return for her funeral. What is even stranger, he never returned to claim the home and other property his mother owned. His father was a big-time gambler...bought the land in 'Sixty,' right before he disappeared, never to be heard from again. Of course, Reed County took the property for back taxes. Willie would have been...oh, about nineteen when his mama passed."

Deborah had faint recollections of Willie Montgomery. She did recall that he approached her and the girls once, during their walk home from school. They rebuffed his advances and he went on his way.

"I am so sorry, honey. I really shouldn't go on like this. It's just that I seldom have the chance to have an intelligent conversation with someone who feels obliged to listen, whether they are truly interested or not."

"No. I'm fascinated. I'm so happy to see you. I love talking to you."

"Do not encourage me," Jasmine grinned. "Tell me something. You ever hear the names, Jude Barsteau...or Florinda Batiste?"

The question seemed an afterthought. Deborah thought for a second. "Barsteau...Batiste. No. Should I have? Who are they?"

"Oh, just folk who used to live around Reedville a long time ago. It's not important." Jasmine stood and motioned Deborah to join her.

"Barsteau," Deborah repeated. I might have heard *that* name once, maybe. Who was he...or is he?"

"Oh, it's not important, dear. I was just wondering."

Neither Barsteau, nor Batiste were names familiar to Deborah. She wondered why Jasmine had mentioned them, but decided not to press the matter. Still, she felt the question was asked to measure her reaction. Something told her she did not want to know more.

"By the way," Jasmine continued, "this place once belonged to an early Governor of Arkansas. And more recently, a former mayor of Reedville. I understand they used to have some wild parties here. Even orgies, if stories are to be believed. Only black folks allowed inside then were maids and butlers."

Miss Jasmine and Deborah continued down a narrow stone-lined path leading toward the main house. "There used to be quarters for them out back—way out back, about a hundred yards from the main house," Jasmine said, pointing. "They wanted them close, but not too close. I never want to forget those things.

"Over there, next to that old abandoned water well," Jasmine pointed to the brick-lined, cemented remains of what was apparently a well. "I was digging...one day, and found some bones and a gold bracelet. Bones looked like part of a hand. I am no forensic expert, but I am sure of it."

"Bones? Human Bones?"

"Sure looked like it."

"What did you do?"

"Stopped digging. Did not want to find anything else. Considering the history of this place, there is no telling who and what is buried here."

"Did you put them back?

"Just the bones." Miss Jasmine raised her left arm to show Deborah a beautiful gold bracelet adorning her wrist.

"You didn't call the police?"

Jasmine chuckled. "My dear, you likely forget the history of the South. I have a feeling the police, past and present, know more about what happened here than anyone. Besides, I did not want to risk having some, plow-nosed bureaucrat declaring this some historical burial ground, ordering me off my land, and plastering some 'Historical Site' placard in my front yard."

The two shared more laughter.

"I am so proud of you," said Jasmine.

"Thank you."

"A real author. And a successful one at that. I guess you know a lot of your readers do not know you're black. And that is the beauty of it. It should not matter one whit. It is the wonderful nature of your writing that really matters. You write with such passion and emotional clarity. And your characters: they are black, white, brown, yellow, good, evil—they are people. What you have is God-given talent. One can learn technique, but one cannot learn or earn talent.

"Of course, as your celebrity grows, many folks will have to confront their internal demons regarding who you are. And I'm talking about black folk, especially. Many will expect your main characters to always be black. The same ones who have read your other novels, and did not care that those characters were just—people.

"Perhaps that's why you do not put your picture on your book jackets. But that is not your worry. You just keep on writing from your heart and soul. And I absolutely love 'Silent Song.' I think there is a lot of you in that story. Probably more than you intended. And I can boast of having had you as a student. Not that I could not before." Jasmine smiled. Deborah blushed with embarrassment.

chapter thirty-nine

Someone's Watching

═══════════════════════════

Jasmine took brief notice of the vehicle...

The interior of Jasmine's home
was inviting, spacious and immaculate. And there was not a trace of
sheetrock or carpet anywhere. The highly polished, lightly stained, birch
floors reflected like mirrors. Fresh flowers and plants adorned nearly
every room, including the five bedrooms and four bathrooms.

The formal living room featured a beautiful Persian rug, a black,
Steinway baby grand piano accented with 24kt. gold-plated pedals and
fittings. Jasmine explained her husband had given it to her on her birthday, only a year before he died. In the evenings, she would often play
and he would sit sipping her tea until long after sunset.

Although Jasmine had added her own special touches, she explained
she wanted to preserve much of the existing flavor of the house. And it
did have a decidedly antebellum feel to it. The gorgeous wall coverings
looked like original artwork. Even the baseboards had hand-carved, floral filigree.

A collection of beautifully framed photo portraits of great musicians and entertainers, displayed in the study, would have rivaled any gallery: Lena Horne, Nina Simone, Duke Ellington, Josephine Baker, Count Basie, Nat King Cole, Dinah Washington, Sammy Davis, Jr., Cab Calloway, Bill Robinson, Marian Anderson, Mahalia Jackson, Miles Davis, Fats Waller, Ethel Waters, Ruby Dee, Ossie Davis, Dorothy Dandridge, even 'Big Mama' Thornton, Howlin' Wolf, Muddy Waters, and more. Jasmine, a onetime aspiring jazz singer, and good friend of Cannonball Adderley, had met them all. Deborah found it difficult to leave the room.

The sprawling kitchen, though warm and inviting, was equipped well enough to serve a small restaurant. On the east side of the room was an area decorated with sofa, two chairs, side tables and a beautiful bouquet of summer flowers. A nearby bay window, unusually large for a kitchen, offered a mesmerizing view of green earth that stretched endlessly.

Deborah fell in love with each room she entered—especially the master bedroom, dominated by a huge canopy bed. A triple dresser adorned with a collection of music boxes caught her eye. At Jasmine's insistence, she sat, or rather climbed, onto the bed, leaned back and seriously considered never getting up.

However, there was one item, normally kept atop the master bedroom dresser, Deborah did not see: A framed picture of her gram—Gram d'lena. Miss Jasmine placed it inside a dresser drawer prior to Deborah's arrival. She had done so, in order to avoid prompting questions she was not of a mind to answer. The two had a warm friendship known to virtually no one. They enjoyed fascinating and revealing conversations over the years. Miss Jasmine saw a lot of her own mother in Gram d'lena.

—

Outside Jasmine Baker's home, and across the highway, a bald, heavyset white man in a blue seersucker suit sat clutching a pair of high-powered binoculars. He watched from behind the wheel of a white, four-door, Ford sedan with Arkansas plates. Deborah and Miss Jasmine eventually exited the house, arm in arm. Both strolled down the length of the long front porch and stepped onto the walkway.

The two embraced, shared brief laughter and warm good-byes. A reluctant Deborah entered and started her car, slowly circled the stone drive, and eased onto the highway.

The portly man in the sedan—with some difficulty—forced his considerable hulk down behind the wheel, and leaned across the passenger seat. Grunting from the discomfort, he waited until he figured Deborah had gone a sufficient distance, then raised himself, started his car, and followed.

While she had not let on, for fear of alarming Deborah, Jasmine Frances Baker had observed the vehicle the instant she exited her house. Few things ever escaped her keen eye. She had immediately surmised the presence of the car was not mere chance. So, as the Ford sedan followed Deborah, Jasmine made a point of intently focusing on the rear license tag. Then, having memorized the number, she hurried inside and entered it on a notepad she kept on a small desk near the door.

For several tentative moments, Miss Jasmine pondered what to do next. She knew she could not simply return to her greenhouse and resume tending her flowers and plants, So, unable to dismiss the matter, she grabbed her keys, locked her door and hurried to her garage. Within seconds, the rear tires of her midnight-blue Cadillac were spinning. Miss Jasmine exited her driveway and followed at a speed her DeVille had not heretofore seen.

chapter forty

Heart to Heart

_____

"I keep wanting to pinch myself."

Inside the still developing
Fulbright Regional Park, along a wide arc in the scenic Arkansas River, a
gentle slope—marked with fledgling pine saplings—led to the calm
water's edge. Nearly an hour after whisking her daughter away, under the
curious gaze of Mabel Davis, an anxious Deborah and an excited Samantha sat atop a picnic table. The river and a captivating view lay before
them. Each was too absorbed in the other to notice the old Ford sedan
idling nearby in the parking lot.

   "I just try not to think about how sick Pa-Pa is," said Samantha. Her
voice broke. "I realize he might not...get better, but I...I don't want to
think about that. It makes me too...too sad. I try to stay busy with school,
and singing, and being with my friends—the one's you met when you
picked me up at school. And thanks for signing all those autographs for
them."

   "I enjoyed meeting them. All one hundred of them."

"They were so excited. I don't think they believed me when I first told them that you...that Deborah Durrell was my sister. I couldn't blame them. It's hard for *me* to believe. Then, when you came for me... Wow! It was sooo unreal. I know I'm talking a hundred miles an hour, but I'm having a hard time believing all this. I keep wanting to pinch myself."

—

Inside the sedan, the driver gripped a 35mm camera with telephoto lens, and raised it to eye-level. He carefully framed Deborah and Samantha in the viewfinder and cranked off an entire 36-exposure roll. A minute later, he drove away. But not before passing within a few yards of where the two sat talking. Neither they nor the driver observed a blue Cadillac DeVille ease away from the roadside shortly thereafter.

"May I call you Samantha?" Deborah asked, easing closer to Samantha and fighting to appear calm. "I know everyone calls you Sam."

Samantha loosed a broad smile, tossed her head back. "Of course. You're my sister. And excuse me for staring. I have to say, you have the most gorgeous eyes."

"Thanks. So do you." Deborah smiled. The word, "sister," rang out, echoing in her ears like cymbals. She was not sure what to say next. "Samantha, tell me...tell me all about yourself. Don't leave out anything."

"What would you like to know?"

"More than you can tell me," Deborah thought, holding her daughter's gaze for—what seemed to her—an eternity. "Ah, whatever...whatever you'd like to tell me. I really want to get to know you."

Samantha tossed her head back, stared skyward then rubbed her chin, thoughtfully. "Well, let's see. I love school, my friends, my music. I also read a lot...almost everything I can get my hands on. I love math, too. And I love writing poetry. Let's see, what else. Ah..."

"You do have wide interests. That's exciting."

"I would love to travel one day. About the only places I've been are Little Rock, Texarkana, Shreveport—places like that. I've always wondered what it would be like to go to New York or Los Angeles or Hawaii, even London or Paris."

"Perhaps we can travel together."

"Are you serious? I'd love that. Maybe I'll be a famous singer, like Whitney Houston or Diana Ross. Or even a doctor, or a famous author like you, or Maya Angelou, or Toni Morrison, or Alice Walker."

"Thanks for putting me in such elite company."

"You belong there."

"Thanks, sweetheart. Time will tell. Look, you can be whatever you want to be. Never limit your dreams. Never."

"I believe in myself. I feel good about me. The only thing that bugs me sometimes is not really knowing who I am, you know? I mean, all the other kids—my friends and all—they know who their mothers and fathers are. I envy them so much."

Deborah's heart sank. She fought back tears. "Is that...is that important to you? To know your parents...where they are?" she asked.

"Yes. I think so. Sure, it is. I mean, how can I really know who I am if I don't know those things?"

"Have you ever asked mother or father about it?"

"A couple of times. I asked them both."

"What did they say?"

"Not too much. It seemed to upset them whenever I brought it up. I felt I was making them feel I didn't love them or something."

"So, you decided not to ask again."

"I didn't want to hurt them. But I do know two things, at least."

"What's that?"

"One of my parents must be white, and the other must be black. Right? I mean, all you have to do is look at me. I do it everyday. I look in the mirror and I know at least that much. Right?" Sam peered into Deborah's eyes.

"Right." Deborah thought about Marie, her beloved doll in the dresser drawer. She fought to remain composed.

"I write to her...to my mother," Sam beamed. Deborah was stunned. "I write her letters, cards—Mother's Day and all—ever since I was about seven. Someday, maybe I'll meet her and I'll give them to her. So, I have to find out somehow. Somebody's got to know something. Maybe you can help me. It doesn't mean I don't love mom and dad. Nothing can change that, not in a million years. It's just that I have to find out. You understand, don't you?"

Deborah was nearly speechless. To learn that both she and her daughter had found the same way to speak to each other, over time and space, was overwhelming. She placed her right arm around Sam's shoulder and squeezed her tightly. "I do understand. I do."

Sam leaned her head against her mother's shoulder. Deborah felt a surge of emotion so intense, her heart raced. She was nearly consumed by it. She felt needed, and by her daughter.

"Why did you stay away all this time?"

Samantha's question struck Deborah squarely in her heart. Her mind went blank. Samantha sat peering into her eyes. "Mom said you had asthma and a terrible allergy. "Hayfever," she called it...said you almost died, living in this climate. Are you better now?"

Samantha had given Deborah an escape route she could not have found on her own. But it was another lie—a lie left to live another day.

"I'm fine," said Deborah. "Especially now that I've met you."

"I'm so glad you're here," Sam shouted. "Everything seems so different, now. You're real cool to talk to. And I really did love reading your book. Now that I know it's you, I'll read it again. That's going to seem so strange. And I want you to autograph it for me. You can say: "To my sister, Samantha."

"I will," said Deborah, forcing a wide smile.

Even as she watched and listened to Sam, Deborah kept reminding herself the moment was real; she was not dreaming. She desperately wanted to reach out, embrace Sam with all the power she could muster, and tell her the whole truth. Deborah could almost hear the words leap from her mouth:

"Samantha, you're my daughter. I'm your mother. You were taken from me when you were only three months old. I'm your mother, Samantha. I'm your mother!"

chapter forty-one

A Place In The Heart

===========================

"What are we looking at," Sam asked.

The area was only vaguely familiar.
Deborah had driven slowly along Crispus Attucks, from its intersection with John Henry Langston Road, hoping for familiarity. There were few man-made structures.

Mother Nature still ruled the landscape. Stands of tall pines remained, separated by expanses of rolling earth carpeted with grass swaying in a warm, brisk summer breeze.

When Deborah reached Drawhorn Creek, a sudden chill coursed her body. She pulled to the side of the seldom-traveled road and stopped. Samantha was curious, but said nothing.

Moments passed. Deborah continued to a place—a spot that just seemed right to her. She turned left onto a narrow bridge spanning a dry creek bed. Several yards ahead, she continued onto an even narrower gravel path nearly lost to vegetation. The pavement soon disappeared from view.

Deborah stopped, nodded to a curious Samantha. The two then exited the car. Samantha hurried around to her mother's door. Both embraced and stood staring in a northwesterly direction. Before them, lay a wide expanse of treeless earth well covered with brush and tall grass.

"What are we looking at?"

"A special place," Deborah all but whispered. Already her eyes were glistening with a hint of mist. "Over there, I think. Hard to tell now. Just about where that old fence stops. Keep looking to the right and far beyond. Follow my hand. There! Right there! That's it. That's it! I'm sure of it. That's it!"

Despite her best effort to restrain them, tears streamed down Deborah's face. Sam wiped them away and gently stroked Deborah's face. She squeezed her mother's shoulder.

"Is that some special place?"

"Oh, yes. It's special. More special than almost any place I know."

"What is it?"

" That's where my Gram d'lena lived...and died. This is the place."

"Gram d'lena?"

"No one ever told you about Gram d'lena—about Gram?"

"About Gram, yes. Aunt Maylene, a few times. Uncle Matthew, a few. Afterwards, he was real sad. I thought he was going to cry. I think that's why he didn't say any more. But they always called her Gram, not Gram d'lena. I could tell she was really special, though."

Deborah smiled and grasped Samantha's hand. "I sure wish you could have known her. She was my...our grandmother—Daddy's mother, Magdalena Morris—an angel on earth. I called her Gram d'lena because when I was little, I had a hard time saying Magdalena. She liked the name I gave her. She was so beautiful, so kind. She treated me like a princess. Used to call me *babygirl*. That was her name for *me.*"

"How old was she when she died?"

"Seventy-two, a young seventy-two. Somehow, she seemed no older than...than Mother."

"Was that because she had a young heart...a young mind?"

"That's it, exactly."

"She had a youthful spirit that would not let her act, or think old. You would have loved her so much. Her little house stood...just about there. I spent so many wonderful hours here with her. I always hated when time came to leave her. I once asked if I could come live with her. I was a little girl, then. Seems so long ago now. So long ago. Too bad, we all have to grow up."

"I've never heard anyone mention anything about my other grand-parents—mom's mother and father. I've never seen pictures or any-thing," Samantha added. There was a sadness in Sam's words—a long-ing Deborah knew well.

Deborah did not respond. A lengthy silence followed. Samantha broke the quiet with more questions about Gram. For the next half hour, Deborah painted a vivid portrait of Gram d'lena that engrossed Sam so much she hardly blinked. Deborah spoke of Gram d'lena, from her ear-liest recollections to the last moments of her life.

And for the first time since telling Aunt Rose years before, Deborah spoke of that early morning, when Gram came to her in what she was certain was the embodiment of an angel.

Samantha watched Deborah's emotions range from uproarious laughter to mournful tears. She saw her face radiate with love and affec-tion at the mere mention of Gram's name. Her own eyes welled; tears spilled.

"I so wish I had known her, too. I wish she were still alive."

"So do I, Samantha. So do I."

A brief silence.

"Come with me," said Deborah. "Come walk with me."

She grasped Samantha's left hand and led her across the open fields, far from the gravel path. The heavily-fragranced country wind blew warm and sweet. The borderless sky was bluer than blue. The two walked for more than a hundred yards. Samantha was struck by the awesome beauty of this expansive area of SB-40. She could not recall having seen this part of it before.

They soon came upon the remains of what appeared to be concrete block supports for some structure. The blocks lay nearly obscured by tall grass. They were arrayed in rectangular fashion, comporting exactly with what Deborah remembered of Gram d'lena's house.

"Samantha, baby, this is...is where my Gram d'lena's house was. This is where it stood. This is it. Right here." Tears raced down Deborah's face. "Matthew and I came here every chance we got. There was almost no place else we wanted to be. We always hated to leave, and she hated to see us go. She would always stand on her porch and watch until we were out of sight."

Deborah slowly moved within the house's imaginary confines, room by room. She stopped, began turning in a full circles, pausing to take in the sight, searching for a familiar view. Then, there it was. The view from Gram's kitchen window.

"Right here," she whispered, pointing. She then framed her eyes with both hands raised before her face. "Gram's kitchen window was right here. I remember sitting at an old leaf table. Don't ask. It had sides that folded up or down. The chairs had woven straw bottoms and high backs. Gram's had a handmade cushion.

"My legs were so short then. We sat here one morning—one summer morning. I was helping her shell peas. Matthew was raking leaves."

Deborah could barely finish her sentence. Sam's face reflected both their shared joy, and sadness. Her expression mirrored the emotions etched on Deborah's face.

"I can see you still love her as much as you did then."

"I do. And I will, the longest day I live. She's always with me. Sometimes, when I'm not expecting it, I almost see her face. She's smiling at me, winking and blowing kisses." Deborah smiled. Sam smiled with her.

"I want to know even more about her," said Sam. I want to see pictures, too, if there are any."

"You won't have any trouble getting me to talk about her. And there should be some pictures. Ask mother if she knows where they are. She should know.

Nearly an hour passed. Deborah and Samantha started for the car. They had not gone five yards, when Deborah stopped cold. Something caught her attention. Something under her foot, deep in the tall grass,.

Samantha watched as her mother knelt and carefully peeled back blades of grass. There it was. A small piece of wood the size of her hand. It had clearly been ripped or broken from a larger piece.

Deborah clutched the treasure with both hands. She instantly knew it was a piece of Gram's old house. A nail hole pierced its center. Deborah traced its smooth side and jagged edges. She cradled it in like some archaeological find of great import. It was. She stood, raised the treasure to her lips, and wept.

"See this? This is a...a piece of wood from Gram's house. It's from Gram's old house. You can see the...the nail hole right there. This is all that's left."

Deborah felt she was finally home. It was impossible for her to leave just now. Through her tears, she stared at the piece of wood, held it to her chest. She and Sam remained for a time, standing quietly. The only sound was the rush of gentle winds caressing the leaves of nearby trees.

With her daughter at her side, Deborah found her way to a nearby oak tree. The two lingered in its shade for the longest while. It was there, she spoke to Sam about her father—the Reverend.

Deborah tried as gently as she could to prepare her for the possibility he would not survive his illness. She relied heavily upon her long conversations with Gram, to help her find the right words.

—

There was one more place Deborah was determined to visit with her daughter: Gram's grave. Not much was said during the short drive to Heming Road, and Shiloh Baptist Church. Samantha knew the route well. She was certain she knew why they were heading there.

With tears blurring her way, Deborah led Sam to where Gram, and Samuel, were buried. And for the first time, she saw her beloved grandmother's grave. Memories and tears overflowed. Samantha held her mother's hand, while they lingered in the shade of ancient oaks.

Deborah shared old memories, even as she and Samantha gave birth to new ones. Later, both entered the sanctuary. Deborah found entering the church especially painful. There were too many memories in this place. She could practically see her father standing in the pulpit; his booming voice rising to a crescendo; perspiration pouring from his brow; a white handkerchief gripped in his left hand, his right hand slicing the air as he delivered the Word.

And she could all but see herself, as a young girl, gazing proudly at her father—a man who commanded such universal respect and admiration. He would end his sermon, glance at the pianist, then nod to her. That meant, he wanted her to sing Amazing Grace, as the 'doors of the church were opened.' Reverend would return to his seat, take a sip of water from a glass handed him by an usher; swipe his brow several times, then close his eyes and wait to listen to his daughter.

Gram d'lena would be sitting on the front pew, smiling from ear to ear, looking on with dancing eyes as her grandbaby prepared to bless everyone within the sound of her voice. The two would exchange knowing winks, then Gram would close her eyes, just as the first note sounded.

—

Enough. Deborah now suddenly felt overwhelmed by her recollections, and forced herself to turn them away. She and Samantha approached the altar, knelt, and prayed silently. Afterwards, she was so compelled to leave the sanctuary; she practically raced toward the exit.

Once outside, mother and daughter sat on the church steps and talked. They talked until evening shadows grew long; until the once brilliant sunlight dimmed and disappeared, and until the symphony of night sounds began its opening overture.

chapter forty-two

Straight Talk

========================

"You been accepted 'cause you learned to look less black..."

Deborah peered through the screen door,
from where she, Maylene and Gloria stood on the front porch. Maylene
had just finished telling them about Ol' Willie's murder. Matthew and
Reginald could be heard inside, embroiled in heated conversation.

Samantha was in her bedroom making entries in her handmade, secret diary, out of earshot of the verbal jousting taking place in the living
room. Normally, she would have remained, aware of the entertainment
potential of her uncle's visits. Deborah had to tear herself away from her.

In the living room—or front room, as such room was customarily
called—Matthew was relishing the moment. He slapped one knee and
leaned forward. Reginald sat on the love seat adjacent to him.

"You sure you're not a Republican? You sure sound like one. Why
you get so bent out 'a shape 'cause I criticize Bush? What I meant was,
all those jobs he had in the past tells me he can't hold a damn job. That's
what they would say about you or me."

"You watch your mouth in there, Matthew Jeremiah Davis!" Mabel Davis yelled from the kitchen. "You know better than to be cussin' in this house."

Matthew cupped his right hand over his mouth and snickered. He may have been joking about the Vice President, but Reginald saw little of the humor.

"You sure sound like a Republican," Matthew repeated. "You even act like one, too. You one of them...them so-called conservatives? You can tell us."

"What's that got to do with anything? What does that mean? I'm not saying, one way or the other. And I'm not suggesting Mr. Bush would make a great president."

"I hope you not. 'Course anybody would be an improvement over that ol' fart we got now. Unless you happen to be white, or maybe think you are."

"I don't know what you're referring to with that last barb."

"Barb?"

"Okay, comment. All I'm saying is, black people cannot continue to put all their eggs in one political basket. One political party keeps ignoring us, and the other one takes us for granted. We have no leverage. None."

"So, one ol' 'Massa' got the rope in his hand, and the other one got his rope in the closet, right?"

"I probably would have stated that view a little less colorfully. However, your point is well taken."

"Fine. I'll take the one with the rope in the closet," said Matthew, hurtling himself back against the sofa and loosing a belly laugh.

Reginald was not amused. "You mentioned Republicans. What do you know about Republicans?"

"I know a lot more than you think. See, you think 'cause ol' Matthew's stuck off back in these woods he's..."

"No. That's not it at all. Tell me about Republicans."

"Alright. Since you asked, I'll give you one example."

"Fine."

"Okay. Let's say there's a man driving a car, right? He has an accident, runs off the road; he's out cold and everything. A minute later, two other cars—one with a liberal Democrat, and the other one with a conservative Republican—drive up at the same time. What do you think would happen next?"

"I know this is some sort of trick question, but you tell me."

"I'll tell ya.' The liberal Democrat rushes over...tries to help the driver. The Republican rushes over, checks damage to the car, first." Matthew cracked up. He was barely able to deliver his punch line.

Reginald just looked at him, shook his head, unsure whether to laugh or frown. "You can't really believe that."

"There might be some exceptions. But, yeah...yeah, pretty much."

"Look, Matthew. Abraham Lincoln was a Republican."

"Right. I know. And even he wasn't all *that*. But there ain't no Lincolns around today. I know that much. You know any?"

"I know there are Democrats—at least one, in the Senate—who used to be a Klansman," Reginald fired back.

"I ain't lettin' them off the hook. Did you know it was senators from the south, who filibustered every attempt to outlaw lynchin' Black folk? Seven times. Seven times they refused to pass a federal law to make lynchin' us...illegal."

Reginald nodded, yes. "I know. They were either klansmen or Klan sympathizers. They didn't want to upset those who kept them in office."

"Hey! They're still out there, especially in the south...even the north," Matthew retorted. "Lot 'a so-called Christians, too. I don't trust any of 'em. They all got sheets with eye holes."

"All?"

"Too many. And...and I'll tell ya' somethin' else. If there was to be a real tragedy in this country, black folk gon' be the last ones helped...or saved. You hear me good. I don't care whether it's a bomb, or...or some attack from out a' space, or a hurricane or somethin', you watch who they save first. That's why we got 'a look out for ourselves...lift each other up."

"Look, Matthew, I agree with a lot of what you say. But all white people aren't bad, and all Black people aren't good. That is an undeniable fact. There are blacks I would not associate with. There are whites I would not associate with. I'm sure the same is true for most Black folk, including you. But you probably won't admit that. You're forgetting there are whites who have been, and still are, part of our struggle."

"To ease their damn guilt," Matthew shot back. "Part-time soldiers, is what they are, if any of 'em are soldiers in the struggle—our struggle at all. That's plain to see."

"Part-time?" Reginald shot back with verve that raised the eyebrows of the sisters standing on the porch. "Remember Schwerner, Goodman? They stood side by side with Chaney...died with him, too. And what about Viola Liuso, and many others? The Reverend James Reeb? Were they all part-time? They gave their lives, and they're full-time dead, Matthew. And what about people like Morris Dees, with his Southern Poverty Law Center? And others I can't even name? They fight racism and injustice, too. The NAACP has always had White folk involved at its core...from its inception."

"What about 'em?"

"What about them? Look, I am just as angry about racists and racism as you. Black people have a right to be angry. But we cannot spend our lives rightfully complaining and doing little else. The world moves on. That doesn't mean the fight's over. We have lives that tick by minute by minute. We have to condemn evil, fight against it, and acknowledge good, whether it comes from Blacks or Whites."

Matthew remained unusually quiet for a long moment. He folded his muscled arms and leaned his head to one side. "I really don't mean to hurt your feelings or nothin', but you been out of touch for a while, my brother. When it comes down to it, no matter how much they pat you on the head and grin in your face, white folks are only for white folks. The poorest, dumbest white man thinks he's better than the richest, smartest brother. If you can't understand that, you in trouble. I don't think you know what brothers like me still have to deal with."

"What do you mean by, brothers like you?"

"You know what I mean. See, me and you prob'ly live in different worlds. To a certain extent, you been accepted 'cause you look less black and learned to act less black to white folks than I have. That's at least a part of it. You don't threaten 'em as much as I do. They look at my big nose, my nappy hair, my thick lips and they see a savage—somebody to be scared of, especially white men.

"But I ain't never massacred Indians, owned slaves, stole land, raped, lynched or otherwise killed nobody yet. So, you tell me who the savage is. It's important for you to show how much like 'em you can be, so you can go along to get along. I understand that.

"So forgive me if I ain't as polished, or as informed as you, and brothers like you. I live down here on the ground. I live down here where sometimes I got 'a kiss their wrinkled asses just to survive. Then, I have to spit, even wash my mouth out with Listerine or...or both. Understand?"

"Amazing."

"Amazin', huh?"

"Yes. I don't believe this. I don't believe it. What you're saying is, I'm not black enough. Right? Is that it? Because my skin is lighter, my hair less kinky, and because I don't eat chitlins, and 'bust' a few verbs, I'm not black? White folk don't have any doubt I'm black. For the bigots and racists out there—and I agree they do exist, and will continue to exist—I am plenty black enough.

"We don't all have to think, act and talk alike to be black, Matthew. I can dig Miles and Mozart. I can groove to Duke and Debussy. I believe you to be a decent and caring person. But it's because of your kind of thinking, that people who look like me have to fight battles on two fronts. I fight racism, and I also have to contend with this internecine warfare. I don't have to *prove* my pedigree. When was the meeting held, and the decision was made that said all black folks had to think, talk, act, and be alike. Should we all look alike, too?"

Matthew leaned back, drew a long breath, and pounded a fist into an open palm several times.

"Don't take it personal, Reggie."

"Don't take it personal? What other way should..."

"My point is, some of us forget who we are, just because..."

"I haven't forgotten who I am!"

"Hold on. Some of us forget who we are, when we get a taste of the good life," Matthew said through clenched teeth. "And I'll tell you something else—and don't take this personally either—white folk ain't the only ones who hate black people. There're some black folk who hate black folk—hate black folk who look like me. Black!"

"What do you mean?" Reginald leaned closer.

"Aw, c'mon. You know what I mean. I'm talkin' 'bout lighter-skinned blacks who don't want 'a have nothin' to do with dark-skinned blacks — even call 'em niggers. Some wouldn't have a dark-skinned brother or sister marry into their families for nothin' in the world. They make some Klansmen look like nigger-lovers. Swear to God. Now what the hell is that? I call it self-hate...black folk hatin' black folk 'cause of the color of their skin. Where the hell they get that from? Where did they learn that?"

Matthew leaned back in his seat. Reginald sat back and drew a long breath. Matthew sat waiting, arms folded. It may have seemed he had been waiting for years to unload on some captive audience unable to escape. Reginald reacted somewhat tentatively, at first.

"Wow. That's a lot. And I know there's some truth...a lot of truth in what you've said about all this. I know you're not directing any of this at me, personally. And that's good, because you don't know me, Matthew. And I just think you should get to know someone as an individual before you make judgements."

"Hold on! Don't go anywhere," said Matthew. "You're right. I'm not talkin' 'bout you, personally. See, if my little sister is with you...you have to be a great guy. Just hold on. I wanna show you something."

Before Reginald could react, Matthew bounded to his feet, bolted through the doorway, and down the hallway to his old room. He knocked and waited. No answer from Rachel. Matthew knocked again, harder this time. Again, no answer.

"I'm comin' in...need to get somethin'."

Matthew entered and found Rachel sitting on the floor—reading. She never looked up. He thought of saying something to her, but decided against the idea. Instead, he raced to the closet and removed a small cedar box from the top shelf.

Seconds later, Matthew returned to the living room, clutching a small, brown, hardbound book that looked decades old. He held it delicately in his brawny hands. Smiling proudly, he sat down.

"What is that?" asked Reginald.

A book. A special book. My grandmother gave it to me when I was just nine years old. I keep it wrapped in linen in a dresser in Sam's room. It's a book by W.E.B. DuBois."

DuBois?" Reginald's face registered his shock.

It's called *The Souls of Black Folk*, published way back in 1911. DuBois autographed it, too. I'm gon' read you somethin'."

Reginald loosed a faint smile. Outside, the sisters were all ears. Matthew turned to page three and began reading in an emotional voice:

After the Egyptian and Indian, the Greek and Roman, the Teuton and Mongolian, the Negro is a sort of seventh son, born with a veil, and gifted with second-sight in this American world,—a world which yields him no true self-consciousness, but only lets him see himself through the revelation of the other world.

It is a peculiar sensation, this double-consciousness, this sense of always looking at one's self through the eyes of others, of measuring one's soul by the tape of a world that looks on in amused contempt and pity. One ever feels his two-ness,—an American, a Negro; two souls, two thoughts, two reconciled strivings; two warring ideals in one dark body, whose dogged strength alone keeps it from being torn asunder.

The history of the American Negro is the history of this strife, this longing to attain self-consciousness manhood, to merge his double self into a better and truer self. In this merging he wishes neither of the older selves to be lost. He would not Africanize America, for America has much to teach the world and Africa.

He would not bleach his Negro soul in a flood of white Americanism, for he knows that the Negro blood has a message for the world. He simply wishes to make it possible for a man to be both Negro and an American, without being cursed and spit upon by his fellows, without having the doors of opportunity closed roughly in his face.

Matthew closed the book and stared at Reginald with a look of profound satisfaction embossed on his face. Not only had he made his point, he felt he had read clearly, and without stumbling over a single word. He smiled, proudly.

"What's your point?"

"If you were listenin', you wouldn't ask me that. All this...it's been goin' on a long time."

Reginald shook his head and chuckled. "Well, I certainly wasn't expecting to have W.E.B DuBois thrown in my face tonight. Look, I don't think we're really talking about two vastly different things. I'd love to discuss DuBois' writings and statements with you. I think some of what you read actually supports my position. But we can continue this some other time. That's a pretty valuable book you have there. May I see it?"

"Sure."

Samantha, who had been standing in the hallway just out of view for several minutes, entered the room as the 'show' reached intermission. Deborah invited her onto the porch, then turned to Maylene. The sisters had been talking, but mostly listening to the fiery discussion taking place inside.

"Has that been going on since we left earlier?"

"In a word, yes. Except for a sandwich and coke break. Even then, Matthew never stopped talking."

"Poor Reginald," Gloria added. "I tried to rescue him twice. But everytime he stands up, Matthew hits his hot button with some statement and it starts all over again. At least Reginald is speaking his mind. Matthew usually has people cowering and agreeing with everything he says by now."

"Samantha and I had a nice ride, got a chance to talk. Right?"

Samantha flashed a gleaming smile and nodded 'yes.' "Most of my friends got autographs. I'm sure they'll be calling me later. Better get my homework done first, though," she said.

"Good idea," said Deborah. "I'll likely leave before you finish. See you tomorrow. And don't forget you're giving me a picture of yourself." Samantha gave a thumbs up and started back inside.

Maylene and Gloria observed the long, caring gaze Deborah gave her. "You've had at least three phone calls since you left," said Maylene. "I took the one from Tommy. He's decided to come right away. Suppose to arrive in the morning. Said he can't wait to lay his eyes on you, girl." Maylene cleared her throat and repeatedly arched her brows.

"I can't wait to see him either."

"I took the other two calls," said Gloria, "both from a sexy sounding guy who seemed pretty anxious to talk to you. I believe his name was Paul...Paul Castle." Gloria and Maylene exchanged mischievous glances.

"I guess he's arrived," said Deborah. "Paul's my literary agent, and a close friend."

"Maylene told me all about your writing...that you're a famous author, Deborah Durrell. I'm...I'm still in shock. I was telling Reginald. He asked me why I hadn't said anything. I didn't have an answer, at least one I wanted to admit to. And I felt so...so stupid. Deborah, I had no idea. And I should have. We all should have, except for things being the way they've been.

"I'm looking at you and...and feeling guilty, ashamed." Gloria dabbed her eyes. " I can't wait to read all your books...for us to know each other again. That sounds so strange to me."

"I know."

"Okay. I'm not going to start crying. Tell us about your agent. Is he English? Irish? Italian? Rich?" Gloria asked. She and Maylene rolled their eyes playfully.

Deborah smiled. "We're working on a special publishing project. Paul must've called from Little Rock," said Deborah. "I really do have to go. Even though I hate to walk out on the live theater going on inside there."

"Knowing Matthew, I'm sure there'll be another performance tomorrow," said Gloria.

Deborah left the room to say good-bye to her mother. She was at the kitchen table drying flatware and humming softly. Mabel Davis seemed reluctant to say much more than good-bye, even as her estranged daughter lingered in the doorway.

"You'll be comin' back tomorrow?" asked Mabel Davis. Only then did she raise her head for a fleeting glance at her daughter.

"Yes, I'll be back. My daughter is still here."

That was the whole of it. Nothing more was said. Before turning to leave, Deborah looked at her mother and was struck by the indelible image of a figure to be pitied, not hated. Yet, she steadfastly resisted any feelings of empathy.

Deborah felt nothing had happened to warrant disavowing her feelings, even if such disavowal were possible. She reasoned that to dispose of them so easily would bestow an undeserved generosity upon a woman who had ceased to be a mother to her. Such magnanimity would require outright condemnation of feelings she was certain she had a right to have.

Even in the forgiving evening light, her mother appeared to have aged far beyond her fifty-eight years. Mabel Davis seemed drawn, weathered, beaten down, deeply conflicted. And her eyes, said to be the windows to her soul, could not be trusted to reveal slightest truth to even the most discerning observer.

Deborah observed her mother's grey hair, her wrinkled brow, her sloping shoulders. They could in no way belong to the proud, strong, vibrant woman she once knew. Her mother's appearance could not be explained by the mere passage of years. Only a diminished, hollowed spirit could explain what Deborah saw.

chapter forty-three

Face To Face

===

I confess I never expected to see you again.

Deborah was aware Rachel was again closeted in her room, patiently waiting for her to leave. She was determined to see her, to speak to her, regardless of her sister's likely reaction to her presence.

Deborah moved down the narrow hallway, steeling herself for what lay ahead. Before she reached the closed bedroom door, she could hear strains of soft, classical music coming from inside.

Just as she was about to knock, the door opened. A somber Rachel filled the space, one hand resting on the doorjamb, the other on the door. It was as if she had known Deborah was standing there.

For a moment, neither spoke. Deborah could not have imagined just how awkward the moment would be. She was first to speak.

"Hello, Rachel." There was no immediate response. Rachel stared at her sister with piercing eyes. "I just wanted to say hello...see how you were. Maylene told me you were living here now."

Rachel, draped in a white, ankle-length linen dress, seemed temporarily disarmed by her sister's soft-spokenness. She was taken aback by Deborah's appearance, her air of sophistication. The off-guard moment quickly passed. Rachel, her face unmade, her twizzled hair mocking mini-dreadlocks, kept the door open only wide enough to permit her to see Deborah clearly.

"Sister Deborah. You're back. Well, well. Sorry I missed you yesterday. What a surprise. I confess I never expected to see you again. How are you?" Rachel asked in an unaffected voice.

"May I come inside?"

Rachel hesitated, before slowly opening the door and stepping away, back into the poorly-lit room. Deborah entered the spartan space, that was furnished with only a double bed and dresser. A small clock radio, flashing 12:00, sat atop the dresser. The room offered no place to sit. A three foot column of neatly stacked paperback books rose against one wall. There were no pictures, no personal items visible—even on the aged dresser top.

The only illumination came from a beam of sunlight that spilled past the partially draped window. The nearly monochromatic hue, combined with the room's drab accommodations, rendered the entire space decidedly depressing.

Rachel's eyes were fixed on her sister. She seemed to be searching for words, as she motioned her toward the bed. Deborah first thought to decline the offer, then walked over to the large, wrought-iron bed and eased down onto its edge.

Struggling to project an air of superiority, Rachel joined Deborah. She sat on the far end of the bed, fingers laced, her hands in her lap. Her eyes darted about the room before coming to rest on Deborah. Silence. Deborah felt a twinge of pity for her sister, though not by choice.

"I'm very sorry to hear about what's happened," she offered. "I can just imagine what you're going through now. Are you..."

"Okay?"

"Yes."

"Of course. Couldn't be better. But I'm more concerned about Father than myself. It's so nice of you to come see him...finally."

The acid nearly dripped from Rachel's lips. Deborah held back an immediate response. She wanted her to talk as much as she wanted.

"I don't...I don't know what to say," Rachel continued. "I could say that I missed your not being here, but that would not be true. I didn't miss you, not after the first year. I told myself God must have meant for things to be that way, and...well, I could do nothing about that."

"Would you have, if you could have?"

Rachel did not answer right away. She drew a deep breath and stood, firmly wrapped her right hand around the metal bedpost and turned toward her sister.

"I know you're my sister, but...but if you think you can simply waltz back into our lives and play the *'Daddy's little lost girl'* role, then perish the thought. What happened to you was brought on by you. You...you did not take Daddy's teaching and preaching to heart. You sinned, grievously. And you paid the price. I call it justice."

Deborah felt raw rage swell within her. Her pulse quickened, but she held her tongue. It was not easy.

"You became pregnant because of your own willful fornication," Rachel continued, seeming to delight in the verbal chastising she was heaping upon her sister. Deborah was certain the tirade was something Rachel had long rehearsed.

"Then, you expected everyone to feel sorry for you. You wanted Daddy to just put his arms around you and tell you it was all right to sin and bring shame upon this family, and a father who had to return to his pulpit, knowing his own daughter was pregnant."

Deborah waited until the tirade ended. She stood and turned to face her sister. She thought of a thousand things to say, but concluded nothing would matter.

"You don't expect to be included in Daddy's will, do you?" Rachel blurted. "Is that why you decided to come back?" Deborah was stunned by the statement. At first, she thought to simply leave the room.

"Sounds like you've already buried your father, talking about a will while he's still alive. Your comment does not deserve a response. I've never felt you had any love, or even a liking for me. In fact, I'm aware you've always hated me. And I've never understood why. But that is your problem—your problem, alone. I pity you. I do.

"At this point in my life, I no longer concern myself with trying to figure out you or anyone else here, for that matter. I'm here to reconnect with my daughter, see about Father, then I'm leaving. You should know that I have rebuilt my life. I've done so with the help of God and my aunt and uncle. I need nothing, want nothing and will accept nothing. I do hope you get better and..."

"I'm fine," Rachel interrupted. "I'm only here to give Mother a hand. Afterwards, I'm leaving to begin reliving my own life. I'm married, you know. I have a wonderful husband. And I'm pregnant. Six months. I'm sure it's a girl, although I haven't had the test."

Deborah wasn't quite sure how to respond, at first. She was certain Rachel believed what she was saying. "I'm...I'm happy for you. Congratulations," said Deborah, belying her deep sadness.

"I don't have anything else to say," said Rachel, slumping back onto the bed. "You may leave, now."

Deborah said nothing more. Even when Rachel had earlier labeled her a twelve year-old fornicator, she declined the opportunity to point out Rachel's own pregnancy was out of wedlock. Such a counterpoint would have mattered little. At that moment, she felt nothing but compassion, and even more pity for her sister. It was clear Rachel was not well and needed psychological help.

After a moment, Deborah turned and left the room, pulling the door closed behind her. She paused just outside the room, and for a moment, whispered a prayer for a sister she never really knew, and would likely never know.

Before rejoining Gloria and Maylene, Deborah interrupted Reginald and Matthew. She gave her brother a long good-bye hug, and shook Reginald's hand, warmly.

Later, Maylene stared into her sister's eyes, searching for some hint of Deborah's reaction to having seen Rachel. Deborah was careful to conceal any reaction.

"It's only six," Maylene noted. "Stay a little longer. We could all sit in the porch swing like we used to...talk about what we want to be when we grow up. Remember?"

"I remember."

Deborah excused herself, explaining she would likely be awake for hours, reviewing contracts. Maylene relented.

"I understand. Tell ya' what. We'll plan a visit to your hotel after we hear back from you. I'm sure you and Paul have a lot to discuss." Maylene smiled and winked.

chapter forty-four

A Revelation

==

You're letting me die here.

Inside the Ashley, the Capital Hotel's five-star restaurant, Deborah and Paul sat across from each other, just beginning a dinner of steak and scampi. Food was great, but this was not Zeno's. Few places were. Paul showed little interest in his meal. Despite efforts to conceal it, the light of anticipation danced in his eyes. Deborah was not unaware.

"So, I took a shower, relaxed a little, watched some television then took a ten minute tour of the hotel," he was saying. "Great hotel, but this is definitely not Chicago. The minute the plane landed I felt the pace slow to a crawl. But that's not a complaint. It felt good. Like I stepped off a treadmill. I need the change."

"Good for you." Deborah's voice was subdued. "I haven't had that luxury, yet. Don't expect I will."

"We've got all night." Paul winked his right eye, arched his brows. Deborah ignored the inference, looking away for a time.

"Just trying to lighten the air a little bit," said Paul.

Deborah hoisted her water glass, took a sip and turned to Paul. "How do you like your room?"

"Room's nice. View sucks. Got hot and cold running water, indoor plumbing, the works. Only one problem."

"Which is?"

"We don't really need two suites."

Paul paused—fork poised at his lips. Deborah kept eating.

"Hello, there! "You're letting me die here. Throw me a rope."

"Hmm. I suppose having two suites is a bit wasteful. Besides, there's a sleeper sofa in my suite."

"Okay. I'll keep my own suite. I suppose we do have to maintain the proper appearance. But I will accept unlimited visitation."

Deborah loosed a quick smile. Paul dropped his fork and raised both hands in mock surrender.

"I took a quick look at the contracts," said Deborah.

"Oh, no. She wants to talk business. I'm crushed. Here we are in this romantic setting in the heart of the *Arkansas Riviera*—a luscious dinner before us. No wine. But there certainly could have been. I wanted wine, but you said no, and I bowed to your wish. Right? Now, you want to spoil this...this wonderful moment with talk of business? Oh! Lift me now from the depths of my despair."

Deborah tried to muffle herself. However, a sudden burst of laughter escaped.

"I don't mean to play Scrooge, but we don't have a lot of time. I just took a quick look at the contracts before coming down. I plan to have an old friend, who's an entertainment attorney, take a look at them as a precaution."

While Deborah spoke, a stocky white man in an ill-fitting beige suit sat alone at a distant table, quietly observing them.

"Who is this attorney friend? And how good is he? What does he know about the publishing business?"

"His name is Tommy Williams."

"Never heard of him. Should I have?"

"He represents sports and entertainment clients. He's highly successful. I've known him since I was in the sixth grade." Deborah didn't intend to sound as defensive as she did.

"Okay, okay, okay. The sixth grade part really impressed me," Paul quipped. "I guess he should be able to review a literary contract."

chapter forty-five

Surprise and Regret

═══════════════════════════

Deborah's Hotel Room—Paul emerged from the bedroom, minus his drink.

P aul and Deborah
sat on the edge of the King-size bed with file folders scattered around
them. Paul, still wearing his suit slacks—the sleeves of his white shirt
rolled just above his elbows—sipped a glass of White Zinfandel. Deborah wore soft-blue, silk, pant pajamas, underneath a blue silk, long-sleeve
robe loosely tied at her waist.

The quiet was broken by a firm knock at the door. Deborah looked
up with a start. Paul hunched his shoulders.

"You expecting anybody?"

Deborah shook her head and rose from the bed. Paul continued reading, while she hurried from the bedroom. Another knock sounded. Deborah peeked out, gasped in surprise then cupped a hand to her mouth.
She unlocked the door and threw it wide open. Standing in the doorway
were Matthew and Maylene.

"Surprise! Surprise!" Both shouted in unison.

Deborah smiled. The three embraced. Matthew then burst into raucous laughter. He lifted Deborah in the air and did a three-sixty before
lowering her to the corridor floor.

"Come in! Come in," said Deborah, masking her surprise. "Come in!
Where's Gloria and Reginald?"

Maylene snickered. "Gloria's feeding her face again. And Reginald
won't move one inch without her. We didn't have time to wait for 'em.
Besides, I think he's seen enough of Matthew for one night. Or should I
say 'Maffew?" Remember that? That's what you used to call him.
I bet he remembers." Matthew smiled and nodded.

"Girl, this is nice," said Maylene, looking around the suite. "I told
Matthew we should 'a called first."

"It's okay. I'm glad you came. Listen, if you're hungry..."

"Mama cooked, remember? We're both stuffed," said Maylene.

"How much this place cost 'a night, anyway?" asked Matthew.
Maylene swatted at him; he backed away.

—

Paul emerged from the bedroom, minus his drink. Matthew's smile
vanished, replaced by a deep frown and a piercing stare. Maylene instantly focused on her brother's reaction. She drew a nervous breath.
Deborah turned to Paul and beckoned.

"Paul, this is my brother, and oldest sister. This is Maylene and this
is Matthew. This is Paul Castle. He owns the literary and entertainment
agency that represents me."

"First sister, not oldest" said a smiling Maylene, her hand extended.

"Pleased to meet you, Maylene."

Paul turned to shake Matthew's hand. A grim-faced Matthew
clenched his jaws, slipped both hands into his pockets. He stared at Paul,
without batting a lash, managing only a faint nod and a barely audible
grunt. Paul slowly lowered his hand, tried to act as if the rebuff never
occurred. A frost enveloped the room. Deborah looked on in disbelief.
Paul cleared his throat, struggled to put the best face on things.

"Good to meet you both," he said, as cheerfully as he could. "Deborah, I think I'll head to my room, give you a chance to enjoy your sister and brother's visit. We'll finish our work later."

Deborah was visibly embarrassed, so was Maylene. Before Paul could leave, Matthew turned on his heels and bolted for the door.

"I'll see y'all," he said. "I'll be in the car!"

"Matthew!" Maylene called out.

Without looking back, Matthew stormed from the room, slammed the door behind him. Maylene's jaw dropped. Deborah gazed at the door, as if she expected Matthew to reenter and announce it had all been a terrible joke.

Maylene had no doubt Matthew was not joking. She was crushed with embarrassment...followed him several steps into the corridor. She watched her brother until he reached the elevator. He turned, looked at her, but said nothing. Maylene reentered the room.

"Deborah...Mr. Castle. I'm so sorry. Matthew is...he's really not a bad person. He's got a real good heart. I mean he's...Anyway, he's not always as tough as he acts."

Deborah eased an arm around her sister's shoulder. "It's alright, Maylene. It's alright. But I am more than a little stunned."

"It's not alright. I'm so upset with him. I'm embarrassed. I wouldn't 'a come if I'd thought he'd behave like this. There's no excuse."

"It's not your fault. I'll talk to him later. It's clear I'll have to get to know more about my brother."

"Deborah, I'd better go. Coming here seemed like a good idea at first. Should 'a known better. Nice meeting you, Mr. Castle."

"No, no. It *was* a good idea."

"I'm not so sure." Maylene's unsteady voice reflected her sadness, shame and anger.

"I'm glad you came." Deborah embraced her sister.

A somber Maylene started to leave, reached the door and turned back to Deborah. "Do we still have tomorrow?" she whispered.

Deborah smiled and nodded, yes.

chapter forty-six

A Dark Place

"You must know how I feel about you..."

Deborah and Paul sat on the bed, again surrounded by a sea of paper. Neither spoke. The events of an hour earlier weighed heavily on both their minds.

Deborah glanced at her watch, stood, and gathered the folders in a neat pile. She placed them on the lamp table and returned to sit. Paul retrieved his wine and took a long sip.

"About your brother. I do understand him. He was just taken off guard by my being here. After all this time, he comes to visit his sister and some white guy pops out of the bedroom. He was only being protective. I'm a big brother, too. I understand him."

Deborah would have expected nothing less from Paul. He was being kind. Too kind.

"Thanks. In my heart, I know it's more than that. But it's nice of you to say so. The plain truth is, my brother hates white folk. It's just that simple."

"Well, it's not like history hasn't given him good reason."

"You're being kind. He doesn't know you?"

"True. Maybe before this is all over, he will."

Paul tabled his drink, leaned back against the wall—fingers laced behind his head, his legs crossed. Deborah started for the bathroom. Paul waited a moment then leaped from bed, dashed to the dresser and filled a second glass with wine. He returned to the bed and turned the three-way lamp down to its lowest setting.

Deborah reentered the room, immediately noticed the altered ambiance and slowed to a stop. Paul was nestled on the bed. A subtle smile crept across his face.

"It's almost midnight," Deborah noted. "Time for bed."

"I've been waiting forever to hear you say that."

Paul reached for the second glass of wine and held it out to her. Deborah refused, shaking her head *no*. Her smile vanished.

"What I meant was, you should go to your bed, and I'll get in mine. That's what I meant," Deborah made clear. She folded her arms and waited for him to make a graceful exit.

"You won't even have a little wine with me...celebrate your new millionaire status?"

"When the check is in the bank, we'll have caviar, champagne—the most expensive we can find. I'm patient."

"I know." Paul placed his drink down. "Come here for a second, please. I want to tell you something."

Paul motioned for Deborah. She hesitated at first then walked over and sat a short distance from him. Prolonged silence followed.

"You know how I feel about you," Paul whispered softly. "I love you, Deborah Yvonne Davis—Deborah Durrell. I love both of you with all my heart. I know this is not the perfect time, but..." Paul fixed his gaze on Deborah and inched closer. She glanced away.

"Paul, I've tried to explain as well as I know how that..."

"I know. But I can't help it."

"Paul..."

"It's true."

"Paul, it's...it's late."

"And it's not that I am a slow learner. Dee, I really do love you. I know I've said this before. The truth is, I can't hide the way I feel about you. You already know that. Dee, why do you think I do all the things I do for you? Tell me. C'mon, you want me to beg?" Paul said, half-jokingly. "Maybe sit up and roll over? Is that it? 'Cause if it is, I'll do it. Ain't too proud to beg."

Deborah turned to face Paul. He was mimicking a puppy—had both hands raised and curled against his chest. She was not amused.

"Wait. Wait! This isn't about some quid pro quo, is it? Compensation for services rendered?"

"C'mon. You know me better than that. Think about it. This is about my love for you, and about your being honest with yourself."

"My being honest?"

"Yes, honest. And admitting you love me, too. What are you afraid of? Why won't you open up?" Paul's tone, though loving, conveyed his longstanding frustration.

"I'm not afraid."

"I hear you. But I think you are. I believe you're afraid of what admitting you love me would mean."

Paul's profession of love only served to remind Deborah of the man who first uttered those words to her: her father. The Reverend loved her. He said so with unquestionable sincerity. She was his "little girl." Everyone said so. Yet, he reclaimed those words. He withdrew his love, replaced it with rejection and abandonment. The mere sound of those three words made her shrink away, emotionally. They stirred awful memories—even fostered resentment.

And Paul's words also forced an unspoken acknowledgment. Deborah heard his words, and admitted an unavoidable truth: she could not imagine truly loving a man, nor making physical love, not in the foreseeable future. Aside from what was a moral issue for her, it was much easier to remain celibate.

Celibacy meant no attachments, no questions about her body—a body she still viewed as damaged—and no questions about the scar. But it was more than a scar. It was a portal—a gateway to her past, a pathway leading to talk of things she wanted to forget.

Even at Northwestern, although Deborah had accepted a number of dates, things always ended far from the water's edge. All this flashed through her mind in an instant.

Deborah brought both hands to her face and paused to think carefully about what she wanted to say. She measured the tone and tenor of her voice. "Paul, I've tried to express this to you before. I care deeply about you. I really do. You might even say love. But..."

"Good. Let's say love."

"But it's not the love you're talking about."

"Why isn't it?"

"It just isn't. And I can't make it be. Neither can you. I would like to think that all the things you've done—things we've done together—were done because we are two people who care for...and respect each other. If there is to be more than that, nothing can stop it. If not, nothing can force it to be."

Deborah stared at Paul, looking for some visible sign he understood and agreed with her. Observing a slightly wounded expression, she leaned over, kissed him lightly on the cheek. He responded by embracing her firmly. He initiated another kiss—a lingering kiss on her lips.

Deborah tilted her head back and attempted to move away. Paul grew a bit more passionate. He guided her gently but firmly back to him, planted a soft kiss on her neck, her ear. She flinched and attempted to move away once more.

"I want you, Dee. I want you so much," Paul whispered. "I've waited so long to...to make you know this in all the ways that matter. There's nothing I can't give you. You know that. " He placed both hands on her shoulders, tried to entice her to him.

"Paul, please. Don't. Please, we can talk tomorrow. Paul!"

Deborah's tone was calm, but serious. She gazed at Paul intently. She searched his face, his eyes—eager to determine his state of mind. He seemed much more persistent, exhibiting a behavior she had not witnessed before. She was certain she had not sent the wrong signal. Still, Paul continued his attempt to seduce her.

Paul next tried to coax Deborah onto her back, while continuing to embrace and kiss her. The move, the level of force surprised her. She firmly resisted.

"No, Paul. Stop! Don't!"

Deborah's tone was firm and unequivocal, but Paul persisted. This was out of character for him. He grew more intense. Deborah was stunned that he did not immediately heed her plea.

"Don't do this Paul! You're ruining everything! This isn't you! Stop!" Deborah called out.

Paul relented, although his hands remained on her shoulders. Desperate to prevent things from escalating, she grasped his hands and quickly forced them downward. But his fingers caught the inside of her pajama top, ripping away the first two buttons, exposing her bra cup.

It may as well have been her naked breasts. Deborah exploded with raw rage. Her eyes flared. She pushed Paul away, struck out at him— flailing with both arms. Paul appeared as stunned as she did. But that's not what Deborah saw. She saw and felt the room spinning. She shut her tear-filled eyes to try and stop the dizzying movement.

This could not be Paul doing this to her, Deborah thought, as blinding tears cascaded down her face. This was not happening. He had never violated her trust in any way. The Paul she knew would do nothing to hurt her, and everything to protect her.

"What are you doing? What have you done?" Deborah screamed.

Paul said nothing. He just stared at her with reddened eyes. He wore a dumbfounded look—an expression that suggested he felt more like a startled observer than a participant. Paul turned his palms up, gazed at his hands, and buried his face in them. But the worse was yet to come.

Deborah's breathing grew deeper; her eyes flared even more. "Damn you, Jonathan! Damn you!" she screamed. She felt shrouded in a dark fog that seemed to envelope her. "I hate you, Jonathan!"

Suddenly, a door—a door leading to a secret place overflowing with painful memories—sprang open with a force that could not be constrained. Deborah was twelve again; Jonathan Reed was sixteen. Both were locked inside his faded blue pickup truck in the piney woods clearing just off Crispus Attucks Road.

It was hot, hellfire hot. Deborah felt on fire. Her heart raced. She struggled to breathe. He was raping her. Jonathan was raping her. And the rape was even more real now. More than it had been all those years before. Now, she saw it all. She felt it all—every unbearable second.

Even in the comfort of her air-conditioned hotel room, Deborah was perspiring profusely. Sweat covered her trembling form from head to toe. It seeped into her eyes. And she was convinced she smelled Jonathan's foul body odor. Sour sputum bubbled up, into her mouth. She spat, repeatedly.

It was May 15, 1974 again, and Deborah was instantly cast into a place worse than hell. The heat was unbearable; the stench was choking. She was nearly blinded by fear, and the perspiration, which Jonathan refused to even let her wipe away. He seemed possessed. He was frothing. He threatened to slice her face and breasts with the razor-sharp pocketknife he gripped in his grimy right hand.

Jonathan cursed in the vilest language, and at the top of his voice. Spit flew from his mouth. He forced Deborah to unbutton her blouse, remove her bra, her skirt, and panties. All the while, she cried out, pleaded at the top of her voice. That only angered him.

"Shut up! Nobody hears you! Look, I don't want to hurt cha', now. Just do what I say and I won't hurt cha'." Jonathan's voice, not Paul's, reverberated in a fiendish tone. A sick smile crept across his face. Veins popped out on his glistening forehead.

"You know damn well you want it. I've seen how you look at me whenever I come around. And I know you were hopin' the rest of your friends wouldn't come with us. So, go on. Look at it, damn it! I said look at it. Touch it. I said touch it!"

"Jonathan, no! Please don't," Deborah pleaded. Tears streamed. Her unlikely tormentor savored every second, delighting in her terror. He forced her to look at his smelly, curved, pulsating, uncircumcised penis.

"Shut up, you little fine-ass bitch. You gon' like it. I promise ya.' Say one more word and I'll slice ya' like a side of bacon. You're gonna do exactly what I say and you're gon' love it. I'll make sure you like it better than Tommy's."

Jonathan's words sounded rehearsed. Deborah saw evil in his eyes; she heard it in his voice. "Please, let me go, Jonathan. I promise I won't tell anybody anything. I promise! Please! Just let me go!"

"Oh, I ain't worried 'bout that. I ain't worried 'bout that at all. Who you think would believe you?"

Deborah trembled the length of her body, as Jonathan forced her tear-stained face down onto himself. She wanted to die. She clenched her teeth, forced her lips closed.

Her resistance enraged Jonathan. He commanded her to take him, full measure. He placed the knife against her neck, forcing the blade against her jugular. A sobbing, weakened Deborah closed her eyes and complied.

Minutes later, Jonathan proceeded to rape her, over and over. Tears covered Deborah's face. She felt Jonathan's sweat dripping onto her. She grimaced and screamed, even as he placed a gritty hand over her mouth. Then, a pain she had never known before coursed her body. With the knife clutched in one hand, Jonathan continued until he had had his fill of her.

Deborah sobbed uncontrollably. She lay twisted on the truck's narrow bench seat, calling out to Gram, and to her father. Salty tears seeped into her mouth.

"Daddy! Daddy, help me!" She screamed. It was the first time she ever needed her father and he was not there. Then, she fell silent. Physically and emotionally spent, and silent.

Momentarily, Deborah was completely passive. Jonathan Reed became mere scenery, not even human. It was then, she felt herself slipping into a gray, swirling mist. For a time, it seemed to have weight and substance. It clutched at her with transparent tentacles she could almost feel. She felt swallowed up by it. Even the monster, Jonathan, melded into its presence.

A drained Deborah was drenched with perspiration. Yet, her body felt neither dry nor wet, neither hot nor cold. She felt neither dead nor alive. Her breathing was spasmodic. She was oblivious to time and space. She drifted in and out of awareness, but was certain she would be alright. She felt she would awaken, at any moment.

Was this the culmination of what Gram had foreseen on that summer morning? Was the horror and violence visited upon her by Jonathan, in 1974, the terrible evil revealed to Gram d'lena that day? Deborah had no recollection of that event, apart from the warmth and love that always embraced her whenever she was with her beloved grandmother. And it was just as well.

—

Deborah lay on her hotel bed, trembling violently. She was there in Reedville again, as surely as she was on that *awful day*. The roasting heat seared her skin. She could practically smell the awful, putrid stench of Jonathan's sweaty body, the stinging odor of his member. Deborah shuttered her eyes, much as she had that fateful day long ago. She winced as she relived the horror of him forcing her down onto himself. She recalled the violent, spasmodic vomiting that followed. Deborah felt ripped inside out.

Then, the worst—the brutal way he forced her onto her back in the cramped cab, still clutching the knife. Deborah cried out as Jonathan thrust himself into her, shoving her head against the door, bending her neck awkwardly and painfully.

It was then, Deborah simply went limp. She realized there was no stopping Jonathan from doing whatever he wanted. Again and again, she kept telling herself it would soon be over. This horror would come to an end; it had to. It couldn't go on forever. "Just pretend he's not here. You're alone," she kept saying to herself. "You're alone."

Deborah shut her eyes as tightly as she could, clenched her teeth, and permitted herself to sink into nothingness. She imagined she was far, far away. A garden. She was in a garden—a place teeming with beauty she'd never seen before. It seemed boundless, without measure, without an end. There were butterflies, hummingbirds, and trees with branches spanning winding paths. The sky above her was bluer than blue. There were pure white clouds that seemed near enough to touch.

And she was no longer twelve, or even twenty; she was ageless. As far as she could see, a seascape of flowers and fauna surrounded her— the colors so brilliant, they nearly blinded her. She imagined turning around and around, desperately trying to take it all in. But the more she saw, the more there was to see.

A gentle wind caressed her face. She felt lighter than air, brimming with joy and peace. Then, a gentle hand on her shoulder, an angelic voice—soft and sweet. Deborah felt a loving warmth that coursed through her entire being. And despite not seeing anyone, she knew she was not alone. In her spirit, she was not alone.

In an instant, reality reclaimed Deborah's consciousness. A face! There was a face pressed against the driver's side window of Jonathan's old truck, then the corner of the windshield. A face—a black face. A sweaty, black face with grimy hands clutching the sides of the head to shield the sun. A face that housed bulging eyes, and an open mouth screaming words that could not be heard.

A man. A man was staring, peering inside, watching. It was Willie— Willie Montgomery. Deborah was sure of it. He was there! She recalled him repeatedly beating on the window. Jonathan turned to face him; he yelled out angrily.

"Okay! You've seen enough, dammit! Go! Go on!

Willie hesitated at first, then disappeared. He just...disappeared. And now he was dead—murdered. Miss Jasmine said he had been viciously murdered. Maylene later confirmed it, providing gruesome details about the unbelievable savagery exacted upon the body, likely done after the murder was committed.

"My God, he saw it! Willie saw it all," Deborah shouted. "Jonathan made sure of it," she thought. "There was no way Willie just happened to be there. The whole thing must have been planned. Willie knew to be there. He knew! Now he was dead. Had Jonathan made sure of that as well?" Deborah had no doubt of the answers.

But there was more. In her emotional frenzy, something flashed into her mind that made her heart race. A shadow—a blurry shadow of some-one else. Not near the truck. Near the roadway.

But who? Was it real, or could it be explained as some psychological artifact stemming from the terror she suffered? Yet, the image per-sisted—like a needle stuck in an album groove, playing itself over and over. Deborah's consciousness had apparently recorded the presence of a moving shadow, accompanied by the sound of rustling leaves.

Someone was there? Watching? Lurking in the trees at the edge of Crispus Attucks road? Hiding as she emerged from the woods en route home? The recall, though limited, was certain. Whoever it was, they were partially concealed several yards away. Deborah turned in their direc-tion slightly; they darted away. Her strong impression now, was that the person was male. Definitely male.

Deborah sat straight up now, struggling to exorcise the last fragment of recollection from her mind. No use pondering the unanswerable. She would never know if someone else had been hiding and observing her that day. More than likely, none of *that* was real, she purposely thought. Far too much of that day *was* real. No need to add any more.

chapter forty-seven

The Awakening

========================

Paul buried his face in his hands and...

T he next thing Deborah knew,
Paul sat hunkered on the floor at the side of her bed. He looked disori-
ented, scared. His hands shook badly. Deborah lay sobbing, curled in
the fetal position in the middle of the bed. Paul buried his face in both
hands for a moment, then began slowly crawling in her direction. He
reached out and attempted to both console her, and apologize.

"Deborah, I'm so...so sorry. Please, please forgive me."

Paul barely touched Deborah's arm. She recoiled—jumped violently
then sat straight up in bed. Her bloodshot eyes flew open. She stared at
him, but hardly recognized him. Deborah was looking at Paul, but was
seeing Jonathan.

"No! Just go. Go! Now!"

Paul flinched, slowly rose to his feet then quickly moved away to stand
at the foot of the bed. Deborah retreated until her back was pressed
against the headboard. She clutched her robe closed with both hands,

still sobbing, breathing in gasps. Paul was breathing erratically. He looked scared; he struggled to find the right words.

"My God, Deborah. Listen, sweetheart. Please, listen. I was...I was wrong. Forgive me!" Paul pleaded in a plaintive voice Deborah could never have imagined hearing. She refused to answer. Still, Paul lingered, even as he knew his words were having no effect. He started away then turned back.

"I'm so sorry. I've...I've never shown you anything but respect—love and respect. I don't know what happened just now. I would never force myself on you."

"Leave, please." Deborah's voice was barely audible.

"You called me Jonathan. You called me Jonathan. Why?"

"Please. Please, leave." Her weakened voice crackled as she spoke.

Paul started away, then took a step back toward Deborah.

"Deborah, I didn't..."

Deborah bounded from her bed and stormed from the room. The mere sound of Paul's voice nauseated her. All she could see was this image of Jonathan. She ran to the door, threw it open and stood with arms folded. Paul, appearing deeply remorseful, followed her with leaden feet. He paused at the door and looked back with a plaintive gaze.

"Deborah," he kept saying.

Deborah was not swayed. She turned away until Paul stepped into the empty corridor. After he had gone, she slammed the door closed then returned to the bedroom and threw herself into the middle of her bed.

An hour later, Deborah had barely changed positions. Later yet, she still sat at the head of the bed with her back planted against the headboard. Her knees were drawn to her chest, her robe cinched around her like a shroud. She sat rocking forward and back, aimlessly staring across the room. Soon, the crying began all over again. Then came a chant. It began softly at first, hardly audible.

"You raped me. You raped me, you bastard," she kept mumbling. "You raped me, Jonathan. You raped me!" Deborah repeated her lament, amid a rush of tears and reawakened torment.

The scarring memory of the unspeakable violence she suffered on May 15, 1974 had been locked away for fourteen years. It had all festered beneath countless layers of fear and guilt. In great measure, Deborah had always blamed herself for the fate she inherited. And she had never wanted to remember what really happened. The truth would have come with a heavy price.

Now, it was all replaying in her mind like a terrible horror movie she could not turn off. Deborah remembered the long walk home. She remembered the physical pain. And she recalled wishing with all her heart she were dead.

"I didn't do anything, Daddy," she murmured, as tears streamed down her cheeks. She kept repeating it, over and over again. "I didn't do anything. I was a good girl. I was a good girl, Daddy."

Deborah's mind was awash in recollections of that fateful day—the day she felt she died. She remembered Jonathan threatening her—threatening to kill her on the spot. In her heart, she felt he had. The storybook life she had known ended that day. Physical death could not have been as horrible as the pain she had endured nearly every moment since.

For the first time in all those years, a thought filled her mind that never had before. Deborah remembered arriving home that fateful day and finding her father waiting for her. But why? Why was the Reverend at home, and not out searching for her? She wondered why that question had never entered her mind before now. There were no answers.

Deborah had later learned from Maylene, that Matthew had done just as she had imagined—taken his .22 rifle and gone searching for her, and for Jonathan. When he returned home to see if Deborah had arrived, and found his father's car parked in its place, he ended his search.

An exhausted, weeping Deborah collapsed forward onto her hotel bed. In a flash, she turned and sat up. Her eyes were fixed—frozen on some place light years away. Her face erupted into deep frowns. Tears flowed, as she ripped off her robe and tossed it across the room. She next tore her sweat-soaked pajama top from her body. Her bare chest heaved with emotion. She sobbed, loudly.

Deborah's anger soared. She struggled to tear off her pajama bottoms, persisting until she was naked. She then stood shaking, gripping herself—both arms wrapped around her with her hands clutching her shoulders. She felt dirty, unclean, and defiled—a thousand times more than she had that awful night she faced the Reverend's violent lashes.

Then, a cold reality descended upon her—one she had resisted acknowledging all this time. In all her twenty-six years, she had never willingly given herself to any man. Her first and only sexual experience was rape. Rape—dehumanizing rape. Such horror should never be the cornerstone of any woman's emotional and sexual history.

Deborah had long escaped facing the truth regarding her initial sexual experience. She kept convincing herself what happened to her was not sex. It was violence. It was hatred and violence—a brutal exhibition of power and dominance.

Still, her self-view had been forever altered. She had long resisted, if not denied, the physical attraction she felt for the men she had known. Physical intimacy was something to be avoided. Deborah knew this tormenting conflict would have to be confronted someday. Someday.

An anxious, fitful Deborah raced from the room. Without breaking stride, she stormed into the bathroom, cranked on the shower and practically thrust herself under the steaming stream of hot water. She flinched from the heat, but held her ground.

With soap and towel in hand, Deborah began washing—scrubbing herself, frantically. It was as if she were desperate to strip away some awful stain that seemed determined to resist her every effort.

Deborah scrubbed her entire body from head to toe, for nearly an hour, all the while sobbing uncontrollably. She washed herself until the soap bar was a mere sliver, and continued. And later, after drying and starting from the bathroom, she returned to the shower once more.

—

At 3 a.m., Deborah still lay wide awake, staring up at the ceiling, unaware of having returned to the bedroom. Her skin felt raw. Parts of her body were bruised. She raised herself slightly and examined her arms, her abdomen, her thighs. The bruises were evident. Events of the past night flooded back, and again the tears flowed.

Then, silence. Deborah lay tightly coiled, her body nestled on her pillows, the covers pulled up to her head. Her eyes were wide open, at first. Her lids closed shut under their own weight. She succumbed to a blank sleep that would leave her no images to recall upon waking, save those that had chased her into blessed slumber.

Six-thirty a.m. found a silent Deborah sitting upright, draped in her top sheet, her fingers laced around knees drawn to her chest. Her eyes were wide open. Her lips began moving, but there was no sound. She kept mouthing the words—searching for her voice. And it came. It came with a melody, a rhythm, time-tested lyrics. It came with a song.

Deborah began singing, softly at first. "Come Ye Disconsolate." She knew it well. As a young girl, she had sung it often, normally just after the Reverend had preached; the 'doors of the church' were opened. And she sang it now, though not with the same verve and volume. But she sang it. *"Come ye disconsolate, where'er ye languish. Come to the mercy seat..."*

When she had sung the last verse, Deborah felt a warming presence that surged through her body, all but lifting her from where she sat. Though only a tiny stream of sunlight now crept past the edge of the drapery, it seemed as if the noonday sun beamed from the ceiling.

Deborah had no doubt it was Gram. Gram's presence had come to her, and she had not come alone. She was in the company of angels. Deborah felt embraced by their presence, humbled by their awesome power, and straightway purified—made whole. A gleam filled her eyes. An inner light filled her being, and she stood, as if resurrected.

—

Two hours later, Deborah's small travel clock glowed: 8:30 AM. Her bed was empty. She stood there quietly, near the living room window, fully dressed—long sleeves concealing the bruises. Deborah sipped coffee, and stared out across the city. She could not explain her feeling of well-being, given her recollections of the past several hours. She simply accepted it, and the renewed sense of mission she felt.

Moments passed. Deborah walked to the small desk, placed the cup down and retrieved the folders containing the contracts. She lifted her briefcase from a nearby chair and slipped the papers inside.

The telephone rang. Deborah froze. It rang four more times, before she answered. It was Maylene, apologizing yet again for Matthew's behavior. Deborah insisted all was forgiven, while struggling to sound cheerful. Maylene was not fooled. Deborah finally gave in.

"I need to talk to you," she said, fighting back tears.

"I'm listening." Maylene was deeply concerned.

"No. I mean face to face. Maybe tonight sometime, after things settle down a bit. I'm meeting Tommy at Riverfront Park downtown. I cannot imagine what that's going to be like. It'll be great to see him again, after all these years."

"I wish I could be there to see for myself," Maylene confessed.

Deborah asked about her father, and learned his condition had not changed. Just as she hung up, a firm knock sounded at the door. She waited. It sounded again. She took a deep breath then started to answer. Another knock reverberated.

Deborah peeked out before opening the door. A young man, dressed in a Khaki uniform, stood panting while holding a long, gold-colored flower box.

"Deborah Durrell?" he asked. Deborah nodded yes.

"These are for you...had special instructions to get 'em to you before nine o'clock. Almost didn't make it."

Deborah stared at the box, oblivious to the young man's banter. She thanked him and he disappeared as quickly as he had come. She closed the door, ripped the note from the cover, looked at it then tossed it and the box into a nearby wastebasket.

The phone rang again. Deborah whispered a weak hello. A soft female voice was on the other end. Deborah could barely hear her.

"Miss Davis?"

"Yes. Who's calling?"

"I'm not quite at liberty to say. But, please don't hang up. I'm sorry, I can't tell you my name."

"Why can't you? Look, I can hardly hear you. You'll have to speak up. What do you want?"

"For one thing, my life could be in serious danger if the wrong people find out I called you."

"Danger? Wrong people? I don't understand." Deborah's head snapped back. Her eyes widened. She eased onto the edge of the sofa.

"Please, ma'am. I don't have long. You're being followed. They've already taken pictures of you and your daughter so the both of you can be easily identified. They know where your little girl is at all times. They always know. They know everything."

"My daughter? What are you talking about? Who's following me? And why? How do you know I have a daughter? Who are you?"

"Ma'am, the Reeds are just about the most powerful and richest family in this state. And you've made some folks real scared 'round here. They're scared you're gonna...well, cause a terrible scandal."

"Scandal? I don't understand. Listen, I'm glad you called. I'd really like to thank you personally. If you tell me who..."

"Ma'am, I've already said too much."

"No, no, no. I really appreciate your calling me. But how did you know I was here?"

"Like I said, you're being followed."

"Followed? Who's following me? Why? Describe them."

"Please, be careful. In case you're wondering, I'm telling you this because I'm a woman. I'm also a mother. And...well, I believe people ought to be treated fairly, regardless of the color of their skin."

———

Miles away, just off the sprawling lobby of the Reed Company, Inc. headquarters building, a full-sized woman—early thirties, about 5'-7," short brown hair, and wearing a beige business suit—stood at a phone bank. She was facing the wall, clutching the receiver, and talking in hushed tones.

"You're...you're white?"

"Yes ma'am. But the point is this. Whatever you plan to do about things, you have to do it quickly. I have to go now. Good luck to you and Samantha."

The woman hung up and turned around cautiously. It was Susan, Jonathan Reed's secretary. She hesitated a moment, cast a wary glance around the lobby, then quickly moved from the phones and toward the elevators.

In Deborah's hotel room, she hung up slowly, and remained on the sofa, clearly disturbed by what she had heard. She had no idea who the woman was or if she could believe her, but had little choice.

"Samantha. Samantha," Deborah whispered. She bounded to her feet, grabbed her briefcase and left. Within seconds, she entered the elevator, just as Paul exited the next car. He walked at a brisk pace to Deborah's room and knocked. There was no answer. He knocked twice more then turned away, dejected.

The elevator bell sounded, just as Paul started back down the corridor. Two men stepped off and started in his direction. Both were white, approximately 6'-4 to 6'-6," 250 pounds or more, and dressed in blue, seersucker suits. Paul had not seen a seersucker suit since Sidney Greenstreet wore one in some 1940s film he could not readily recall. He stepped to one side of the corridor to permit the oversized pair to pass. However, they stopped directly in front of him, blocking his path.

"You Paul Castle?" asked the man nearest him.

Paul was surprised but recovered in good form. "Apparently, you already know my name." The second man moved even closer. Paul got an overpowering whiff of his Aqua-Velva aftershave. The man had obviously fallen into the bottle, Paul thought.

"Sir, I wonder if we may prevail upon you to join us in the restaurant for coffee and a little conversation?" he asked.

Paul took a couple of steps back and took a deep breath to clear his lungs. "What's this about?"

"I'll be happy to answer that," said the first man, "But I don't think we should discuss it here in the corridor. Surely, you wouldn't refuse a little southern hospitality. Caffeine aside, what harm can a little coffee and friendly conversation do?" As he spoke, the man patted the bulging left breast pocket of his jacket. Paul got the message.

chapter forty-eight

The Lioness's Den
=========================

"I'm due at a meeting in Governor Clinton's office this afternoon. So..."

It was nearly 11:00 am.
Deborah's car crept down the quiet residential street shaded by magnificent magnolias and stately oaks.

She lowered the driver's window and peered out at addresses adorning gate columns. Mammoth, sprawling estates in Little Rock's exclusive River Oaks area stretched endlessly on both sides of the wide, winding streets.

Deborah arrived at 10919 Cypress Creek Circle. In the distance was an immense, white-columned, two-story, white brick structure with antebellum facade. It was set on acres of lush grounds, well behind ornate walls ten feet tall. Attached, L-shaped, stair-stepped wings extended from the main house on either side.

Deborah was awed by the view. She slowed and pulled to the gate. A shimmering, polished brass, French script "R" sparkled in the sun. Deborah leaned through the window, and lifted the column-mounted phone.

"Who's calling, please?" Boomed a rich baritone voice.

Deborah cleared her throat and swallowed hard. "Davis. Deborah Davis," she answered. "I spoke to Mrs. Reed a short time ago. She's expecting me." Deborah waited, hardly breathing.

"Hang up the phone, please. The gate will open."

Deborah returned the receiver. The heavy gate swung open, slowly. She entered, drove along the meandering driveway to the main house, and eased to a stop in the huge, circular, courtyard driveway. Deborah sat a short while with the car idling, absorbed by the sheer size and beauty of the place.

"No wonder these people can isolate themselves from the rest of us so completely," she thought. "This is like another planet."

After taking a much-needed deep breath, Deborah killed the engine, exited the car, and walked toward the main entrance. Her steps echoed on the stone walkway. She was met at the door by a tall, uniformed butler—a distinguished-looking black man. His salt and pepper hair was neatly cropped. He appeared to be in his early sixties, alert, shoulders squared. His strides were long and sure, though his pace permitted Deborah to keep up.

The man was cordial but unsmiling, as he escorted Deborah past the high domed, chandeliered entry, and the cavernous, formal, living room. A couple of Hockneys and a Pollock adorned one living room wall. He continued to a somewhat smaller, more informal living room—no less stately, and equally well appointed.

"May I get you coffee, tea or lemonade?" he asked.

"No, thank you," said Deborah, accepting a seat on the Duncan Phyfe sofa just behind her. The butler smiled for the first time, nodded to her then left the room.

It was hard to miss the large, heavily framed family portrait hanging prominently over the fireplace. It included a woman Deborah assumed to be Mrs. Reed, along with Richard Reed, Jonathan, apparently Jonathan's wife, and...Susan? Deborah did a doubletake. There was Susan. Jonathan's secretary was a family member?

Deborah was confused. Even when she and Jonathan entered his office, she was never introduced to Susan. Her name was never mentioned. But here she was in the Reed family portrait.

Jonathan's son and daughter were also in the picture. It was a striking portrait, notable for the fact that only the men wore smiles. Susan, Mrs. Reed and Jonathan's wife all appeared remarkably somber, even subdued.

Susan? Deborah was still pondering Susan's presence in the portrait, when Mrs. Reed sauntered into the room. She was a tall, attractive, lightly grey, elegantly dressed woman. She was much too elegantly dressed for 11a.m., Deborah thought.

Mrs. Reed wore a faint smile, a haughty air, her nose aimed well above sea level. As she neared, Deborah stood to greet her, but was motioned to sit. Mrs. Reed moved to a nearby chair, but remained standing.

"Miss Davis?"

"Yes. Deborah Davis. My parents live..."

"On SB-40. Yes. I'm Virginia Reed."

"Pleased to meet you." Deborah extended her hand, which Virginia Reed barely grasped before releasing it.

"Yes. You mentioned all that in your phone call. I'm sure Mac offered you some refreshment. Sure you won't change your mind?"

"Yes, he did. And yes, I'm sure. Thanks."

Virginia Reed took her seat, easing about three-quarters of the way onto the seat cushion. Her back was as straight as an arrow.

"Beautiful morning," said Deborah. "You have a gorgeous home."

Virginia Reed only nodded. She appeared extremely impatient. "Miss Davis, I agreed to see you this morning for only a moment, and for only one reason: my son."

"I appreciate your seeing me on such short notice."

"Well, you convinced me you knew him years ago. Of course, that's possible. Jonathan was always such a gregarious sort...loved animals, made friends easily, irrespective of backgrounds and ethnic origins. It's his nature. Now, convince me of the difficulty you infer he is in. But first, you should know that my son is a United States Senate candidate. He is also a highly respected member of this community, a lifetime member of the NAACP, even helps raise money for the United Negro College Fund. So, you have apparently made some grievous error. I welcome the chance to set things straight. Now, what is it you have to discuss with me?"

Deborah listened and quickly realized she was hearing the words of a devoted mother. She had expected nothing less. But she, too, was a mother, and equally devoted to her daughter.

"You're kind to see me."

"Of course. Miss Davis, I really am pressed for time. I'm due at a meeting in the Governor's office this afternoon. So..."

"I'll get to the point." Deborah cleared her throat, took a deep breath, and looked directly at Virginia Reed. "I wish there was some delicate way to put this," she said.

Mrs. Reed's eyes flashed. She appeared offended. Her freshly coiffed head snapped back a bit. She then leaned forward.

"Miss Davis, I assure you there is no cause to concern yourself with my need for delicate treatment. If you have something to say, I must insist you put it in whatever way is most direct."

"Very well, Mrs. Reed. I'll speak directly."

"Thank you."

"Mrs. Reed, I have a wonderful, beautiful, young daughter. Her name is Samantha. She'll be fourteen years old this coming February. I brought her picture with me."

Mrs. Reed watched as Deborah removed a small color photo of Samantha from her small purse and handed it to her. She accepted it with some reservation. The photo, given to Deborah by Maylene, was one of Samantha in a model-like pose. She stood near the old log fence at home, flashing a broad smile. Mrs. Reed hardly looked at the photo. She handed it back to Deborah almost immediately.

"She's...she's your daughter?"

"Yes. Samantha. Her name is Samantha."

"She's attractive. You should be proud."

"I am. She's beautiful, smart. I love her dearly, just as you love your son." Mrs. Reed glanced at her wristwatch, conveying her mounting impatience. Deborah took notice. "Mrs. Reed, before you came in, I was admiring that portrait of your family. Is the woman next to you...your daughter?"

Mrs. Reed seemed surprised. "Why do you ask?" Virginia Reed sounded defensive. Her eyes flared. She leaned forward again. Deborah knew she had pricked a raw nerve.

"No particular reason. Is she?"

"Yes, Susan is my daughter. But I don't understand. Why are you so focused on the portrait?"

"The portrait is incomplete."

"I know."

"You know?" Deborah's was not sure she had heard correctly.

"Of course. My daughter-in-law is expecting another child in only a few months. We'll have to commission another portrait," she said.

Deborah's look of surprise faded into a faint smile. She hesitated before continuing. "I'm sorry. That's not exactly what I am referring to. What I meant..."

"What do you mean? What are you saying, Miss Davis?"

"What I'm saying is, *my* daughter belongs in that portrait as well. Samantha—*my* Samantha is your granddaughter. Your son is my daughter's father."

Deborah's explosive words detonated in Virginia Reed's ears. Her eyes nearly popped from their sockets. Her face turned ashen. Her jaw dropped. She slumped back in her chair.

For a time, Deborah thought the woman would stop breathing. Mac peered into the room from just outside the doorway where he had been waiting. He raised his hand to his chest and shook his head repeatedly.

"On May 15th, of 1974," Deborah went on—her trembling voice filled with tempered emotion—"Jonathan...your son, Jonathan, raped me. Your son raped me, Mrs. Reed."

Virginia Reed clutched her bosom with both hands. "Raped?" she wheezed, nearly swallowed her tongue. "You said...you said raped?"

"Yes. Yes, raped, Mrs. Reed."

Deborah had not anticipated the swell of emotion that rose within her. She fought hard to steady her quaking voice, while riveting her gaze on Virginia Reed's reddened face and bulging eyes.

"My God. You are insane! You are most surely insane. Mac!"

"He offered me a ride home in his old blue pickup that day."

"Stop! Stop, this instant! I want you out of here. Mac!"

"Instead, he pulled off the road, drove down a trail into the woods and out into a clearing." Deborah's eyes narrowed; her jaws clenched; her speech slowed. "He forced me to perform certain...certain acts on him. Then he...he raped me!" Deborah fought to not cry, even as horrendous images filled her mind once more.

"Lies! Damnable lies! My God, woman! I want you out of my home this instant. Mac! Get in here, now!"

"He threatened to slit my throat with a sharp, black pocket knife he held to my neck. His initials were engraved on it.

"Out!"

"I was only twelve years old, Mrs. Reed. Twelve years old! As a mother, I am sure..."

Virginia Reed gasped. Her eyes looked like eggs. Deborah grew even more concerned for her and moved to the edge of her seat. She looked around to see if the butler was in view. Virginia Reed struggled to regain her composure. Her crimson face contorted. With great effort, she practically willed herself to her feet.

"Mac! Mac!" she kept screaming.

Mac, who had been listening all the while, and leaving his employer to twist in the wind, took a short step back. He hesitated a moment more before entering the room.

"Mac!" yelled a furious Virginia Reed.

"Yes," Mac calmly answered, casually gliding into the room.

"Mac, I want her out of here now! Get her out this minute! Miss Davis, you are a damned liar! I might have known you would come here and spew god-awful lies about my son. Who is putting you up to this? Who's paying you to spread these damnable lies about my son?"

Deborah remained calm, kept her gaze aimed at her fuming host. She rose and moved slowly toward the doorway. Mrs. Reed followed, pointing angrily. Mac held his place.

As she passed a small table, Deborah observed something she had not noticed earlier: a hardcover copy of her novel, 'Silent Song.' There it was, her embossed name—Deborah Durrell. It leaped out from the glossy jacket. Deborah paused to enjoy the moment, smiled, and walked on past.

"I don't know what your purpose is, Miss Davis. But I warn you, do not show your face here again! Do you hear me? You'd be much better off, if you caught a flight back to Chicago as soon as you can. People who engage in character assassination are severely dealt with down here."

Deborah wheeled around to face a livid Virginia Reed.

"Are you threatening me?"

"Take it any way you like. And if you repeat one word of this foul garbage, I'll have our lawyers sue you for libel faster than you can say watermelon," warned Mrs. Reed.

Deborah's teeth clenched. Her fists formed and she took a step toward Mrs. Reed. The latter flinched and stepped back, raising her right arm defensively.

"I cannot deck this woman in her own house," Deborah thought. She took a deep breath and forced a smile. That seemed to enrage Virginia Reed more than anything.

"Mrs. Reed, you know what I have told you is true. I can see it in your eyes. I hear it in your voice. You do believe me. In your heart, you I know you do believe me. You do."

"That is a damnable lie. And don't think for a moment I'm going to mention something so...so preposterous to my son. Get her out of here, Mac! Get her off my property this second!"

"You don't have to tell Jonathan, Mrs. Reed. He already knows. He has always known. You see, he was there. Your son is a rapist. That fact is irreversible, no matter how much power, wealth, and influence you have. You will never be able to change that fact. I was twelve years old, Mrs. Reed. I've carried this with me every moment since. I love my daughter with all my being.

"But what happened to me changed my life forever, changed me in ways you cannot begin to imagine. Rape, Mrs. Reed. Rape is a hell I would wish on no woman, not even you. What your son did to me was violent, by its nature. Yet, he chose to be even more violent and brutal. For the longest time, I wanted him to suffer, too. I wanted him dead!

"I don't blame you for trying to defend your son. However, the truth needs no defense. Only lies require such a defense. I have spoken the truth to you. And I want you to know, that despite what I have endured, I refuse to be defined by what happened to me. I am all cried out now, Mrs. Reed. All I want is for the truth to be known. And it will be known. It will. I promise you."

The veins in Virginia Reed's neck and forehead appeared ready to burst. Even her ears were now blood red. "If this did happen—and there is no way I believe a single, malicious, word of this—why didn't you say something back then? Why? Get her out of here, Mac!"

Deborah stared back at her. She raised her right hand and pointed her finger. "He was uncircumcised, Mrs. Reed. At sixteen, your son was uncircumcised. Do you need to hear more? I feel so sorry for you. And one more thing, who is Susan? Who is she? She doesn't look at all like *you.* She's your *husband's* daughter, not yours, isn't she? She's his love child. Am I right?"

"For the last time, show her out, Mac, before I call the police. I will not be spoken to this way! Get her out, or you can leave with her!"

Mac froze. His eyes narrowed. Deep frowns gorged his brow. His employer's angry words resonated in his ears. Mac bristled at Mrs. Reed's intemperate statement. He rightly felt it was absolutely uncalled for. It accorded him no respect for his twenty-five years of faithful service.

Mac clenched his jaws angrily, as he escorted Deborah toward the front entrance. A seething Virginia Reed trailed them both. Mac opened the heavy door. Deborah stepped out into the bright sunlight and never looked back.

Virginia Reed was distraught and teary-eyed. Veins in her forehead stood out in bold relief. Mac closed the door and turned to find himself less than three feet from her. He looked at his longtime employer with deep concern. She seemed almost pathetic. Mascara streaked down her face. Beads of perspiration covered her brow. Mac had never seen her appear so unsightly, not even after one of those tearful, explosive arguments she often had with her husband.

Touched with a twinge of sympathy, Mac approached to offer her comfort. Virginia Reed raised both hands, palms out, turned her head away, and stepped back. Mac halted in his tracks, gave her a 'go to hell' look and stalked past.

Virginia Reed planted herself, with fists clenched, rooted to the spot just inside the entry. She appeared unable to move. Minutes passed, before she started toward the library, then stopped when she saw Mac approaching with a purposeful stride.

Mac wore a look of determination. His black Kangol cap rested smartly atop his head. He carried a black windbreaker and a plastic tote bag in one hand. Mrs. Reed waited, attempted to make eye contact with him. But Mac stared straight ahead without blinking.

"Mac, where are you going?" Virginia Reed demanded. "I am talking to you, Mac. You answer me!"

Mac said nothing, never looked in her direction. Instead, he strode right past his now former employer, and out the front door. He left it wide open.

"Mac!" she shouted. "MacArthur Jenkins!"

The only voice Virginia Reed heard was her own. Staff Sergeant, MacArthur Alexander Jenkins, III, U.S. Army, Retired, lifted his head, squared his shoulders, kept walking, and never looked back.

chapter forty-nine

Another Reunion

"You're not smiling anymore."

Even from the parking lot
of Riverfront Park, overlooking the Arkansas River, the view was spectacular. A stone-columned street bridge, above the park, spanned the river, insuring a picturesque shot for even amateur photographers.

The facility was site of the 1863 river crossing by Union forces, under Major Frederick Steele. His troops were en route to the Old State House and the capture of Little Rock.

Even on weekdays the place was never crowded, despite being only blocks from downtown. On weekends, except for a few homeless, and several vagabond chess players, it was virtually abandoned. Same was true for most of downtown Little Rock.

An anxious Tommy Williams, 29, wearing a cream-colored suit, sat at the wheel of his black, Mercedes 450SLC. He alternately glanced at his watch, then the park entrance. He had just turned toward the river again, when Deborah wheeled into the parking area and drove slowly along the front row. When she spotted the Mercedes, her heart leaped to her throat. She could make out the image of a man behind the wheel. It had to be Tommy.

Tommy peered into his rear view mirror. He saw the car slow behind him, turned in his seat, certain he recognized Deborah. It *had* to be her. His eyes widened.

Deborah eased into the space alongside Tommy's car. Before she could kill the engine, he climbed out wearing a subdued smile. He started for her car, just as she opened her door and stepped to the ground.

"Tommy!" Deborah called out. "Tommy!" The two rushed to embrace each other. After several moments, both stepped back for a long, fuller look, then embraced again.

"Amazing. God, this is amazing! You are still the most beautiful girl I know," said Tommy. "And those eyes..."

"You never told me that before."

"I was shy...had a limited vocabulary. Remember? Wow! Let me look at you. You are certainly not twelve anymore."

Both laughed, kissed lightly then embraced again. Tommy lifted Deborah, did a three sixty before easing her down.

"It is so good to see you!" said Deborah. A tear stole down her face. "I always wondered what you'd look like all grown up...tall, handsome, no longer shy and retiring."

"Well, now you know. The same, just a little heavier, taller, older, not quite as shy. And no afro!" Both laughed. "I thought of you often. I missed you...wondered how you were. And I was in Chicago several times over the past few years. Started to look you up."

"You should have."

They embraced again, then lingered in brief silence. Tommy shut his eyes and grimaced. His smile faded. He placed both hands firmly on Deborah's shoulders and peered into her eyes. She saw the change in his demeanor right away.

"Deborah," Tommy started. His voice was different.

"You're not smiling anymore. What is it? Something's wrong. What is it?" Deborah waited.

Tommy was silent, but his eyes answered.

"Tell me," said Deborah, her voice filled with trepidation.

Tommy held both her hands in his own, even as she tried to wrest them away.

"Deborah."

"It's my father, isn't it?"

Again, Deborah tried to free her hands. Tommy released them, then wrapped his arms around her. She resisted at first then grew stone still, and quiet. Tommy relaxed his embrace.

For a long moment, Deborah stared across the park toward the river's shimmering blue water, then fixed her gaze on the ground at her feet.

"Deborah, listen to me. Maylene says your father has taken a turn...a turn for the worse. That's all she said. She tried to reach you on your car phone. When she couldn't, she found me at my mother's. Listen, leave your car here. We can get it later. I'm sorry."

Deborah suddenly felt cold. She shuddered, badly. Tommy removed his jacket and placed it around her. After assisting her to his car, he retrieved her briefcase and purse, locked her car and returned.

chapter fifty

The Calling

Deborah moved slowly to the head of the bed.

Just under an hour later, Tommy was less that a quarter mile from the Davis home. Deborah wore a pained expression. She stared directly ahead...had not spoken since leaving the park. Several yards from the turnoff, she caught sight of an ambulance, and a Reed County Sheriff's vehicle, parked directly in front of the house.

Tommy wheeled hard onto the yard. The car had barely stopped, when Deborah threw the door open and stepped out. Paul was on the porch, just left of the doorway. He had called for her earlier and learned of her father's downturn.

June Boy stood near the porch swing. The instant Deborah saw him, her pace slowed involuntarily. She was not conscious of it at all, although others noticed. A cold shiver sliced through her body like a frozen stiletto. She barely remembered June Boy from her time in Reedville. But there was something about his face, his form, his aura.

What was even more chilling, the next image that leaped to her mind was that of a shadowy, male figure standing near a clump of pine trees. But what did it mean? June Boy approached, stopped, then looked away. The unnerving sensation Deborah felt passed quickly. June Boy stood there, shifting back and forth, wringing his hands and mumbling something. Deborah moved toward the steps, and onto the porch. Paul rushed to meet her. "Paul." Her voice trailed.

Paul turned to her. He was about to speak, when Maylene—her own eyes reddened from crying—stepped out onto the porch. She shook her head mournfully and threw both arms around Deborah. Maylene wept on her sister's shoulder while Paul looked on.

"I wish I had been here," Deborah whispered.

An emotional Maylene shook her head sadly. Tommy reached Deborah, just as Gloria stepped outside to embrace her sisters. He watched as the three held onto and consoled each other. Rachel stood in the doorway with arms folded, swaying rhythmically, staring blankly. Paul walked over to Tommy. The two introduced themselves, each having surmised whom the other was.

June Boy kept mumbling to himself. "I...I just wanted to see him, touch his hand, pray for him. I could 'a made him well," he repeated, over and over. No one gave him much notice. He finally stepped from the porch and headed across the yard toward the road.

As Deborah entered the house, Rachel stepped aside, well beyond arm's reach, declining to make eye contact. Rachel's behavior, coming at such a time, surprised Deborah more than she would have expected.

Once inside, Deborah was greeted by the presence of death. A somber air hung over the crowded living room. Two uniformed EMTs and a deputy stood to one side. The deputy had already called for a coroner's unit. Matthew was consoling a distraught Samantha. Sam saw Deborah and rushed to her waiting arms.

"Papa's gone," she kept sobbing. "I prayed real hard for him to be okay. I prayed for him."

"I know," said Deborah, stroking Samantha's face and fighting back her own emotions. "I know, baby."

"I hurt all inside. I can't make it stop. It won't stop." Samantha's words brought a rush of tears to Deborah's eyes. She wished with all her heart she could absorb the pain her daughter was enduring.

A somber Yvonne and Charles, holding hands, sat quietly on the sofa. A short time earlier, Maylene had spent time alone with them, comforting them, and they, her.

Matthew looked angry and distant. Frowns lined his brow. He approached Deborah and embraced her tightly. He shook Tommy's hand while Paul hung back.

"Mama's still in the room with him." Matthew's voice thinned. "He just...he just never woke up again. I never had a chance to say anything else to him. Not s'pose to be like that, Dee. Should at least have a chance to say good-bye."

Maylene grasped Samantha's hand and led her outside, while Deborah began the long walk to her father's bedroom. As she did, she was revisited by every thought, every emotion, every pang of fear she had known over the past fourteen years. No amount of imagining could have readied her for this moment. Deborah reached the closed bedroom door and paused, shut her eyes tightly and brushed tears from her cheeks. However, they were quickly replaced.

Forcing herself forward, Deborah entered her parents' bedroom. She found her mother seated in a rocking chair, next to her father's bed. Her eyes quickly focused on the Reverend's still form. Deborah felt condemned—haunted by angry thoughts that reflected years of hurt and anger. She recalled cursing her father and wishing him dead.

Rebecca and Reginald stood a few feet away, looking on with great empathy. The instant Deborah crossed the threshold, something happened to her. Aside from the self-condemnation she felt, a bizarre sensation coursed her body. It was a feeling she could not understand then, nor been able to explain since.

The air was ether-like, unnatural, difficult to breathe, at first. Deborah saw her mother, Reginald, and Rebecca. She saw her father lying under the crisp white sheet pulled up to his chin.

But the room seemed empty—devoid of life. At Deborah's core, there was the realization her father's spirit had escaped the natural world. His body was there, but his soul—his substance was gone. His physical form now seemed only a hollow shell. He was gone.

Mabel Davis held a large, tattered Bible in her lap. It was the one she had recently removed from the pulpit at Shiloh. Reverend had kept it there since his first sermon in 1959. Mabel sat still, staring at her husband, one hand on the armrest, the other on the Bible.

Rebecca and Reginald offered Deborah their condolences and embraced her warmly. Rebecca held on to her; she seemed reluctant to let go. It was as if she were literally feeling Deborah's pain.

"I'm so sorry. He just...he just slipped away," said Reginald.

Deborah eased closer to the perfectly made bed—too perfectly made. The sheets were the whitest she had ever seen. They were too white. Flawless. The whiteness suggested the absence of warmth. It reminded her of ice—a coldness, bleak and impersonal.

Mabel Davis sat motionless, staring at her husband's now hollow form. Only her lips moved, as she rocked back and forth, silently reciting the 23rd Psalms. There were no tears. Not yet.

Deborah watched her mother for a time, before she walked over to her, touched her shoulder then slowly moved to the head of her father's bed. Reginald left the room.

Rebecca came to stand beside Deborah. "Miss Deborah. I already took care of cleaning and dressing him and everything." Deborah mouthed a thank you. "To be absent from the body, is to be present with God," Rebecca whispered.

Deborah understood and appreciated what Rebecca was saying, but she was not of a mind to hear it. She gazed down at her father, struggled to focus through misty eyes. And despite the enduring hurt she felt, despite the Reverend's diminished appearance, Deborah pictured the face that was once his—the full, smiling, beaming face she had known as a young girl. That was the image she hoped she would keep.

Deborah made a point of wrenching the most minute detail from each surreal moment. She catalogued every sensation. Everything took on an amazingly vivid quality. She observed that her father's hair had been neatly combed, his hands crossed at the lower part of his chest. A look of serenity covered his lightly bearded face. Deborah spoke to him.

"Father," she whispered. "Father... Father." The word, softly spoken, echoed deep in her heart. She repeated it, again and again. "Father. Father." Then, another word found its way to her lips—a word she had not spoken in all those years: "Daddy."

Ignoring tears winding down her face, Deborah peeled back the edge of the sheet and touched her father's left hand. She noted the gold wedding band that had never once been removed.

She traced the long scar on his left forearm—the one he "earned" playing baseball, at the age of thirteen. An opposing player, wearing metal cleats, slid into third base and was tagged out. Reverend wore the scar like a badge. He would roll up his sleeve, proudly show it whenever he retold the incident. He told the story exactly the same way everytime.

At that moment, Deborah's past pains and hurts seemed to evaporate, or at least retreat. They were quietly overwhelmed by the onslaught of emotions now enveloping her. Minutes slipped by as she stood staring at him—staring and remembering.

"I love you, Daddy. And I forgive you. Please, forgive me. Forgive me for not being here to say good-bye, for the hate I've felt, for the thoughts I've held onto for so long." Deborah leaned over and kissed her father's brow. A lone tear fell onto his face.

Shortly thereafter, at Mabel's direction, the entire family gathered in her bedroom. All entered with emotions worn on tear-stained faces. Mabel stood near her deceased husband's side. Everyone, including Yvonne and Charles, held hands and formed a circle around the bed. Deborah held Samantha's hand, leaned close and whispered something in her ear. Mabel took notice. She particularly noticed Samantha's look of surprise.

Mabel Davis set aside her curiosity, closed her eyes and began speaking in a halting, emotional voice. "Dear God, I don't know the right words just now. Only you know what I feel in my heart. Part of me wants to curse your Name. But Lord, I've served You too long to question Your will. So, in my sorrow, I thank You. I thank You and praise Your Holy Name. I thank You for the life of this, your faithful servant, my devoted husband, and this lovin' father.

"I know You have already received his soul and spirit into Your kingdom. Father, give us all a portion of your strength, as we face the days ahead. Bind us with Your abidin' Love. Comfort us, I pray in the blessed name of Christ, Our Savior. Amen."

A tearful Maylene began reciting the Twenty-third Psalm, her voice barely audible. The others joined her, as Matthew eased an arm around his mother's shoulder. She clung to his waist for support.

Rachel was first to leave the room, slamming the door behind her and rushing to her own bedroom. Gloria felt compelled to go to her, but did not do so. A maelstrom of emotions was swirling now. Even Gloria dared not risk an outburst from her sister.

A half-hour later, the coroner's team arrived, and the EMTs left. The team performed a brief investigation, mainly to rule out foul play, but also to make an official death declaration. Tommy stood in the living room speaking in hushed tones with the lead coroner investigator. Transport of Reverend's body would be made within a few minutes. It would be an hour or so before his body's release to the designated mortuary.

"We don't wanna rush the family," the man explained. "We understand these things. And if you prefer, we won't cover his face 'til we're inside the van."

"That's very thoughtful," said Tommy, who turned to Maylene and informed her. She nodded yes and both started for the bedroom.

A short time later, the Reverend Davis' body was carefully removed to the coroner's van. Everyone fought back emotions. Some lingered on the porch, others in the front yard. Paul had second thoughts about having come. He felt conspicuous and useless.

Mabel Davis and the others followed to within a few feet of the vehicle. They waited as Reverend's body was placed inside. Soon, the shiny, white van quietly eased down the grassy driveway and onto Crispus Attucks road. Matthew followed in his pickup. Mabel wanted to come with him, but he suggested she not. Not yet. This was something he wanted to do alone.

A surprisingly composed, but silent Mabel Davis stood on the porch. Her right arm was draped around a nearby support column. Long after the ambulance disappeared from view, she remained there, staring blankly into the distance. Only a feet away, Gloria slipped an arm around Samantha, who had begun crying again. Mabel Davis took notice and beckoned to Sam. Yvonne and Charles sat watching quietly from the porch swing.

Hardly anyone seemed eager to abandon the yard and porch. Deborah stood transfixed, staring down the road where the ambulance had taken her father for the last time. With the sun in full retreat, and her pulse pounding in her ears, she turned and started across a yard now covered in evening shadows.

Deborah struck out toward the old fence, walking briskly, her eyes cast far beyond her footsteps. Tommy and the others watched as she reached the partially open, half-hinged gate and moved past. Without a word, she struck out across the vast field of knee-high grass, her image silhouetted against the backdrop of a fleeting sunset and darkening skies.

Tommy quickly grew concerned. He removed his jacket, tossed it aside, and started after her. As he passed Maylene, she grabbed his arm, shook her head 'no,' then started after her sister. Seconds later, Paul whispered something to Tommy, then reluctantly started for his car.

In the evening sky, flaming bands of color now stretched to infinity along the horizon. It was a brilliant sunset, unlike one anyone could remember. The sun's crown topped the horizon, and appeared to linger far longer than customary. In a moment, it disappeared, leaving fiery remnants of its spectacular display.

Deborah, now a few hundred yards from the house, reached towering Samuel's Oak. The grand tree, its branches lazily swaying, stood out
against the evening sky. She knelt, plucked a handful of wildflowers, and
leaned back against the massive trunk. The world and all its heartaches
had always seemed a little smaller here. She prayed that would be true
this day. But it was not to be.

For the moment, Deborah was alone, with only the sound of the wind
caressing her ears. Yet, every unwanted thought she had known for the
past fourteen years seemed set on assaulting her. Every wrenching emotion seemed bent on invading her heart. She felt overwhelmed, to the
point of feeling faint. And it dawned on her, that any hope of engaging
her father in any way...was now gone, forever.

The words. It was then Deborah remembered the words she had spoken to her father the day she arrived. She had desperately wanted for
him to speak to her, or at least hear her. But it was never to be. It was
then, Deborah remembered the last words her father spoke to her. The
intervening years had not erased them, yet she abandoned the recollection. They had not been words she wanted to hear the night before she
left Reedville...all those years ago.

But what if the Reverend *had* heard and understood her words spoken only days earlier? What if he *had* fully comprehended everything
she said, but was unable to emote or respond. The thought was nearly
too much to contemplate. Were it true, she imagined it would have been
a maddening experience for him.

Yet, while acknowledging that fact, Deborah could not help hoping
it *were* true. She prayed her father, even for a moment, had recognized
her—that he had heard her voice and understood her. It was a faint hope,
yet one she felt worth clinging to.

chapter fifty-one

The Powerbrokers—Reed Company Headquarters

"I can't blame you," he said.

Inside the 16th floor conference room,
nearly two dozen men—most dressed in business suits—were gathered
around an oval conference table. The large, black marble-top table was
laden with beer and overflowing snack trays.

Jonathan sat next to his father. An impatient Richard Reed stood
with both forearms resting on the back of his chair.

"Gentlemen. Gentlemen!" he began, waving a hand in the air. "I'm
not gon' pull any punches here. Most of y'all know me well enough to
know I'm not good at being subtle. Besides, we don't have time for fore-
play. Television time is expensive as hell. We got 'a do unto our opponent before he *do* unto us. We got a candidate here that's gonna make us
all proud."

A round of raucous, glass-rattling, laughter and backslapping
erupted. Jim Tinker, a longtime business associate of Richard's, stood
clutching a can of beer.

"Dick, ain't no doubt John's gon' win. We're lookin' at the next U.S. Senator from the state of Arkansas, no doubt. And if it's more money you need, you got it, dammit. All I wanna know is when you gon' break ground on that big development in Reedville. Tell us real quick, before we all get way too drunk to remember what you said." Tinker's comment brought even more raucous laughter.

"Listen, before you all get bombed," said Richard, "I want some signatures on some fat checks. The more zeroes, the better. To hell with the F.E.C. And don't y'all worry 'bout Reedville. It's gon' be the showpiece of the entire South. I guarantee it.

"And I'm happy to say we're in good position to have that environmental impact study waived. We may have to contribute to some select political retirement funds. But what the hell. Money has always been the mother's milk of politics. You just have to know which tit to yank on, and which bucket to fill."

—

Inside his Capital Hotel suite, Paul wore his pajamas. He sat forward on the sofa with the phone clutched in his left hand, his right hand supporting his head. "It's not that. No, no. I just felt you needed time alone with your family. I wish I could do more than say I'm sorry about your father," Paul explained. "I just want to help in some way. What about accommodations for out of town relatives? I could reserve some rooms."

There was a long pause, as Paul listened to Deborah. "I can't blame you," he said. "I understand. There's no excuse at all. None. The fact that I was consumed by what I was feeling, by being close to you, by the way you...well, I'm sorry. That wasn't the me I really am. You know that's true. I just hope you can find a way to forgive me. I called because I just wanted to make sure you're okay. Please convey my deepest sorrow to your family, again."

Long after the conversation ended, Paul held the receiver in his hand, staring with empty eyes across the room. He knew nothing he could say would erase the memory of what happened in Deborah's hotel room. He felt deep remorse and offered himself no excuse for his behavior. The last thing he ever wanted to do was damage their relationship. Ironically, that's what had happened.

Momentarily, the pulsating alert blasting from the phone receiver jolted Paul back into the present. He hung up then slouched back into the corner of the couch.

chapter fifty-two

Moment Of Truth

Nothing could have prepared her.

Four hours had passed.
Samantha had not left Deborah's side. Mabel Davis had waited unsuccessfully to speak to Sam alone. Before retiring to her room, she abruptly requested her daughters, and Sam, gather in Sam's bedroom. There was now something she needed to say.

Rachel was last to enter. Her eyes were red from crying. She hung back, appearing reluctant, even angry. Deborah riveted her gaze on her mother, prepared for whatever she was about to say, and wondered why it had to be said just now. Everyone was exhausted.

After all these years, it had come to this. Deborah and the others noticed their mother had not yet exhibited any grief. She and Reverend had *appeared* to be inseparable. The impact of his passing had not visibly affected her. Deborah observed that Mabel Davis appeared nervous, uneasy. Her mother avoided direct eye contact with her.

"Mama," Sam whispered.

Mabel Davis shook her head.

"But Mama..."

"Samantha, hear me out, baby. This ain't easy. I just hope to God I can get through it. I knew...someday I would have to say these words to you. I kept puttin' it off, hopin' the time would never come...knowin' it would. After what's happened now, the old reasonin' behind things just don't matter any more. I don't want to heap more pain on you right now, but there ain't no other way to say it, than to just say the truth...say it and hope you can forgive me."

Maylene and Deborah exchanged hard glances. Maylene then moved to stand next to her sister.

"I don't understand," said Samantha. Her expressive eyes widened with expectation.

"Baby, you must know how much we all love you...how much Reverend loved you. We wanted you from the beginning. You have to know that. We always did what we thought was best for you."

"I know that, Mama."

"Sweetheart, you can't...you shouldn't call me that."

"Why not? You're the only mother I have," said Sam. "You'll always be my mother."

"Samantha..."

"I don't understand what's going on."

"Samantha."

"Tell me!" Sam demanded, moving closer to Mabel.

"Samantha, we haven't been honest. None of us were honest with you. We haven't told you the truth, baby."

"What truth? What are you saying?" Samantha's face erupted with deep frowns. Her eyes widened. She gazed at Deborah then Mabel Davis. Every eye in the room was filled with tears.

"Please, just tell me."

"I'm tryin'. It's just...Samantha, baby you're...you're sittin' next to your...your real mother. Deborah is..."

"What? What? I...I don't understand." Samantha's eyes flared. She was clearly stunned. "What are you saying? What do you..."

"Baby..."

Before Mabel Davis could finish, Samantha wheeled around to face a speechless Deborah, then back to Mabel. Her lips parted. Her hazel eyes widened even more. She clutched at her chest. Nothing could have prepared her for this. "No! I'm not a baby. Just tell me!"

"I'm tryin' hard. God help me. Baby, please listen to me. Just listen. Deborah...Deborah is not your sister. She's...she's your mother."

Samantha was now hearing a truth denied her all these years. She tried to speak, but words failed her for a time. When Deborah reached to embrace her, Samantha took a step back. She stood trembling, staring at her mother—her grandmother, then Deborah.

"You're...you're my mother? What is she saying? You're not my sister? You're my mother?" she asked, stroking away tears. Sam's eyes glazed over with shock and confusion. "And you're my grandmother?"

Deborah reached out to her again. "Samantha, baby. Please let me explain," she pleaded.

"No! No! No!" Sam screamed, then tore from the room.

Deborah turned to follow, but her mother grabbed her hand, shook her head, and motioned her to wait.

"Leave her to herself for a while."

"What? All this is too much for her to cope with all at once...and alone," said Deborah. "You...you have done enough! You should've spoken to me before finally deciding to tell the truth. She just saw her...her grandfather die, and now she learns her entire life has been one big lie. I cannot imagine what's going through her mind."

"I know. That's why she needs time to herself, right now. We may lose her for a time, but I had to tell her."

"Lose her for a time?" Deborah was incredulous. She stepped closer to Mabel. "I lost my daughter once, when you came and took her from me...claimed her as your own. I've been without her for fourteen years. I have no intention of losing her again to anyone, and for any reason!"

Deborah's words were resounding. She did not wait for a response. She hurried from the room to search for her daughter, and found Charles a short distance down the hallway. Before she could ask him if he had seen Samantha, he pointed toward the front door.

Seconds later, Deborah found her daughter standing at the edge of the front yard, only feet from the roadway. Except for the light spilling from the front porch, spotting her would have been impossible. Deborah saw her, and in many ways, saw herself.

Samantha was sobbing, pacing along the roadside—her fists angrily striking the night air. She was clearly lost, trapped between the real and unreal, unable to fathom any of what she had just heard.

Deborah's instincts were to rush to her side. But against those instincts, she remained a short distance away, yet kept a watchful eye. No matter what her daughter was thinking and feeling, Deborah was determined she be the first person Sam saw when she turned to look back.

—

An hour later, Samantha returned with her mother. Both appeared subdued, drained. Charles and Yvonne remained at the kitchen table, where Maylene had prepared them peanut butter and jelly sandwiches and cold milk. She knew they were curious about what was taking place. She would sit with them later and explain as much as she could.

The others reentered the bedroom, just as Samantha unleashed a flurry of questions. Both anger and confusion laced every word, every gesture. She was now left to sort through everything she had been told, everything she had ever perceived as truth. The interrogation continued for more than an hour, before all sat on Sam's bed, cloaked in an uneasy silence.

Samantha dabbed her bleary eyes with a crumpled handkerchief, then reached tentatively to touch Deborah's hand. Deborah lost it. Pent up emotion and regret spewed out like a geyser. There was no script for this moment. She threw both arms around Samantha and whispered her name over and over again. Mabel Davis sat sobbing and mumbling something. Deborah noticed, and doubted the tears were real. She resisted the urge to tell her so. Her need to vent her anger and frustration nearly overwhelmed her, but she held it back. It was not concern for the likely affect on her mother, rather it was respect for her father's passing.

"I'm so, so sorry." Mabel gazed into her lap, laced her fingers. "I hate everything happened the way it did. I'm sorry for all the years you weren't here with us, Deborah. Me and Reverend thought we were doin' the right thing. Shouldn't 'a taken his gettin' sick, to try and set things right. I just wish he was here now. You have to forgive him...him and me. All of us."

"I want to forgive, for my own sake. The day I arrived, I told father I forgave him, although I know he couldn't hear me. But this was not some long weekend for me. It was fourteen years. How many years did it take to figure out that...that something wasn't right?" Deborah waited.

"He felt your presence...your words. I'm certain of it. And as hard as this is to tell, I want all y'all to know 'bout what happened that night."

"Guess I'll wait longer for an answer. What night?" Deborah insisted.

"The night...the night everything happened. You know."

"The night I arrived home late and was beaten? What about it?"

Mabel Davis turned to look at Samantha. She was staring at her grandmother, listening to every syllable.

"Some of what I'm gon' say is pretty bad."

"It couldn't be worse than I remember," Deborah interrupted.

Mabel Davis nodded with resignation. "Well, it was after I was done examinin' you. There was no doubt what had happened. Your underclothes told the story. The signs were all there. You were hurt pretty bad. Then after your daddy had...had finished, I tried to cover all the tender spots you had all over you.

"Later, I had to tell your daddy what I found. I have never seen a man so filled up with anger. God, he was angry. Forgot all about bein' a man 'a God. Took all I could do to keep him from takin' his shotgun and drivin' out to Reed Manor. 'Course, by then, they'd prob'ly taken that boy to their main place in Little Rock for the weekend."

Mabel Davis recounted the details in a halting voice. Deborah was pained and angered. The others were gripped; they listened intently.

"After a while, I got him to pray with me. We went in our room and we prayed—we cried and prayed. A little while later, he calmed down a bit. Later on, he called Sheriff Lucas Darden at his house. The man was more angry your father got him out of his bed, than 'bout why he called...wanted Reverend to explain everything over the phone.

"Your daddy refused...insisted on seein' him face to face. The sheriff said he could come. So, Reverend drove over. It was 'bout midnight when he got there. Even though the sheriff had no family, he had your daddy wait outside while he threw on some clothes and came out onto the porch. Pro'bly had that bleach-blonde hussy, Joella Wainwright, inside.

"Anyway, they talked on the porch for a few minutes. Sheriff Darden did not want to hear your Daddy's bad news...kept askin' if he was sure. Wanted to know if the boy had forced you...if you would say so. Since you told us nothin' had happened, Reverend had little to say about that.

"Sheriff said there was no reason to believe you weren't a willin' party. And it didn't much matter that you were only twelve. Made a big point of the fact that the Reed boy was sixteen and also a minor. But your daddy didn't believe what the Sheriff was sayin' was true, legally.

"Then Sheriff Darden made it clear there was nothin' he could do. Wasn't even gon' talk to the Reed boy without you first accusin' him of somethin'. Certainly wasn't gon' talk to Richard Reed. Said no way anybody was likely to believe the boy did anything anyway...that he would never have relations with any 'cept his own kind. All your daddy had was our word sayin' the boy had been with you. Sheriff said he needed proof, and that there was none. Least nothin' he could hang his hat on.

"Besides, if your father insisted on pressin' the matter, you would have to be brought in and questioned. Told Reverend the county doctor would be brought in to examine you the followin' mornin'. It was clear they would 'a put you through pure torment. Then, would 'a done nothin' after all was said and done.

"Sheriff even asked if we were sure it wasn't Tommy who'd taken advantage 'a you. Things would 'a been turned upside down around here, if we had tried to press things. 'Course, we all learned you were gon' be a mother...later. That just made everything even worse—a thousand times worse. Doctor Samuels mentioned takin' the baby sometimes during the first three months. Me and Reverend told him there was no way we would do such a thing. We would 'a lost Sam."

Samantha sat motionless, appeared numbed by what she was witnessing. Deborah took in every word, every inflection.

"I should have forced this thing to resolution long before now. I should have confronted you and Daddy, years ago. I tried, but I failed. I never told Aunt Rose, but I came back here in eighty-one...took the bus. I came for my baby. The next morning, I couldn't get close to this place...couldn't find it. And I had so little money with me. So I left, without doing what I came to do. I should have forced both of you to tell the whole truth.

"Back in '74, I was a scared little girl—a little girl who knew the truth would mean a lot of trouble for everybody. I thought we would all have to move away, and it would be my fault. No one was going to believe me! And Daddy was so angry. I have never understood how he just...just threw me away." Deborah's anger swelled; it bubbled over. "I know I shouldn't have gotten into Jonathan's truck, but he was wrong. He was wrong for what he did to me."

"What do you mean?" asked Mabel, frowns rippling across her brow.

"There's something I need...need to tell all of you, especially Samantha. And it is the most difficult thing I can imagine, right now."

Deborah choked back her emotions. She exhaled, with a loud whoosh. Then she said it—said it aloud. Said it as plainly as she could.

"He raped me, Mother. Jonathan Reed raped me. I did not consent to have sex with him. He raped me! Do you understand? Do you?"

There was stunned silence, looks of shocked disbelief.

"He what?" Mabel Davis screamed. Deborah's words had exploded like a bomb. Her sisters were speechless, especially Rachel. She dropped her arms to her side and stepped back, eyes widened, lips apart.

Mabel Davis sat straight up. Her eyes seemed ready to bulge from their sockets. "Lord, what are you tellin' me? You sayin' that the Reed boy forced himself on you?"

"No. He raped me, Mother! The word, as awful as it is...is rape. He threatened to kill me...held a knife to my throat, and he raped me. It's a nightmare I have kept buried all this time." Deborah's voice brimmed with passion. "And because of that—the suppression of what happened that day—it is now all so...so fresh in my mind. In some ways, I'm dealing with it, as if it...as if it just happened."

"My God! My God! Why didn't you tell us?"

"Tell you? I shouldn't have had to tell you. A real mother would have known. Why didn't I tell you? When could I ever come to you and tell you anything—anything about anything that was troubling me, things a girl should be able to confide to her mother? When could any of us? Did Maylene? Did Gloria? Did Rachel? I mean, heart to heart. When I was small, it was Gram I could go to. She would listen to me and talk to me with her whole heart.

"After she died, what did you do when you found me talking to her? You told me to *stop it—stop talking to the wind. Your grandmother is gone on home now.* But I didn't stop it! I kept talking to her, and she answered me in so many ways. She still does. When I grew older, I turned to Maylene. She always made me feel I meant something to her. I'm sure she did that for everyone, but she made me feel like I was the only one. It was later, that I realized just how much of a blessing she was. So, why weren't you the mother you claimed to be? I wish you had been." Deborah looked at her sisters. All were stunned silent. None came to their mother's defense.

"As for being raped, I regret having to talk about it even now, but I must. I have no choice. But back then, I just couldn't face what had happened. I couldn't. Everything seemed to be happening at once."

"We asked you for the truth, the plain truth of it. We could 'a done somethin' then. We could 'a had him brought up on charges for sure, if somebody hadn't killed him first."

"Killed him? You're not really hearing me. Killed him, Mother? I'm listening to you, and I wonder how...how you could have forgotten what happened to me that day, what happened to me that evening when I got home." Deborah moved closer to her mother. Raw anger surged within her. "I wasn't whipped. I was beaten—beaten and scarred inside and out. Can you understand that? My father, thinking that my only sin was taking a ride home and arriving late, took a belt to me as if I had...had killed JFK. How could I say more? And you, Mother Dearest, you. What you did afterwards, in this room, was...was as painful, if not more painful, than what Jonathan had done.

"Jonathan only had concern for what he wanted to physically take from me—my virginity. But you two were the people who had given me life. You saw me every day, knew me from my first breath. You heard me laugh, heard me cry. And that night, I cried. I lay in my bed...in pain, trying to find a position that didn't hurt, and wished I were dead. And that night was not the only night I felt death was the only answer for me.

"Standing here, it's like...like I've just awakened from some coma. In many ways, I still see things through the eyes of that twelve year old who left here. She is always with me, and she is owed a debt. I'm expected to adjust to seeing all of you through the eyes of a twenty-six year old? I can not tell you how hard that is to do. It is impossible.

"I wasn't sure I was coming at first, but felt I had no choice. I had to come...for me, for my daughter. And I know...I know as sure as I am breathing, it will never be...it can never be as before. I can never be your daughter again, Mother, not really. There is no resurrection for the person I was then. She's dead. There's no recalling of innocence that dies so completely. You just...you just find a way to go on. It's not resurrection; it's a quest for new birth—a rebirth.

"You ask me why I never spoke up. I'll tell you. I was twelve. Twelve, Mother. Later, I blocked it all out. I had to. To protect myself, my mind didn't allow me to remember the horror of that day. I knew something happened. But I kept hoping you and Daddy would somehow know I would not have done that willingly, and would figure it out. Didn't you know me? All that time with me, and you never knew me.

"I was scared. I was scared to death. I was scared of old man Reed; scared of Daddy; scared of everybody...you, too! And that night...that night, lying on that bed, completely naked, my legs drawn to my chest, you inspected me like I was a piece of livestock. There was no love or caring in the way you examined me. And I just wanted it all to go away. I wanted to be gone, completely.

"I wanted everything to be like it was before. I knew something terrible could've happened if I said a single word. Daddy could've done something and...and been hurt, taken away. He would've been lost to us, the church, the people who needed him. Gram had always told me about what happened to black men who stood up for themselves, and their families. I could hear her words."

Mabel listened to words that convicted her. Their impact showed on her face, in her eyes. For a second, her body appeared to go limp.

"Lord, Jesus. You kept all that locked inside you all this time? My God! That boy should 'a been arrested, should 'a been put in jail. He ain't worthy to walk this earth even now. I can't even imagine somethin' so...so awful. My God! Whatever y'all do, y'all can't ever let Matthew know 'bout this. Samantha, don't ever breathe a word of this to your uncle. And if Reverend had known, I don't know what he would 'a done. He might 'a killed that boy. Lord we would 'a had trouble down here."

It was clear, Mabel had heard only what she chose to hear. Either that, or she was without any defense regarding Deborah's indictment of her mother's actions or inactions, especially those of May 15th, 1974.

Deborah had not expected a much different response. "After all these years, there are times when all this feels...feels like something I imagined. I try hard to push it out of my mind. Most times, I'm successful. I tell myself that this did not happen to me. It was someone else. In a strange way, that's true. But real truth can't be destroyed. It's always there. Always." Deborah aimed a long glance at her mother. "Recently, something happened that...that brought everything rushing back to me."

Deborah cupped her hands over her face. A tearful Gloria and Maylene rushed to put their arms around her and Samantha. Rachel held her place, her expression nearly unchanged.

Mabel Davis responded with indignation. "And he's runnin' for office? You locked all this up...never told? What made you remember?"

Deborah was slow to answer. "Nothing I care to talk about."

"Ain't there somethin' we can still do? He shouldn't be able to get away with somethin' like this, no matter how long it's been."

"Do what?"

"I don't know. Somethin' for sure."

"For me, the most important thing is facing the whole truth, and being honest with my daughter. It sounds so strange, just saying, *my daughter.* My daughter. You're...you're my daughter."

Samantha threw her arms around Deborah and held on as tightly as she could. Gloria and Maylene remained close by them, sopping away tears. Rachel hung back. Then, just when it seemed she was about to leave the room, she walked slowly to where her sisters stood. Her eyes teared, even as she resisted them. For the moment, even Rachel appeared to be sharing the pain they all felt.

Rachel quickly turned to leave. Gloria blocked her path and refused to budge. It was clear that Rachel had been affected by what she had seen and heard. And while she did not verbalized her thoughts, that initial reaction had not been expected.

A moment later, Deborah rejoined her mother and Samantha at the side of the bed. There was a long silence. The room remained thick with emotion. It was Mabel Davis who broke the quiet.

"I'm sorry I was such a...such a terrible mother. I don't know which one of my sins to ask for forgiveness for first. It's hard for me to believe we handled everything the way we did," she said. Her voice was halting. "Right now, more than anything, I wish we had been able to say we were wrong—wrong for not bringin' you back home...for not tellin' the truth. We wanted to tell you this long before now. It's like we were trapped, too scared to face things.

"Reverend loved both y'all more than anything. Your grandfather loved you so much, Samantha. And you should 'a been free to call him Grandpa...to see and know him as your grandfather. And your daddy loved you, Deborah. He loved you—loved and cared about you. He knew that if you hadn't gone to stay with Rose and Jack you would 'a faced stares, whispers, and maybe even a lot worse. He wasn't worried 'bout what people would 'a said about him. That was not it at all. Reverend just had a hard time sayin' what was in his heart, sometimes. A lot 'a people are like that. But I knew what he felt.

"After Samantha was born, your father wanted her here, same as me. That was so you could go to school. Rose could do a lot more for you than we could. But the years just went by so...so fast."

Deborah listened, and heard. The years had not passed quickly for *her,* she thought. Despite wanting to be moved by her mother's words, they still rang hollow. They explained nothing. She doubted there was anything Mabel Davis could have said that would have sufficed, or provided the slightest basis for real healing.

Samantha sat shaking her head, struggling to reconcile what she was hearing, with what she had always believed. "I don't exactly know what to say about any of this," she managed, facing Deborah and wiping away tears. "I prayed to God I wouldn't grow up never knowing my real mother. I would see women in places we'd go, and often thought I could be looking at my mother and...and never know it. Now, I find out my real mother was no stranger. She used to live here...in this house! And I also find out...I have three aunts and an uncle, not four sisters and a brother. How am I supposed to understand all this? Am I suppose to just say: "Okay. Gee thanks. Glad we had this little talk. What's for dinner?

"I thought love was supposed to be about truth...about honesty. I'm...I'm confused. I don't know whether to be happy or sad. I'm both. But I do know I'm not happy about how I was conceived. I can't even imagine how scared you must have been. I'm sad, and I'm so angry about it," Samantha continued. "Right now, I'm...I'm not sure who I am."

A tearful Deborah embraced Samantha for the longest while. For years, she had imagined this kind of moment—the moment Samantha would learn the truth. She had both longed for it, and feared it.

"You're my daughter, that's who you are. Samantha, I have never for a moment regretted your birth. You have to know that I love you more than anything in this world. All these years, it broke my heart, not being allowed to be a…a real mother to you; to not have changed you, fed you, nursed you—all the things mothers do. No matter how long it takes, no matter what has to be done, you *will* know the truth. You *must* know the whole truth. No more lies, no more excuses, no feeble explanations."

Mabel Davis' tear-stained face glistened in the light. Her tears seemed real enough. Deborah turned to face her eye to eye. "Mother, I have to be honest. It may take another lifetime for me to reconcile all that's happened, if at all. I'm not the same person who left here. My life changed. Samantha's life—all our lives have changed. And Daddy's gone now. Funny. Just now, I was thinking he was still in his room."

Following a long silence. "We did wrong," Mabel Davis admitted, standing slowly. "We both talked about it right before Reverend had the stroke. I know there's no real explanation. I guess we just got lost and couldn't find our way out. I know none of it makes any sense. We were wrong. That was a hard thing to face…the way we did things, not tellin' the truth—him bein' a preacher and all; me bein' the First Lady of the church. We were supposed to set the example of what bein' true Christians meant. And we didn't. We thought we did right."

There was little left to say. Deborah and Samantha made their way to the doorway, paused, and shared a long embrace. Deborah glanced back at her sisters…at her mother.

Mabel Davis had just heard words that should have torn at her heart, filled her with shame and genuine remorse, prompted answers to every question, no matter how long it took. For Deborah, her mother's rambling explanation was woefully inadequate.

"Everything's already been arranged," Mabel said, changing the subject at an awkward moment. "Your daddy left strict instructions 'bout what he want and don't want. I plan to follow 'em to the letter. Said he don't want no long church funeral. Said preachers talk way too long, especially at funerals. Said it wasn't necessary for everybody in the church to try and say somethin'. And he didn't want no whoopin' and hollerin' and fallin' out in the aisles. Funny thing for a Baptist preacher to say, huh?" Mabel Davis forced a weak smile.

No one said a word. She went on. "He told me to have a short funeral, and a even shorter graveside service. And that's what I plan to do. You children can take care of callin' kinfolk and distant friends."

With that, a worn-looking Mabel Davis, supporting herself with the help of the nearest bedpost, turned to leave. Everyone's expression, excluding Rachel's, was one of stunned disbelief...grave disappointment. After all that had happened, after all that had been said, this was all their mother would say? If she had felt convicted by anything she had heard, it appeared she was on the road to recovery.

"I want to be alone for a while," Mabel whispered.

Samantha and Deborah stepped to one side as Mabel Davis reached the doorway. She stopped, turned to face Deborah, and rested her hand on her daughter's shoulder. Mabel said nothing more before leaving the room, leaning on Maylene for support.

Rachel and Gloria were next to leave the room. Deborah and Samantha returned to sit on the edge of the bed, arm in arm. Neither spoke for a long time. Not until long after the aura of the others had faded from the room.

—

Mother and daughter shared silence. Pure silence. A silence both joyous and sad. Tears amid lingering glances. Prolonged gazes. More silence—embracing, thought-filled silence. A quiet that permitted the faintest sound to be heard and felt. Audible breaths, inhaled and exhaled. A touch. A mother's loving touch. Another. Hand on hand, hand in hand. A gentle grasp. A shared knowing. An embrace that spanned the years. A daughter, with her eyes closed, cradled herself in her mother's arms—arms that had longed to hold her all her life.

Mother and daughter spent hours alone, speaking, listening, feeling. Hours that seemed but minutes. A reunion of two hearts, two souls, two spirits now one. And both came to know what neither fully understood: their eternal bond remained, undiminished by distance or time. This was not a beginning. It was the continuation of a relationship begun long before.

chapter fifty-three

Into The Night

===============================

Then, without warning...

It was after one o'clock in the morning.
Nearly every heart, nearly every soul in the Davis household was emotionally drained. The avalanche of phone calls, the visits from scores of neighbors, friends, and Shiloh members had slowed to a trickle.

Reverend Eldrick Robinson was, at seventy-five, Reverend's best friend and mentor. Just before 10 p.m., he arrived from Phoenix for a long-delayed visit. He was heartbroken to learn of his friend's death.

Deborah and Tommy sat in the porch swing, serenaded by swing noise and a cacophony of night sounds only heard in deep country. Tommy noticed a pair of bouncing headlights approaching from down Crispus Attucks.

A slow-moving, dark-colored, 4dr sedan eased to a smooth, whisper-quiet stop in front of the house. The vehicle appeared to be a late model automobile. It was too dark to make out much more, except for the faint silhouette of a male driver. Tommy and Deborah watched from the swing, expecting the vehicle to pull onto the drive and up to the house. She guessed the driver was likely an acquaintance, or Sticks resident looking to offer condolences. Despite the late hour, visitors were expected throughout the night, and into early morning.

However, instead of pulling onto the yard, the car remained parked and idling at road's edge, for nearly two full minutes. No movement could be detected inside.

Tommy stood and started down the steps toward the roadside. No sooner had he reached the bottom step, than the vehicle sped away. Surprised and curious, Tommy watched until the car disappeared into the night, then returned to the swing. The mysterious driver's behavior was more than a little curious to Deborah. She remembered the phone call from the anonymous caller, warning her to be careful.

"After a couple of years, I knew corporate law was not what I wanted to do the rest of my life," Tommy continued. "I wanted more. But I owe that experience for the success I'm enjoying now. I love what I do. I've got associates who handle the west coast for me, except for Hawaii, of course," he chuckled.

"Your father must have been extremely proud of you."

"Yep, he was. And I miss him. My father was a strong, proud man who loved his family more than anything. I owe him and my mother so much. They sacrificed a lot to get me where I am."

"I envy you."

"*Me?* You envy *me?* Why? I envy *your being* an author, New York Times' Bestseller. I always wanted to write. I'm flattered you feel that way."

"You have a wonderful, loving, uninterrupted childhood to remember. I can only wonder what that feels like. But I'm not wallowing in self-pity. In spite of everything, I have a lot to be thankful for. At least, I was able to see Daddy again, touch him, speak to him." Deborah looked away, paused to steady her voice. Tommy caressed her hand, and she leaned her head softly against his.

"I'm going to promise you something," he said.

"You're going to make all this go away?"

"Wish I could."

"So do I."

"I will promise you...your mother will leave this place only when she's good and ready, not a minute before. And when she does, I have a feeling it will be to a big fancy house you'll have built for her."

Deborah smiled and squeezed Tommy's hand. He had no idea of the unlikelihood of such a gift. A warm silence followed. The two then talked well into the early morning hours. They spoke of the past, the present, even dared to wonder about the unknowable future.

Then, without warning, the two found themselves locked in a magnetic gaze, each unable to look away. Both appeared surprised. Deborah nearly panicked, but fought to keep it from showing. Before either understood what was happening, their lips were touching. The kiss lingered. Tommy immediately apologized.

"I'm sorry. I..."

"No. Don't be. I'm not." Even as she spoke, Deborah felt as if her whole body were in a spin cycle.

Tommy leaned back, smiled sheepishly. "I'm speechless. And I'm not often speechless. Few lawyers are."

"No. There's no need to say anything."

A long silence.

"There's something I'd like you to do for me before I return to Chicago," Deborah all but whispered.

"Whatever you want."

"It's going to sound dumb."

"Ask me anyway."

Deborah started to speak, but hesitated. Tommy could see the tears in her eyes reflected in the moonlight.

"It's alright," he whispered. "It's okay."

"I'll look and see if mother...if I can find a couple of my sixth grade books. And I was wondering if, before we both leave here, you would...if you would carry my books and..."

"And walk you home, from where you left us...that day?"

"Yes. Yes." Deborah dabbed her eyes.

"How can I refuse? Yes, ma'am, Miss Deborah. I would be most honored to carry your books and walk you home." Tommy summoned his best portrayal of a southern gentleman. "In fact, I already have. Over the years, I've made that walk with you a thousand times...in my mind."

Another brief kiss. More silence.

Without warning, the full weight of her father's passing—the undeniable finality of it—pierced Deborah's thoughts anew. It wrenched more tears from her. The realization her father would never speak to her again, never stand to answer her questions, landed on her foursquare. It all left her feeling empty, turned inside out.

Tommy sensed Deborah's inner torment. He held her close, as the swing gently swayed, and the night grew old. Deborah was surprised by her reaction to Tommy, and by what she was feeling. It was all so new to her. Perhaps her feelings were owed to the weight of the moment, she thought. Still, she was amazed she did not feel threatened. To the contrary, she acknowledged the comfort of Tommy's presence, and it mattered. It mattered a lot.

chapter fifty-four

A Celebration—Shiloh Missionary Baptist Church Cemetery

Four Days Later

T here was no wake.

Deborah was surprised, and her heart warmed by the unexpected presence of Steve Bono, Julie Amada, and Janet Luu. All had flown in for her father's funeral, and would be returning after the interment.

Honoring Reverend's longstanding instructions, funeral services at Shiloh lasted just under an hour. Prior to the official start of services, the one odd occurrence came when June Boy, dressed in his trademark overalls—accented by long-sleeve French-cuffs and a black bow-tie—lingered at the Reverend's casket. He purposely waited, so as to be last to view the body. Everyone watched nervously.

For the longest time, June Boy stood with his right hand resting on the Reverend's hands, his eyes shut tightly. He appeared to be praying. The music stopped. No one moved, not even the ushers. A few moments later, with tears in his eyes and his head lowered, June Boy turned away, walked briskly down the middle aisle and out of the church.

Longtime friend and fellow pastor, Reverend E. R. Curvey, delivered the eulogy. He was Pastor Emeritus of Sunnyside Missionary Baptist Church of Houston, Texas. Scores of mourners, unable to find room inside the church sanctuary, spilled out onto the grounds.

There was a brief delay before the service began. Mabel Davis had insisted upon remaining in the 'family funeral car' until nearly everyone, including her daughters, were inside and seated. With everyone waiting, she had Matthew escort her inside. June Boy exited, just as they entered. Sister Jeter, a longtime usher, motioned everyone to stand. However, more than a dozen mourners remained seated.

All eyes were on good Sister Davis, as she proceeded to the Reverend's casket, where she stood quietly for a long moment. She lifted her veil, leaned over, kissed the Reverend's forehead, lowered her veil, then slowly raised herself. She repeatedly dabbed her eyes. Her chest heaved. A solemn Matthew embraced his mother, before assisting her to her seat.

Service was brief. No long speeches, no windy testimonials. Near the end, Mabel Davis requested Deborah sing "Amazing Grace." It was the Reverend's favorite, a song she had sung at Shiloh countless times. At first, Deborah hesitated responding, but stood when Samantha grasped her hand and proudly gazed into her eyes.

While Deborah made her way to the front of the church, to stand near the Reverend's casket, Rachel sprang to her feet. She said nothing, as she made her way to the center aisle, and practically ran for the door. Deborah showed no reaction. She waited until the door closed, then turned and nodded to the pianist.

For Deborah, singing Amazing Grace was emotionally painful. Yet she managed to hold back her tears. And she sang with all her heart and soul. Her voice soared, filling the church. It soared beyond the walls, and the vaulted, exposed-beam ceiling, to those gathered outside. Everyone was deeply moved.

Deborah sang with a power and verve that surprised even her. And she could all but see Gram—sitting on the front pew, right aisle, where she always sat. Gram's face would always beam like a thousand suns.

She would lean back with eyes closed...tears trickling, despite a gentle smile, whenever her 'babygirl' sang. She would lift her right arm high above her head, and slowly wave it from side to side.

After Deborah returned to her seat, Mabel composed herself, glanced down at the printed program and waited for Reverend Curvey to give the benediction. But Matthew sprang to his feet and stepped forward, surprising everyone. A hush fell.

"I...I have a few words to say. I may not be the most faithful Christian here today, but that's alright. I don't remember ever standin' up and speakin'...at Shiloh before, except on 'programs,' back when I was little. I don't mean to keep everyone longer than necessary. But, as my father's son—his only livin' son, I want to...No, I need to say somethin'." Matthew finally exhaled. "I loved my father. He was a good, and righteous man—God's servant. He served this church, and this community through good times and bad times. We didn't always see things the same. A lot 'a times, fathers and sons don't agree on things. Some folk think I have a pretty strong mind about most stuff. But he was the father, and I was the son. And I respected him.

"Our father would be the first to tell you that...that he wasn't perfect. No. But he tried everyday to...to be the man God wanted him to be. I think he would want all of us to learn from his successes and, most of all, his failures. If he could speak now, I know he would apologize for any wrong he did to anyone, and he would ask for forgiveness."

Matthew glanced at Deborah. She lowered her eyes briefly and fought to not tear up.

"There's just one more thing. I know the program don't mention this, but I know we're not gon' leave here without openin' the doors of the church...invite sinners to Christ. All a' y'all know my father would not want us to leave here without doin' that."

A chorus of amens rang out, as Matthew took his seat. Reverend Curvey smiled and approached the microphone. He was clearly pleased Matthew had pointed out the oversight, saving him from doing so.

—

The largely black crowd of mourners gathered at graveside. The site was less than a hundred yards from where the Reverend Henry Bertram Davis had led his congregation for more than thirty years.

There were dozens of Whites present, to be sure. The Reverend had touched the lives of many peoples. And they came. Nearly the entire official congregation of five hundred seventy-six Shiloh members turned out to pay final respects.

The day began under a canopy of gray skies, ominous clouds, and the threat of rain. However, just before the start of services, the clouds retreated and a beaming sun broke through.

The Hoages were present. Jasmine Baker, Rebecca, Reginald and Tommy sat in the row behind the Davis family, including Aunt Rose and Uncle Jack. Rose sat next to Deborah, caressing her shoulder, comforting her like the mother she had become. Deborah grasped her aunt's hand tightly, gazed into her eyes and smiled.

Dozens of members of fraternal, social, and religious organizations were present—organizations Reverend had belonged to, and supported for years. They came from all over the country.

Somber music rose. Aunt Rose sat back in her seat and lifted her eyes. She froze—stunned by the sight of a familiar face. A face she had not expected to see again in her lifetime. Rose gasped, leaned forward. Her heart throbbed wildly.

The man stood several yards away, at the right edge of the throng, which had gathered in a semicircle around the grave. The tall, wiry, light-skinned, black man appeared to be in his late sixties. He cut a striking, distinguished-looking figure, in his tailored black suit and custom black fedora—cocked just so. The hat crowned wavy, nearly shoulder-length, salt and pepper hair gathered in a ponytail.

Rose was certain she saw an evil aura about the man. There was little doubt in her mind who he was. She was sure she saw him smile thinly, and aim a cold, piercing stare in her direction. Rose felt it slice right through her. She returned his gaze, arming her opposing stare with a lethal message she prayed he would receive.

But surely Jude Barsteau had not broken his promise to never return to Arkansas, let alone Reedville. That promise had barely spared his life before. What on earth would possess him to take such a risk?

The Reverend's passionate threat to dispatch Barsteau to hell had not been an idle one. There were righteous men, still living, who were willing to enforce the terms that extracted his promise more than twenty-five years earlier.

"My God, It's him! It's him! If only my gaze could stop his old heart mid-beat," Rose thought, "the bastard would die instantly, or at least vanish under threat of death, just as he had before."

Rose turned to nudge Jack. When she looked back, Jude Barsteau was gone—vanished. She was at a loss to explain his sudden disappearance. Had Mabel seen him? Had anyone, other than she?

An anxious Rose looked about the crowd. There was no hint of Barsteau. He was gone, if indeed he had been there at all. Rose began to have doubts. "But I saw him," she told herself then placed her hand over her pounding heart. She released an anxious sigh, and prayed she had only imagined the sighting.

—

Meanwhile, Paul stood just beyond the gathering. He appeared nervous. He kept glancing down the narrow gravel road leading to the cemetery. Seconds later, he and Kevin Davis, Uncle Melvin's estranged, twenty-four year-old son, slipped away. The two jogged briskly toward a nearby tree line. Kevin, a recent Southern University grad, was the only Davis cousin to frequent his Reedville kin. He and Matthew kept in touch. They were ideological soulmates.

Kevin had left home at fifteen, following a deep rift with his father. He never returned, despite Reverend's attempts to bring him and his father together. Kevin wanted no part of it.

Paul came to a stop, well out of view of the mourners. He turned to Kevin and pointed toward a rusting, white, Ford sedan parked several yards off the road. The vehicle was partially hidden in a stand of pine trees. He motioned Kevin to follow him at a spacing of several yards.

Reverend Curvey was a distinguished, widely-respected cleric, well-known throughout the country. He wore a flowing, navy-blue robe, and held a leather-bound Bible in his right hand. He moved to the head of the Reverend's slate-gray casket and waited. Silence fell. He began speaking, in a comforting but resounding voice.

"We are all gathered today, not to mourn and be sorrowful in the passing of God's faithful servant, Reverend Henry Bertram Davis, but to rejoice in his having lived. As young Matthew so beautifully said, during the service, he would be the first to tell you he was not perfect. Like all of us, my good friend possessed his share of imperfections. But lacking love and concern for his fellow man are not among them."

—

Paul circled to a point just behind the old Ford. Kevin suddenly appeared out of nowhere. He nonchalantly approached the car, from the front, appeared to be walking past.

The surprised driver, unaware he had been 'made,' sat clutching a modified assault rifle. He held it across his lap, affixing a high-powered scope. A .44 Magnum pistol, equipped with silencer, lay in the passenger seat next to him.

Before the man could raise the rifle, or reach for his pistol, Kevin reached the front bumper, leaped onto the hood, and crashed his right foot down onto the windshield.

Simultaneously, Paul rushed the driver's door. The man loosed his grip on the rifle and lunged for the .44. Paul ripped a 9mm handgun from his waist, thrust it through the open window and jammed the barrel to the man's neck.

"Don't move. Don't twitch. Don't even breathe," Paul ordered in a deep, guttural tone.

Kevin leaped from the hood, dashed to the passenger door, yanked it open, and grabbed the pistol.

"Asshole! You...you planning to smoke somebody, huh?" Kevin demanded—biting into his lower lip, his eyes bugging. "Ought 'a cap your dumb, fat ass right here...leave you in the damn woods."

Paul threw open the driver's door and dragged the man out by his collar. He fell to the ground, collapsing onto his face.

"Get the hell up!" Paul hissed, ordering the man to his feet.

With fingers interlaced, trembling hands resting atop his head, the driver—who had taken photographs of Deborah and Samantha at the park—was marched to the rear of the vehicle. Paul cuffed him.

"What we gon' to do with him?" Kevin's excitement was evident.

"Just watch. Get the keys."

Kevin hurried to the driver's side, grabbed the keys from the ignition and dashed back to the rear of the car.

"Hold this on him." Paul handed Kevin his 9mm. "If he breathes too hard, shoot him between the eyes." Paul winked.

"Can I just shoot him anyway?"

Paul took the .44 Magnum and placed the muzzle against the curved portion of the trunk lid. He turned his head away, grimaced, and fired. The only sound was a sharp, muted pop. He fired twice more.

Kevin motioned their frightened captive to step back. Paul glanced around to make certain they weren't being watched, inserted the key and popped the trunk.

"Get in," Paul ordered.

The beefy man, sweating profusely and no doubt realizing the futility of pleading, climbed inside. His legs were hardly in, when Kevin slammed the trunk closed.

"We gon' leave him here?"

"For now. We'll call the Reed Company tomorrow...let someone know where they can find this clown. Probably wouldn't do much good to call the sheriff."

"What about the .44 and the rifle?"

"Merry Christmas," said Paul.

Kevin grinned. "Thanks. Merry Christmas to you, too. You from Chicago, right?" Kevin exchanged handguns with Paul.

"Yeah."

"Are you a mobster or something?"

"Naw, I just don't like creeps."

"You're alright." Kevin patted Paul on the back. "I like you."

"Same here. Pleasure working with you, too."

"Cool."

"Yeah, cool."

Kevin was having the time of his life. As they parted company, Paul swore him to secrecy. To protect Deborah, he had no intentions of sharing this with her. Given the visit from the 'goons in the seersucker suits,' he had come to one conclusion: better safe, than dead. Paul relied upon skills learned long before he turned to more passive pursuits. Others had also made the mistake of taking his nice-guy persona for a weakness.

A short distance away, a black P.I., wearing a black suit, had sat watching from behind the wheel of his black, Chevy Impala. A smile gripped his face. As Kevin and Paul left, he holstered his .45, and retrieved—from the dash—a handwritten note containing the license plate of the Ford sedan.

—

Reverend Curvey concluded the service. "We embrace his family, his friends, and those who were touched by this man of God. We will all leave this place today, knowing that we are all made better by his having passed our way."

Everyone was standing. Only the distant sound of chirping birds pierced the silence. Reverend Curvey bowed his head and prayed. Moments later, after the flowers were removed, he grasped a handful of soil and slowly sprinkled it atop the casket.

"Father in heaven, as we return our brother to the dust from whence he came, we humble our hearts, knowing you have already received the soul of thy servant to reside in your presence forever more. Amen. Go with God, Go in love."

Amidst sounds of gentle sobbing, the Davis family was surrounded by friends and well-wishers. The full sun still shone through. 'Come Ye Disconsolate,' a stirring gospel duet, performed by Roberta Flack and Donny Hathaway, rose from the P.A. system. Everyone clasped hands and sang along, until the last note sounded.

chapter fifty-five

A Family Gathering

===========================

"Saves me or those churchmen from having to kill him."

Dozens of vehicles
were packed in tightly along the edge of Crispus Attucks. Others were
parked along the driveway and across the Davis front yard. Scores of
family, friends and neighbors—black and white—arrived in a steady
stream. More than a dozen ministers—Reverend's friends and associates from over many years—were present to pay their respects.

Keeping with tradition, nearly everyone brought food, mostly genuine soul food, for family and guests. A virtual human blanket covered
the yard and the front porch. Guests congregated in pockets along the
old log fence and beyond. Many were renewing old friendships. Some
were discovering, or rediscovering family members, as often happens
on such occasions.

Charles and Yvonne joined dozens of other children playing games
in the front yard. Fortunately, their resilience had left them relatively
unbowed by the somber reality that had brought everyone together.

Inside the cramped living room, Mabel Davis still wore her funeral dress. She stood talking with Jasmine Baker, and James Penrice, a former Carver High School principal. Aunt Rose busied herself, making certain everyone signed the book of condolences, and insuring the food made it all the way to the kitchen.

A short time later, Rose took her sister's hand and led her to the master bedroom. Mabel was curious, but compliant. She closed the door behind them. The two moved to the bed and sat down.

Mabel was anxious to know Rose's purpose for stealing her away, but waited. Both stared across the large, sunlit room toward the open window and beyond. They saw blue sky, white clouds, bright-green landscape that stretched endlessly. Full-length lace curtains, framing the double-wide window, danced in a steady breeze.

"I'll stay here as long as you want me to," Rose promised.

"I'll be alright. I will." Mabel sounded anything but convincing.

Rose studied her sister's expression, especially her eyes. "I've already told Jack I'm staying for at least a couple of weeks. We've spent too much time...too many years apart. Things have to change, Mabel. Families should act like families. Life is far too short for anything else."

Mabel Davis smiled and nodded. "I know you're right. But you go on home. Maybe we can visit with each other later this summer."

Rose studied her sister for a long moment. She smiled, then nodded reluctant agreement. Mabel glanced toward the window. Rose sat quietly, for a moment, then placed a hand on Mabel's shoulder and turned to face her.

"Mabel, there's something I...I have to tell you. 'Cause if I don't, I'm afraid I'm gonna burst wide open."

Mabel grinned. "Well, we sure don't want that to happen. What is it?" Her grin quickly faded.

Rose took a deep breath. "This is hard."

"Just say it."

"Alright, Mabel. Alright. Look, I know this is gonna sound plumb crazy, but...but this morning, I swear I saw Barsteau at the cemetery."

"What?" Mabel was incredulous. She bounded to her feet, took a couple of steps, then turned to face Rose. "Barsteau? You can't be..."

"Just hear me out. I am as sure as I am sitting here. There is no doubt in my mind, whatsoever. I could never forget what he looked like, even after all these years. There is nobody like him. A merciful God only made one of him for sure, and probably regretted that."

Mabel Davis' eyes popped. Her lips parted. She shook her head from side to side, clenched her fists. For a few seconds, she appeared to stop breathing altogether.

Finally, "No. No, Rose. That's impossible. I'm sorry. I don't know who you think you saw, but it was not Jude Barsteau. He wouldn't dare come back here. He'd be a fool to come back here, after all these years."

"Mabel, listen. Just listen to me. He was standing at the edge of the crowd. I looked up from where I was sitting and...and there he was."

"No. No, Rose."

"Yes. I know I saw him. He was standing there, looking all full of himself. I could almost see that blue-gray ring around his pupils. At least it seemed that way, although I know I was too far away to see *that* much detail. But, it was him! Girl, my heart jumped to my throat. You cannot imagine what went through my mind."

"Rose, I hear what you're sayin,' but you must 'a made a big mistake. I would 'a seen him...would 'a felt him."

"All I know is, I saw him as plain as day. I started to show Jack, but when I turned back he was gone. Gone. No trace of him."

"Oh, My God!" Mabel gasped.

"What is it?" Rose observed her sister flinch violently then shudder. She clutched her chest. It appeared a sharp pain had struck her.

"He's dead," Mabel emphatically declared. "He's dead. Jude Barsteau is dead." She spoke with the confidence of someone just presented a revelation.

"What do you mean?" Rose was not expecting such a spirited response. "I'm telling you, I saw him with my own eyes, plain as day."

"He's dead. I feel it in my spirit. What you saw was...was not really him. You saw his evil spirit. Rose, I'm not wrong 'bout these things. What you saw was his spirit. Jude Barsteau is dead."

"How do you know that?" Rose stood and moved toward her sister.

Mabel retreated a couple of steps. "I just know. It came to me this instant. He's dead for sure. Jude Barsteau is dead!"

"Mabel, I know full well what I saw. Unless he fell dead within the past two hours, Jude Barsteau is very much alive. But if what you say is true—and the bastard truly is dead—that's proof that there really is a God in heaven."

"You shouldn't talk like that, Rose."

"Saves me or those churchmen from having to kill him."

"Vengeance is mine. I shall repay, sayeth the Lord," Mabel quoted.

"The man tried to destroy you, tried to destroy Henry and this family. And for what? Vengeance! Pure vengeance. He set out to destroy you. Henry should 'a put a bullet in him the day he first started those lies about you."

"Only God gives life, Rose. Only God should take life. And you're right, they were lies. And his lies came close to destroyin' my marriage."

"You ever plan to tell Deborah and the rest of the children about him? About what happened? The last thing you want is for them to hear it from somebody else. That would be the most awful thing."

"I know. But some things are better left unsaid. Somethin' tells me I should let the lies and the pain be buried with him."

"I sure hope you're right. 'Course, you don't have *kids* anymore. But what if you're wrong? What if he is still alive?"

Mabel Davis had good reason to hope she was right about Jude Barsteau being dead. The two had known each other back in Texas, years before she married the Reverend.

After a romance that began when she was in high school in New Orleans, Mabel moved to East Texas. Barsteau, nine years older, soon followed. She later refused his longstanding offer of marriage. Barsteau felt spurned, but vowed to never give up.

Years later, Barsteau surfaced in Reedville, Arkansas. A stunned Mabel Davis knew it was no coincidence. She felt he had tracked her down for sure. Barsteau even joined Shiloh Baptist Church, and soon became an ordained deacon.

Barsteau's charm, and his devoted service to church and community, won everyone over. He had style and panache. One would have been hard put to find anyone with an unkind thing to say about him.

For a time, Mabel's reaction to him suggested she felt Jude Barsteau was a changed man. That is, until he began making advances—a fact she belatedly explained to the Reverend.

In 1961, not long after the time she became pregnant with Deborah, rumors soon surfaced that Barsteau was claiming to be the father. Without ascertaining the truthfulness of the rumor, the Deacon Board quickly moved to 'set him down'—remove him as Deacon. Barsteau was vocal in his defiance. He made it clear he would not accept the board's actions.

Mabel Davis felt ashamed, by being forced to deny such a "hateful and ridiculous" claim, as she put it. However, what gave the rumors even the slightest credibility, was the fact Mabel had never told Reverend of her past relationship with Barsteau. It was only after Barsteau, himself, made that fact known, that Mabel was forced to reveal "all."

Mabel's belated admission sowed fertile questions in the minds of many eager to keep the matter alive. Most amazing, was how—in such a small town—all this seemed to have escaped the ears of the Davis children. And if it had not, neither of them ever let on.

Reverend was thoroughly embarrassed—consumed with anger. One rainy, Sunday morning he confronted Barsteau on the steps of the church and turned him away from services. Barsteau insisted it was God's house, not Davis' house, and that he had a right to enter if he chose.

The Reverend, normally a peace-loving man, warned Barsteau that if he so much as crossed the threshold, a quick eulogy—Jude Barsteau's own—would be given on that day. Furthermore, Reverend made it clear, if the vile rumors persisted, he would "install"—Reverend's word—a bullet in Barsteau's skull, pray for both their souls, then call Sheriff Darden, himself. His reputation for nonviolence notwithstanding, few who were aware of the heated exchange, doubted the sincerity of Reverend's passionately stated warning.

Before sunrise the next day, Reverend and several deacons rousted Barsteau from his bed, and ordered him to get dressed. Deacon Board Chairman, Brother Poe Simpson, Jr. held his .410 shotgun at the ready, while Barsteau loaded his 1959 Pontiac Star Chief with whatever personal belongings he could cram inside.

A surprisingly cool and collected Barsteau was then escorted to the Reedville city limits, and given clear understanding: if he ever returned, he would next leave Reedville County in a two-foot long pine box. The implication was clear. Barsteau, a man of considerable analytical ability, had no doubt of the sincerity of the promise.

Since that day, April 16, 1962, Jude Barsteau had not been heard from nor seen again. Those events, all those years earlier, explained why Rose's perceived sighting of him put such fear, loathing and anger in her otherwise forgiving heart.

But was he dead? Was Jude Barsteau really dead? How could anyone be sure? No one knew where he claimed to live, or was aware of any surviving family. All the old folk back in Texas and Louisiana, who may have known of his whereabouts, were likely dead.

Rose had never suggested she doubted her sister's denial of involvement with Barsteau. She never once asked her if his claims were true. Still, there were moments, following the events of May 1974, when she wondered if those ugly questions would someday be raised again.

About the same time, Rose had heard rumors of Mabel's frequent solo trips to Little Rock—trips made when Barsteau's whereabouts were likewise unknown. Such whisperings had come during a time when no one knew him, other than as a well-loved deacon.

No one knew whether Reverend had ever directly confronted Mabel about those rumors, although they clearly disturbed him. The strain in their marriage appeared later, following her belated acknowledgment of her past relationship with Barsteau. And she avoided explaining why she failed to inform her husband, even after Barsteau arrived in Reedville, joined Shiloh, and became a deacon.

In 1962, days following Deborah's birth on the third of April of that year, a steady stream of visitors filed through the Davis house, past her crib. All brought gifts and probing eyes. The birth was about the most awaited event the Sticks had ever witnessed. Deborah received more visits and more gifts than all her siblings combined. Fortunately, she bore a notable resemblance to her paternal grandmother. Still, some were not convinced of her lineage.

There were those who labeled the resemblance a mere coincidence. Many, who delighted in the speculation, had little doubt the baby's skin color, the color of her eyes, the shape of her nose, and her curly hair came from Jude Barsteau.

"Honey, that child's got some 'geechie' in *her*. You hear me? She got a lot more cream than coffee in her cup, that's for sho'," some "busybodies" were heard saying.

Rose stood and quickly moved to grasp her sister's hand. "Mabel, I've never asked you whether any of that old gossip about Jude Barsteau being Deborah's real father was true. Didn't have to. It was the most...the most ridiculous thing I'd ever heard. I've always felt if any part of that was true, you would have told me yourself." Rose stared at her sister intently. She observed Mabel look away, then back.

"Rose, I..."

"It's okay, Mabel. You don't have to say anything."

Rose placed her right arm around Mabel's waist. Both then vowed to never speak of such things again.

A moment later, Rose left the room, closing the door firmly behind her. Mabel Davis remained. Her mood was pensive, reflective. She stood quietly, fingers interlaced, looking about the room wistfully,

Soon, tears were streaming down her face. She stroked them away, fought against emotions stirring within her, but to no avail. Mabel's tears persisted. She began clutching at her heaving chest. She closed her eyes, raised her head.

"Daddy," she whispered, her voice faltering. "Daddy, why? Why? How could you...how could you say you love me and let 'em kill my baby? I could 'a died, too. All these years, I tried to understand; I tried not to hate you. I could 'a taken care of her. Me and her father would 'a taken care of her. I was almost eighteen. I wanted to *have* my baby, but you..."

With each word, Mabel's voice had grown louder, her voice more pained, more anguished. She tore at her chest, pressed both palms to her tear-stained face. Then silence.

It was as if Mabel Davis abruptly became aware of her uninhibited state of mind. She stopped, gathered her emotions, dried her eyes and composed herself. After a lingering look in the dresser mirror, Mabel powdered her face, drew several deep breaths, turned and started from the room. After reaching the door, she paused, cast a look back then left.

A perspiring Rachel waited, hunkered inside the bedroom closet. She wanted to be certain her mother and aunt had left the bedroom. Unconvinced she was now alone, she waited, afraid to emerge from her hiding place.

Before her mother and aunt had entered the bedroom, Rachel had been standing near the large window, staring out over the green expanse toward the distant tree-line. When she heard approaching footsteps, she scurried to conceal herself inside the closet. Now, her heart pounded fiercely. What she had heard, confirmed thoughts and feelings she had harbored most of her life.

Despite the implied denials she heard her mother express to Aunt Rose, Rachel had little doubt Jude Barsteau was Deborah's real father. She had no real proof, but she needed none. She *wanted* to believe it. She *had* to believe it. It justified her hatred.

At age eight, Rachel first overheard Barsteau's name. It was spoken in anger during an argument between her parents. She was never sure what the argument was about, but it all made sense to her, now. She had long-felt Deborah had been undeserving of the attention heaped upon her by the Reverend, and Gram d'lena. Those feelings now seemed validated. Nothing would ever convince her otherwise.

However, Rachel was not certain of just what she had heard. She had no idea what had just brought on her mother's surprising, emotional reaction. And what baby could she have possibly been referring to? It did not make sense to her. Rachel had never seen or heard her so overwrought, and she was dying to know the reason.

Several more minutes passed. A nervous Rachel waited. Just when she thought it was safe to exit, she started to open the door, then paused. A noise. She thought she heard someone reenter the room.

Fearing being discovered, Rachel retreated into the large space, and attempted to conceal herself behind the double-tiered clothing rack. In doing so, she nearly tumbled over a large, bulky object on the floor. She reached out and broke her fall by thrusting her extended left hand against the rear wall.

Breathing and perspiring heavily, Rachel waited another several minutes. Nothing. Silence. Hearing no one, and curious about the object, she felt around blindly, searching for the dangling light cord. Found it, pulled it, illuminating the closet.

A box. A large cardboard box was set behind the clothing, next to the far wall. Rachel could not resist examining it. She maneuvered to step out of her own shadow, which had obscured the top. There it was— a name. A name was handwritten across the top, left corner of the taped flaps. It was barely legible, but unmistakable.

"For Deborah—Mother's things," it read. She instantly recognized the handwriting. It was her father's. "Mother's things?" she wondered aloud. "For Deborah?" Then it dawned on her. It was Gram's things, not Mabel's. It was Gram's.

Apparently, Reverend had taken some of Gram's things from her ol' house, placed them inside the box, and had intended them for Deborah. The thought angered Rachel. She bit into her bottom lip, traced her right hand over the inscription. She wondered what was inside. What things had been set aside for Deborah? And why? Why was she deserving of anything at all? Had the Reverend planned to give them to her?

"No damn way! I'll destroy everything here, first," she vowed.

chapter fifty-six

A Family Gathering Continues

===

"Now what the hell's come over you?...

M eanwhile,
the tantalizing aroma of food wafted throughout the house and beyond
its doors. Deborah and Gloria were greeting more guests, thanking them
for coming, accepting their condolences.

Rachel joined them, though it was obvious her mind was on other
things. She kept casting furtive glances at Deborah, watching with dripping scorn, as her sister was besieged by longtime Reedville residents
surprised and happy to see her again. Her blood boiled.

Tommy, Paul, and Reginald were gathered at the hallway entrance
leading to the bedrooms. All kept inching closer and closer to the food-
laden kitchen.

Paul was happy to see at least a few more whites arrive. He had to
acknowledge feeling a bit self-conscious, being one of only three or four
white folk in a sea of black folk. Paul had never been in such a large gathering of black folk, except for the annual Soul Train Music Awards Show

he always attended. But this was much different. That realization came as a big surprise to him.

—

Miss Ruby Jean Dandridge, and three of her well-proportioned female employees, entered the house, all carrying large containers of food from her cafe. They struggled under the weight of their treasure. Maylene took a large roaster from Miss Ruby. A half dozen men, all under the watchful eyes of wives or girlfriends, rushed to assist the others. The entourage moved through the living room, the dining room, and into the rapidly shrinking kitchen.

Matthew, who stood near the kitchen counter polishing off a second chicken drumstick, moved to one side. He paused long enough to clear a spot for Maylene to place the roasting pan and other containers. She glared at him. He was not sure whether it was because she was looking to see if he recognized any of Miss Ruby's employees, or because he was munching on another drumstick.

"Should've known where you'd disappeared to," Maylene teased. Matthew smiled and swallowed the last mouthful.

"Ahh, just trying to make more room. Everytime I turn around y'all keep packing in more. This is a hell of a lot of food. Too bad Mr. Rainey died last summer. I could sure eat some of his barbecue."

Gloria and Deborah entered the kitchen. Both stopped in their tracks, when they saw Matthew gripping the bare bone.

"Guess y'all gon' stand there and watch me eat?" He then carved a giant slice of sweet potato pie.

Gloria groaned. "I'm starving, too. But we're suppose to wait." She moved toward the counter. "I need to eat something. If I don't, I'll start thinking about why all this food is here and start crying. Daddy said he didn't want folks crying."

"Food's ready for the dining table," said Maylene, "The men are setting up folding tables and chairs under the trees. We can start serving in a few. There's plenty of paper plates and plastic ware."

Your agent friend sure is cute," Gloria blurted. Deborah shrugged.

"I thought we were talking about food," said Matthew. He finished eating and moved closer. "I just wanna' make sure I hear all this."

Maylene aimed a scalding glance at Gloria. Matthew placed his pie on a napkin and folded his arms.

"He's my literary agent, and a close personal friend." Deborah and Maylene exchanged knowing glances. All eyes were trained on Matthew.

"Y'all stop lookin' at me like that," said Matthew, "This ain't got nothin' to do with the fact the guy is white. Today, out of respect for Daddy, I'm filled with love for all of God's creatures. But since Gloria brought it up, he is just a little too slick for me. He may be a good agent, whatever. Anyway, I'm just thinkin' 'bout Daddy and Mama, today."

Matthew finished his sweet potato pie in no more than three gulps. Maylene was desperate to change the subject.

"Daddy got his wish," she said. "Nobody whooped and hollered and passed out cold. Everything was classy and dignified."

Matthew wiped his hand on a cloth towel, tossed it onto the counter, and left the kitchen. Seconds later, Deborah exited the kitchen and started for the front door. An apprehensive Paul intercepted her. He reached for her arm, but quickly pulled his hand away.

"Dee, can we talk for a second?" he asked, smiling uneasily.

Deborah hesitated a bit, nodded "yes." The two stepped into the hallway. "This is about as private as I can offer."

"DeeDee, I want to apologize again. Forgive me. I'm truly sorry for what I did."

"You don't have to say anymore about it."

"No, I do need to. I have to say this: I deeply regret my actions, alright? It was stupid. It was wrong. There's no excuse. And I won't blame you if you want to end whatever relationship we have left. I think you've outgrown me anyway. You're well on your way to unimaginable success. I'm just happy I had a hand in helping you in some way. And one other thing. I think I understand so much more about you...why you called me by Jonathan's name that night, what you've gone through...about your daughter, Samantha. But I realize there's a lot I don't know. Perhaps you'll share that with me someday."

Deborah allowed Paul's words to settle on her. She was tentative, visibly uncomfortable. Paul sensed it, too. The moment was awkward for both of them.

"Perhaps I will. There's a lot you deserve to know. Listen, Paul. You're a great agent...a great person. And you've always been a wonderful friend and mentor for me. One great agent is plenty, but one can not have too many friends. I regret what happened. It did cast our relationship into a unwanted place. But I know your heart. I know you've always wanted the best for me. I truly thank you for that. So, let's just. Let's just see."

"I understand."

"All that's happened: the deal with Simon and Schuster, the national book, and media tour—it still doesn't seem real. But it's lost much of its luster and excitement, given what has happened here. Later, we'll have to celebrate in some way."

Paul smiled, grasped and kissed Deborah's hand. "I'm catching the red-eye home tonight. Will you call me when you get back to Chicago?"

"I will. I don't know when that will be, though. I've got major decisions to make. I'm a real mother, now."

"You light up when you say that."

"It feels so wonderful."

"Amazing how so much happiness and unbearable pain can exist within the same moment," said Paul. The two warmly embraced. Deborah watched with mixed emotions as he walked away.

Matthew, who had watched from the hallway entrance, wore a deep scowl. Paul reached him and stopped. He placed a hand on Matthew's shoulder, shook his hand. Then, to Deborah's surprise, the two began talking—even walked away together. Deborah stared at them and smiled.

—

"You! You are not my sister!" A scream. Rachel was screaming at the top of her voice. "I know *who you* are! You can sing Amazing Grace all you want. But I know the truth. God knows the truth, Amen."

A startled Deborah wheeled around. Everything stopped. She felt as if she were yanked right out of her body—left standing alone in the far corner of the room—watching and listening. Disbelieving.

Rachel kept yelling, even as she approached her sister. "You are not my sister! You -are-not-my-father's daughter! No, no. You are a...an imposter! A fake! And I knew it all along! My father knew it, too!"

Rachel's eyes seemed on fire. Spit flew from her mouth, as she came closer. Her left fist was clenched, her right index—pointing. Everyone stopped talking, whatever they were doing. Mabel and Rose rushed into the room, so did Maylene, Gloria, Matthew, Tommy, and several children. Paul was dumbfounded. Folk outside, crowded onto the porch.

"Rachel!" yelled Rose, but then stopped. She turned to Rebecca. "Mrs. Miles, please take these children out of here...outside, and away from the porch, too. And anyone, not family, please wait outside. Somebody close the door." She held her tongue a moment, then turned back to Rachel. "Now what the hell's come over you? What are you doing?"

"Telling...telling the truth! Somebody's got to do it! Will you, Mother? Will you? We talked about this. You know better than anyone, that I'm telling the truth—the truth everybody has whispered all this time. Tell them her real father is Jude Barsteau. Tell them, Mother!"

Deborah was brought back, by the sight of a startled and frantic Samantha standing near the door leading to the hallway. She was desperately trying to get to her mother, but could not make her way past the mass of humanity now jammed into the small room.

She's finally cracked. But that...that name! Deborah thought. *Jude Barsteau! Why is Rachel yelling out the name of someone I've never heard of before? But, wait. Miss Jasmine asked me if I knew who he and...a Florinda Batiste were. But why? And why is Rachel saying all this? In all her raving in the past, she never mentioned that name, until now.*

Mabel stood shaking her head, while a fuming Aunt Rose advanced on Rachel. With fists clenched, she stood within a foot of her. Jack, knowing his wife well, called out to her.

"Rose! Rose!

Rose reluctantly stepped aside. Mabel eased forward. All eyes were on her. She now stood only inches from Rachel, who was breathing spasmodically. Her eyes were bulging, like someone possessed.

Deborah saw the stunned reaction on the faces of her siblings. All appeared petrified, unable to move or speak.

"Tell everybody, Mother!" Rachel boomed. "Tell us all who her real father is! I'm my father's *real* daughter. He loved me, not her. He knew who she was. I talked to him...told him I knew the truth. He didn't say anything, but I knew. Just look at her! Look at her! She doesn't look like us. And I was smarter. I had the best grades, but she...she was 'daddy's little girl'? I don't think so. It's not *his* blood in her veins! It's not his..."

A slap! A thunderous slap halted Rachel in mid sentence. Mabel raised her right hand, and brought it full force across her daughter's mouth and face. The blow rocked her—set her back on her heels. The sound reverberated off the walls. The moment was surreal.

"Enough!' Mabel shouted. "Enough! The Devil's got a hold 'a you for sho'! You stand here, and defile this house, dishonor me and your father...and on this day? I want you out 'a my sight. Now! Right now!"

Mabel struggled to catch her breath. Rachel stormed from the living room, repeatedly slapping her face with both hands. She bolted down the darkened hallway, and into her shadow-bound room. The door slammed shut with a force that rocked the walls, rattled windows. Immediately, she could be heard wailing, in a chilling, sustained, unearthly voice.

Then, silence. Everyone was quiet, gazing at each other; for a time, too stunned to move. Then, all eyes trained on a mute Mabel Davis. She appeared shaken, self-conscious, but struggled to not display the effect. When she found her voice, she felt compelled to apologize. But her voice was weak, wavering—barely audible, at first. She cleared her throat, squared her shoulders, and clasped her hands in front of her.

"I'm...I'm so sorry, everybody. Lord, have mercy. Seems the devil is busier than I thought. I'm gon' ask for the prayers of the righteous. Y'all please keep prayin' for that child...prayin' for us all. She ain't as...ain't as well as the rest 'a my chil'ren. She been through a lot, losin' her husband

and her baby. And losin' her daddy ain't helped. It just sent her over the edge. As a mother, I feel the pain that my child feel. I understand why she would say things—things that she wouldn't say if she was in her right mind. So, please pray. Prayer is the answer. We all know that."

Minutes later, the crowd outside was still buzzing. Most drifted from the porch, and back onto the grounds. Maylene and Gloria embraced Deborah, who appeared outwardly calm, but she was anything but calm inside. Mabel quickly came to her, placed a hand on her arm. Samantha hurried to her mother. She threw both arms around her waist.

"What was she talking about?" Deborah demanded of Mabel. "Tell me the truth! Even Rachel couldn't hate me this much. What was she saying about Father? Who is this...this Jude Barsteau? Who is he?"

Mabel's brow dripped with perspiration. "Listen to me, Deborah...all 'a y'all. I know I don't have to say this, but, there is not a shred 'a truth in any of what was just said. Deborah, your sister was trying to hurt you in whatever mean way she could. For the life of me, I do not understand it. Don't give the devil the victory. That wasn't Rachel y'all heard talkin' just then. That was the Devil—pure evil. We *buried* your father today. That's the truth. I never wanted to admit this, but Rachel is sick. She needs help. There's no doubt about that now."

"Who is he? Who is Jude Barsteau?" Deborah's tone was demanding.
"Deborah..."
"Tell me! Tell all of us. Or am I the only one here, who doesn't know who he is? Am I?"

Deborah panned her siblings for a reaction. All appeared eager for their mother to answer. Rose waited as well. After enduring her sister's prolonged silence, she could be quiet no longer.

"Mabel, it's time for you to deal with this. Deborah, Matthew, Gloria, Maylene...you all meet me and your mother in Samantha's room.

Rose and Jack exchanged knowing glances. In an instant, they conveyed understanding and agreement, in a manner only possible between two who are truly one. Rose then started down the hallway to Rachel's bedroom.

A forceful knock. Rose waited. No answer. She knocked again, louder this time. "Open the door, Rachel. Open it, or I'll break it down!"

Still no answer. Rose gripped the doorknob. It turned. She entered the poorly lit room, and saw no one, at first. Then, she saw a sight that stopped her cold: Rachel. She saw Rachel. She had ripped off all her clothing, and was seated on the floor, in a corner—completely nude. She sat there, arms wrapped around her lower legs, her hands gripping either forearm. She was moaning, and rocking back and forth.

Aunt Rose started to approach her, then stopped. She turned to look for a robe—something, anything. She found a black bathrobe draped over the bedrailing. She retrieved it and slowly approached Rachel. Rachel, who continued mumbling and rocking. Rachel never looked up, never acknowledged Rose's presence.

Rose delicately draped the robe around Rachel's shoulders, then stepped back. "My God," she whispered. "My God."

—

Outside, few took particular notice of the long, white, late-model, Cadillac DeVille steaming through the Crispus Attucks offset, and onto the roadway fronting the Davis place. They were still buzzing. Despite the yard being filled with people, and more cars than space would allow, the driver drove onto the grassy drive and stopped smack in the middle. The man made no attempt to find space along the road, as had others.

The long, sleek, shiny, *white on white with white* Coupe DeVille—with high-beaming headlights, wide sidewalls and tinted windows—sat idling as all finally took notice. The driver appeared to be waiting to make some dramatic exit, and an even grander entrance.

—

Rose, with Samantha at her side, entered Samantha's bedroom. They found everyone waiting in silence. Deborah appeared emotionless, as she stood near the lace-draped window, bathed in the spill of afternoon sunlight. Just before Aunt Rose and Sam walked in, she had all but decided she did not want to hear another word from Mabel Davis. She would say her good-byes, pack her daughter's things, and they would leave.

Matthew was propped against the wall nearest the door—arms folded. Maylene and Gloria stood at opposite ends of Sam's bed. Mabel sat on the edge of the bed, but stood, when Rose and Samantha entered. Mabel had come to a moment she had avoided for decades. All watched, and waited for her to speak.

"Jude Barsteau is...was someone who...Rachel is not well. That is clear to me, now. Ever since Jamile died, she's been diff'rent, not herself. And I don't know why she hates you the way she does. But—and I should not have to say this—all 'a y'all had one father. The same father. The one we laid to rest this afternoon. I want everyone within the sound of my voice...to hear me. Now that's all I have to say 'bout that, now or ever. I refuse to dignify the kind 'a evil that poured out 'a that girl's mouth. Yes, I knew Jude Barsteau. He and I were friends long before I met your daddy.

"After me and your daddy were married, he followed me here, joined Shiloh, and became a deacon. I had not said a word to him for years. I was shocked when he started spreadin' lies about us. Then other people, full 'a the devil, started right in with him. There was always a handful that was against me and your father. This was all they wanted to hear. There are people who do nothing but try and bring down those who try to serve God. It was all meant to tear down your father and what he had built. They figured the best way to do it...was through me.

"Then, after Barsteau was run out 'a town by some deacons loyal to your father, I thought that was the end of it. But not long afterwards, the same rumor-mongers started up again. They tried to say that because Deborah looked diff'rent in some ways, she was not your father's daughter. I want to say here and now, that was and is a bald-faced lie. She just happened to favor her grandmother a little more than the rest 'a y'all.

"People can be so evil...used as tools of the devil. But my God is faithful. He is faithful to those who put their trust in Him. I have always put my trust in the Lord. And He has always seen me through."

Mabel took a needed breath. The silence was roaring; furtive glances were exchanged, breaths exhaled. Most eyes turned to Deborah, who moved slowly to stand near Samantha and Aunt Rose. More silence.

Mabel tried hard to appear calm. She actually looked relieved, as if she had bared her soul and was free, at last. "I'm willin' to answer any questions from anyone who doubts the truth I've laid out about all this," she added. "I'll understand, and do my best to answer."

No one spoke. All the while Mabel was talking, Rose stared at her sister, hardly blinking. Samantha turned to her mother, gazed at her, and saw tears welling in her eyes. She embraced her, kissed her cheek. Nothing more was said. No questions. No reactions. Nothing.

Momentarily, Deborah was surrounded and embraced by everyone, except Mabel. She was either unable or unwilling to step forward and join the others. Soon, everyone left the room. Only Rose and Mabel re-mained behind the closed bedroom door for nearly fifteen minutes.

—

Down the drive, and a few dozen yards from the front porch, the occupants of the Coupe DeVille had alighted. The two were greeting guests and onlookers as if they were the King and Queen of Botswana. The man with the gleaming gold tooth, and three silver crosses hanging from around his neck, could only have been Uncle Melvin. The whisper-ing and pointing began immediately.

Uncle sported a white suit, white shirt, white felt hat, and matching, white, patent leather shoes. He stood every bit of six feet-four, and would certainly have tipped any scale at more than three-hundred pounds.

The attractive, young, blonde-haired black woman stapled to Uncle Melvin's side was blushing like the new bride she was. She could not have been over twenty-five. She wore four-inch spikes, and had poured herself into a shocking-blue dress that cut her mid-thigh. And shapely thighs they were. Her plunging neckline all but revealed her melon-like breasts, nipples and all. A bra was nowhere in evidence. She was instantly in the crosshairs of practically every woman within sight of her.

Meanwhile, Mabel Davis was determined to reestablish the atmo-sphere that existed prior to Rachel's verbal bloodletting. In the living room, she and Rose resumed entertaining guests, and helping serve food. Hardly anyone had left. To the contrary, the crowd was even larger.

Shortly, there was a commotion outside the front door. Comic relief had arrived in the form of Uncle Melvin and his bride. The duo reached the steps and prepared to make entry. Melvin's boisterous voice boomed out greetings to those nearby. A surprised Aunt Rose, now standing nearest the door, took a hard look. She turned to Mabel, who stood directly behind her, and let loose a bellowing sigh.

"I don't believe it. Look at this, Mabel! Look! I'm either going crazy, or there's a polar bear with three silver crosses hanging around his neck. And he's standing on your front porch."

Mabel, along with everyone within earshot of Rose's comment, let go with howls of laughter. Rose stepped forward, opened the door just as Uncle Melvin reached for the handle. Both he and his voluptuous bride stepped inside. By now, Gloria, Maylene and Matthew were straining to see what the excitement was about.

A somber-faced Melvin, now unsuccessfully trying to conceal his gold tooth, draped an arm around his young bride and reached out his right paw to his sister-in-law.

"Hello there, Mabelline...ever'body. It's a sad occasion, but good to see all y'all. This here's my wife, Rodessa. Rodessa, this is..."

Melvin never got a chance to finish his introduction. Mabel stepped forward, refusing to accept his hand. She stood within inches of her erstwhile brother-in-law. "Brother, Melvin. Brother, Melvin Van Horn Davis. Your timing ain't exactly perfect. And you call me Mabelline again, we'll have another homegoin' today."

"Didn't mean no harm, Mabel. You know that's what I always..."

"Right. What a surprise," Mabel interrupted. "Well, not really. Somehow, I knew that even without a call, or a notice of any kind, you'd be here. I knew that much. We haven't heard from or seen you since...since Paul was Saul, but here you are. Well, you missed your brother's funeral, and his burial. But you sure know how to get to the feedin' trough on time. Well, the cafeteria is closed. All the food is spoke for. And we don't want whatever you're sellin'. You can turn the sails on whatever boat you rowed in here on, and head right back out to sea."

"Mabel, I just came to express my condolences and ask forgiveness for everything that's happened in the past. I truly..."

"Sorry. But the man you should be tellin' this to...he can no longer hear you. He's gone. The time for pullin' weeds and pickin' flowers is done. You may try to speak to God, if he still hears you. And I'm so sorry your young bride had to experience this. What number are you, child?" Mabel turned to Rodessa. "Four? Five? I think he wears a cross for each ex-wife. One more and he won't be able to stand up straight. So you try and stay with him, for his own sake. Thank God most black men are not like you, Melvin. Good-bye to the both of you. And God's speed."

Melvin stood his ground, until Matthew stepped forward and stood next to his mother. Uncle Melvin doffed his hat, forced a weak smile, grabbed his bride's hand, and the two made their exit. All watched until the two reached the Cadillac and finally drove away, leaving a plume of dust in their wake.

It was then that poor Kevin came out of hiding. He had understandably disappeared for several minutes. In a show of kindness, no one made an unkind remark about his estranged father and his new "stepmother."

—

No sooner had Melvin and his bride left the scene, than another vehicle approached. This one caught nearly everyone's attention, but especially that of three people.

The shiny, red, Peterbilt bobtail, with it's glistening, chrome exhaust stacks, wheeled into a space at the side of the road and hissed to a stop. Maylene spotted the vehicle from the doorway. She loosed a loud yelp.

"My baby's home!" she yelled, as she stormed out onto the porch and down the steps. Charles and Yvonne were not far behind. John Rollins had finally made it home.

J.R., tall, lean and dark, dressed in starched and creased jeans, white, long-sleeve French cuffs, and cowboy boots, leaped from the steps of his rig. Smiling from ear to ear, he waited with outstretched arms. Maylene reached him in seconds and bounded into his eager arms. Charles and Yvonne followed. The four stood locked in a bouncing embrace.

chapter fifty-seven

The Conversation

═══════════════════════

"Who was the man...?"

Long after Rachel's explosive tirade,
Deborah was still in no mood to smile. However, she smiled anyway as
she weaved her way through the crowded living room. The excitement
of meeting Maylene's J.R. still lingered. And everyone was still buzzing
about Uncle Melvin's and Rodessa's truncated visit.

Rose waited for her niece, near the front door. The two had managed only a brief conversation, since she and Jack arrived. But there was
much more that needed saying. A smiling Rose grasped both Deborah's
hands in her own, embraced her tightly.

"You okay?" she whispered.

"Yes...and no, is the only honest answer."

"I understand, baby. I completely understand. Walk with me."

Deborah nodded *yes* and followed. Rose wound her way past several
people huddled near the front door. She greeted and shook the hands of
those she passed. Soon, she and Deborah were down the steps, and

headed for the winding fence trail leading to Samuel's Oak. The now seldom used path was the one that led to where Gram's house once stood. It did not take long to reach the massive tree. Rose turned to Deborah, grasped her hand.

"I'll try to say this without...without crying," Rose joked.

Deborah smiled. "And I'll try to listen without crying. But I won't hold *you* to it, if you don't hold *me* to it."

"Deal. You know, it feels so strange being here. Must have been a thousand times more for you when you first arrived."

"It was. Still is."

"I know." Rose forced a slight smile. "I cannot imagine how you're dealing with all this, including this craziness with Rachel. If someone had told me I would ever have to cope with mess like this...in my family, I would've looked at them like they were nuts."

"I know. I just...I pray a lot. And I keep focused on those who love me, not on those who don't. Gram helps me, too. She really does. I hear her speaking to me all the time. She had a *lot* to say, today."

"I'm sure. Baby, if there is anything you want to ask me...anything you need to talk about, just let me know."

Deborah smiled. "Right now, all I can think about is Samantha, about packing my things, getting away from here...back to my life—my new life, now that I'm...I'm really a mother."

"You always were. Life is full of changes. Some expected, some not. That's the way it is. We've come to a new place now, in our lives, I mean. And no matter what effect it has on us, we have to deal with the change and go on." Rose glanced away. Deborah squeezed her hand and waited.

"When you graduated from college, I was so scared you were going to leave us right away. I didn't say anything, but Jack knew. One day he just came right out and asked me. He asked if I thought you were going to move to your own place right away; maybe even move to some other city to work, to start your own life. I could tell he was scared too. It's not that we expected you would never want to start out on your own. I mean, you were grown...had accomplished so much.

"We just wanted you to understand that...that we would be alright with whatever you decided you wanted to do. But I can't tell you how happy we were you stayed with us old folk this long." Rose laughed. "And now, we're at another bend in the road—this journey we're on. You and Samantha are...you *are* each other. She is definitely her mother's child. The instant I saw the two of you side by side, I wept. I cried on the outside, but I wept on the inside. I wept and I rejoiced. I thanked God for both of you."

Then the tears came. Each reached out simultaneously to dry the other's cheeks. That brought a sudden burst of laughter from both.

"Look at us. Are we a mess or what? Now, about home. I can't wait to help you decorate your new condo when we get back. How's that for changing the subject. And I promise to not change your old room at the house. I spoke to 'Mr. Fixit' about that very thing. There'll be plenty of times when you'll visit and we won't let you leave. All you need now is a new car. I can't believe you still won't trade your old 'Bug' in on a new one. The thing will soon be ten years old."

"I love it. And it's been loyal to me. I'll get another car, soon. But I'll never sell my *Bug*. As for the other things you mentioned, you'll get no argument from me. You're right. Things do change. People change. They say everything changes. But my love for you and Uncle Jack will never change, not in two lifetimes. I would not be alive, if it weren't for the both of you. I wouldn't be who I am."

Deborah was about to say more, but Rose smiled and raised an index finger to her lips to silence her. For a long moment, neither spoke.

"She's all over this place. You can feel it. Talking 'bout your Gram."

"I know. I feel her presence, too." Deborah cast a sweeping glance.

"She was the heart and soul of this family, especially to her grandkids. Some family, huh?" said Rose. "I wonder if we can still call this a real family. I think we stopped being a family years ago. And I often wonder what Gram would've said about all this."

Silence. A long moment to hear nothing except the whoosh of the wind, the clanging of thoughts, feelings working their will.

"I am still shaking from our conversation last night. I'm trying not to feel hatred. What happened to you should not happen to any woman, but especially a child. And there's another thing: I never once felt that what happened to you was anything but...but rape. My blood boils when I say the word out loud. I never believed you were willing. It couldn't have been anything else. And I've often wondered: Where was God on May 15, 1974? But in my heart, I know it wasn't God's doing. It was the evil—the evil in humankind."

Deborah brushed away tears, and embraced her aunt. Rose's words resonated through both mind and soul. She could not help remembering that her own mother and father had doubted her innocence. It was a painful reality that would last her lifetime.

Little more needed be said to convey how Rose felt. Despite her own anguish, she seemed anxious to not stir more unwanted pain and emotion in Deborah than could be avoided.

"I was just thinking," said Rose, "In a way, I'm a grandmother. I've been a grandmother ever since Samantha was born. All this time, I've looked at you as my own daughter. So, that means..."

"My God. You're right. You *are* a grandmother. How does it feel? You certainly don't look like a grandmother. We could be sisters, fine and feisty as you are?" Both laughed.

"You only say that 'cause it's true. I do look pretty good, huh? Thanks, baby. Look, I hesitate to ask this question," Rose went on. "Something tells me I'm gon' regret it later, but I feel I have to."

"What is it?"

Rose exhaled. "All these years, did you ever...ever hear much said about your other grandparents—your mother's folk, my folk?"

A surprised Deborah weighed the question. She took a moment before answering. "No. No, we never did. When we were kids, we asked mother, but she always said as little as possible. We knew their names, but we never saw pictures or anything. "One time, I remember her saying they—meaning you all—were from Tennessee, and that Grandpa David and Grandma Annabelle divorced soon after the two of you grew up and left home. That's all I know. You and I have never talked about this before. What made you think about it just now?"

"Oh, just thinking about Gram d'lena. Like I said, her spirit is all over this place...every single blade of grass, every leaf, it seems. Listen, the truth is long overdue. Of course, I'd feel better if your mother told you all this, but I know she wouldn't."

"I agree. And I want to know everything. This has always been a missing part of our lives. It's like we only had one set of grandparents. That's all we ever knew. So, we accepted that. When you're a child, you're at the mercy of what grown-ups tell you. They write the history for you, and they choose to either include, or leave out whatever they decide they don't want you to know."

"So true."

"But after all that's happened, we all deserve to know everything. What is it you want to say, Aunt Rose? Tell me about your mother and father—about my other grandparents."

Rose's expression suggested she was regretting having raised the matter. She looked away for a long while, drew a deep breath.

"Baby, Mabel and I...we don't share the same father."

Deborah's lips parted; she leaned forward. Rose's words struck her ears like a thunder clap. Had she heard correctly?

"Not the same? You mean..."

"Yes, I do mean just that. Mabel's father, David Mack, left Mama when Mabel was only four years old. He never came back, although Mama waited for nearly two years, hoping he would return. He never did. For all we know, he's dead. 'Course, in a way he died the day he left. I'm sure that's the way Mabel felt about it, on the surface, but not deep down. She was only four then. I have no idea why he left, but he did. Mother never said why. It was like...like Mabel had no right to know; we had no right.

"Mama finally remarried, although I'm almost certain she never got an official divorce. She couldn't afford one. I was born a couple of years later. Her husband, my father, Albert Strong, adopted Mabel and raised us both. Daddy died in his sleep. It was the day after my ninth birthday.

"But three years earlier, Mabel had run away. She was desperate to find her own father...never gave up on believing he would come back home. I've always wondered if she ever blamed me for Mama giving up on waiting for her father. Then, I think she probably felt *she* was somehow responsible for her Daddy's leaving. Mama let slip the fact he never really wanted to be tied down with children. Mabel never said right out that she felt responsible, but I believe she must have thought about it a time or two. Must have."

Deborah was unable to speak. Not a word formed on her lips. She simply listened. Every word Rose spoke had weight and form. They spilled from her lips like pictures—like aged, frayed, but still vivid photographs, not words.

"Mabel somehow found out, or at least was told, that her father was probably in Louisiana—Baton Rouge or thereabouts. She got there somehow, but couldn't find hide nor hair of him. Someone suggested he might be in New Orleans. I'm not sure how she did it, but that's where she found him alright. Don't ask me how. New Orleans is much bigger than Clarksville, Tennessee where we were born and raised."

"Clarksville? Not Chattanooga?"

"No. Clarksville. Why?"

"Nothing. Clarksville. That's where Mrs. Baker—Jasmine Baker is from. Did you all know her and her family?"

"No. No, I'm pretty sure we didn't. I would have remembered her for sure. She is something special, I'm telling you. Makes me think about Lena Horne, everytime I see her, and vice-versa."

"Funny you would say that. I've always thought the same thing."

"Maybe they lived near Clarksville, but not *in* Clarksville. Anyway, Mabel found her way around New Orleans. She was determined nothing would stop her from finding her daddy."

"So...so what happened when she found him? What did he say?"

"Well, he met with her, talked to her, but didn't want to have anything else to do with her beyond that. He was living with this 'Cajun' woman and *her* three kids, and one of their *own*—a boy with Downs."

"He rejected her?"

"You might say. Strangely enough, it was the woman—his common-law wife—who insisted they take her in. They did. She enrolled in school...even graduated. That's when she met someone...when she was still a senior."

"A classmate?"

"No, he was older. A guy who fell in love with her, wanted to marry her, even though she was still in school."

"Who was it? Was it...was it Jude Barsteau?"

Rose hesitated.

"Was it?"

Reluctantly. "Yes."

"Interesting."

"Why you say that, baby?"

"Because it is. So, what happened after that?"

"He insisted on marrying her...gave her no peace. He even got into a tussle with her father. Her father threatened to kill him. Mabel left New Orleans to get away from him—Jude, that is. She dearly loved this man, but said she just...just wasn't ready to get married.

"I think she was scared of him. He was older, demanding, firm in his ways, she later told me. Said he seemed to have some sort of spell over her. Mabel once told me that he could just...just look at her and she would nearly melt...forget what she was thinking before, or what ever she meant to say. But she never told me all I wanted to know."

"Where did she go next?"

"Well, she left New Orleans and came back to Clarksville for six or seven months. That's how we learned what had happened to her. I think she told me a lot more than she told Mother."

"What *about* your mother? I'm sure she was happy to have her daughter back home."

"She was, but they never really seemed like mother and daughter again. Something had changed You have to understand, your mother was a real daddy's baby."

"Like me?"

"You might say. Her father could do no wrong. Mama was crushed to find out about the new wife, and the child and all."

"But *she* had remarried."

"True. And even though she loved my father, I could see Mama was never the same after Mabel came home again. And I think Mabel always blamed Mama for driving her father away. It's entirely possible each blamed the other, in some odd way."

"How long did she stay home? Where did she go after that?"

"Texas, I think. I know she ended *up* in Texas."

"Did your mother—my grandmother—try and talk her into staying?"

"Yes, but it didn't do any good. Mabel moved to Texas anyway. Now, she has never filled in much of that time between leaving Clarksville, going to Texas, and when she met your father."

"This is...like a novel, like...like fiction; like part of my own life. Did she ever see Jude Barsteau again...before he showed up in Reedville?"

"Not as far as I know. Baby, you've got to decide whether to believe your mother or not. Personally, I have no reason not to believe what she's said about Barsteau. But I'm treading on ground that should be left to your mother to reveal. Sit her down, one on one, and ask her every thing you can think of. And demand she answer you. Don't let her play Houdini. She does that a lot. And she's good at it. Then, you can determine if what you hear is true."

"She's said all she's going to say."

"Maybe. "

"She has."

"Just sit her down and put all this to her, point blank. I don't mind your letting her know any of what I've told you. If she gets mad and...and stops talking to me for another fourteen years, then...well, I guess them's the breaks, huh?"

Deborah did not press Aunt Rose further. Already, she knew more than she ever expected to know. She was not sure how it all impacted her. But there was one glaring thought that would not go away: how could her mother, given her own unfortunate history, allow her own daughter to suffer such separation and pain for so long? It defied reason. It made no sense. Why? And then there was...The Reverend.

In some strange way, Deborah wondered if she had been the better for not knowing any of what she had learned from Rose. What flowed through her mind—a mind still struggling to heal—was impossible to immediately digest, now or perhaps at anytime in the near future. She was left with a thousand swirling questions. She had an immeasurably more complex view of her mother, and felt she would likely never know more than she now knew.

But what to do with this new knowledge about her mother's past? Should she at least share it with Maylene? Should she speak to her mother, first? But how could she share this with Maylene and not the others? How would her long-held view of her mother be altered by what she now knew? Should she even care about what happened so long ago? Should she simply wait, for now?

Deborah was certain she would know what to do, and when it should be done. For now, her main concern was Samantha—for her daughter. *Her* daughter. She was more determined than ever that her fate and her mother's fate not be Samantha's fate.

Rose stood watching Deborah and questioning the wisdom of having shared so much with her. Yet, in her heart she knew it was the right thing to do. She had always felt this part of the Davis family history belonged to all the Davis children. Rose had long ago concluded they had been cheated of that knowledge. She could not have returned to Chicago without sharing it with Deborah—her only child, her daughter.

Deborah embraced Aunt Rose as tightly and warmly as she could. She felt her aunt's body quake, and realized Rose was crying. Tears soon filled her own eyes again. The two remained in the sprawling shadow of Samuel's Oak, as the wind swelled, creating a symphony of rustling leaves on swaying branches.

chapter fifty-eight

Vengeance

=====================================

Matthew's eyes widened. His nostrils flared.

Deborah entered Samantha's bedroom and found her sitting in the middle of the bed, staring at the television set. Deep frowns gouged Sam's brow. A concerned mother eased down beside her and waited. A full minute of silence passed.

"Why are you in here alone, sweetheart?"

"Watching my father."

A commercial break ended. Deborah turned toward the small television set atop the chest and saw Jonathan Reed being interviewed by a local TV news reporter. She grasped Samantha's left hand and held it firmly in her own. Reed's wife and children were at his side. Deborah quickly recognized the Richard Reed Estate in the background.

"All the polls continue to show you with nearly a thirty point lead over your opponent. That is...is unheard of, given the interest, and the investments by both Democratic and Republican national parties in this election. So, would you care to predict a margin of victory?"

"Please, let me be clear. I am not taking this election for granted," said Jonathan, exuding charm. "There are several months to go. I recognize that the people of Arkansas have yet to speak. They will provide the final poll numbers—the ones that count.

"Now, while I feel good about our chances, I am expecting this election will be a lot closer than you pundits and pollsters are predicting. I have a lot of respect for my opponent. It's just that I believe I am better able to represent the people of the great state of Arkansas."

—

Deborah's and Samantha's eyes were cemented to the screen. Neither spoke. Reed turned to answer another reporter's question.

"Well, there you have it," said the first reporter. "Democratic Senate Candidate, Jonathan Reed, while careful to not appear overconfident, is expressing belief he will be the next Democrat Senator from Arkansas. And well he should. Recent Harris and Gallup polls show him with a 25 to 38 percent lead over his Republican opponent.

"However, experience shows that all it takes is a major gaffe, or hint of scandal, to evaporate any lead. This is Kaye Riley reporting for News at Noon, from the sprawling Reed Estate, where the big fund-raiser continues. Back to you in the studio."

"He is my father, isn't he?"

Deborah placed her right arm around Sam and caressed her. "Yes, sweetheart. He's your father."

"He looks so skinny and so pale. I just can not imagine him being my father. And what about that little boy and girl?"

"They are your sister and brother. Samantha, you must understand that what happened to me, happened a long, long time ago. Jonathan Reed grew up, got married and started a family. Now he's running for the U.S. Senate. And he has a good chance of winning."

"But how does it make you feel...seeing him, seeing them, knowing what he did to you?" Samantha's tone reflected her anger.

Deborah hesitated, resisting the urge to give Samantha a completely honest answer. "Darling, what is important...is how *you* feel."

"I hate him."

"No, Samantha. Don't hate. Remember what I told you Gram said about hate. Plus, hate destroys *you*. It's like cancer. *I* had to learn that."

"He knows about me, right?"

"Yes. He knows. He knows."

"I'll bet his wife doesn't know."

"Perhaps."

"And I'm sure he doesn't want to see me. Doesn't want his wife and his kids to know. Doesn't want the world to know, ever."

Deborah embraced Samantha again and planted a gentle kiss on her forehead. "I love you. I love you."

"I love you, too."

—

Outside the Davis home, folk still crowded the yard, enjoying the great food and each other's company, the solemn occasion notwithstanding. Reginald and Paul, stood on the porch, near the swing, eating from paper plates.

At first, few noticed Jeb Liddy's red BMW 320i slowly approach from north on Crispus Attucks. Following him was a small convoy of heavy equipment transporters, loaded with mammoth earthmovers and other 'destruction' equipment. Their awesome weight left deep wheel grooves in the already deteriorated asphalt roadbed.

Several hundred feet from the house, the behemoths pulled onto the shoulder and stopped. Liddy, and a passenger, parked several yards in front of them. Seconds later, he climbed out and stood staring toward the Davis house. The heavy-set black man, who appeared to be in his thirties, had difficulty extracting his hulk from the small car.

Scores of guests, standing near the roadway, looked on. Liddy noticed the attention he and his associate were receiving, and felt more than a little uneasy. The latter appeared even more uncomfortable, but said nothing, even as sweat beaded on his heavy brow. Maylene walked out onto the porch, just as the two men reached the edge of the crowd and began making their way toward the house.

"I don't believe this," she said aloud. "They fire his big butt, and he's still playing their flunkie."

Matthew overheard his sister, came out from the living room, and joined her on the porch. "What's wrong?"

"Matthew, don't get upset. Okay? Let's see what they want."

"They who?"

"Those two coming toward the house. The short guy works for Reed Development Company. He brought your friend with him—Big Baby Jesse. Promise me you'll stay calm, Matthew. Please?"

Matthew's eyes bugged. His nostrils flared. "I'll be damn. That's the asshole that brought those papers. Right? And he talked that fat fool into comin' with him. That ain't gon' help him none."

Liddy stopped a few steps from the porch and doffed his hat. Big Baby Jesse stood a few steps behind him, looking around nervously, trying to appear calm. He nodded to Matthew. Matthew ignored him.

Inside, Mabel Davis and Aunt Rose stepped to the screen door. Kevin, who had been in the kitchen, dashed out onto the porch and stood next to his favorite cousin. Matthew moved to the center step.

Liddy swallowed hard, wiped his beaded brow with the back of his hand. "Howdy folks." He flashed a silly grin that quickly faded. "Sorry to barge in on y'all here...today. I truly am. Got my orders, though."

"Sorry, Matthew...Sister Davis," Jesse sheepishly offered. There was no response. All eyes were glued on the two men. Despite the size of the crowd, hardly anyone spoke. A nervous Liddy glanced around, reached into his rear pocket and removed a piece of white paper.

As Baby Jesse spoke, Kevin whispered into Matthew's ear. Deborah, Tommy, J.R. and Samantha, who had been watching from the living room window, stepped out onto the porch.

"Won't take long," said Liddy, his voice breaking. "I wonder if I could trouble Mrs. Davis for just a minute? I got a demolition permit, effective Monday morning. Now, this is..."

Before Liddy could finish his sentence, Matthew leaped from the porch, ripped the paper from his hand and tossed it to the ground. With-

out looking back, he next bolted for his truck like a man possessed. The
crowd parted for him like the Red Sea. Mabel Davis thrust open the
screen door and hurried out onto the porch, with Aunt Rose close by
her side. She knew trouble was only minutes from her front door.

"Matthew! Where you goin', son? Matthew!"

 Matthew continued on a laser line to his truck. His only response
was a clenched right fist thrust high into the humid air.

Mabel Davis aimed a pointed glare at Liddy and his cohort. "I see
you brought your protector with you. Good thing. 'Cause you just might
need one. I pray to God y'all leave. Get away from here, right now. You
couldn't a' picked a worse time. We just buried his father—my husband.
And now you come waltzin' up here with this mess. You ain't too smart,
orders or not...neither one 'a y'all."

"Let's get out of here, man," said Big Jesse, "Matthew's crazy. I know
him. Ain't no tellin' what he might do."

Maylene bounded down the steps after her brother. Liddy and Big
Jesse were rightfully concerned. Both turned to gaze in the direction Matthew had gone. Paul and Reginald stood near Rose and Jack. Neither could
believe what they were witnessing. There was more to come.

Meanwhile, Matthew threw open the driver's door to his truck,
ripped off his suit jacket and flung it onto the passenger seat. He next
tilted the driver's seat forward and reached behind. Those nearest him
watched in nervous anticipation. A buzz swept through the crowd.

Matthew stood straight, kicked the driver's door closed and wheeled
around. A collective gasp erupted. Gripped firmly in his hands, and held
at port arms, was an assault rifle with a thirty round banana clip in place.

Matthew looked like a man possessed. His eyes flared like flaming
spheres. A reverberating groan erupted. Dozens of onlookers broke into
spontaneous applause, including June Boy. He was jumping up and
down, clapping his hands wildly. Still others scurried for safety behind
vehicles and trees. By now, Maylene was only a few feet away.

"Don't do it, Matthew!" She pleaded. "Think about Mama. Please!
There are children here, Matthew!"

Matthew, stoned-faced and steely-eyed, stood at the road's edge with the rifle pointing skyward. Liddy and Big Jesse scurried onto the porch, positioning themselves behind Mabel Davis and Aunt Rose. Maylene called out to her brother, pleading to him. Tommy dashed down the steps and moved cautiously toward Matthew with both hands held at his sides.

"Lord, have mercy," Mabel Davis whispered.

"Matthew! Matthew!" Deborah pleaded.

Matthew did not respond. Instead, he turned and headed toward the construction vehicles parked along the roadway. When he reached Liddy's car, he stopped, raised the rifle to hip level and opened fire.

Fiery flashes leaped from the muzzle in a steady, hot stream. An earsplitting cacophony crackled through the air. Rapid-fire blasts blew out the windshield, side windows, side view mirror, and flattened the tires facing the roadway.

Frantic drivers inside the transporter trucks leaped from the vehicles and beat a quick retreat down Crispus Attucks Road, as fast as they could.

One chubby man wearing coveralls crawled under his vehicle, as Matthew ejected the empty clip, reloaded and continued firing. The enormous tires on the mammoth transporters collapsed, as multiple rounds ripped through them.

Matthew returned, then strolled to the other side of Liddy's BMW. Tumultuous cheering erupted again. He resumed firing. He began at the rear and calmly strolled alongside, until he reached the front grille.

He stopped and stood staring at the red heap in front of him. The cheering was deafening. Matthew turned and walked slowly back toward the house, with his gun barrel pointing toward the ground. Scores of the curious ran to survey the destruction.

A shaking , red-faced Jeb Liddy, and an anxious Big Baby Jesse cowered behind Mabel Davis and Aunt Rose. A furious Uncle Jack grabbed Liddy by his collar, while Paul seized his right arm and twisted it behind his back. The two forced him out into the open. Cousin Kevin gleefully shoved his .44, minus the silencer, into Big Baby Jesse's broad back. The latter let loose a high pitched yelp likely heard in several counties. Both men, raining perspiration, were forced out onto the bottom step. Kevin then reluctantly concealed his weapon.

Matthew turned and strode toward the house—the rifle now held at port arms. Only feet onto the yard, he came face to face with Tommy. The two men stood briefly staring at each other, before Tommy slowly extended his right hand. Matthew caught a glimpse of Jesse and Liddy approaching. The sight of them angered him even more. He hesitated, clutched his rifle.

"They're not worth your going to jail, Matthew. Let them go. They've already peed in their pants, and God knows what else. You've made your point," Tommy reasoned. "Look at them. They were both hiding behind women and children."

"He's right," echoed Mr. Peabo, who had arrived minutes earlier and was standing nearby. "Got 'a know when you already won your battle, son. Don't waste your ammo. And go hide that cannon for a while. Even if the law do show up, I don't think they gon' find any witnesses 'round here."

Tommy nodded his agreement. Matthew stood motionless for what seemed an eternity. His eyes appeared to glaze over. His jaws were clenched. Everyone held their collective breaths. Matthew removed the clip, ejected the chambered round, and left to find a secure place for the assault rifle.

A seething Aunt Rose turned to a trembling Jeb Liddy, grabbed his shirt sleeve and yanked him toward her.

"Mister, only a couple of fools would have come out here on this day. And you *purposely* chose today. Now, I don't know how fast you two can haul your...*your you know whats,* but I think *now* would be a good time to find out. Wouldn't take but a second for my nephew to lock and load that thing again. And I have a feeling that next time, his targets won't be sitting on wheels. They'll likely be wearing shoes, like the ones you two have on."

Amidst mock applause and a chorus of jeers, the two frightened men bolted from the step and made an inspired dash for the road. Liddy reached the roadside first, spotted the remains of his car, and broke into tears. He ripped his hat from his balding head, flung it across the road.

"Goddamn! Look at my damn car! Look at my poor car. He shot my damn Beamer! He shot my car...shot it all to hell! My God! Look, Jesse! He shot my goddamn Beamer!"

Liddy fell to his knees with hands uplifted, bawling like a baby. Jesse was not at all sympathetic.

"Piss on your damn Beamer! Let's get the hell out of here, fool!

"I can't leave my car like this."

"Your damn car is dead. You wanna join it? Either you come with me or I'm leavin' your ass."

Big Baby Jesse yanked Liddy to his feet and practically dragged him down Crispus Attucks Road past the flattened transporters. Liddy kept wailing and resisting. Fed up, Baby Jesse released his grip. Liddy crumpled to the roadway. Jesse trudged on, never looked back.

A stern-faced Deborah gazed out over the crowd. She struggled to absorb what she and the others had witnessed. *All these people gathered here for one reason,* she thought. *To honor and pay respect to my father. This is neither honor nor respect.*

Deborah now feared for Matthew's safety. Something had to be done. She had no doubt that by Monday morning, even more heavy equipment would appear with orders to reduce every structure to rubble. Orders may now be given to level all of Oakwood Manor. That would mean war, for sure. Few in the Sticks would stand for that. And this time, crews would surely be protected by scores of heavily armed deputies.

Deborah threw both arms around Samantha. "No more, baby," she whispered. "No more. There's something we have to do."

chapter fifty-nine

Birthright

======

"No one's noticed us yet," said Samantha.

The Reed estate,
with its brilliant white structures, stood in majestic relief against a backdrop of bright blue sky. Perfectly manicured grounds and floral fauna surrounded the sprawling compound.

Hundreds of $2000 per-plate guests, and media, continued pouring onto the property past the ornate entry gate. Nearly two dozen uniformed security personnel were in evidence.

Deborah, with Samantha happily and excitedly at her side, slowed her car and pulled to the opposite curb, just short of the entrance. She turned to her daughter, stroked her face and smiled.

"God, I sure hope I'm doing the right thing...and for the right reasons. I don't want you to be hurt in any way. How do you feel about this?"

"Let's go for it!" Samantha beamed.

Deborah chuckled. "Alright. Let's go for it."

Deborah realized the fifty-plus mile trip had exposed both to unknown dangers. If the mysterious woman caller was correct, they were likely being followed. During the long drive, Deborah kept glancing into her rear view mirror, wary of every vehicle that followed, or passed her. She had been careful to not transmit her concern to Samantha.

"You still look worried. Don't worry. I'm a little scared, but I'm okay." Samantha appeared more excited than frightened.

"Tell you a secret. I'm scared, too."

Deborah squeezed Samantha's hand, turned onto the driveway and eased up to the gate. A female security guard stepped forward and peered into the car.

"You're with the catering company, right? They're waiting for you. Just pull up and park up there," she said, pointing.

Deborah thanked her, while struggling to contain her amusement. The young woman waved her on through then turned her attention to the next car.

"I guess we're hired help because we're black," Samantha snapped.

"Maybe. The fact we're wearing all black probably helped that assumption along. I really don't think she thought twice about it."

"That's what I'm talking about. Why didn't she assume we were guests? She has no idea who we are," Sam protested.

"True. But save your ammunition, sweetheart."

Deborah drove on to the main house, pulled to the edge of the driveway, and parked next to a large catering truck. The two exited the car and joined a throng of arriving guests moving toward the east end of the main building.

The sound of music and the buzz of conversation grew louder and louder with each step. Deborah and Samantha reached the corner, turned, and stepped onto the lawn.

Ahead, on the sprawling rear grounds, were a trio of large, white tents, and a virtually all-white crowd of at least five hundred. With few exceptions, most of the nonwhites in evidence were an army of Black and Hispanic service personnel, and the black drummer in the live band.

Deborah held Samantha's hand as they neared the largest tent.

"No one's noticed us yet," said Sam.

"Believe me, they will." Deborah had no doubt.

Her words were hardly out when a female guest blocked her path, thrusting an empty glass to her face.

"Could you get me another one of these, dear?" she asked, even as she glanced away. "A Margarita."

Deborah took the glass, tossed it to the ground and stepped on it, crushing it and leaving the woman stunned—her mouth wide open.

"Did you see her face? This should be interesting," said Sam. "I feel like I'm in some sort of demonstration or something."

"We are," said Deborah. "We are."

—

Virginia Reed was radiant in a free flowing, sleeveless, white, Versace dress. She stood with her husband, and Jonathan and his wife. All were chatting with a small cell of well-heeled guests near the center tent entrance. None saw Deborah's and Samantha's determined approach.

The two were about twenty yards away, when a startled Virginia Reed caught sight of them. Her heart nearly burst through her designer dress. She stopped speaking mid-sentence, clutched her chest.

"What is it, dear?" asked Richard.

"My God!" she gurgled, barely above a whisper.

"What is it?"

Deborah and Samantha were only a few feet away and approaching fast. Richard and Jonathan wheeled around to face them. Both men were rendered mute. Samantha stared at her father; he turned away.

Virginia Reed was fully aware the crowd was laced with media. She fought to quickly recover. Several, beefy, black-suited, Reed security people watched from close by.

"How dare you," Virginia Reed hissed, while trying not to draw attention. "How dare you show your face here again? You people have no shame, no shame at all. Richard, get her away from me. Get her, and her albino offspring off this property, this minute."

Richard was beside himself with anger. "Sonofabitch," he wheezed in a guttural tone. He turned to his wife. "Sweetheart, we do not want a scene here."

Deborah was in full rage, angered by Virginia Reed's intemperate insult. She bit into her bottom lip, tightened her fists, and fought to remain calm and nonviolent. She moved to within inches of Virginia Reed. She glared at her.

"You listen to me, and you get this straight," Deborah fired back, pointing. "This beautiful child—my daughter—is your granddaughter. Whether you or I like it or not, she's a Reed heir. And she has as much right to be here as you or any other Reed. Do you understand? Right, Jonathan?" Jonathan was practically trembling. "Neither she, nor I are going anywhere until we get a few things straight, once and forever. What you want or think does not interest me in the least.

"Since TV cameras are here, perhaps we should hold a press conference and let you repeat your foulmouthed comments. Maybe we can even discuss your own past life as a New Orleans hooker; your husband's past infidelity, and your son's rape of a twelve year old girl, fourteen years ago. And there's more."

The music stopped mid-note. It seemed no one dared even breathe aloud. A news cameraman, and reporter approached on the run. They were intercepted by several of Jonathan Reed's political operatives. However, one young female reporter broke past and approached.

Deborah again turned her attention to Jonathan. He was ash white. His stunned wife seized his right forearm with both hands.

"Who are these people, Jonathan?" she demanded. Jonathan never answered his wife.

Richard was ready to explode. He turned first to Jonathan, then Deborah, and back to Jonathan. "You lied to me, son. Your ass is ruined if you don't do something, and right damn now. And keep smiling, everyone. Just keep smiling."

The reporter was now less than three feet away. She turned to Deborah. Her eyes flashed a look of recognition.

"Excuse me," she said, smiling and lifting her note pad. Her camera-man waited directly behind her. "Aren't you Deborah Durrell, the au-thor. You are, aren't you? So, you're a supporter of Mr. Reed's. May I get a comment from you. Charlie, bring your camera around."

"I'm sorry, no interview, no camera. Please, I'm here on another mat-ter," Deborah responded. The reporter respectfully backed away.

By then, Virginia Reed's face was tomato red. Her jaw practically dropped to her navel. She turned to her husband with a look of astonish-ment. "Durrell? Deborah Durrell?" she chortled in disbelief.

"I'll be damn. Your favorite author, right dear?" Richard murmured through teeth clenched to stifle outright laughter. Jonathan could only manage a mindless stare.

Samantha burst with pride, watching her mother. Deborah turned to Richard and smiled broadly, clearly relishing the moment. Yet, she wept inside. This moment did not stand in isolation. It had its genesis in a life-altering event nearly a decade and a half old. Amongst other things, it proved to her just how complex a tapestry, this life.

"We can all go inside," Deborah announced. "Or we can conduct our family business in public. Personally, I don't care which you choose."

Before the Reeds could react, Deborah turned and was startled to see Matthew charge past several of Jonathan's handlers. Samantha yelled to her uncle. He reached them in all of four strides.

"What are you doing here?" Deborah whispered.

"You alright?" Matthew grasped her shoulders with both hands.

"We're fine. But how did you know? How did you know where we were? You didn't have to come."

"Yeah, I did. I couldn't miss this. Wouldn't want to miss out on a big family gathering like this one. But I didn't come alone."

Tommy and Paul suddenly broke past the crowd to join them. Deborah's jaw dropped. "You, guys, too?"

"Us too. The Three Musketeers, right?"

"Deborah smiled, turned back to Matthew. "Ah, you're...you're not carrying anything, are you?"

Matthew smiled. "Am I packin'? No. Just my driver's license. I'm clean. I just wanna get to know all my new kinfolk here."

A perspiring Richard Reed turned to stand nose to nose with Jonathan. Jonathan's wife appeared ready to faint.

"Let's get the hell inside," Richard groaned. "We've got 'a talk, right now. You've got a lot of damn explaining to do." He took a tentative step toward Deborah. "Please. Let's go inside," he said, swallowing a healthy helping of his hidebound, southern pride, "I'm...I'm sure we can resolve this matter in a manner you will find more than acceptable." The words nearly stuck in his craw.

"Well, I do declare, Mr. Reed, sir. Are you offering to buy my silence?" asked Deborah, summoning her most convincing southern drawl. Richard clenched his jaws mightily. His eyes squinted. His face turned red.

"Miss Davis, I am simply of a mind to do the right thing. I am an honorable, southern gentleman. Please, let's take our discussion inside. No one will benefit from a public airing of this...this sordid story."

However, before they could start for the main residence, a roar erupted from the stunned crowd. From the rear, the throng began to part. Reporters turned their attention toward the commotion. Cameras trained on the disturbance.

The cause of the excitement soon became clear. Within seconds, a half-dozen State Troopers, five local police officers and four Pulaski County Sheriff deputies, appeared. As the law enforcement contingent approached, a black, plainclothes officer, along with a member of the Republican, State Attorney General's office, led them.

Deborah, Samantha, Tommy, Paul and Matthew watched with amazement, as the young officer approached a stupefied Richard Reed. All hope of avoiding embarrassment was about to be shattered.

While cameras rolled, and shocked guests looked on, the cadre of officers encircled the Reeds.

"What's going on here," Richard demanded. "What the hell's going on here? What's the meaning of this?"

The plainclothes officer, badge in hand, stepped forward, stopped directly in front of Jonathan and displayed his identification.

"Mr. Jonathan Andrew Reed. My name is Major Bruce Davenport of the Arkansas State Police. On behalf of the State of Arkansas, I'm here to place you under arrest, sir. You have the right..."

Jonathan was incredulous. He wheeled around, traded gazes with his father and mother. Both were enraged.

"Arrest? Arrest? This is absolutely insane! Under arrest for what?" Screamed an indignant Jonathan.

"You're under arrest for conspiracy to murder one William Montgomery. Two of your father's employees, a J.D. Fogle, and a Roger Hill are already in custody."

"This is crazy," Jonathan insisted.

"Please, I have to say this first, sir. Mr. Reed, you have the right to remain silent. If you give up that right, anything you say..."

As Jonathan was being Mirandized and cuffed by Officer Davenport, the crowd watched in disbelief. Reporters grabbed their notebooks, scrambled to get to phones. Cameras rolled nonstop.

Richard Reed was almost passive. "Officer," he managed, as Jonathan was being led away. "I think I can save the State of Arkansas a good deal of trouble, if I could ahh...borrow your sidearm, for just a moment."

Dozens of people within earshot of Richard, burst into grim laughter. But Richard never cracked a smile. Those who knew him well, would later say they were convinced he was not joking.

———

Within minutes, Governor Bill Clinton was approached on the State Capitol steps, as he walked toward his limousine. He waved his security detail aside and issued a brief statement:

"As most of you know, today I've been meeting with leaders of major Civil Rights organizations. I am not fully aware of the facts relating to the questions you're asking me about. And if I were, it would be injudicious of me to comment on this matter at this time. But, let me just say that I have full faith and confidence that the facts will come out, and that justice will prevail. I want to affirm my belief in the principle of innocence before proof of guilt. Who knows, I may need the same affirmation some day. Look, I have unwavering faith in the rule of law, and have no doubt the truth will be revealed. Thank you very much."

"Governor! Governor! Does that mean you still support Jonathan Reed for U.S Senate?" shouted a reporter.

"Thank y'all very much. By the way, I noticed no one had a single question regarding my meetings on fostering racial harmony in this country. It's something all of us have to be committed to."

That said, the Governor, flanked by members of his security team, smiled and entered the rear seat of his car.

—

Meanwhile, as Jonathan's world unraveled, Deborah thought about May 15, 1974. Once more, she remembered Ol' Willie's face pressed against the truck window. And she recalled Jonathan showing anger, not surprise. He was not at all surprised. It was as if he had fully expected Willie's appearance.

Deborah turned to her right and saw Susan, Jonathan's half sister, emerge from the crowd. The two made brief eye contact. Deborah started toward her, then stopped. Susan gave a knowing smile, and started away.

It was then, Deborah fully understood. It was Susan who was responsible for what they had just witnessed. Susan and a Republican Attorney General wielding a sharp political axe.

Richard Reed had made at least one enemy he could not control: Susan—Jonathan's gatekeeper. Susan, the one privy to all his comings and goings. The one person who was aware of his phone calls, his meetings, most of his secrets.

It was Susan, the outsider. Susan. Never fully accepted as a Reed by her half brother. Susan. Often ridiculed for not possessing the beauty or social graces that would have made her socially acceptable.

It all made sense. Willie had often boasted of being a friend of Jonathan's. Few believed him, although in years long past, they were seen together on a number of occasions.

Willie apparently saw it all. He knew everything. That likely made him expendable. Deborah remembered Miss Jasmine's musings regarding Willie's death. He had disappeared almost the same day she left for Chicago, and never returned until now, showing up dead.

Ol' Willie knew. He knew! And Jonathan, the Reed clan, and their cohorts, wanted him never to reveal a word. Most likely, he had returned to try and cash in on his knowledge, only to end up dead. There was yet no solid proof of her speculation, but Deborah hardly needed proof.

chapter sixty

Purpose beyond pursuits.

....as only a country boy, raised on beans and cornbread, knew how.

Deborah spent the rest of the day, and most of the night, sorting through the storm of emotions swirling in and around her. She forced lesser matters, such as Rachel's inexplicable hatred of her, far into the background of her concerns.

And while Deborah was sure the law, and public opinion, would later deal harshly with Jonathan and the Reed family, she focused her heart, mind and soul on Samantha. It was clear to her, recent traumatic events would have a lasting impact on her and her daughter. Deborah was especially concerned about the effect Samantha's seeing her birth father would have on her, now and in the future.

Tommy assured Deborah that Samantha would get everything she had coming to her from the Reeds. He was certain a generous settlement offer of both land and money, would be provided Deborah and Samantha. However, if it became necessary, he and his civil law partners were prepared to file a lawsuit.

While all that was gratifying to hear, Deborah had other issues weigh-ing on her heart—business and personal matters she discussed at length with Tommy. And there was one surprise that surfaced: he was reluc-tant to say good-bye, unwilling to have their paths diverge again. Before leaving for New York the next morning, Tommy said so as plainly as he could—as only a country boy raised on beans and cornbread knew how.

"You should know something, Miss Davis," he declared. "I'm not let-ting you disappear on me again. I'm not taking a chance that it'll be an-other fourteen years before I see you again."

"Is that right?" Deborah was surprised. She had not expected this.

"That's right."

"That's...that's quite a statement."

"I know. We'll have to...to talk. First things first," he said with a seri-ousness Deborah did not mistake. She would later recall those words with a fondness that only intensified each time she remembered them.

—

Samantha did not attend school on Monday, the day following her grandfather's funeral. Deborah spent the entire day with her daughter. By evening, she had made a decision that set everyone on their heels.

The school year would end on Friday. The following Sunday, Saman-tha would leave for Chicago with her. Aunt Rose and Uncle Jack were thrilled. They would return home Tuesday afternoon, and promised to have everything ready when Deborah and Sam arrived.

Deborah's decision began to form, the day she arrived and had the long conversation with Maylene. From that moment on, she struggled to interpret the discordant voices in her head and heart. Maylene had asked her what she planned about Samantha. There was now an answer.

Deborah had been asking herself why she had come to Reedville at all. Part of her questioned the wisdom of disturbing the life she had, at long last, created for herself. Was it only to see her dying father? Was it to simply experience some brief reconnection with her daughter? Was it to confront her mother and the others, as part of some feel-good attempt to exorcise pent-up frustrations, while effecting nothing? No!

For years, Deborah had known that if she wanted lasting, inner peace, she had no choice but to confront and resolve her past. No amount of success could ever mask the pain, guilt, hate, and feelings of abandonment that tormented her.

Samantha was her *daughter,* not her *sister.* And she was certainly not her mother's *adopted* daughter. Deborah kept recounting the lies. She questioned *her* own role in their perpetration. Should she have come back sooner, after her earlier failed attempt? Should she have come, no matter the consequence, no matter having created a new world for herself?

But all that aside, what was her responsibility now? Forget her head, what was in her heart? That was the question Deborah realized she had to confront head on. Time for being concerned about anything except truth, and for anyone other than her daughter, was past.

That meant subjugating her own desires and aspirations, when and wherever they conflicted with Samantha's needs. That was not a commitment she felt deserving of plaudits or accolades, not even in her own mind. She was a mother—Samantha's mother. Deborah wanted nothing more than to be just *that*. Nothing was more important.

Deborah wrapped both arms around her daughter, literally and figuratively. The two spent hours trudging around the grounds at Gram's old homesite. Deborah took great care to make her Gram d'lena come alive in Sam's mind and heart.

Mother and daughter traveled country roads that stretched like asphalt ribbons, through postcard views drenched in brilliant sunlight. They strolled through woods alive with the sights, sounds and fragrances of unspoiled nature. They saw rippling streams teeming with life.

Near day's end, on what would be a fateful Monday, it was Samantha who raised the subject. She brimmed with excitement and anticipation as she tried to word her simple question:

"May I...may I go back with you, Mother? May I come to Chicago?" Sam's voice was filled with trepidation. At first, Deborah simply basked in the glorious feeling that attended the sound of the word, "mother." The joy the word brought to her heart could not be measured.

It was clear that Samantha was afraid the answer would be anything but "yes." Her plaintive gaze, the way she reached out and touched her mother's arm as they walked. Samantha was now placing all her dreams and hopes in her simply phrased question.

"I would love for you to come visit...anytime." Deborah's response was carefully calculated. "All you have to do is say when you want to come." She fully expected Samantha's response to her.

"I don't mean just for a visit. I want to come *live* with you. I want to come stay with you. Please?"

Deborah stopped, turned and grasped both Samantha's hands. Her daughter's words burrowed down to her soul. Her face exploded into a wide smile. After allowing her heart to slow down a bit, she assured Samantha nothing would please her more.

Mother and daughter talked for hours about what all that would mean. Samantha would have to give up her friends, her school, the people and places that meant so much to her. They shared their hearts and souls. Sam bubbled as she spoke excitedly of her expectations. Deborah listened. She listened with a heart, filled to overflowing.

So, after a day unlike any other in their lives, the two agreed. Samantha would return with her mother to Chicago, and would remain for the summer. Afterwards, both would discuss whether she wanted to, or should stay longer.

Samantha beamed. She was ecstatic. She had a thousand questions about what lay ahead. Deborah had never seen such happiness in the eyes of a thirteen year old—soon to be fourteen—as Samantha was quick to point out. Deborah was patient, eagerly answering all her daughter's questions.

Then came the time to reveal all, to those who had assumed only Deborah would be returning to Chicago. Maylene was thrilled. It was the decision she had prayed for. Matthew hugged Deborah, and in an emotional voice she had not expected, he whispered: "This...this is the best thing you could 'a done. I'm so proud 'a you. Take me, too!" He then loosed a reverberating belly laugh.

A stunned Mabel Davis, clearly conflicted, was left grasping for a response. Her natural instinct was to object in the most forceful manner. However, she did not. She managed to hold her tongue. Still, one could see the sudden change in her expression and demeanor.

Mabel's initial understanding was, Sam would be leaving permanently. Then came the clarification. That decision would be left for Sam and Deborah to make later.

Mabel Davis forced a smile. "Well, she's...she's your daughter. Whatever you think is best." A lone tear stole down her cheek.

As for Rachel? Well, Rachel was Rachel. Upon hearing the news, she called her mother aside and pleaded for her to intervene. She questioned Deborah's motives, questioned her ability to devote the proper time and attention to Samantha.

When Maylene learned of Rachel's reaction, she stormed into her sister's room, slammed the door shut, forced her onto her bed and read her the "Riot Act." Maylene made it clear to Rachel, if she did anything to cause the least bit of trouble for either Deborah or Sam, she would *wish* she were crazy, if she were not already. After her outburst during the family repass, few had any question regarding her mental state.

"She's not my sister," Rachel defiantly yelled, as Maylene turned to leave the room.

Maylene wheeled back to face her. "We've heard that crap before. What's your problem? Is it because Deborah is a bigger person than you? Because she's survived all these years, become successful, and hasn't let lies destroy her? Because your petty, self-centered attitude toward her hasn't affected her? After all this time...daddy's death, and all the crap this family has been through, I cannot believe you have not changed one single bit. You haven't learned a single thing. Not one friggin' thing.

"Now, you listen to me! You're my sister by birth, not choice. I love you, but I do not have to like your crazy ass. And I don't. You need some serious help, girl. Truth is, you're lucky; we're all lucky that Deborah still claims us as her family. If I was her, I'm not so sure I'd have a thing to do with anybody 'round here, except Sam."

Rachel started to fire back.

"Don't *even!*" Maylene warned, pointing a loaded index finger inches from Rachel's twitching nose.

Maylene slowly turned and exited the room, leaving the door wide open. No accident. She remembered that even as a young girl, Rachel hated open doors, especially bedroom doors.

Mabel Davis was approaching Rachel's bedroom. She stepped aside, as an exasperated Maylene stormed past. She started after her, but continued toward Rachel's open bedroom door. When she reached the doorway, Rachel raised herself to a sitting position. She aimed a look at her mother, so fraught with evil and venom, it halted Mabel Davis in her tracks. She took the measure of Rachel's hate-filled gaze, then turned and walked away.

chapter sixty-one

The Journey Home

════════════════════════════

Deborah remembered standing before the same mirror...

Deborah canceled her return airline ticket.
Instead of flying, she and Samantha left for Chicago in the same manner *she* had on that Sunday in 1974. Her decision came as she was about to purchase airfare for Samantha. At first, Deborah resisted the idea, then realized theirs was a journey that had to be made. She hoped the trip would help Samantha understand some of what she had experienced that day. When told of the plan, Sam was solemn, but embraced the idea.

Mother and daughter departed Reedville on Sunday. It was as bright and outwardly peaceful a day as that day in 1974. Except for Gloria and Aunt Rose, everyone was present. Of course, Rachel was not there. But one could argue, she had not been there in 1974.

The air was thick with memories. It was difficult to hold emotions in check. Mabel Davis appeared especially affected. Deborah questioned her mother's sincerity, but embraced her. She mourned the missing heart and soul connection that should define mothers and daughters.

Nearly everyone thought about the Reverend on that day. While he had not been present *that* fateful Sunday, all were certain that, were he alive, he would have joined them on the platform on this Sunday. It was a thought Deborah clung to.

Happily, she and Samantha boarded a more modern Greyhound bus than she and Aunt Rose had endured. The journey, while reminiscent of the fateful trip taken years before, had one distinct difference: Samantha. Deborah closed her eyes, held her daughter's hand. The irony was overpowering. In 1974, a scared twelve year-old Deborah sat next to her aunt. And she was pregnant with the daughter who now sat next to her, smiling, enthralled by the beauty of a pastoral countryside. The view had been there before, but Deborah hardly saw it then.

—

When Deborah and Samantha arrived in Chicago, Uncle Jack was waiting—camera in hand. He and Rose insisted on a brief, night-tour of downtown. It was the beginning of the most exciting summer in Samantha's life. She was awed; could not take it all in quickly enough.

When they reached home, Samantha was given Deborah's old room. It was a deeply emotional moment for both, especially when mother and daughter entered the room together. It had been decorated in much the same way it had years before.

Uncle Jack had even retrieved the bassinet and placed it in the room. But when he saw the emotional effect on Deborah, he apologized and rushed to remove it. Deborah stopped him, insisting she was okay. The moment provided an opportunity for her to explain everything to Samantha. Jack and Rose excused themselves.

Deborah mostly shared her happiest recollections. She and Sam talked, laughed and even cried into early morning. Deborah showed Samantha baby items she had held back from her mother: diapers, booties, the hospital I.D. bracelet. Samantha reacted with joy and sadness.

This was, in fact, her *second* time being in the home of her great aunt and uncle. It was surreal for her. She confessed to having a feeling of familiarity with the room, one that could not be explained.

"It's almost like...like I remember being here."

Samantha spent countless minutes staring at the bassinet that had once held her. She kept touching it, slowly tracing her fingers along its edges. Once, she turned to her mother. Tears broke free, and both wept without reservation.

A time later, Deborah took Samantha's hand. Both moved to stand in front of the full-length mirror—the same mirror where Deborah had once stood crying, examining her cesarean scar and wishing herself dead. Samantha asked to see the scar for herself.

Deborah was taken aback by her daughters request. At first, she hesitated before reluctantly consenting. Samantha gently traced the scar's length. Deborah wondered what she must be thinking. Again, tears sprang from the eyes of both. Even so, smiles appeared, as the two embraced and clung to each other for the longest while.

—

Before sitting down to a late dinner, Deborah made sure Samantha called home to speak to everyone, even Rachel. The latter declined to speak to Deborah, surrendering the phone to Maylene. The two spoke for nearly a half hour. Deborah next spoke to Matthew. At her continued urging, he at last promised to enroll at the University of Arkansas at Little Rock. Deborah assured him she would cover his tuition and expenses, as long as he remained in classes and maintained at least a 'C' average.

Aunt Rose later sparked a tearfest, when she produced a picture of Samantha and Deborah, taken by Jack the day Mabel Davis took Samantha away. The film negatives had been thought lost. Uncle Jack had recently discovered the roll in a basement desk drawer, only days before Deborah and Samantha arrived.

Although the years had caused the film to slightly degrade, it yielded a remarkable and priceless set of photos. Deborah and Samantha could not stop gazing at them.

Meanwhile, Jack disappeared. He soon reappeared in the doorway, carrying his 35mm camera. He had Deborah, Samantha, and Rose stand together in a loving embrace, then snapped all twenty-four exposures.

A cautious Rose insisted he immediately remove the film and give it to her. Everyone laughed, except Jack. While he and Rose discussed the matter, Deborah led her daughter down to the basement. There was an old, well-worn, brown leather suitcase she was anxious to show her.

—

Within days of returning to Chicago, Deborah spoke to Paul's secretary. He was in Europe, but called later, promising to get in touch when he returned. During their brief conversation, Deborah learned that contracts were ready to be signed. The final package was worth a little over three million dollars, plus a heavy promotion budget.

With her financial future on a sound track, Deborah's rapt attention was focused on Sam. Her daughter was her priority, and would remain so. The imposing demands that writing, and promoting her novels would exact, would simply have to conform to whatever was demanded of her as a mother.

During that first month and a half, Deborah, Rose and Jack treated Samantha to practically every Chicago attraction of note: museums, Wrigley Field, the lakefront, Sears Tower, Soldier Field, the United Center—home of the Chicago Bulls. They also attended an Oprah Show taping. To avoid being recognized, Deborah wore a disguise. It worked.

The next week, Uncle Jack proudly arranged a visit to Ebony Magazine, where he still worked. Samantha met the magazine's distinguished managing editor, Mr. Lerone Bennett. He informed Deborah of their upcoming cover article on her—scheduled to appear in three months.

One of Samantha's biggest thrills came when she accompanied Deborah on an inspiring visit to her mother's alma mater, Northwestern University. She fell in love with the place. It was love at first sight. Days later, she declared she wanted to attend Northwestern. Deborah was flattered.

—

Time passed far too quickly. At summer's end, Deborah returned to Reedville with Samantha, in time for her freshman year enrollment at Carver School. Samantha's friends were thrilled to have her back.

Deborah frequently returned to Reedville to be with Samantha. During semester breaks, Sam spent time in Chicago. On one occasion, an ecstatic Charles and Yvonne accompanied her.

Over the months, Samantha accompanied her mother on portions of her book tours whenever possible. There were trips to Paris, Spain, France, Germany, and London—places Samantha had only dreamed of seeing. Knowing she was the most important person in her mother's life, was evident in Samantha's behavior, in her voice, in her scholastic performance. She brimmed with self-confidence.

Even when Deborah could not visit, or arrange Samantha's visit, she called. In fact, it was rare if more than two days passed without them sharing a long phone conversation. Their well laid plans called for Samantha to spend summers with her mother, graduate high school in Reedville, then move to Chicago to attend Northwestern University.

—

In quiet moments that would follow, Deborah sometimes found herself looking back over the months, the years. She often revisited that awkward moment when she stood in her mother's living room, and gazed with disbelief into the eyes of her daughter. *Her* daughter.

Deborah was deeply saddened, whenever she recalled the years of lies and deceit. She tried to avoid thinking about them at all. However, despite her long suffering, reestablishing the bond with Samantha had made all that suffering worthwhile. Having her daughter look into her eyes and call her "mother" was reward enough.

The love Samantha and her mother now shared, gave Deborah the strength she needed to force the dark memories to the rear of her consciousness. Her life now had purpose beyond her own pursuits.

Still, Deborah wisely sought and received counseling. It was long overdue. Not surprisingly, she also provided much-needed funds, and gave of her own time to help counseling programs serving other rape victims. Her days were now filled with meaning; her nights, with resurgent hope—hope for an even more fulfilling tomorrow.

chapter sixty-two

A Walk on the Dark side - Six Weeks later

===========================

"My baby! Get him out! "

T he awful news came near midnight.

A nearly two hour conversation with Tommy, now in California on business, had ended. Deborah had just fallen asleep in the master bedroom
of her twentieth floor, lakefront condo. It was her second night in her
new home. She and Rose had spent two weeks decorating the place.

All was well. Samantha was doing great...making straight A's, sounding more grown-up every time she called. More than a month had passed
since Deborah had taken her back to begin the new school year.

Then came the call. The phone rang, yanking Deborah awake. It was
Maylene. Her emotional, tearful tone signaled it was not good news.
Words tumbled from her lips—a fusillade of apologies for calling so late.

Deborah assured her sister it was alright. Then Maylene delivered
the news. It was Rachel. Rachel was near death. Another suicide attempt.
This time she appeared to have finally succumbed to demons that had
been tormenting her for so many years.

From the instant she said hello and heard Maylene's tortured voice, Deborah sat straight up. Now she was standing, clutching the phone, straining to understand what her sister was saying.

"Near death? What do you mean? What's happened? Maylene..." Deborah interrupted, even as Maylene's words flowed without allowance for her response. Deborah halted her.

"Maylene, wait. Stop! Start over. What's going on?"

Maylene explained she and her mother had been in the kitchen, while Matthew was busy devouring half a chicken. Suddenly, bone-chilling screams rang out from Rachel's room. Hearts nearly stopped. She was screaming at the top of her voice. Just what she was saying was not immediately known. Whatever it was, it was clear she was in agony.

Matthew was first to bolt from the room. One step beyond the doorway, he tripped, crashed into the wall, but braced himself just before tumbling to the floor. Maylene and her mother quickly followed. Earsplitting screams continued as they raced down the hallway.

Rachel's door was locked. Matthew motioned his mother and sister aside, took a couple of quick steps back then laid into the door, full force. The facing splintered; the door nearly popped from its hinges.

What greeted him inside momentarily froze him in his tracks: blood. Blood was everywhere. A demented, wild-eyed Rachel sat on the side of her bed, flailing a pair of scissors. In a crazed frenzy, she was stabbing, ripping and scoring her abdomen. Her gown was a sea of bright red.

"My baby! Get him out! "He's dead! He's dead! My baby is dead! My Baby!" She kept wailing, referring to her baby, lost years earlier. "He has to come out!" Rachel yelled. Foam crept from the corners of her mouth; her eyes bulged in their sockets, the veins in her neck were in full relief. "He's inside me...inside, and he's dead. I've got to get him out! My baby!"

"Don't come in here!" Matthew yelled to his mother. He immediately lunged onto the bed, seizing Rachel's blood-drenched hand in both his own. Mabel was shocked by the sight, as was Maylene. Despite Matthew's size and strength, and notwithstanding Rachel's blood loss, he had difficulty wresting the scissors from her hand. Stunned disbelief gripped Maylene and her mother. Rachel kept screaming, resisting Matthew with adrenaline-induced strength. He had to summon every ounce of his strength. Even so, his arm was nicked several times, drawing blood.

"My baby! Get him out! He's got to come out!" Rachel yelled. "I've got to see him! I want to...to hold my baby. Please, help me!"

Maylene confessed to Deborah, she and her mother were petrified. The stark reality took several moments to register. Mabel moved to Matthew's side, just as he tossed aside the blood-drenched scissors. Mabel Davis desperately tried to comfort a raving Rachel, who was inconsolable. However, she appeared oblivious to her gaping wounds.

Matthew had Maylene call for an ambulance, while he and his mother ripped strips of white bed linen. He banded them around Rachel's wounds and applied pressure to stem the bleeding.

Samantha arrived amidst the commotion. She rushed toward Rachel's bedroom, but Maylene held her back. Thankfully, both Yvonne and Charles were away in Little Rock with Clarise Harris, Maylene's close friend and co-worker.

Minutes later, Matthew grew impatient, unwilling to wait any longer for an ambulance that would likely take more than a half hour to arrive. He carefully swept Rachel up in his arms and made his way outside to Maylene's aging Ford stationwagon.

With Maylene at the wheel, and Matthew and Mabel Davis in the rear seat with Rachel, they all headed down Crispus Attucks Road en route to Reedville County Regional Hospital.

Samantha remained at home, to prevent Charles and Yvonne from returning home and finding everyone gone. Deborah was deeply concerned about the impact of all this on all three. Maylene assured her they had all been spared any exposure to the gory scene.

Maylene remained extremely emotional. Deborah tried to calm her, only succeeding near the end, managing to get Maylene to pause for a moment. A short while later, she learned Maylene had left Matthew and her mother at the hospital. Samantha later joined them.

Doctors had made it clear, Rachel was in a critical, and unstable condition. She had suffered massive blood loss, and severe internal wounds, including a perforated large intestine. Doctors could make no promises, regarding a prognosis for her survival.

Silence. Brief silence followed by rapid-fire questions and incomplete answers dominated the minutes that followed. Deborah found herself wishing she had never ventured from the cocoon that had protected her for so many years.

"Will she...come through okay?" Deborah struggled to mask her absence of passion, and the follow-on guilt. "What did the doctors say?"

Maylene repeated what she had said earlier. "They don't know. They gave her blood, stabilized her enough to do the surgery. She's pretty stable now. It's touch and go. We just don't really know."

"Are you sure Samantha is okay?"

"Sam's fine."

"I'll call and talk to her first thing in the morning. I just want to be sure. How's Matthew and...and everybody"

"'Matthew's in a...a stupor. He's hardly said a solitary word since Rachel went into surgery. He just sits in the waiting room, doesn't say a word. And Mama? She's devastated. 'Bout what you would expect. I think she feels guilty, too. She's denied the seriousness of Rachel's condition for so long. It was a sight—the blood, her stabbing and ripping at herself. I was even scared for Matthew, too...the way she was flailing around with those sharp scissors."

"Was Samantha there at the time?"

"No. Like I said, she came a little later. She wanted to call you, but she's at the hospital now, with Mama and Matthew. I'm back here with my kids. Sam kept trying to comfort Mama and the rest of us. She was more calm and grown-up than we were. I'm so proud of her. I know she's gon' have a lot of questions. Thank God, she wasn't in that room. And thank God, Matthew was here at the time. There's no way me or Mama could 'a done what he did."

Silence.

More silence.

"I'm coming."

"What? What did you say?"

Deborah hesitated. Was Maylene's not understanding her... God's way of giving her a chance to reconsider? "I'll be there," she repeated.

"Where? Here? You're coming here?"

"I'll be there as soon as I can. I'll make arrangements as soon as we finish talking. I should be able to leave tomorrow."

"You sure? I'll tell Matthew and Mama."

"Of course, I'll have to call Aunt Rose and Uncle Jack. He's due for prostate surgery in the morning. Otherwise, I'm sure Aunt Rose would come with me."

"I know. But is Uncle Jack gonna be alright?"

"I pray he will. You never know. any surgery is serious."

"Deborah, Deborah. I'm so sorry to have to call like this and...I know you have so much to do and..."

"Don't, Maylene. Don't. It's alright. I'll be there."

"I sure hope Rachel will..."

"Not for Rachel, nor for mother, to be honest. But for me...because of who I am, and my concern for Samantha and the rest of you. Period."

—

Deborah never slept, following her conversation with Maylene. Despite the hour, she called Aunt Rose and broke the news to her. The two prayed for Rachel, right over the phone, then said little else. There was little else to be said. Deborah informed Rose of her plans. She insisted Deborah not worry about Uncle Jack.

"He's tough as boot leather," Rose joked. "At least the surgery will give me a little break. Sometimes, that man acts like we're both teenagers." Rose laughed, so did Deborah, although she heard more than a smattering of concern in her aunt's voice.

The next morning, before dawn, Deborah arrived at 97th and Yale streets, not O'Hare Airport. Aunt Rose was not surprised, but Deborah clearly saw the joy in her eyes the instant she entered the house.

Notwithstanding Rose's comforting words regarding Jack, Deborah was determined to be there for him. He had always been there for her. The trip to Reedville would have to wait until she was certain he would be alright. And he was. She left for Reedville on the afternoon of the following day.

—

Deborah decided to not visit Rachel in the hospital. She was determined to avoid any likelihood of a confrontation with her sister. Uncle Jack was recovering well from surgery. No cancer was found. That gave her great peace of mind.

Being in Reedville gave Deborah invaluable time with Samantha. She remained there for two of the three weeks she was in Arkansas. During the third week, Sam joined her mother on the Texas-Arkansas leg of her book tour.

After nearly three weeks, Rachel was released from the hospital. With Mabel Davis' encouragement—unthinkable earlier—she agreed to an indefinite stay in a Little Rock mental health facility. Deborah underwrote all costs, insisting Rachel not be told of her involvement.

Then, the day before Deborah was to return to Chicago, an unexpected request from Maylene turned her world in a direction neither could have anticipated.

chapter sixty-three

Things Remembered

═══════════════════

"Deborah...Daddy. That's Daddy's handwriting..."

The request was a simple one, yet it was not at all simple. Maylene did not anticipate the emotions it would spawn in Deborah. They had just finished the eggs, waffles, ham, grits, and home fries breakfast Maylene had prepared. Both washed the dishes and put them away, sharing little conversation. Deborah sensed her sister had something to say, but chose not to ask what.

Maylene waited until they were done and seated on the front porch swing, before revealing what was on her mind.

"Mama's hardly able to stand going into her closet anymore. She needs to move Daddy's things, but she can't do it herself. You think you could help me? There's plenty of space in the closet in Matthew's old room. Rachel only uses part of it. It'll hold most of Daddy's stuff."

For the moment, Deborah's voice abandoned her. Maylene's request came hurtling out of deep space. Before she knew it, she had nodded yes, even as her brain was saying, "No, no way." It took a few seconds for

the disconnect between response and intent, to fully register. But
Maylene's reaction—her quick "Thanks," told Deborah she must have
answered in the positive.

In an instant, Maylene bounded to her feet, clearly expecting Deborah to follow. When Deborah hesitated, she took a short step toward
her. "It won't take us long," she assured her sister.

Earlier, Mabel Davis had left to visit Rebecca, who had taken ill the
week before. Her condition did not appear to be serious, but doctors
had ordered several days of bedrest.

A solemn Maylene and Deborah entered their parents' bedroom,
after making sure Matthew's closet was absent any surprises he may not
have removed. There were none. Now both stood in the middle of their
mother's room. Deborah still sensed her father's presence. Her pulse
spiked. Maylene noted her reaction. Both hesitated before going farther.

It was as if Maylene was only now aware of the emotional magnitude
of the task. What they were about to do was not as easy as it may have
initially appeared to her. The possessions of the departed carry with them
a special aura, a nearly tangible sense of the person's having been, and
now having gone. It often evokes a level of emotion one cannot anticipate. Perhaps Mabel Davis had been so affected, and unable to remove
her husband's belongings.

Maylene was first to enter the closet. She yanked the dangling, light
cord, turning on the incandescent bulb overhead.

"There's a lot of stuff in here. Fortunately, Mama's is off to one side.
They kept things separated like that. That'll make it a lot easier. Just
look at all these suits, robes, shirts, and shoes. Daddy sure loved him
some Stacey Adams."

Deborah nodded. Maylene forced back a section of suits, clearing
space to move forward. Deborah was not certain she could do this. What
she saw, resurrected thoughts she had worked hard to ban from her mind.

Her eyes quickly focused on a pair of dark, cuffed slacks with suspenders still attached. She saw a wooden rack holding at least a dozen
leather belts. And she remembered. She remembered May 15, 1974. A

shudder coursed her spine. She remembered the Reverend's long sleeve white shirt, those dark, cuffed slacks, the suspenders, the belt. It was what he wore on that day he ushered her into the bedroom and slammed the door shut behind them. She could practically see him in those clothes, towering over her again. Deborah's breathing grew labored; perspiration beaded on her brow. She turned to leave, when Maylene spoke up.

"Deborah. If this is...is too much for you, right now, I can probably get Matthew to help me later. I should have thought about that before asking you to help me."

Deborah nodded yes, and stepped back into the room. Maylene started to follow, when her glance caught sight of the cardboard box, now visible through the space she had created.

"Hold on a second. I'll be right there."

Deborah waited. Shortly, she heard Maylene speak to her in a surprisingly subdued voice.

"Deborah. Deborah, you need to see this. Come here, please."

A reluctant Deborah reentered the closet and found Maylene tugging a box toward the closet door, and into the light. The latter stood erect, and pointed. It took a moment for Deborah to focus on exactly where Maylene intended she look.

"Here. Right here," Maylene whispered.

"The box?"

"Yes, and what's written on the box."

Deborah moved closer. Then she saw it: her name. She saw her own name scribbled on the box flap. She looked up. Maylene's eyes were riveted on her. Deborah leaned even closer, staring at her name—the entire, handwritten inscription.

"Mother's?" she managed.

"Deborah...Deborah, that's Daddy's handwriting. It's hard to read, but it's his. I have never seen this box before. It says, 'Mother's things.' This is from Gram, I'm...I'm sure of it. Looks like somebody's already started to rip this tape off. Look here! In fact, the tape *was* removed, then put back. Somebody opened this."

Deborah and Maylene dropped to their knees, on opposite sides of the box. Neither moved to open it right away. Both were too stunned, unable to take the next step just yet. Deborah traced her fingers along the words...over her name. She grasped the tape and hesitated.

"You scared?" Maylene's eyes were like saucers. "'I sure am. I'm scared and nervous. Girl, look at me shaking."

Deborah nodded. "You think it's...it's some of Gram's things? You think Daddy put this here for me?" Her eyes teared. "Thought I was done crying." She stroked the tears away and took a deep breath.

Maylene moved closer, draped her left arm around her sister's shoulder. Deborah took a deep breath and began lifting the tape, slowly, at first. Then quickly. A single rip. It came off easily.

A long pause. Deborah lifted the top flap, then the second, then the others. A loud gasp. Her eyes nearly bulged from their sockets. Maylene's grip on her shoulder felt like pincers. There, in front of them, was a treasure neither could have imagined.

Maylene noticed something: an envelope. A business-size envelope had slipped down along the edge of an interior side of the box. She lifted it. It was empty. She gazed at the front, pressed one hand to her heart then handed it to Deborah.

Deborah immediately saw what had caused Maylene's reaction. Her heart raced; more tears trickled down her cheeks. The envelope was addressed from Reverend...to her. It read: *To Deborah Yvonne.*

It was clear, the envelope had been carelessly ripped open, and the contents removed. But what had the Reverend written, after all those years? What had he written, but failed to verbalize. Deborah stared at the empty envelope and realized she would never have those answers. But who would have taken the letter? Rachel's name immediately sprang to her mind. Rachel. Deborah then wondered if that name had come too easily. Perhaps it was a bit too obvious. Was there someone else? Who?

chapter sixty-four

More Precious Than Gold

═══════════════════════════════

Once uncovered, she held it delicately with both hands.

Gram's Bible, her English lace curtains
that had once adorned her kitchen window. Her horn-rimmed eyeglasses
with scratched lenses, the picture of Grandpa George—the one that always hung over the divan. Her sewing kit, her white shawl she had knit-
ted, herself. More than a dozen storybooks—the ones she loved reading
to her grandbabies. It was all more precious than gold.

And there were more treasures. A hand-sewn, patchwork quilt Deborah would often lie on during summertime, afternoon naps. A small jewelry case filled with mostly costume jewelry. They were pieces Gram seldom wore, but valued because they came from her beloved, George.

Deborah could not contain her joy; her surprise, her deep sadness.
Maylene was likewise awestruck. It was like Christmas—a Christmas
Deborah could not have expected. She had hardly discovered one remarkable item, before spotting another, and another. She felt five years old
again; could not examine everything quickly enough.

A small photo album lay near the bottom of the box. It was wrapped in a swath of aged linen and bound with white-lace ribbon. Deborah gingerly unwrapped it as if it were the Emancipation Proclamation; The Holy Grail. Once uncovered, she held it delicately with both hands. An emotional Maylene looked on.

With a deep sigh, Deborah lifted the thick brown cover and saw what she had not expected to see again: a photo of Gram. There she was, in all her beauty, elegance and charm. Tears now streamed down Deborah's face. She held the album away, to avoid damaging this priceless prize. Maylene shared her sister's tear-filled joy.

The black and white photo was less than three inches by five inches. There was Gram, smiling at them, her eyes sparkling. They could feel the warmth leaping from the image. Deborah held the album to her chest and closed her eyes.

There were more aged photographs: a picture of Gram with Deborah and Matthew. Maylene was certain Reverend must have taken it. It appeared his hat was on the sofa next to where Matthew was seated. Deborah guessed she must have been no older than four.

Several other loose photos. Some were of Gram's ol' house. In one, a wreath of smoke could be seen rising from her chimney. Another was of Gram's summer vegetable garden. She was always rightly proud of her garden, and her green thumb.

Then, there was the Bible. While it was not her large, black, family Bible, it was one Gram used nearly to the point of destruction. The loosely attached cover opened to reveal names and birthdates of her grandbabies. And there were other scribblings, some barely legible.

But there was one name that instantly caught both Deborah's and Maylene's eyes: Barsteau. In the lower right-hand corner, the name 'Barsteau,' with a question mark next to it, was clearly visible. A stunned Deborah looked at Maylene. Neither said anything, at first.

"There's that name," said Deborah. "Barsteau. Why is it in Gram's Bible, of all places? I don't understand. Why does the name of a man I had never heard of before, now seem to be everywhere?"

Maylene was slow to comment. She shrugged. "I don't remember hearing his name before...before Rachel blurted it out. Anyway, this is just...amazing. Daddy actually set all this aside for you. He meant you to have this."

Maylene's determination to redirect the conversation did not escape Deborah. "But when? When was he planning to give this to me? Had he intended to mail it...send for me and give it to me then? When? Was it simply intended to ease his own guilt...some act of atonement? I don't understand, Maylene."

"I don't know."

"But I am so happy this...this is all here. I have always wondered what happened to Gram's things. And I know this is just a few of them. I'm happy, I'm sad. Just look at this picture of Gram. Oh, my God. I can't wait to show this one to Samantha. It's like she's looking...looking directly into my eyes. This is more valuable than anything I own."

An excited Maylene hugged her sister tightly. She then grasped her right forearm with her left hand and peered into her eyes.

"Daddy must have done this before he got sick. He must have. But this could not have been here all the time...before then." Maylene seemed certain. "I wonder who tried to open it before. Whoever it was, I hope they didn't take anything out. "Course that letter is missing. "

Maylene had barely finished speaking, when Mabel Davis appeared. She stood only feet from where her daughters sat, and said nothing. Her sudden entry startled both.

However, it was Mabel who seemed the most stunned. She tried to conceal it, but her eyes gave her away. The contents of the box were clearly visible. Mabel stared in silence. She neither frowned nor smiled. The fact she said nothing, made it clear she was not surprised by seeing the box.

chapter sixty-five

A Gathering

===============

And it would always be so.

T he warm wind gently swept
through knee high grass that swayed but never surrendered. A boundless blue sky shared its domain with but a single, billowing, cottonball
cloud, and a gleaming sun.

Buoyed by warm, steady wind currents, a pair of hawks soared ef-
fortlessly, like majestic kings of the air. The day was reminiscent of another day and time. It was as if some distant yesterday had returned to
give hope to the present, and to inspire tomorrows to come.

In the distance, two jean-clad figures strolled side by side. Their shadows often appeared as one. Both stood out boldly against mother nature's
sun-drenched backdrop.

Matthew and Deborah gazed far beyond the moment, into yesterday, into a time when all seemed right with the world—their world.
Theirs was a time when discordant sounds and disparaging voices were
muted by a chorus of joy, by songs of hope—a symphony that should

serenade the heart of every child. The joy, love and innocence of youth should fortify and undergird children for their journey through life.

Matthew and Deborah now stood on hallowed ground. Even the sound of the wind seemed to bear witness to same. Gram's house had once graced this land. Her spirit was still alive in the hearts of two who loved her beyond the limits of human expression.

While their voices could not be heard across the expanse, it was not meant to be otherwise. A brother and sister communed with each other without concern for time and its ceaseless demands. It was a true family gathering symbolized by just two.

It was in this setting, at this place, that Deborah decided to share some of her darkest secrets with Matthew. She told him the truth about Jonathan having raped her. He had to know. His reaction was fully predictable. He vowed to see Jonathan pay. What was not expected, was the depth of his hurt, not for himself, but for her. He cried unabashedly, wondered how Deborah had endured so much, and yet had survived and succeeded.

Deborah exacted a promise from Matthew that he would do nothing violent. She knew she could not leave without sharing more time with him—time both needed. More than five thousand days had passed since that Sunday. Lives had been altered in ways that could not be quantified. No confession, no apology could atone for that. But this, too, was their time. On this day, in this place—a place where so many wonderful moments had been shared, they shared yet again.

As the day grew short and shadows lengthened, the two reluctantly turned to begin the trek back along the old trail. And while it was no longer the well-blazoned pathway it had once been, the way was still clear. There was no denying things had changed; they had changed. Yet, the ties that had always bound them—remained. And despite neither being able to recapture a single stolen moment, those ties would always be there.

—

Deborah left the next morning, just before noon, and only minutes after a shipment of two dozen books arrived for Charles' and Yvonne's personal library. The collection included autographed first-editions of their aunt's three novels, a number of classics, including the works of several African American authors. The kids were overjoyed.

Rachel's suicide attempt, and the angst that followed, had severely drained everyone. However, the time Deborah spent in Reedville had brought her even closer to Samantha. At the airport, Sam clung to her mother until the last moment. Deborah loved every second, good-bye tears and all. As for bridging even part of the chasm remaining between herself and her mother, only time would pronounce a final verdict.

Deborah left Reedville with unexpected treasures, including a small snapshot of Gram that was mysteriously delivered to her by courier, two hours before she was set to leave. And there was one other special possession making the trip to Chicago—one she had intended to take with her more than fourteen years earlier: Marie. During the night before, and without a word to anyone, Deborah simply removed Marie from her place in the dresser drawer, and lovingly packed it away. Finally.

—

Deborah acknowledged there were now even more questions about her mother, her father. Why had the Reverend kept Gram's things for her all this time? Had he expected to give them to her himself? What was it he wanted to say, but never said? Why had he never come for her, called her, returned her calls, written to her? What was in the missing letter? What answers had he taken to his grave?

As for her mother, Deborah had long ago grown weary of trying to fully understand her. She tried to resist thinking about all this. The questions were unanswerable. Nonetheless, they were never far from her mind, and would likely always be.

With the exception of Rachel, everyone expressed disappointment Deborah was leaving, even her mother. Mabel Davis never actually said so, but one could see it in her eyes—the fits and starts in her speech; the way she touched her daughter's hand and embraced her at the depot.

Deborah allowed for the likelihood something profound had emerged from Rachel's near tragedy. She sensed something, though she could not define it. But how would all their lives be changed by it, if at all?

Book Three
In Her New Life

With every breath I take, I am born again.

—*gene cartwright*

chapter sixty-six

A Dedication — April, 1990

He was shocked...in stunned disbelief.

T wo years later, under a gleaming,
April morning sun, a smartly dressed Deborah stood embracing a beaming Samantha. Matthew, Mabel, Maylene, J.R., Charles, Yvonne, Rebecca and her husband, Lincoln, were close by. Rachel was unable to attend. She claimed to have suffered a reaction to depression medication. Reverend Alton Patterson, the new Shiloh Pastor, greeted the family.

Reginald and Gloria, married weeks earlier, arrived barely a half hour before the ceremony. The two had wed in a brief civil service, but planned a large June wedding at a church Atlanta. Gloria made it clear, the entire Davis family was "invited and expected."

When Reginald spotted Matthew, he nearly passed out from shock. A dapper, smiling Matthew—sporting a dark blue, three-piece, pin-striped Italian suit—stood holding hands with a gorgeous young woman he introduced as Brenda Russell. Ms. Russell, 29, was an associate English professor at the University of Arkansas. Both were clearly in love.

A wide grin covered Matthew's clean-shaven face. Every hair on his head was in place. He greeted Reginald with a smile and a bear hug the latter never expected. This was not the Matthew Reginald had last seen. At his core, he was the same, and would always be. But his manner and appearance was stark contrast to his earlier incarnation. The family struck a handsome pose for a phalanx of both news and personal cameras.

The Sticks, and even Reedville itself, was well-represented. Scores of folk, wearing commemorative hard-hats, gathered on the edge of twenty thousand wooded acres of prime SB-40 real estate. Deborah and Samantha gripped the gold-plated shovel, smiled for the cameras, then thrust it firmly into the rich black sod.

Applause erupted from the large crowd that included local and state dignitaries. Still cameras flashed; television cameras rolled. Folk embraced and congratulated each other. This dedication was the culmination of a dream few dared dream. When completed, the facility would provide area residents access to much-needed healthcare.

At Deborah's insistence, the substantial Reed family settlement would finance more such dreams. A lifetime trust fund was established for Samantha. And not only had the twenty thousand acres of prime SB-40 land been deeded, so had the land where the Davis home stood. Even more meaningful to Deborah and Matthew, was that the land where Gram's house had been, was included in the twenty thousand acres.

The two agreed on developing a park and recreation facility, complete with a man-made lake, swimming pool, playground, picnic areas and a baseball diamond. "Magdalena Davis Regional Park" would be the first facility of its kind for residents of the Sticks, and Reedville.

The southwestern phase of the proposed development would include Samuel's Oak. A granite marker would be erected to honor their brother, and the importance the majestic tree had played in all their lives. Reed family funds would finance the entire construction.

A still youthful-looking Jasmine Baker, and Dr. James Penrice were present. The large, racially mixed crowd presented a picture of harmony few in the area ever expected to see.

Another newlywed couple was in attendance: Bryson Peabo and Ruby Dandridge. The two had 'merged' six months earlier. Miss Ruby purchased Peabo's in '89. Now the only thing left to negotiate was, whose last name would be used. Not an easy matter, given the strongheadedness of both. For now, each kept his and her own.

Mr. Lonnie would no doubt have been present, except he was dead. He died on Christmas Eve night in 1989, shot and killed in his Blue Room while trying to break up a fight.

One man got into a violent argument with another male patron over the continuous play of a single song on the juke box. One fellow selected fifteen straight plays of Wilson Picket's 'Midnight Hour.' It should have been an omen. About that time, one annoyed man, thoroughly sick of the song, unplugged the Ol' Wurlitzer. A fight ensued. Mr. Lonnie stepped in to mediate. A gun went off. He dropped dead.

It was a full week before the killer, Benny 'Snake-Eyes'—a tattooed, icy-veined craps shooter, whose real name no one knew—was arrested and charged. As it turned out, *her* real name was Doris Jean Jackson.

Black on black crime was not a law enforcement priority, as long as it stayed in the Sticks. That was true under Sheriff Lucas Darden. But that had changed. In February, Darden lost his umpteenth re-election campaign to Jesse James Williams, Jr., a Desert Storm veteran whose parents were longtime Sticks residents. Jesse, a UA graduate with a degree in Law Enforcement, had earned a Bronze Star.

Williams' deputies made the arrest, in Texarkana, Texas, less than a month after he took office. A week after Benny's...Doris' arrest, Ronnie Cooper, Mr. Lonnie's only known son, took over the Blue Room. The only apparent change: a hand-lettered sign placed over the juke box, limiting to three, the consecutive plays of a single song.

—

The crowd quickly swelled. Samantha never strayed far from her mother and Maylene. Charles and Yvonne were being entertained by June Boy, who wore his trademark overalls—fresh from Mr. Winston's cleaners. His wagon was loaded with flowers he intended to plant on the site.

While cameras rolled, Reedville Mayor elect, David Lee Washington, Jr.,—Reedville's first black elected official—tugged on a braided gold rope. The Mayor loosed a large blue drape that fell away, revealing a massive sign, mounted on steel supports. It read:

FUTURE HOME OF THE HENRY B. DAVIS EDUCATION,
SCIENCE & HEALTH COMPLEX Phase I, SB-40 Development.
A Project of Davis -Williams Development Corp.
Davis-Williams Construction Company: General Contractor

Deborah refused interviews, determined to draw as little notice as possible. And while Mabel Davis expressed excitement and elation, she made no mention of the fact that, were it not for Deborah, none of them would have been there this day. Deborah did not need for it to be said.

Hardly anyone noticed a latecomer—the lone occupant of a shiny, new, midnight blue GMC pickup. He arrived shortly after the ceremony began. The man, dressed in a tan suit, wore a white, western-style hat, cocked just so. He alighted from his vehicle, with a bounce in his step, and remained several dozen yards away from the throng. Matthew saw him first. He frowned, nudged Deborah and directed her attention toward the man.

"I'll be damn. What the hell's he doing here?" he bristled.

Deborah smiled. "Hmm. That's a surprise."

"Why is he just...just standing there."

"It's okay. It's okay. I'm sure it took a lot for him to come witness what's going on here, considering all that's happened."

"I reckon," Matthew reluctantly conceded.

Others soon noticed the man, even as speeches and applause continued. A short while later, as many of the Davis clan observed him, Richard Reed doffed his hat, returned to his truck and drove away.

In less than an hour, the ceremony had ended, and the crowd was gone, except for June Boy. He had flowers to plant. Deborah and Samantha had gone for a "long drive in the country." Things were not perfect, not even close, but Deborah recognized that through it all, her faith—instilled in her as a child—was what had sustained her. It was a faith reaffirmed in her by Gram, by Aunt Rose, by her own spiritual DNA, even Uncle Jack—the loving agnostic. When she had questioned, and even doubted God, it was her faith that gave her strength. And she was determined to share that faith with her daughter.

The financial security of the Davis clan was now secured. The eviction order for Sticks residents had been rescinded, and SB-40 development plans scuttled.

And Deborah was certain justice would finally come to Jonathan Jefferson Reed. For her, it was no longer a matter of vengeance. Jonathan had more to fear from his father, than from Deborah.

In 1988, Richard Reed had declined to post Jonathan's one million dollar bail—unusually high, considering the victim was black and poor. But Richard's stony refusal was more about anger than principle. Jonathan was forced to use his own assets, which had been severely limited by his father's attorneys.

Compounding injury, Jonathan's name also showed up on a number of call girls' customers lists. His wife filed for divorce almost immediately. Except for the possible emotional impact recent developments may have on Samantha, none of it mattered to Deborah.

—

Only a dark blue Corvette remained parked at the side of the road. Several yards away, Matthew stood next to the large sign, gazing up proudly. He appeared lost in thought, as he stared out over the Eden-like expanse that would soon buzz with construction activity.

Moments later, he turned and started toward his 'Vette. The bounce in his lengthy stride suggested authority and self-confidence. He reached his car, and the eager embrace of the beautiful charmer with the deep mocha skin, shoulder-length black hair, and curves to rival his Corvette.

Matthew opened the young woman's door, buckled her in securely, retreated to the driver's side and slipped behind the wheel. He fired the powerful engine and sprinted away, leaving a plume of dust in his wake. June Boy, no longer fearful of Matthew, had observed him all the while. As the latter drove away, June Boy stood, smiled and waved.

chapter sixty-seven

The Message—G.W. Carver High School Auditorium—May 1993

"Tragically, some of you will die..."

O n this night, three years later,
a newly rebuilt George Washington Carver High School complex was
the center of the universe. The halogen-lit parking lots were filled to overflowing. Four mobile TV satellite trucks were parked at the rear of the
main building. Their antennae made them appear more like alien pods
awaiting instructions from their home bases.

Inside the main structure, the state-of-the-art auditorium was filled
to capacity with graduating seniors, parents and friends. The racially
mixed audience applauded, as the principal, Mrs. Diane Washington,
approached the podium.

On the stage, seated behind the podium, were school administra-
tion officials and special guests. Samantha, wearing her admiral-blue
and gold grad gown, adorned with a red and gold Valedictorian sash, sat
next to a proud and glowing Deborah.

A noisy media horde crowded the area just below the front of the stage. Mrs. Washington adjusted the microphone and raised her right hand to quiet the capacity audience.

"Thank you. Thank you. Seniors, that processional was The Bomb!" Laughter and applause erupted. Mrs. Washington waited. "See? I can be cool, too. You know, we haven't had this much media attention in Reedville County since Joe Cumby's cow, Millie, gave birth to a barking calf."

The crowd erupted again.

"Of course, we know why the media are here in such great numbers, and we're thrilled about it all. I'm happy and honored to have the privilege of introducing your speaker—a beautiful young woman who has made us all indescribably proud.

"She certainly needs no introduction to most of you who know the wonder and joy of reading. She is a gifted author whose insightful, emotional, inspiring novels are read by millions. A couple of months ago, she came within an eyelash of her first Pulitzer Prize for Fiction. But there's next year. Trust me. It will happen. She is a super-talented, warm, dynamic and genuinely caring person, who serves as a bonafide role model for people, young and, ahh...seasoned. And she was born right here, in Reedville Arkansas. Ladies and gentlemen, please join me in welcoming our own, Deborah Davis-Williams, the real Deborah Durrell!"

Roaring applause greeted Deborah. Camera flashes flickered like a thousand silent explosions. After what seemed minutes, the audience was finally seated again.

Deborah appeared genuinely embarrassed by the emotional reception. For nearly a full minute, she stood basking in the glowing warmth being showered on her. *If only Gram and Father were here,* she thought, as the applause continued.

"Thank you very much and good night," she said. Audience applause exploded all over again.

"I thought I'd quit while I was ahead." She paused. "Before I begin my brief remarks, I'm going to ask all my media friends to refrain from unnecessary distractions. While I certainly enjoy the attention, this ceremony is for *you*—our graduating seniors." Energetic applause signaled the audience's approval. Deborah waited.

"I have often thought that, when seeking individuals to speak at events such as this, we would do well to choose one of *you* to stand here and offer encouragement and inspiration to your peers. After all, each of you must summon the courage to face whatever awaits you beyond these protective walls. Still, I am honored, thrilled, and humbled to have been asked to stand here.

"The message to you need not be complex, nor too simple. But it must be honest. Above all, it must be honest. Yet, it is that determination to speak honestly that leaves me deeply conflicted.

"You see, I would love to declare that all of you will be successful in your future endeavors, but that would not be true. Some of you will succeed beyond your wildest dreams, while others will fail.

"I would love to tell you that all of you will be judged solely by the content of your character, not the color of your skin. Yet, while the latter need not deter you, it is not true. This is still America, land that I love. I would love to infer, if not declare explicitly, that racism no longer exists in this great country. However, my love of truth will not permit me to falsely proclaim that the Dreamer's dream has been realized.

"I would love to gaze out over this beaming crowd of graduating seniors and declare that all of you will live healthy and useful lives, and die of old age. But that would also be untrue. Tragically, some of you may die at the hands of others, perhaps just like yourselves. Regrettably, if statistics hold true, others of you will perish by your own hands—by either suicide, illicit drugs, or disease resulting from promiscuous sex.

"I cannot stand here and blithely serve up empty platitudes and forecasts of the good life forever more. I will not, like so many politicians, past and present, simply tell you that it is 'Morning in America;' *that* 'America is a shining city on a hill,' or that all I see are a 'thousand points of light.'

"It would sound wonderful. And were I running for President, it may even garner me a few votes. However, there are nearly two-hundred, and sixty million people in this country. To see only a thousand points of light would be a profound disappointment to me.

"Were I to make such proclamations, I am certain many would think well of me, perhaps even quote me. If I were to say that the only thing that counts is the will of the majority, many would agree. But that would be dangerous. In America, notwithstanding those who would repeal them if they could, our Bill of Rights protects the minority from the tyranny of the majority. In my America—our America—we rightly declare our belief in the sanctity and power of the individual. The power of the many arises from the power of 'the one.'

"We are free, to the extent that our freedom does not abridge the rights and freedoms of others. To blindly diminish personal freedoms, even in the pursuit of National Security, is to grant victory to the enemies of freedom.'

"Class of 1993, I have enumerated several things that I will not, and cannot tell you. But what *will* I tell you? What *can* I say that will, hopefully, challenge and inspire you? I will tell you that the strength, the ability, the guts, the fortitude, the burning desire, the sustained motivation for whatever you desire, and for whatever you will be, must and can only come from within you. It must all come from the depths of your soul.

"By that, I do not suggest the influence of family, friends and others will not, and should not be a factor. What I do suggest and declare is that it must not be the only, or the final determinant.

"I challenge you to never consign your thinking to the minds of others. You *must* be an *agitator* for positive change. Do not fall prey to those so-called leaders who cynically appeal to your patriotism and Faith, in order to simply advance their own selfish, political agendas. I challenge you to be a true patriot by challenging those who rule over you. I challenge you to be healthy skeptics. I challenge you to not merely seek out role models, but seek to be a role model.

"All of you, in ways large and small, will help to determine all our futures. So, will you succeed? Will you go on to live lives that serve humankind? Or will you live a life that will cause others to cheer, rather than mourn your passing? The answers lie within you. So, boldly go from this place. Find your passion, live out your dreams, and make this a better world. Thank you, and God bless you. I love you, Gram," Deborah whispered, and glanced upward.

Carver auditorium rocked with thunderous, standing applause. Cameras flashed. Reporters surged toward the stage, but were restrained by security personnel. Samantha rushed to embrace her mother, and a proud Jasmine Baker. Others on the stage rose to congratulate Deborah who turned and beckoned to someone waiting offstage.

A beaming Tommy approached his wife, proudly carrying their six month old son, Henry Matthew Williams, cradled in his arms. He joined the entire family: Mabel, Maylene, J.R., Charles, Yvonne, Matthew and Brenda, Gloria and Reginald, Aunt Rose and Uncle Jack—all had been seated on stage. Aunt Rose and Uncle Jack beamed. They were as proud as any parents, and grandparents could have been.

Even Paul, who had arrived from Chicago only minutes before Deborah's address, joined the family in celebration. Rachel was noticeably absent. She remained in the mental health facility, but was scheduled for conditional release in three months. Those on stage stood arm in arm, while applause continued, unabated.

Precisely then, two attractive, smartly dressed young women approached from stage-right. Both appeared to be in their early thirties. One was slightly taller and a bit heavier than the other.

Smiling, and struggling to contain the excitement and anticipation each felt, the two approached Maylene. She saw them heading toward her and stopped still. Despite the emotion of the moment, her heart instantly knew who they were. Maylene turned. Her eyes widened. She stretched out both arms, and yelled out two names, at the top of her lungs. The crowd noise nearly drowned her out.

"Kay! B.B.! Oh, my God. Mama, Gloria, would you look! Look! I cannot believe this. My God! Tommy, I think you know these two."

Tommy, cradling the baby, turned to look. His jaw dropped; he shook his head in disbelief. "No way. No Way!" he kept repeating.

"Tommy? Is this Tommy? Hmm, you *look* like Tommy, but where's the afro?" Karetha joked, then loosed her patented laugh.

A flurry of hugs and kisses. Uninhibited laughter. A shower of tears, more hugs. Introductions to those who did not know them. A thousand questions. More hugs.

Samantha Yvonne Davis was aglow, amid congratulations and hugs from her mother's long-lost best friends. The only one unaware of their presence was Deborah. A short distance away, well-wishers were still mobbing her. Maylene and the others conspired to shield Kay and B.B. until Deborah was done. No one wanted to miss *this* reunion.

—

None in the Davis family would argue, that the four and a half years preceding this night, had been uneventful. There had been joy and celebration, unfamiliar in earlier years. Yet, the renewed family conflicts that had surfaced, often threatened to make earlier conflict seem tame, by comparison.

And through it all, one enigmatic personality had employed extraordinary means to stay abreast of what has going on in Deborah's life. As he had been in 1988, at Reverend's funeral, Jude Barsteau was present this night. His tall, wispy frame was bedecked with a tailored black suit; a white, French-cuff shirt with open banded collar. His snow-white hair was combed back in a ponytail.

During the ceremony, Barsteau had gripped his trademark, black fedora in his right hand, while he applauded. His eyes never left the stage, even as he inched his way toward a near wall. He appeared to be taking great care to remain in the shadows of the semi-dark auditorium.

While raucous applause continued, Barsteau moved stealthily toward the near exit, unnoticed by even the eagle eyes of Aunt Rose. Yet, a hint of discomfort crept onto Mabel Davis' face.

But the moment, the night—all belonged to Samantha, her proud mother, and her family. A wave of thoughts streamed through Deborah's mind as she looked on. She beamed. Her heart brimmed. It was a night none would soon forget.

Hundreds waited to greet and congratulate Deborah. The line snaked along the stage, and out to the center of the auditorium. Many, seeking autographs, held copies of her third, and latest novel, 'Where The Winding Road Ends.'

Then, a face. A man near the front of the line caught Deborah's attention. He stood out. He was a man of regal bearing. Perhaps it was his crisp, neat, manly appearance, his daunting presence. The man stood tall, shoulders back. His gaze was laser-like; his head held proudly. He exuded an air of certainty and self-confidence. Whatever other intangible qualities were evident, Jude Barsteau possessed them in abundance.

Within minutes, Mabel caught sight of him. Her heart quickened; she nearly lost her footing. She grew faint, but luckily made her way to a nearby chair and sat down, clutching her chest.

Barsteau, wearing his hat now, was only steps away from Deborah when she saw him. It was as if the sea parted, and there he was. He smiled, removed his hat with his left hand, extended his right, while securing a copy of Deborah's new book against his body with his left arm. Something about his eyes commanded her attention. They were a deep, black-brown with a distinctive light, gray-blue corona.

Deborah was a bit unnerved by what she saw and sensed, but could not figure out why. In the next heartbeat, the *only* face she saw was Barsteau's. And while a dozen news cameras flashed, the only sound she heard was his resonant baritone.

"I've been waiting a long time...to meet you."

———

The saga continues.

Who can say where the winding road ends,
where the dark night fades, and the light begins
to reveal the path to places unknown,
and the promise of harvest for seeds long sown?
Who can say where the winding road ends?
Who can say?

I Weep No More

I weep no more.
    Well of tears—bone dry,
    bed of thorns now lies empty,
    absent my presence, waiting, hoping, expecting,
    foretelling my return to its piercing embrace.
    But I have moved on.
I weep no more.
    Wall of fear—once stone,
    blown asunder, now gone forever,
    reduced to dust, crumbled, shambled,
    unable to thwart my will, nor prevent my escape.
    'Cause I have moved on.
I once longed for the serenity of death, the solitude of nonexistence,
    the eternal peace of unbeing—as in never having been. But no more.
    I once sought the tomb of a mindless darkness, unacquainted with
    the informing nature of memory, or the gift of light. But no more.
    I have found my voice, heard my song, seen my spirit leap
    like a geyser toward heaven.
    And I have moved on.
I weep no more.
    Well of tears—bone dry,
    bed of thorns now lies empty,
    craving my presence, waiting, hoping, expecting,
    predicting my relapse to its cruel embrace.
    But I have moved on.
I weep no more.
    Wall of fear—once stone,
    blown asunder, now gone forever,
    reduced to dust, crumbled, shambled,
    unable to shunt my will, nor stay my escape.
    'Cause I have moved on.
I weep no more,
    'Cept for joy, aloud I cry,
    now yearning to be, to live, not die.
    Now cleansed of shame, I weep no more.
    My soul is free. I weep no more.
    My soul is free. I weep no more!

Confound your enemies: live long, live well.

—*gene cartwright*